WOLFSONG

Wolfwalkers! the wolves howled.

Come! Dion shouted joyfully. *We run with you. Now run with us.*

The packsong swept in, catching Dion as if she were a leaf before an autumn wind. *Wolfwalker!*

Dion howled, an inhuman sound. *Come!*

The gray tide shifted. From den to ridge, the summons swept. Wolves roused, stretched, cocked their heads, listened to the silent wind. Voices joined. Packs merged. Deep in the earth, deep in the forest, that howl grew, rising to the wind and carrying across the canyon, east to the desert, north to the mountains, south to the sea.

Howl with the wind, wolfwalker! We come!

By Tara K. Harper
Published by Ballantine Books:

Tales of the Wolves
Wolfwalker
Shadow Leader
Storm Runner

LIGHTWING

STORM RUNNER

Tara K. Harper

A Del Rey Book
BALLANTINE BOOKS • NEW YORK

A Del Rey Book
Published by Ballantine Books

 Published in the United States of America by Ballantine Books, a division of Random House, Inc., New York, and simultaneously in Canada by Random House of Canada Limited, Toronto.

Library of Congress Catalog Card Number: 93-90176

ISBN 0-345-37162-3

Manufactured in the United States of America

First Edition: August 1993

To Mom and Dad, with love

Chapter 1

The intriguing of a voice,
sung in shadow;
pierced with a breath that
caught
in her throat . . .

Dion eased forward another meter. The smell of damp earth between the new, spring grass caught in her nose. The gritty edges of the old, stiff leaves sawed on her wrists while brittle weeds brushed against her ear. One of the hollow stalks slipped up inside her warcap, poking her temple sharply until she shifted forward again. Quietly, slowly, one knee, then an elbow, then her body another length. Her heart pounded, but she knew the raiders could not hear it; she had learned her stealth from the wolves themselves. Across the river, watching from the edge of the forest, Hishn's yellow eyes gleamed. Separated by the canyon, they were linked with their senses. The Gray One breathed through Dion's lungs and saw through her eyes, while the wolfwalker's slow stalking filled Hishn's lupine mind with the lust of the hunt. When the gray wolf growled low in her throat, Dion froze. The scent of the raiders' camp was faint, then stronger as the wind brought it to the wolfwalker's nose. When the breeze rose again, shifting the weeds in ragged waves, Dion dug her toes into the ground and crawled forward again.

Behind her, Yagly moved softly in the late afternoon shadows. The shifting stripes were his guide, stretching out and hiding his lurking figure in the long black fingers of the trees. To the raiders' eyes, he and Dion were ghosts in the grass. Three days earlier, Yagly had gotten within ten meters of the raiders' guardpost. Watchful as they were, the raiders looked to the boulders and shrubs for their enemies—they did not expect a scout to slither across a near-flat stretch of ground.

Yagly's faded brown eyes flickered from the raiders' camp to the bridge they guarded. The raiders were wary. They were right to be: for a year, Yagly and the other Ariyens had been sneaking across the river, stealing back their people, and trying to drive the raiders on. The dark-haired man grinned. The bridges might not be open to cross, but he and Dion did not use those high, stone roads: they forded the river below, then climbed one of the canyon chimneys to reach the raiders' land. The raiders were not of the mountains; they did not think to watch the cliffs either.

In front of the other scout, Dion edged between the root clumps of two shrubs, and Yagly's gaze followed her with approval. The wolfwalker was as silent as a thought in the brush. Her black hair blended with the shadows as if it were part of the dark itself, and her lithe body wriggled from shadow to shadow as if she were made of supple rope, not lanky bones. Behind her, she left only a faint worm's trail where the grass did not spring back before Yagly bent it down again.

With one hand on the hilt of her sword, Dion drew her blade forward beside her, hiding its long length beneath her body when she stopped. A stone gouged her knee and she shifted around it silently. She eased sideways for the other scout to join her, and a moment later, Yagly's long body lay next to hers.

Dion scowled, adjusting her warcap with a slow shift of her shoulder. The healer's circlet was well hidden beneath the leather-and-metal mesh, but her braid was frizzing between the two. The rising wind whipped loose hairs into her eyes and across her nose until her face was tickled from brow to chin. She blinked as old leaves whirled up and past, followed by the long, hollow threads of winter grass, straining to break free. The pale, spring sun slipped down in the sky. They had an hour, no more, before they would have to ease back and cross again into Ramaj Ariye. She narrowed her eyes. From here, she could see ten, maybe even twelve raiders in this camp. Their shelters were sturdy; their supplies stacked neatly—this looked more like a soldiers' fort than a raiders' stakeout. She eased forward another meter, stopping at the edge of the shadow in which she hid. If there had been no wind, they could have heard every word the raiders spoke, but the gusting breeze brought, then stripped away, the sounds. A word, a phrase—that was not enough to tell anything.

"I can't make anything out," Yagly said in her ear, "but I would bet on all nine moons that something is up. Look at their stance. For the last nine days—an entire ninan—they have been guarding the bridge against Ariye. Now they stand as if they guard the crossing from those in their own county."

"But the refugees are not due for three more days," Dion breathed in return. "How could the raiders know to guard the crossings early?"

"Maybe it is some other poor fool, running from the camps."

"But if the raiders are wary now," she whispered, "the refugees will never make it through to the Devil's Knee."

"If they even know to go there," the dark-haired man returned as he eyed the raiders' camp.

"They know," she whispered back. "The north scout crossed back into Ariye yesterday. He got the message through. It was not easy, though—there were raiders everywhere."

"How did you pick that up?" Yagly glanced back over the river. "The wolf?"

She nodded almost imperceptibly. Her bond with the Gray Ones was strong enough that, like the other wolfwalkers, she could hear the packsong at a distance. Even now, the faint gray voices echoed through her thoughts like a winter wind in a forest.

Yagly turned his gaze back to the raiders' camp. "Must be nice," he whispered. "I have to wait for the message birds or the runners to find out anything important."

She smiled wryly. "At least you're not assigned down south. Gamon said that the mud there is so thick that even the runners have to walk."

"You will be walking in mud yourself if we don't start back soon." The scout's gaze flickered to the sky. "Rain will be here in an hour."

Dion followed his glance. "I've still got forty kilometers to go to meet the next scout on the line."

Yagly gave her a sly look. "And ten kilometers more after that?"

She blushed slowly. "Yes," she said steadily. "Any news to pass along?"

The other man hid his smile. When Dion worked in the hospitals, she might be as serious as any other healer, but out here, he could make her blush like a girl. "Tell Aranur—and Gamon," he added while Dion's flush deepened, "that there are four more camps like this above and below this bridge. Further south, they are thicker than flies on a dead dog. From now on, we won't be able to use any crossing below the Sky Bridge."

"The crossings above the bridge aren't safe anymore either," she said slowly.

Yagly gave her a thoughtful look. "The raiders are massing there, too?"

"They have not set up permanent camps yet—that we know of," she amended, "but Gamon thinks that is just a matter of time. Even the Slot is no longer completely safe."

Yagly's lips set in a grim line. "The refugees would never make the Slot anyway—not with children in the group. The raiders will be hot on their trail when they escape. Wherever it is they run, they better be able to get to a crossing fast."

"Which means," Dion agreed, noting the clouds that swept up over the horizon before turning her attention back to the camp, "that their only choice is the Devil's Knee."

Or death, Yagly added silently.

In the dim, gray morning, the river's surface flashed dully each time the water surged against the soil of the bank. The slapping sounds were like the smacking of a badgerbear as it eats, sending a shiver down Moira's emaciated back. The roiling waves in the deeper stream refused to hold the reflection of the sky; they turned black instead with the shadows of the canyon. There was no warmth to this dawn. Moira, shivering uncontrollably, hugged herself as if she could hold onto the thought of warmth. Yesterday, the flat, pale sun had disappeared into thin clouds and chill winds, raising bumps on Moira's bare legs and forcing the children to huddle into the moss as they had huddled through the night. Now, standing on the trail, Moira glanced back at them, her eyes dull and sunken in her face. Like the others, she had wrapped her feet in rags and bark. She wore only a thin tunic. No leggings, no jacket against the bitter chill of the canyon wind that whipped her shirt against her skin and slapped the cold further into her body. Only the tunic that hung to her thighs and left her bruise-striped legs pale and blue in the wind.

She stared up the canyon. The overcast heights were more gray than green now, but there was safety in those stones—she knew it. Her calves burned as she forced herself forward on the trail—her feet were numb from the mud; her breath rasped through the gaps in her teeth. Gods, she prayed, let her body hold out a little longer. She could not stop now: there were the children to think about. Children, with their haunted, hollow eyes . . .

Old Jered, his knobby hands pressed hard against his ribs, stumbled up beside her. The stitch in his side had gone beyond pain, and the gesture was now reflex. He wondered when he had ceased to care. He motioned downstream with his chin.

Moira shook her head vehemently. The wolves followed them—she was sure she had seen a Gray One just before dawn, though there had been no tracks when she and Jered went to look. Tracks? Her face twisted. As if she could read the marks in the dirt as she once read her council books. Did her ignorance of the woods matter? Even if she knew how to hide their trail, the wolves would scent them out. All she could do was run—run to the river and pray the wolves did not attack while she waited to be seen. Waiting—it would bring their death upon them. Moons help them all, but she had fled the camp too early. The Ariyens would not expect them for two more days, and the raiders had been on her heels from the hour she and the others had escaped. Her group had gained some little time by hiding in a bog. They gained more when they crawled into an old lepa's den: the wolves had passed them by. Jered said the oily stench of the predator birds was still strong enough to mask the scent of the children. But, Moira worried, her eyes flickering from tree to stone, where could they hide here, at the river's edge? The trees were thin at this altitude, and the cliffs rose with the trail—soon there would be only rocks to conceal them.

"Two days," Jered whispered, echoing her thoughts. "Sixty-two hours to hide and pray the wolves will pass us by."

Moira stared at the river—the one, thin border that taunted them with the safety of its other side—watching it thrust and tumble the spring snags like matchsticks.

Jered followed her gaze to the river. "We could never cross it here," he muttered. "We would be swept away like leaves."

But might it not be better, she asked herself, to let the children drown rather than give them back to the raiders? Eight young ones behind her, and not one of them without the same purple marks that marred her own face. The six-year-old who clung to Moira's aunt would bear the burn scars for the rest of her life. Jered's own grandson, a boy only five, clutched another elder's hand, his left eye swollen in an angry, reddish-pink cyst. And Eren, Moira's last living child, with the blisters broken across her small feet, and her dull voice no longer even whimpering—Eren should have grown this year, Moira thought wearily. She should have sprouted like a speedgreen in a garden. But there had been no meals of substance, no hours of easy sleep—just the beating sticks and the whip-spurred work and the tortured fear at night. Something blinded Moira for a moment. It was not until Jered's whisper brought her back that she realized it was hatred. Fury, not so much at the raiders, but at those who had placed them in her county. Fury at the faceless ones who built their futures on the soil of children's graves. She bit her lip violently this time, tasting the sweet blood with a savage satisfaction.

Jered glanced at her, then over his shoulder, taking in the blackheart trees, the bright green edges of the undergrowth, the clumps of rotting leaves that buried themselves in the mud-swollen ground. "This county was my family's home for sixteen generations," he said softly. "But home it is no longer."

"Leave it behind, Jered," Moira said flatly. "Leave it behind with your heart. It belongs to the raiders now."

"Raiders, yes," he agreed slowly, "and the man who claims three of the nine counties as his own: the Lloroi, Conin." He spat the name. "A Lloroi like his father. A Lloroi who takes other men's land, other men's lives for his own. A Lloroi who bleeds his people for his own gain."

"They say his father was killed—and swiftly—by an Ariyen sword." Moira smiled without humor. She looked down at her bony hand, clenching it tight and pressing it to her stomach. "I hunger," she said softly, "for the fire or the sand snakes to bring the justice of the moons to this new Lloroi. I hunger for anything but the quick release his father felt."

"That he has come here now—to the borders—to see his handiwork, to gloat in his control . . . Gods, but I curse him. I curse his name to the ninth hell. Damn you, Conin," he whispered vehemently. "Ruler of the raiders. Ruler of the wolves."

Moira stirred. "Not all the wolves, Jered. Only those who stayed behind. The others fled to Ariye just as we do now."

"Does it matter?" he demanded. "Whatever bond was bred between them and the ancients, it no longer holds true. The wolves hunt us here like rabbits—and they do it for the raiders."

"We have survived a night, a day, and another dawn," she said flatly. "The moons will give us a few more hours." She looked into the shadows, daring a pair of yellow eyes to watch her. The hunters were there, she knew it. Why they did not betray the refugees to the raiders, she did not know, nor did she dare question it. It was enough that she was still free.

She took a step toward the fork in the trail and caught her breath as her aching legs pulled against the motion. Gritting her teeth, she cursed the strength of the wolves. The Gray Ones who had left this place had had strong legs to carry them to the borders—strong legs and fangs to chase the hunger from their bellies as they ran. These children had neither the Gray Ones' strength nor their skills. They had no food to sustain them; no clothes to keep them warm. And they could not run much farther.

Which way to go? Which way to safety? It was two kilometers to the Sky Bridge; eight to the Devil's Knee. Two kilometers—even the children could make it that far. Peyel, the tavernkeeper, had told Moira that the Sky Bridge was safe now—safe enough to cross. No raiders for three days, Peyel said—they were being moved north, to the new camps. Moira had to believe her. Peyel had been helping people flee the camps almost as long as there had been camps to flee. She had suffered enough at the hands of the raiders to make her resistance a vengeful one. The Sky Bridge, she had told Moira.

What if Peyel was right, and the raiders would not be guarding the whole bridge? It was a wide arch, a hundred meters of smooth stone, three hundred meters long. The raiders could be camped on one side only, letting the traders through, letting shadows—skinny, bruised shadows—creep along the edge . . .

No, Woss must have gotten through to Ariye. His message ring and the map delivered to her just three days ago proved it, and they promised safety only at the Devil's Knee. Moons, she prayed, was it Peyel or Woss who was wrong? There were no fighters here to protect the children should Moira choose badly. The resistance group that fought the raiders—their leader, the Siker herself—would not know that Moira had taken the youths and fled. Woss could not come back to help. The Ariyens would not be ready for days. "By all the gods," she whispered, "if there is just one moonwarrior left to cross the stars, if there is one ancient fighter to come from the First World, let him come to Bilocctar now. Let him crush the raiders with the weight of the gods and avenge the deaths of my people."

She stared at the fork in the trail. To go north—to go higher in the mountains—meant the Devil's Knee. To go south would bring less wind, she knew; less cold, and a crossing only an hour away. Gods, but what was one hour when the eyes of the children had haunted her for months? Their small bodies dogged her footsteps like frail ghosts. Would the moons give them any more strength to climb this trail? Any more will to make it to the canyon of the Devil's Knee? The falls at the Knee were legend, a bogeyman to elders and children alike. Dangerous beyond a badgerbear, it was said, where the stones rose up toward the gods, and the moonmaids played with a man's balance to see if even the brave would slip and plummet to their deaths. Menacing, too, was the rim, where the shadows of the cliffs promised footholds that were not there. She closed her eyes. Even now, she could see the blasting waterfall they called the Devil's Knee—the torrent that swept from the heights of the river to the booming rocks at the base of the plunging cascade.

Yes, deadly was the Devil's Knee; deadly and daring. Daring her to ignore Peyel's whispered advice. Forcing her to hope that Woss was alive. Taunting her to play god with their lives.

There were ghosts in her eyes: her own sons, her eldest daughter . . . Grief made her choke, and she fought to breathe so that Jered would not guess. She clenched her jaw and cursed herself silently, using epithets that a year ago would have made her reel in shock. In anger, she regained some measure of control. Death was only another step, a moment, a small event, she chanted to herself. Death was irrelevant. Death was a circumstance, nothing more. For there were living children still to worry over. Children still to flee the raiders' swords. And somewhere, hidden beneath her death-dulled chant, was the prayer that when those here with her were safe, there would be time for her own tears.

Moira stared at the trail, hearing the oncoming raiders in her mind as surely as if they were beside her. One mistake, one loud sound to draw the eyes of a hidden hunter, and how many more would she lose from this group? Annoc and young Lyo had been left behind that first night, dead of the war arrows through their backs. Little Nita, with her bruised blue eyes and tangled hair, had died from snakebite the previous dawn, when she had pushed Jered's grandson from the viper's path. The two youngest boys, hungry beyond reason, had fed each other the sweet leaves from a burrberry plant, and their twisted, frothing bodies had been left in the shelter of the blackheart trees last noon. She had held the youths and watched them die, screaming silently at the moons for the hope of Ovousibas—for the miracle of the ancient healing. She had cried out to the gray-damned sky for a healer—for anyone—to stop the agony of the poison clutching at their nerves. Her soul, she had promised; she would give her soul for a healer who knew the miracle of Ovousibas, the ancient healing that went beyond the warbarbs and poisons, beyond the cut of the sword, and made the body whole. Last night—and she clenched her shaking fists as she remembered—it had been Yana's daughter who died. Quietly, quickly—no one had even noticed until they tried to rouse her. Only then had they seen the nest of nightspiders crouched behind her knee, the blackened edges of the bite marks making Moira gag as she watched them lay their eggs in the hollow carved in the little girl's flesh. Today, Luter's leg was still bleeding where his thigh had been deeply slashed. If gellbugs set in, they would lose him, too. Gellbugs, she snarled silently in fury. Such a simple thing for a healer to prevent, but Moira had no healer. Even now, the tiny bugs were probably swarming in his veins, thickening, clotting his capillaries, planting their eggs in his blood while he dragged himself onward. A healer who knew Ovousibas—such a person could use the ancient arts, she prayed hopelessly, such a healer could save him. But there was no such thing. Ovousibas was the "farce of the faith healers."

Once, perhaps, the miracle of Ovousibas had been real—a skill, learned from the birdmen who once flew over this continent. But the birdmen had gone north since that day, eight hundred years ago, when the humans had come down from the stars and made this world their own. That miracle of their healing, that ancient skill, could have been kept alive so that children like little Nita did not have to die—so that wounded men like Annoc did not pour their lives out on the dry and hungry dirt. But Ovousibas had been lost.

She looked at the group bleakly. There had been a dozen children and half that many elders who fled the camp beside her. Now only thirteen were left. Of them all, she and, surprisingly, old Jered were the most able. Able. She snorted. Able to do what? To run? She limped. To fight? Her fist tightened around the hilt of her stolen knife. Two dull blades for thirteen lives. She stared at the children, and Jered followed her gaze.

"The Sky Bridge, Moira," he said softly. "It is only two kilometers. We could all make it that far. And you cannot be sure the mark on the message ring was not at the bridge—Peyel said the bridge would be clear. You got only a glimpse of the ring and the map before they were burned."

She shook her head stubbornly.

"Look, Moira, even if we reach the Knee, we have no way to cross the canyon. The raiders are too close—we cannot hide for two days and hope they will not see us. The Ariyens do not even know we are coming." He clutched at her arm. "It is dawn now. We can make it to the bridge in two hours."

"No." She shook free of his twisted fingers. Sharply, she motioned for the others to follow her to the trail. They got up dully, moving with dragging steps. Had they known they were slated to die? Young Tomi's blank gaze caught her memory with the image of his father's eyes, sightless and still as she had last seen them, and it was with a fierce wrench that she saw again those of the child. To choose wrong for these babes . . . Gods help her. "No," she repeated stubbornly. "The map was real. The message ring was real. We trust the moons to protect us."

Jered's hands caught her again, halting her. She glanced down at fingers digging like talons into the thin flesh of her upper arm. "How far do you think we can get with the raiders only two hours behind us, and the wolves even now scenting our tracks? Look at you. You are no more hero than I. How do you think to stop them when they catch up?"

"You question my judgment too far, Jered," she said softly.

One of the elders behind them glanced warningly at the woods, and Jered, his lips tight, dropped his voice. "We have only two knives and not one sword between the five of us elders. Even if we had better blades, how could my one good arm"—he gestured at his wound-withered limb—"stand against that of a trained raider? What words of yours will stop the ones who find us?"

Moira's heart beat in her throat, and she shook with more than weariness. She glanced deliberately at the fingers on her arm, then back to Jered's face, challenging him silently until he released her and rubbed his hands on his own ragged tunic.

"They expect us at the bridge," she said softly. She knew she was right. There had been no answers from the other refugees who had fled the camps because no one else had made it across the border. She stared at the roiling river. "No one could suspect we head for those falls—they know as well as we that the Sky Bridge is the only crossing safe enough to attempt with children. Besides," she added wearily, "the raiders could have arrived at the bridge long before we did. They are not limited to running game trails on blistered feet when they have riding beasts and the safety of their own roads."

"And if there are no Ariyens waiting for us at the Knee?"

She stared at him. Did Jered guess what she would do if the Ariyens could not help them? Did he know that even now she prayed for the moons to give her the strength—and the will—to release these children from this world herself? "If they are not at the Devil's Knee," she said quietly, "we were lost before we started. There can be no refuge for any of us"—she steadied her voice—"in a county that turns its back on children."

Jered ran his tongue across his dry lips and regarded the ridge that blocked the northern view. "You still reason with the weight of council, Moira," he said slowly, heavily, "though the body of your words lies in those shallow graves behind us. If, for no other reason than that your daughter is with us, I must trust your judgment."

"If, for no other reason than that your grandson is with us, Jered, I trust you to follow." She turned and stepped out onto the path, trying to jog again. She took only a few steps, dropped heavily back to a walk, and tried again to pick up the pace. Behind her, one of the boys whimpered, and the soft tones of an elder's voice soothed the child. "Come now. See those rocks? Just to the top of the red one," she heard the old aunt say. "It is only a little farther. You can be strong another ten meters. Strong as the moonmaids who protect us." The elder pointed to the moon ghosting out from behind a thin cloud, and the children dully followed her finger. "See?" she said. "The moons are still with us. Now you know you can make it to the top of that little hill, yes? Come."

On the eastern side of the river, the gray wolf, Hishn, picked up the other scout's scent long before Dion would have seen the man. She waved at the brush in which he crouched, and he stood up with a grin. "Can't never fool the Gray Ones," he called softly, gesturing for her to join him.

"Not as long as you eat spiceweed for breakfast," she returned with a smile. They gripped arms in greeting, and as the gray wolf faded back into the forest, Dion nodded toward the river. "I've come from Yaglv's site. Anything new?"

He grimaced. "They still squat on the Sky Bridge like they grew roots into the stone itself."

The two turned to stare at the white expanse that stretched across the canyon. "They're thick down at the next bridge, too," Dion said slowly.

"I don't like it," the other scout said. "They don't usually get this wary until after someone makes a break for the border. If the group we contacted tries to run through this mob, they'll die before they get a kilometer from their camp. We might have to change our plans."

"We can't," Dion said flatly. "It took three days to get word to them the first time. They will be starting their run tonight. There's no time to reach them before they break free."

"You're a wolfwalker. Couldn't you use the wolves?"

She chuckled without humor. "From what I can tell, the people in Bilocctar are as afraid of the wolves as they are of the raiders."

"Afraid?"

She nodded. "Remember I told you about that man we picked up way to the north—up at the Slot? He is as terrified of the Gray Ones as if they were beetle-beasts. Said they ran with the raiders."

"He was feverish?"

She shook her head slowly. "He was lucid enough to describe the roads to his camp and how to get word to the last of the elders there."

The man frowned. "But wolves and raiders? That doesn't make sense. I thought the Gray Ones could run only with someone who was sensitive—like you, or Sobovi. You can't tell me that the raiders have empaths among them? How could anyone with feelings burn off a woman's hands? Or stake out a child for the lepa to tear apart?"

Dion hid her shudder in a shrug.

"Awe, I could understand," the man added. "Hells, I've felt that myself when your Gray Hishn looks in my eyes and makes me feel like I've just jammed my head full of scents and sounds. Wolves running with the raiders? No way in the ninth hell that that could be." He motioned for Dion to follow him, then led the way toward the canyon. "What if there is someone on the border now?" he asked over his shoulder. "Could you tell?"

Dion considered that. "When the wind rises, maybe." She reached out mentally to the Gray One in the forest behind her. There was a thick, sweet scent in Hishn's nose, and Dion's own nostrils flared as she recognized the smell of a digger's burrow. The hunger in the gray wolf's belly clutched her own stomach. Dion forced herself apart.

". . . what about the crossing at the Devil's Knee?"

She caught the end of the other scout's sentence and shook her head. "It will be two more days before it is finished."

"So until then, anyone running to the border is on their own."

They halted just inside the edge of the trees. "They surely can't cross here," said Dion softly, eyeing the distant group of raiders who held the other end of the stone expanse.

The other scout followed her gaze. "You know, I've lived in Ramaj Ariye most of my life. Until a year ago, the raiders were not organized enough to track a riding beast gone astray. Now look at them: They're a goddamned army." He shook his head slowly. ''I never thought I'd see the day when raiders rode for a Lloroi.''

Dion glanced at him. ''They don't ride for Lloroi Conin. They ride for Longear.''

''Longear? The one in charge of his security forces?'' He pursed his lips, thinking back. ''You met her once—she had you whipped.''

Dion nodded, her face expressionless. ''If ever there was one person who embodied all the evilness of the raiders,'' she said softly, ''it is Longear.'' She shook herself. ''Just saying her name gives me the shivers.'' She forced a laugh.

''It ought to.'' The other scout's eyes flickered to the back of Dion's left hand. The torn flesh had never healed completely, leaving the skin twisted and ridged, like worm trails. ''If you had not been a healer, Aranur said you would have lost the use of your hand forev—''

Dion cut him off. ''Aranur talks too much,'' she said shortly. She shrugged at his look. ''I am a wolfwalker. I always heal faster than other people.''

The other man watched her silently for a moment, then returned his gaze to the Sky Bridge. ''If Longear is behind the raiders here,'' he said finally, ''we will be lucky to see even one refugee at the Devil's Knee.''

Dion settled her warcap more firmly on her head, tucking the silver circlet on her brow back under the leather mesh. Her violet eyes were hooded. ''We will be lucky. The moons would not allow it to be otherwise.''

The children made it only two kilometers before they had to stop again. Luter's leg gave out as the path rose, and Jered half carried the other man the rest of the way up the ridge until his own shoulder knotted and cramped so badly he could not extend the one good arm he had. Moira stared at the sky—it was already only an hour till noon. Had the Ariyens watched the riverbanks as they promised? Or would the wolves who hunted her group betray these children before they could reach safety?

She nodded reluctantly as her aunt asked a question with her eyes. Yes, they could stop. The children dragged their feet, suffering silently. She could do nothing about their hunger, but they could at least drink; this was the last place the river met the trail.

Upriver, the stone walls rose more steeply until the canyon looked like the narrow cut of a knife in stone. There, the rocks turned blue with shadow and black with the wetness of the falls. The water was deep enough even here, she worried—dangerously swift and silver with boulders bursting from its surface.

A soft touch brought her back to the present, and she forced her lips to soften as Eren's small hand crept into hers. "Aunt Giela will take you to the water in a minute," she said, squeezing her daughter's hand. "Then I'll rewrap your feet and see if we can make them feel a little better, all right?"

The small girl pushed her tangled hair from her face and tugged silently at Moira's hand again.

A fist clenched the tall woman's heart. "Go with Auntie, child," she managed. "I will come over in a minute."

She stared at the stumbling group that followed her aunt to the bank. Jered, already there, pulled two bark cups from a knot in his tattered tunic and passed them to Giela. Moira almost smiled. Jered could not take even a day on the trail without carving his message designs on some object he must insist on carrying. Even with Luter's weight knotting his shoulders, he would not let go of his wooden cups. She could almost understand. The crudeness of those cups must make his hands ache to smooth the chipped surfaces, to place in them the designs of his craft, his lineage. Two years ago, Jered had been one of the foremost craftsmen in her village; his message rings were beautifully simple, carved and dyed in wood and stone, mixed with cloth sometimes, and even used in the ring dances at the solstice feasts. Now, the twisted fingers of his left hand dangled as uselessly as his withered arm. She watched him, squatting on a rock, dipping the cups into the river and handing them back to the young ones. He waited patiently while they drank. It would take some time for each child to take his turn—time enough for all to rest. But Moira, though her legs trembled with numbness, stayed on her feet.

How long had it been since she closed her eyes last? How long without dreams or nightmare? There had been one night to plan, to steal those torn tunics from two of the tortured bodies—tunics of the dead for the rags that made their boots. Then a night, and a day—that nightmare day when she watched the others dragged away—others that would have been running now, had they survived the fires. And then there was the night itself in which she stole the children from their threadbare bunks and led them through the shadow-black woods. A dawn, a day, another night . . . Four more dead. And now? This morning had come with only a fitful doze between the rising of the second moon and the fifth, but it was a morning she had never hoped to see. She stood swaying, not quite believing she still breathed from her aching lungs. She would not be able to rise again if she sank down to rest. She squeezed her eyes shut to ease their burning, and listened, her ears strained to catch the sounds she dreaded. No howls. No shouts in the distance. The river drowned all noises except Aunt Giela's "Slowly. Drink more slowly."

Moira finally stumbled to the bank herself and took her turn with the cup as one of the elders drew a dull smile from her daughter with a playful splash.

"Do not soak your feet too long," she warned quietly. "It will make them soft for the trail. Dry them now, and let Auntie tie the rags back on." Two of the other children were slowly stripping bark from a string tree to stiffen their rude footgear. Counting the small faces as she looked around, Moira glanced to her right. "Cal, Eren, the water is too deep there. Come back."

Obediently, Eren clambered up, her wet toes glistening in the dull, overcast light.

"Cal, be careful," Moira said sharply.

"Eren!" Auntie cried out as the girl's feet slipped.

"Momm—" The little girl's shriek was chopped off as she fell. Water splashed out, then closed over the child's head.

"Tomi, grab her!" Moira's despairing cry cut off abruptly as Tomi flung himself down the bank below and into the river, past the other boy.

Eren bobbed to the surface with her face streaming water. Her tiny scream, her mouth twisted in terror, was cut off as the river sucked her under again. Her arms thrashed at the surface. She swept by. Waist-deep in the surge, Tomi grabbed at her thin arm. Beneath him, the river sucked at his legs. He slipped, and as he was pulled under, his mouth and eyes filled with water. His knees slammed into a rock, and he kicked wildly, thrusting himself up, slipping by the boulders. He grabbed at Eren—at anything. The river sucked him smoothly under again.

Moira was already moving, jamming her numb legs against the ground and throwing herself after the boy. Tomi was bare inches from her straining hands. His arm thrashed, grasping at the slick space between them while his other hand tangled in Eren's hair. The desperation in his eyes terrified Moira even as he swept past, choking, a handspan, then more, out of reach. Eren's hands dug into his arms. The river surged. The children went under. Moira, not yet realizing the frozen shock of the mountain river as it iced her skin and burned that frozen burn inside her womb, slipped and slid as the run of water grabbed her legs and slammed her against a rock. Her ankle, then her calf, jammed with crushing pain. She gasped, swallowing water. The current forced her under before she could fight her way back to the surface. And then she was choking herself, and the nails of Jered's fingers were digging through her shoulders. He jerked, then tore her free from the river. But she struggled against him, her eyes staring after the current; she did not notice his desperate strength. Aunt Giela opened her mouth to scream as the two children were thrust back up to the surface just ahead of a deep standing wave. Moira, clinging to Jered with one hand, lunged at the bank, clamping her other hand over Auntie's mouth. They watched in horror as the tiny heads swept up, swept over, and were gone.

Jered looked at her expressionlessly, and her aunt choked back her sobs. "Eren—Tomi—"

Moira, her eyes hollow, stared after the river, then got to her feet. She helped her aunt up, then motioned to where the other elders had hauled the rest of the youngsters away from the water.

"Moira," Jered began urgently.

She pivoted on her heel, the expression on her face silencing the old man.

He licked his lips.

Beside him, Aunt Giela ventured, "Moira, they will . . . they will drown."

The tall woman stared at them, unseeing. "They are dead already. Not one of us could keep up with the river's pace. The waters of the Phye will—will drown them or give them back to the raiders before we could reach their bodies."

"We could go after them. Jered and I—"

"Jered and you and I are all that are left to carry the rest of these children who still trust us with their lives."

"Moira," the elder pleaded.

"There are other, living children." Moira's voice was harsh.

Jered wiped his hands on his tunic, smearing their wetness into mud against the dirt. "It's a hard trail you lead, Moira," he said, his voice flat, devoid of accusation.

"Jered," she started. She stopped when he turned back, and stared into his eyes, but as he saw the grief and horror deep within, it was Jered who looked away.

Chapter 2

There, above the blackheart trees;
There, where the sky lifts up;
Just above the thinnest branches,
Where the air itself is pale;
Ice hangs with your breathing;
Ice clings to your hands.
Climb there—
Climb up,
Where the rhythm of the bull elk calling, calling
Is only your heart beating, beating up the trail.

It was midmorning now. Where Dion stood, the sounds of the woods were almost buried under the canyon wind. Until she moved back from the river, even when she strained, she could barely hear the howl of the wolf pack on the ridge. Warily, she made her way back to the main trail. A twig snapped; Hishn's ears pricked, and Dion froze, her eyes flickering to the right. It was only a small chunko, its rodent teeth chewing up the stick and stuffing it into his mouth. Dion did not move. Death came in many forms here: raiders, badgerbears, worlags, snakes . . . As many years as she had run the woods, there was one danger that still chilled her blood to ice: worlags. The beetle-beasts could tear her skin like paper—she had the scars to prove it—and the tracks she had come upon an hour earlier proved that they were near.

Silently, she melted into the undergrowth, away from the canyon's edge. Her gray cloak was its own shadow, and the greens and leather browns of her tunic and leggings hid her in the colors of the forest. Cold, the canyon's breath brought color to her cheeks, and the violet of her eyes flashed as the pale sun lit them between the movements of the leaves. With her hand in Hishn's thick fur, Dion acknowledged the Gray One's impatience softly. The wolves in the pack sensed no danger, but the wind for them was wrong. Hishn sniffed the air first to one side, then the other, then glanced back at the wolfwalker.

One last time, Dion's wary gaze swept the forest and the broken ridge. "All right," she said softly. "Let's go on."

The wolf's yellow eyes gleamed. *We run with the pack?* she sent, her gray voice echoing in Dion's mind.

"There's no time to join them," Dion returned. "We have come only halfway."

When you see through my eyes and hear through my ears, you cover twice the distance in half the time.

Dion cuffed the Gray One lightly. "As long as there is something in your belly, you don't care how far we have to run. I, on the other hand, have my feet to consider; and my feet still have five kilometers to go before I can take a break."

Hishn growled softly in her throat, and Dion grinned. The Gray One's impatience was with more than the trail. Hishn's mate was running to join them. He was near already—the gray threads of his thoughts rang through Hishn's mental voice almost as strongly as if he were standing there beside his mate.

Hishn's eyes gleamed. *Yoshi and I have better ears than you,* she sent persuasively. *Why do you not use my senses to hear the song of the pack?*

"I want to hear through human ears, Gray One, as the refugees must do two days from now." Dion scratched Hishn's ear. "If they could hear the packsong as I do, there would be no need to worry about them on the trail." She glanced fondly at the wolf. Three years they had been together, and she could no longer imagine what it was like not to have the gray threads in her mind. Hishn went almost everywhere with her. Only when the wolf felt the need to run with her mate did she leave Dion behind. At least Gray Yoshi had his own wolfwalker; otherwise, Hishn might have run with a mate far from Ariye. The wolves, not just the humans, made concessions when they bonded. Dion gave Hishn one last scratch, then shoved the wolf away, brushing ineffectually at the winter fur left behind on her leggings.

Faint sweat sharp in my nose. Sweet leather. The wolf sent her images to Dion automatically, letting the woman smell herself through Hishn's senses. The wolf dug her nose into the dirt. *Fresh rabbit dung—like a call to the hunt* . . . The gray voice echoed wistfully. Dion sighed, breathing in the scents with flared nostrils. This forest, these sights and sounds and smells—Hishn could not let Dion live away from them: the bond of a wolf forced its own changes. With all the wolves fleeing Bilocctar, they swept across Ariye like a gray storm, catching up in their passing the senses of half the county. There had been four more wolf-bondings in Ariye than had been seen in two decades. At least, Dion thought, she herself had been a forest runner before she found Hishn as a pup. The changes for her were not as radical as the changes forced on some of the businesspeople in Aranur's town. She smiled at the memory of one of the more portly men trotting after his Gray One and sweating like a winter hare in summer.

Her own stomach growled, and Hishn's eyes gleamed in triumph. The wolfwalker shook her head. "We will both hunt later," she promised. "Right now, I have to listen. If I can hear the wolves as clearly here as I do now, the wind might carry the sound clearly to the refugees across the river. And if that is so, the refugees might forget the Devil's Knee and bolt like deer to the Sky Bridge instead. And the Sky Bridge," she added, "as we saw—"

Smelled, Hishn inserted strongly, sneezing into the dirt.

Dion made a face at the yellow gleaming eyes. "—stinks with the number of raiders who lurk there like rats on a wharf." Most of the time, the gray creature projected images, rather than words, filling Dion's mind with a voice like a soft and constant rain. Sometimes, the power of the smells and strength of the instincts of the wolf made her cringe.

Hishn scratched her belly with one of her hind legs, then shifted and scratched the other side with her other rear leg. *I could howl,* she suggested, *and you could ask those who run now on the other bank if they hear me.*

Dion's smile faded. Those people running now—the marks they had left at the riverbank were deep, as if they did not know how damning those signs were. And the springtime rush of the river was subsiding, not rising—the marks would stay until the next heavy rain. Dion glanced at the sky. The cloud cover was thin, not building with the thunderheads of spring. The marks would not be gone quickly. She could only hope the runners two days from now would be more careful with their feet.

Hishn trotted ahead on the trail. . . . *Dust and blood,* she sent from her memory. *Dried sweat. The acrid smell of fear and rancid breath.*

The image of the battered man who had crossed the river a ninan—nine days—ago made Dion nod slowly. "Some other poor fool," she said echoing the words of the scout she met with yesterday. "Heading upriver, though," she added to herself. North—the direction of the Devil's Knee.

There is less thunder in your ears above the falls than below it, sent the wolf.

Dion nodded. "If I could contact them there, above the Knee, I could direct them further north—to the Slot."

They could not wait in their den until you are ready to help them cross?

Dion almost laughed. "There is no den to keep them safe from the raiders, Hishn. Could you hole up if worlags were on your heels?"

The gray wolf wrinkled her nose, baring her teeth. *You cannot survive the hunter by hiding where it can easily go.*

"No." Dion pursed her lips. "If they are moving as slowly as I think, it would be two more days of travel to the Slot, but they could gain a fair degree of safety crossing up there."

If the raiders are like worlags, they will track your runners to the Slot and back.

"Not if Gamon sends some riders to meet them. Once they cross below the Slot, they are in Ariye, and we can protect them." She settled her bow across her shoulders and automatically checked the thong across the hilt of her sword.

Hishn's yellow eyes gleamed. *We hunt?*

"We run. Only to the Devil's Knee."

The water pulls like a mudsucker at the Devil's Knee.

"We're not the ones who have to cross the Phye," she reassured the wolf. "All we have to do is pass the scouting news on to Aranur." And spend some time alone together, she added silently. Hishn gave her a sly look. Flushing, Dion cuffed the wolf's soft ears. "No snide remarks," she admonished.

Your mate is close, the wolf returned, dodging out of reach.

But my mate—Gray Yoshi—is closer. I will have my greeting long before you have yours.

Dion grinned after the wolf. The Gray One—Yoshi—who even now raced to meet Hishn would be here in perhaps ten minutes; Aranur was still an hour away. Dion forced her jog to drop back to its calm pace, smiling ruefully as she realized she had, as usual, quickened her steps at his image. But it had been days, a tiny inner voice reminded, causing her to speed up her pace again in spite of herself.

Days—two days, the thought came back. Dion could not help imagining a ragged group of people running for the border, running for a hidden crossing they trusted to be there. Racing north, stumbling perhaps, beside the river that blocked their escape. In Ariye, Aranur and Gamon had had only nine days to build the crossing—one ninan to make good on the promise of safety. But there were people fleeing now: people whom she could not touch, could not help.

Her hand reached up to the silver circlet that had slipped out from under her warcap. Carved with the language of the ancients, the language of the First World, it affirmed her skills. Most of her skills anyway, she admitted silently. There was one skill omitted from the carvings of the circlet—one skill she had to hide from the people of Ariye themselves. Not even Ariye's Lloroi knew she had healed his son with the ancient secret of Ovousibas. "Look to the left," it meant: Ovousibas. Only Aranur, and perhaps Gamon, knew how much it took out of her to do it.

Aranur. Her hand dropped to her chest where a tiny gem had been set into her sternum. With every running step, her fingers jerked and grazed its edges. Purple it was, for the Waiting Year—a year that was nearly over. She smiled to herself. She was Promised. In two months, Gamon would no longer be just a friend, but an uncle. In two months, she and Aranur would be mated.

Promised. She repeated the word like a chant. Aranur, so tall and lean, with the broad shoulders of a fighter, and the narrow hips of a runner. He had cold, gray eyes that could freeze to ice when he was angry and darken with emotion when they were together. His humor, sharp as his sword, made them both laugh, and the force of his person was like a wind whipping through the woods. They argued—probably more than they should, she thought wryly—but she could not expect a mating without conflict when both of them were as stubborn as winter oxen. She could only be glad that even when he disagreed with her, he stood by her decisions and backed her when she faced the council, even as she did for him. Their mating would not be a calm one, she admitted; but perhaps, she realized with sudden insight, she preferred the storm.

She reached the top of a rise and stretched her legs against the cold canyon air. Her gaze flickered back, automatically searching the path for movement behind her. The river canyon split the forest to her left, making a dark line through the vertical shafts of the trees. To her right and ahead, the ridges rose further, taking themselves up into the mountains of Ariye. The other scouts were right—the trail here was lonely of men and women; the dawns were still damp and chill, and the nights near-black and sightless under the cloud-heavy skies of spring. But only here, along the middle border, was she close enough to Aranur. One hour, she promised herself. One hour to see him, report on the raiders, ask him about the fear of the refugees for the wolves. And then, when their duties were done, and the forest could give them privacy, there would be some time for each other.

In Bilocctar, last autumn, when the dying leaves still clung to the trees, and spring was just a dream of the new year . . .

The man behind Conin was like the young Lloroi's shadow. Nervously, Namina stared at the guard. Shadow Man, she called him in her mind. He was carefully not listening to their words, his ears and eyes turned instead for sounds of danger, and Namina, hating herself for a coward, knew he ignored her because she was the last person anyone would consider a threat. Even holding the power that went with being the Lloroi's mate did not make her dangerous; she could not assert herself to anyone, including Conin, her mate.

She shifted her gaze to her husband. She should be grateful he had Promised with her, although she did her best by him: as she had been a dutiful daughter, so now she was a dutiful mate. She went with him everywhere, listened to his councils, heard his speeches, worried when he was away. In return, he gave her a home, a position, respect and fondness, pretty curiosities from all three of his counties . . . Her hand rose to touch the two gems that studded her sternum. After a year of marriage, she supposed she loved him.

Was her Promise such a prison? She raised her eyes. If so, then here, in Bilocctar, Conin was as trapped as she. He was Lloroi of Ramaj Bilocctar, but he did not control his own counties. He was only a figurehead. It was Longear who held the real power—Longear, that small, dark-haired woman who ran his secret service, ordered his soldiers, and controlled the raiders on the border. She dictated Conin's every move. With Longear behind his seat, Conin's hands were tied as surely as if they were bound with steel.

Namina frowned at the paper Conin was holding. His hands were young, like his face. His hair was wavy and brown with a hint of red, his eyes dark black, his bone structure delicate. But since they had been married, two grooves had grown between his eyes. He no longer smiled, but carried in his gaze the fatigue and bitterness of a man haunted with the destruction he had wrought by his own good intentions.

Namina was like enough to him to be his sister. Her thick brown hair was dark and wavy, and her fine bones gave her a prettiness that would age into beauty. Her eyes were blue and wide, not tired like Conin's, but wary and somewhat timid, like a rabbit who does not know if the field is safe. Watching the faint disdain on the Shadow Man's face, Namina knew that her lack of confidence showed. She could not do any of the things at which her sister or cousins excelled. She was lousy at business. She was useless on the council—she could not open her mouth to discuss an issue if her life depended on it. Organizing people took authority, and no one had ever accused her of having that. Her fingers were clumsy in any craft that required dexterity—which was just a polite way of saying that she lacked even the most basic eye for design or detail. She could not even manage a fighting knife as one of her cousins had learned to do. The riding beasts scared her, the mining worms gave her shivers, and although other livestock did not actively dislike her, she was frightened enough of their unpredictable ways that she could not even take charge of feeding them. As for traveling, she had had enough of that to last a lifetime. With its stinging insects, cloying mud, and burning blisters, she hated traveling more than the thought of gellbugs in her bed. The only thing she did well, she thought derisively, was listen. Listen to the council, listen to Conin. She had come to hate the word.

Conin glanced up from the letter and saw her eyes dart from her feet to his face and back down. He frowned, reading the paper again.

Namina watched him furtively. The wilted, crumpled letter had not suffered her anxiety well. It was not her first letter from home—in the last year, her mother had written six times, her cousin twice. Namina had not answered them before; but this time, the contents of that paper could not be ignored—even by her.

When Conin finished reading, he handed the letter back. "She sounds as if she is fine," he said politely. Namina took the paper but did not move, and Conin looked at her sharply. His mate never asked, never demanded, anything. He supposed that was why he tried so hard to please her. After her sister died, she had withdrawn—that was what her cousin told him once—but he guessed that she had always been shy. Now, he recognized the struggle in her to force out her words.

Namina hesitated. "My mother . . ." Her voice trailed off. She tried again. "She said . . ." She cursed herself silently, hating her cowardice, hating her inability to speak. She had rehearsed the words for days, and now she could not say even three of them at once.

Conin watched her patiently. She was fragile, like a siker flower, he thought. She made him feel strong—almost powerful. It was, he thought bitterly, probably the other reason he needed her so much. While Longear made him a puppet, Namina made him feel like a man. Namina, watching him, bit her lip, and he tried to smile.

"As usual," he prompted, "your mother said that your brother is fine, your uncle Gamon's leg is bothering him less because the weather is warmer, the mining worms look like they are breeding well, and"—he gestured at himself—"your father would like to see you and meet the man who Promised you a year ago."

Namina looked down at her feet. That was not all her mother

had said, she told him silently, willing the words to spill out of her mouth.

Conin watched her closely. He could swear that she was trembling. He almost barked a laugh—what could Namina have to fear from him? He was Lloroi, and he was the least powerful man in the county. "Namina," he said softly, "what is it?"

"My mother says that—that the border is closed between the outer county and Ramaj Ariye," she stammered.

He stiffened slowly. So, Longear had done it. Taken the border with her raiders, trapped the people within the county. Just as she said she would, with his seal on the orders, she took his word to the border with the blades of her raiders. Trade, mail, travel—she controlled them all now. And how long had it taken her to do it? Two months? Three? How many people had resisted? And how many deaths was he responsible for now?

Namina gathered courage at his silence. "She says that it brings trouble to both our counties."

Conin stared at her bleakly. "The borders are not your concern," he said curtly. Namina blanched, and he cursed himself again. Damn Longear, he thought vehemently. Damn her to the seventh hell. Namina was the only person in the county who believed in him—loved him, even—and because of Longear, he could not even keep Namina safe from his witlessness.

Namina did not look up, but her voice, when it came again, was stubborn. "I worry," she said quietly, "when my family has to risk their lives just to send me a message."

Conin regarded her in amazement. Namina was disagreeing with him. Namina, who didn't know the meaning of the word *argue*.

"Your mother is mistaken. They hardly risked their lives," he said finally. "The borders are not closed, just controlled. The trade caravans still go through. The mail has not been stopped. Anyone delivering that—or any other—letter would not have been harmed for it."

Namina clenched her fists in the pockets of her loose trousers. "You're wrong. People in Ariye have been killed."

"Namina—"

"No, you listen, Conin." Namina surprised herself with her outburst. Her stomach quailed, but she faced him bravely. "What is this?" Her hands shook as she held out the letter. "People fleeing across the borders? Raiders killing anyone except traders who try to cross the Sky Bridge?''

Conin shrugged uncomfortably. ''We have not had good relations with Ariye in almost three years.''

Good relations? That was an understatement. The words rolled through Namina's head, but when she spoke, she said only, ''I want to go home.''

Conin stared at her.

Her resolution fled, and she trembled. ''I want to see my family,'' she whispered.

Conin stood up. He sat down again without a word. He opened his mouth, shut it, then got up again and strode to her, looking at her closely. ''This is your home,'' he said finally. ''I am your family.''

''I want to go home to Ariye.''

''No!'' he exploded. With a muttered oath, he motioned abruptly for her to follow him. He stalked toward the door that led to their private apartments. Namina walked after him silently. Behind them, the shadow fighter followed the young Lloroi until Conin threw a venomous look over his shoulder. The guard subsided into the shadows.

As soon as the door was closed, Namina spoke. ''Conin,'' she said softly, ''you won't lose me.''

He spun on his heel and burst out, ''I will. You'll go back to them—to your parents, to your cousin Aranur—and they will fill your head with lies about me. You'll make one excuse after another to stay, and finally, you will refuse to come back with me. To me.''

''We are mated,'' she protested.

''Longear said—''

''Longear.'' Namina's voice was small and hard. ''It's always Longear, isn't it?''

''I don't know what you mean,'' he muttered.

''She—she poisons you against my family,'' she said stubbornly. ''She poisons you against me.''

Conin did not meet her eyes. ''She is important to my control of the county. She knows everything about my father's rule over Bilocctar. I—need her.'' He choked on the last words.

''Longear is the head of your secret service,'' Namina whispered. ''Nothing more.''

"She advises me on everything: the crafts, the housing, the economics—"

"And the borders."

"And the borders," he agreed bleakly.

"Why did you take her back?" The despair in Namina's voice was palpable.

"Because," he whispered, "if I had not, she would then have taken the county—taken everything away from me. She would have taken you, too."

Namina stepped forward. Hesitantly, she laid her head on his shoulder. They held hands loosely at their waists. "I Promised to you," she said in a quiet voice. "I mated with you. My vows bind me to you more strongly than steel itself."

Conin winced at her words. It had been steel, not love, that had brought them together a year ago. The steel of the sword, the iron of the chains of his father's prisons. He had never asked Namina about her time in the jails, and she had not volunteered. He could have found out everything—how she had looked when she went in, if the guards molested her, how she suffered the stench and sickness of the place. He did not want to know. After that first meeting, when he saw her for the first time and recognized that lost look as his own expression, he begged his father for her. And after she had been released, she had stayed with him. Even when her family returned to Ramaj Ariye, she had stayed—stayed and Promised with him, so that her family could go free. Moons damn his weakness, but it had been Longear who had imprisoned Namina in the first place. It had been Longear, too, who had convinced his father that the Ariyens plotted against the Lloroi. And Longear it was who tried to kill Conin himself a ninan later—just after he took power.

Longear. A dark-haired woman with a sharp tongue and a bitter knowledge. A woman who stood barely to his shoulders, but could destroy his dreams in a few words as completely as if she had smashed them with an ax. When she failed to take his life, he sent troops back to kill her, and she disappeared. She showed up again a month later, laughing and mocking his puny efforts at leadership—when the county was in chaos, and he could not manage even one of the craft guilds, let alone deal with simple problems like the traffic of produce into the city, or the relocation of two of the cramped schools onto vacant property. Every problem was connected. He could not answer one question or commit to one favor without destroying someone else's livelihood. And then there were the big issues. The tonnis root, the dator drugs, creeping into the city like a tide. The dissatisfaction of troops that were suddenly bored, broke, and violently restless. The gangs that looted the shops, burned homes, stole children and left their bodies to be found on the steps of his own council room. The problems that dragged him down as soon as his father was dead.

The old Lloroi had been no hero, Conin knew. But he had been a leader. No one had questioned his father's judgment. They jumped at the chance to follow his father from one campaign to the next. He paid them, fed them, housed them, and gave them pride. They worshipped him like a god. Even if that pride was built on the bullying and deaths of others, it did not matter. It was theirs. Hells, even the counties he had taken over had not resisted. The troops the old Lloroi had commissioned never once saw battle; they occupied the counties like police. When trouble rose, it was twenty troops to three or four people. The few who dared to complain were now dead. Conin shook his head. His own father, a tyrant. Longear bringing the raiders in by droves. And no one questioned it.

And what of himself? What of Conin? He strangled on his bitterness. He was a bastard—a child accident. No notice from his father did he get growing up. No roughhousing down at the weaponhall. No encouragement for his studies. No advice to grow with, to live by. Only two things had the old Lloroi given him: the rule of the county for his twenty-third birthday, and a grave to mark his father's passage. That, he snarled to himself, and the memory of the people who would not let Conin forget the man in whose steps he followed.

What was it that let his father rule where he could not? His father had not worried if a man here disagreed, if a woman there was hurt by a decision. But one order from Conin, and a dozen voices argued. He tried to listen. He tried to make good decisions. But he was nervous, and they were sharks. They sounded out his uncertainties and explained to him that he needed help here and there, until he had so many people running the county that he did not even know who represented the guilds. That each was as corrupt as the next, he did not doubt. But how to replace them, get rid of them? If he could beg the moons for an answer, he would, but he did not think the moons looked kindly on him now. Not since he had become Longear's puppet.

It had taken only four ninans to become her marionette. One month after he became Lloroi, he had stood on his balcony and stared at the city, watching as another fire blazed a kilometer away. He could not stop the raids. Of the two people he had originally trusted to help him rule, one had disappeared after an argument with another leader, and the other had suddenly resigned. The first had certainly died. The second, Conin was sure, had been threatened into resigning. Who was behind it? Who had engineered the collapse of his authority so cleverly that he could do nothing about it?

There could be only one person.

Longear.

And Conin was her slave. As surely as if he had put her chains around his neck himself, he did her bidding. He had no choice.

It had been almost a year now. An entire year of hell since she had showed up again. She had let herself into his study, when he was alone. He could not even have called for help, because while she faced him, she had her men holding his mate, Namina, hostage.

Why had he not resisted more? Why not risk the knife? Why not fight? Why, as Namina asked, had he given in and taken Longear back? Every night, in the hours before the first pale tones of dawn crossed his windowsills, he woke from his nightmares and wondered if he could have taken the rule of the county by himself. And every morning, when the shadows that marked the day grew clear, and he could no longer toss and turn the night away, he slept again, knowing he could not have remained Lloroi without her. Longear had been his only choice. He could have stepped down, yes. And his enemies would have swarmed like vultures, tearing each other apart in their greed for power. And Longear would have waited until they made each other weak, and then would have taken everything.

Yes, he might be a figurehead, he admitted angrily—but he was not completely helpless. He looked at Namina. Her blue eyes watched him steadily. How could she be so calm? How could she ignore what it meant to have Longear hanging onto his back, choking him with her advice?

''I understand, Conin,'' she said softly.

His face softened. Namina knew him. It was the reason she had stayed. They knew each other as if they had found in each other another part of themselves. She was the daughter of the Lloroi of Ariye. She had taught him how to be Lloroi of Bilocctar—how to resist Longear, work around her, even when the woman seemed to hold every key to the county in her hand. And to Namina, he was stability. Strength. A way of life. He protected her, gave her a home to replace the one from which she had been stolen. He looked at her now and clenched his fists. She was not a strong person, perhaps, but she was his.

''All right,'' he said suddenly. ''We will go to Ariye.''

She reached up and touched his lips lightly, and he almost smiled.

Chapter 3

Stretch deep in the forest greens
Fill your nose with its senses
Run with us—
Hunt with us—
Wolfwalker!

Hishn turned back on the trail and nudged Dion's thigh. Once more, they stood on the lip of the canyon, staring down at the river, watching the white water burst over the rocks. Dion had seen no more sign of the travelers on the other side of the river. Whether that meant they had already been captured by the raiders or were still running, she did not know.

For what do you listen? Hishn asked. *I hear only the flickers in the trees and the sound of the ant-largons chewing at the bones of a rat.*

Dion did not shift her gaze. "Gray One, are there wolves on the other side of the river?"

Hishn cocked her head. *Yes,* she returned, *though the pack is small.*

Dion nodded slowly. She could swear she had heard the howling of a wolf, but the wind was deceptive. She scraped her boot against a rock, knocking mud from her heel. Sometimes, she admitted wryly, she wished she had not fallen for a weapons master. Aranur was an even harder taskmaster than his uncle

Gamon had been before him, and this scout line was proof of that. Back and forth along the river, up over the ridges, down along the cliffs; reading the signs of the animals brought across the stars by the ancients; tracking the signs left by the creatures of this world; noting the human prints on every trail; hauling herself across the frozen waters of the Phye just to see that the raiders were, indeed, still sitting on the bridges . . . She ran a longer trail than any scout except Sobovi, the other wolfwalker. She grimaced. No one, she thought sourly, could say she was favored because Aranur and she were Promised.

She grimaced at the mud that still clung to her footgear. At least Aranur no longer insisted on scouting with her, she thought. When she had first come to his county, he had not believed that the bond of the wolves brought its own protection. It had taken some ingenuity to discourage him from dogging her heels—ingenuity, plus a fireweed meadow, a stingers' swarm, a nest of blue adders . . . She grinned to herself. She had not realized how stubborn he was. Four ninans of surviving the lepa and nightspiders, the badgerbears and the wild pigs, and it was the poison sleyva that finally did him in. It had taken twelve days for the swelling to go down, and his face had been pocked like a plague the whole time.

She looked up now, at the mottled forest across the river. What would he think of the wolves that ran on the other bank? It seemed odd that there were still Gray Ones there. So many wolves had fled Bilocctar in the last year. Why had those few not moved on?

As if her question had triggered them to cry out, the wind lifted the Gray Ones' howls, and Dion cocked her head, listening intently, trying to reach far enough through Hishn to read the thread that pulled at her attention. *Grief,* came the faint sensation. *Sorrow like the death of a pup, like the loss. Frustration—like a caged and hungry wolf looking at the carcass of an elk, hung out of reach and still warm from the kill . . .*

Dion glanced at Hishn. The creature's yellow eyes gleamed back, as she passed on the packsong for Dion's mental ears.

"Hishn," she said softly, "I have heard those notes in the song of a single wolf—like the mother we came upon who lost her litter. But this—you are singing the song of the pack, not a lone wolf, and it is not a song of grieving that is anything like what we have heard before."

Hishn sneezed in the dirt. *Once, when a wolfwalker died,* she returned, *we heard the pack howl together.*

"This is not sorrow for the loss of a partner," she murmured. "This is different." She shivered, then wrapped her cloak more tightly around her, but her chills were in her mind. For now that she had identified the note in the packsong, she realized that it was not just grief that she heard. It was a terrible despair. "Can you speak with them, Hishn? Ask what makes them howl like that?"

Hishn's ears flickered back toward Dion. *They are closed to me—tight against my voice.*

Closed? The Gray Ones might not welcome another wolf in their physical pack, but they usually welcomed all to their mental song; there was no such thing as a self-contained pack. Puzzled, Dion reached out to the gray storm on her side of the river, the dim voices growing as she focused on their tones. Hishn's voice was strong in her own pack, Gray Yoshi a solid line of gray threading around his mate's tones. Then the rest of the pack: six males, five females, three yearlings. But there was a hurt in their memories, too—a deeply buried hurt that spoke of more than simple pain. Their racial memories reflected the song from the other side of the river, too. Dion scowled, trying to put words to those images. What they felt was more than hurt, she realized. Betrayal was closer, but who could betray the Gray Ones? The ancient bond with humans was sacred—no one harmed a wolf. Neither could a wolfwalker force a wolf to do his bidding—the Gray Ones honored humans with their senses, but were not pets or slaves; they were partners. What they did, they did with love. When that love was gone, so, too, were the wolves.

Dion shifted her stance as the wind brought the song more faintly across the canyon. She hiked slowly back to the trail, picking up her pace again when she reached the smooth path. Only a raider, she thought bitterly, could bring that much grief to a Gray One's soul.

She halted abruptly.

Ahead of her, Hishn stopped and looked back.

Raiders?

No, she reasoned, that was not likely. She had heard rumors of raiders trying to control the wolves, rumors that had started long before Dion came to Ariye. There was no truth to them. Run with a raider—a murderer, a torturer? The wolves would never do it.

But somewhere over there, somewhere on the rim, in the trees beyond her sight, the Gray Ones hunted. They hunted . . . humans. Could it be true? That note in the packsong—the betrayal—could it be the song of a wolf betraying itself? Running with a raider? She had never heard of such a thing. Perhaps, she thought, her lips curling in distaste, even the raiders had one sensitive among them. But a whole pack? No, she rationalized, even a single wolf partnering with a raider did not make sense. Raiders did not fight in self-defense—they fought for gold, for weapons, for goods. They attacked villages, they took prisoners, they tortured their captives for sport. How could a wolf honor a murderer? Would it not sense the difference? What the raiders did went against the bond of the wolves as no other actions could. But, and Dion's eyes scanned the opposite bank restlessly, somewhere close, sometime soon, the raiders would be running refugees to ground. Perhaps even now, those on the west side of the Phye were running for their lives, running from the bridges the raiders guarded, running from the wolves the raiders controlled.

Dion knelt in the trail, reaching for Hishn with both hands. She buried her face in the fur. "Gray One," she whispered, "do you know? The wolves across the river—who do they run with? Why do they grieve?"

Hishn's yellow eyes were puzzled. She nudged Dion until the wolfwalker sat back, frustrated. After three years, Dion should know better. The Gray Ones could make no sense of human views. If a wolfwalker was a raider, the wolves would not know it. They would see only that, like Dion, the runner was a member of the pack.

Hishn nudged her thigh again, trying to understand Dion's need. *Their song is dull,* she sent. *They do not wish me to sing with them.*

"But why?" There were few wolves running the hunt on the raiders' side of the Phye, but then again, it only took one to find a human's heavy trail. Dion stretched her senses into Hishn, reaching with all her concentration to the three beasts who howled on the canyon's other side. Dark gray and dull, their song was faint, even through Hishn. Dion touched it, wove her voice into the threads—

—and was cut off as if she were not even a wolfwalker herself. Even her ears were rejected from the howls as the gray tendrils tightened into a distant wall of fog. Dion sat back slowly, stunned. Rejected. Hishn was not welcome in their pack, and Dion was closed out completely? Never since she bonded with Hishn had she been denied the song of the wolves. A core of anger sparked deep in her gut. No wolf in its right mind would deliberately cut a wolfwalker from the packsong.

No wolf in its right mind . . . A slow shiver crawled down Dion's spine. What if the wolves ran, not by choice, but by coercion? What if the raiders had somehow forced the Gray Ones to do their bidding? She got to her feet slowly and stared back over the canyon. Hells, but it made no sense. The Gray Ones' code was strict. There were cases of wolfwalkers who had turned, and then been abandoned by their wolves. What would force a wolf to run with a raider?

"In eight hundred years," she muttered, "what has changed?" Eight centuries ago, when the ancients first landed on this world, bondings between them and the wolves had been common. But the disease in the Gray Ones' genes—the disease planted by the birdmen—had been passed from generation to generation until now the wolves were few, and the humans they bonded with even fewer. In all those centuries, though, whether the wolves were many or few, they had never broken their trust with their humans. Never had they hunted men; never had they attacked except in defense of their wolfwalkers. So, Dion asked herself again, what had changed? Or, she thought suddenly, to ask it differently, what would make Hishn herself hunt refugees for a raider?

She regarded the gray creature with a frown. Hishn blinked at her, and the wolfwalker stiffened.

There could be only one reason Hishn would run with a raider: Dion.

Her lips thinned into a grim line. If she were captive—if she were in pain—Hishn would do whatever Dion asked. And if Dion asked her to hunt down humans, to betray that ancient trust between the wolves and humans, would Hishn do it—to keep her wolfwalker alive?

I run with you, Wolfwalker, Hishn growled. *I hunt as you wish it.*

"Hishn," Dion said urgently. "The wolves over there—" She pointed with her chin. "Do they run because their wolfwalkers are hurt?"

The pack runs where it must.

"Is their hunt unhappy?" she persisted.

Hishn hesitated. *The hunt is as it is.*

"Do they—is the pain in their song . . . normal?"

The wolf looked at her in puzzlement. *The song is as it is.*

Dion bit her lip. Hishn did not understand her questions, and the wolfwalker could not read the packsong. "But then," she muttered, "what difference does reading the packsong make?" Whether the wolves had bonded with raiders or were hunting by coercion, either way, Aranur would have to know. And if the wolves were being betrayed, Ramaj Ariye could not stand silent. The trust of the Gray Ones was something that humans, too, must honor.

Hishn yelped softly, and Dion realized that her fists were clenched in the gray pelt. She released the wolf, scratching the thick fur gently to ease her unconscious tugging. The wolves on the other side of the canyon moved away, their voices growing dim, while the song of the pack on this side grew stronger. They were closer now; their lupine feet padded against the earth in her mental ears, their voices like a gray din behind Hishn's sharp images. As Dion glanced at the broken ridge that rose above the river, two of the nine moons hung beside one of the rocky spires, waiting, it seemed, for her to follow them. Even the moons, she thought wryly, called her to run with the wolves. She made the sign of the moonsblessing. The refugees, she thought, shaking out her cloak and welcoming the chill blast that curled inside her jerkin and cooled her trail sweat, would need it.

Gray Hishn's voice touched her mind, troubled, and Dion looked down. Hishn's image of the other wolves was too close, too real, even though their song rejected her comfort. *Wolfwalker,* the Gray One snarled, unable to express the pain she sensed.

Dion gripped the gray fur. The voice in her mind was more real to her than the feel of the coarse hair against her fingers.

The gray bond thickened and became taut. "Gray One," she whispered, "you honor me."

Hishn whined, and Dion shook the fur from her hands. "Come," she said resolutely. "If the crossing is close enough to being done, I could climb into Bilocctar today."

The wolf growled. *The land across the river is a worlags' den. You will no longer go there.*

Dion glanced at her. "But if I see the Gray Ones who run the hunt in Bilocctar, I could speak to them. I could ask them about their packsong—find out why they reject us."

Hishn balked. *No.*

"Someone must," she asserted. "You cannot reach them from here, so, neither can I. And I—no, not just me, but all of Ariye needs to know if the Gray Ones are being somehow betrayed."

You will not run with them. Hishn's mental voice was adamant.

Dion looked at her in surprise. "I will not leave you for long, Hishn. I would rather you came with me, but you cannot cross under the falls as I can. And by the time you ran to the Slot and down to the Knee again, I would be back in Ariye."

Hishn growled, her once-clear images degenerating into an instinctive chaos. She could not articulate her stubborn denial.

"Don't worry, Gray One," Dion soothed. "Even if they do not want me in their county, I am a wolfwalker. I will be safe with the other wolves."

. . . hunter lust in my gut. Hot scent of blood burning, burning in the flames. Meat, fresh, human. Warm oils on the trail, hot scent on the ground, on the leaves. Cries and screams that fill my ears and do not end. And hunger, hunger tearing at my gut . . .

Dion frowned slowly. Hishn's concern was more than mere worry—it was a warning. "All right, Hishn," she soothed. "I will not run with those across the river." The creature's images calmed, but remained turbulent, and Dion wondered at the near panic her suggestion had caused.

Though her muscles had tightened already from standing, she hurried along the trail, hiking, then jogging, as the trail fell and rose. Ahead of her, the gray wolf ran, her growls still constant in the wolfwalker's mind. Dawn had come late that day, and even now, at midmorning, the small, pale sun of the mountains hid behind the gray-cast sky. Glancing at the heaviness above her, Dion pursed her lips. It must have rained up north—the east fork of the river was unseasonably high, though it was dropping by the hour. Even this distance from the canyon, she could hear the river's voice clearly as it crawled up the ravine and growled as strongly as the wolf by her side. The noise was welcome. In two days, there would be children at the crossing, and the river's sounds would drown their noise as it drowned the unwary within it. It would mask the sounds of her own movement on the trail, too. For with deer and other game driven away by the humans haunting this stretch of water, the worlags were hungry. Dion stifled her shudder. She would not use her voice again. Sound, which bounced off both rocks and water, could triple in seconds the number of hunters who would seek her.

She rubbed her sternum absently as she paused and studied the trail, tracing its familiar path by memory up the ridge. Underneath her jerkin, on her chest, the purple stone itched where it had been set into her flesh last fall. Beside her, Hishn suddenly stopped and hooked a rear leg onto a furry chest to scratch deeply. Tripping over the wolf, Dion realized that she was still rubbing her sternum. She made an irritated exclamation. Giving her an injured look, the gray wolf scrambled to her feet.

''That's not a flea, Hishn; that's me,'' she told the wolf curtly over her shoulder.

Hishn scratched again. *It still itches,* she protested.

Dion snorted, and Hishn, after a baleful glance at the wolfwalker, loped on ahead.

Dion made a face after her. She fingered her water bag, then broke into a jog again. It would be wise to reach the river soon—her bota bag was nearly empty, and Hishn's thirst was growing, too. There were places up ahead where the river fanned out shallowly and it was easy to get down the cliffs to the water. Beyond those places, there were streams that rushed down to the river. And there were the falls, where Aranur waited.

Aranur. She smiled to herself. Only one more hour. The wolves in Ariye, of course, had known the minute he had left camp. Even before Hishn picked up his image, Dion had felt their song blend his familiar scent into the gray mental trail. He should meet her on this side of Devil's Knee by midday. She absently brushed her hair from the silver healer's band that crossed her brow and peeked out from under the edge of her warcap. Wolfwalker and healer . . . Fighter and healer. Her hand dropped to her sword. There was a struggle in her to acknowledge both sets of skills. Both were for survival; both let her fight for life. Neither one left her without ghosts.

Images rose: a boy who died in her arms of fever; two men crushed beneath the rocks, screaming as they died. A woman writhing from the poison of a fireant, begging and pleading and promising anything if Dion would only stop the pain. People she could not help. People who had died because Dion had not yet learned Ovousibas. There were the other faces, too. Faces left behind by the raiders: discolored, cut with blood; eyes, sightless, staring at her soul. Dion clenched her fists suddenly, shoving down the memories. If she had had the skills then that she did now, she could have saved those lives. Ovousibas, the healing art of the ancients. Like her stealth, Dion learned her healing through the wolves. Ovousibas was her skill now—or her curse, as Gamon called it.

It was no miracle, as most people thought. Just a skill that tapped into the threads of gray and focused through them to heal bodies human and not. Few people knew that Ovousibas was real. Even when Dion dealt now with the trauma injuries from a rockfall, or the deep, mortal gouges of a badgerbear, she was careful to hide what she did, disguising it under the semblance of surgery and therapy and deprecating comments. The few that had seen her perform the healing did not speak of it. There were only two other healers that she knew of who had learned the skill, and they used it as sparingly as Dion. She fingered her sword again. Here, surrounded by the forest eyes, it was not the band of silver she used, but the blade of steel.

Ahead of her, out of sight, Hishn growled low in her throat, and Dion sent her a thought of reassurance. The gray creature lived through Dion's senses as much as Dion did through hers; when Dion thought of danger, Hishn's scruff would rise. The wolfwalker laughed softly, a bitter note creeping into the sound. There was little safety in knowing both sword and scalpel. Those skills that had saved her from the raiders before now made them want her life most bitterly. As a fighter, she thwarted them. As a healer, she negated their handiwork. And as a wolfwalker, she threatened them with every reach of her senses. She shoved the healer's band back up under her warcap. If there were raiders who watched the Ariyen border as closely as she did theirs, Dion did not want them to know her by sight.

Hishn's voice went taut suddenly. *Wolfwalker—*

Dion stiffened at the wolf's tone. She halted, searching the forest with her eyes, stretching her ears. "What is it?" She did not wait for the answer before she reached with her mind to the gray wolf's senses.

Hishn's mental voice reflected surprise and concern. *A cub.* She reappeared on the trail, her lips pulled back from her gleaming teeth.

Dion was startled. Casting through the chorus of gray voices that strengthened with Hishn's warning, Dion read the acrid scent that marked a human's fear. "A boy?"

Hishn's image was clear. *He runs like a rabbit who bolts beneath the lepa's talons.*

"Where?" Dion breathed, her eyes and ears with the wolves.

By the river, where the water is strong on the tongue. The gray wolf paused. *There are hunters on his scent.*

The image of the worlags was unmistakable, and Dion's hand clenched her sword hilt. Who could the boy be? And from where? No one could have tried to cross the river here—the refugees would not find the hidden ropes without help, and they were not even due for two more days. The people whose sign she had seen at dawn? Perhaps, but she was not happy with the answer. They must know how treacherous the river was. Even if they had their own ropes, they could not try to cross below the falls.

"How many worlags, Hishn? And how close are they to the boy?"

A band large as a wolf pack. Hishn's answer was uncertain. *They are close. They read the heat of his feet and legs in his trail. They smell the heat of head and hands.*

The oils, yes, by which the Gray Ones tracked. The boy must be near naked to leave so much scent—and sweating with fear. The images, sent through other lupine eyes, were confused with moving shadows, but the message was clear. Dion gathered her cloak and coiled it tightly around one of her arms, gripping the flapping end in her fingers. "Hishn, hurry—ask your brothers and sisters to guide him away from the worlags."

Hishn growled low. *He does not listen.* Her nostrils flared as she communicated with the rest of the pack. *His fear is thick in his throat like a bone.*

Dion was already moving, running in the direction of the wolf pack. "Then we must find him ourselves."

See with the eyes of the pack, the Gray One commanded. *Run with me, Wolfwalker.*

Dion, her feet pounding across the ground, opened her mind. The song of the Gray Ones swept in. In the din of their voices, her senses expanded. There were fourteen wolves on the ridge; Gray Yoshi close-by, and two more to the east. Dion could feel them all. And distantly, deep in the fog in the back of her mind, she could hear the other wolves—the ancestors, the racial memories that passed down their howling like a dull thunder lost through time and lives. She closed her thoughts to all but Hishn and Yoshi and the two nearby. Even with only those four in her mind, Dion felt the hairs on her free arm ruffle like fur. Her nose, suddenly sharp, picked up dust and sweat and the sweet scents of plants that whipped by her face. Hishn, running to her left, was downwind, and Dion felt her own odor fill her nose. Gray voices from other packs crowded into her mind, and her feet stretched in a long lope.

Acrid fear, sent the packsong. picking up the boy and passing the knowledge of him to the other wolves. *Sweat stench. Mud thick and stinking with the crushed duckfoot new from spring. Sudden sharp scent of the whitewood tree . . .*

Turn him, a gray wolf up ahead called to another. *The worlags gain . . .*

He falls . . . a female voice returned.

A yearling wolf picked up Dion's song in his own and, recognizing her voice, shouted gleefully, *Wolfwalker!*

You honor me, she sent breathlessly.

The first two voices chimed back in. *Your cub runs blindly,* sang the deep voice of a male.

He runs in fear, the old female howled.

Dion clenched her jaw. *Stay with him, Gray Ones.* Her urgency was a spear in the center of their song, and the gray beasts spurred themselves around the fleeing boy.

Run with us, Wolfwalker, they howled at her. *Sing with the pack . . .*

The voices blended and meshed in her mind so that she saw the river, the rocks, the worlags scuttling in the shadows. The boy stumbled and fell again. A Gray One lunged onto the path from behind him and he cried out in terror, scrambling to his feet and falling again before he fled. Dust dried in Dion's nose. Her ears seemed to lie back against her fur as she sensed his flight through the wolves. And to the east, paralleling their track, close enough now that the Gray Ones could hear the clicking of the beetlelike jaws, the worlags hunted.

Dion's feet slid in the damp dirt. Wet humus and soft, new leaves and old tree needles glommed onto her boots and were gone again when she raced through a clearing of stickgrass, the brittle leaves stabbing painfully at her ankles and snapping beneath her feet. Gray shadows moved in her sight. Fear—the worlags? No, not yet. Only wolves. The boy was near—she could smell him. She could taste his scent in her mouth as the Gray Ones sang it. The river's voice surged suddenly as she skidded around a huge boulder and slid into a dew-slick meadow that stretched to the water's edge. The boy? Where?

To the east—away from the river. The gray voice was Hishn's, picking up the song of the other wolves. *He has turned.* Her voice was urgent. *He runs toward the worlags.*

A chill struck through Dion's sweat. *Head him off, Gray Ones—hurry! We are almost there!*

Wolfwalker, they sang. *His fear is a stink that draws them close.*

A loop of Dion's cloak slipped off her arm and flapped, catching on the branches. She gave it a quick twirl to secure it again, ducking the leaves that slapped her face as she did so.

Now the trees thinned, and she could see further. The wolves swept up a rise like a gray flood, and Dion raced after them. Her wind was buoyed up by the wolves, and she gained the top without pain, her lungs free and full, before she saw him. A boy, yes, and running terrified.

''Stop!'' she cried out. ''Not that way!''

He did not hear. His ears were closed in terror. He stumbled, sobbing as he landed in a clump of redbrush. When he staggered out of it again, he cried out and threw himself back from the Gray One who tried to block his path.

Dion sprinted forward. She was gaining, but so, too, were the worlags. She could almost see them now, shadows in the Gray Ones' minds. Their acrid scent clogged the wolves' nostrils. Their chittering filled her ears.

The boy disappeared behind a thick stand of trees, and a cloud of spotted birds rose up screaming, fleeing to another roost.

Hishn dodged to her right. *This way—it is clear this way—*

Within the stand, the trail petered out, and the boy thrashed into the brush, rodents and reptiles alike scurrying away from his clumsy feet. The Gray Ones swept around the trees. Dion and Hishn skirted the bushes. He would come out there—where it was thinnest. Dion could see the branches snapping and jerking with his panicked run. She dodged one of the wolves who cut across her path, and skidded to a halt. The boy lunged out almost at her feet.

"Stop! Stop now—"

At her words, the boy froze, then cried out and flung himself back at the brush.

Dion lunged at his arm. "No—there are worlags—"

The boy shrieked and yanked back, jerking Dion off balance.

"Stop—stop fighting me!" Dion pulled him against her, but his feet kicked wildly against her shins and legs. "There are worlags—dammit!—do you hear? You are running right into them—"

"Raider-rat!" he shrieked. "I'll die before I give in to you!"

Dion grabbed his arms in a pressure hold and the boy screamed again until she forced him to the ground, helpless. "I am not a raider," she said urgently. "I am a wolfwalker—"

"Raider-rat—" he sobbed again.

"Listen!" she shouted. "We will both die if you do not get up and run with me. I am not a raider. I am from Ariye. I am here to help you and the others. I will answer your questions later—do you understand? There is no time now. The worlags are almost on us."

The boy stopped struggling, the terror on his face unrelieved. Dion's heart tore at his expression.

"Worlags?" he stammered.

"On your trail. They are almost here. We've got to run—now." She dragged him back to his feet.

"But the wolves . . ."

"They were trying to guide you away from the worlags." Dion shook him. "You must trust me. Do you?" She did not wait. "Hurry. Follow the Gray One in front of you." She shoved him after Hishn, but he balked. "I will run behind you." She tried to reassure him, but her voice was sharp with fear as she coiled her cloak around her arm again. "Do not stop, no matter what. The Gray Ones will protect you as best they can. Go. Now! Oh, dear moons—"

He hesitated again, looking back, and she screamed, "Go!"

The gray voices tightened suddenly in her head, their song hardening into the hunt. As the surge of it hit her, the worlags threaded through the trees like a tapestry of blackness. Hishn lunged away, the boy stumbling after, then running as Dion shoved him again. "Faster," she snapped. "Fast as you can! Don't look back!"

Behind them, the worlags' chittering broke into the shrill singsong of their hunt. The Gray Ones scattered. Even the wolves could not face the razor-sharp pincers of the beetle-creatures.

Dion's heart was in her throat. The boy's fear, sharp in her nostrils through the Gray Ones, was as nothing compared to hers. The boy knew only the tales of the worlags. Dion knew their reality. "Faster!" she screamed as he staggered up the rise. She grabbed his arm and flung him before her until he regained his feet. She did not look back. The three Gray Ones, racing in front of the beetle-creatures, sent their urgency to Dion as if they shouted it in her ears.

Where do we go? There is no den here . . . Hishn's question was almost desperate. The battle fever in her blood all but overwhelmed her desire to commit to Dion's command.

The river—there was a boulder. Beyond the clearing. Behind her, a Gray One snarled and a worlag screeched. The old female dodged the worlag's claws, and the beetle-beast came on, wanting soft, hot human, not lupine, flesh.

Hishn veered right, taking them toward the meadow Dion had skidded through earlier. There had been a boulder—its image was still clear in her head—and it was high on one side. If they could climb the other, the boy might be safe, and Dion could defend their position until help came. Worlags could not climb rock as well as they could climb trees.

"The boulder—up ahead," she managed. She loosened the thong on her sword and yanked her long knife from its sheath. She did not draw the sword while running—its weight would exhaust her arm even before she swung it. The chittering behind her grew more excited. Through the Gray Ones' eyes, she could see the worlags closing. First on six legs, then on two, the worlags scuttled, then rose up and sprinted as they found Dion and the boy in their sight. They ran like men now, their hairy forearms swinging through the brush like machetes, their scrawny middle arms tucked in against their bodies. Forty meters. Thirty-five. The boy was flying ahead of her, fear making his feet into wings. His hoarse breathing matched her own. "To the right," she gasped. "There, where the rocks come together—"

He did not answer, but pelted after the wolf toward the cliff. The thunder of the roiling water below drowned the sound of their breathing, and Dion shouted, "Climb! Hurry!" He reached the boulder and struggled to get a handhold in the smooth stone until Dion caught his knees and roughly threw him up. He slid backward, and Dion screamed. "Climb!"

She whirled, her back to the rock. The worlags, their red-black eyes on her, fanned out, charging the stone.

Chapter 4

Stoke the fire in the heavens,
Because the moons are rising fast.
The wind is blowing, boiling down;
The hunters run at last.
Where you seek your haven,
Where you find your den,
There face you the hunters dark,
There face you your fear
With blade bright silver;
Blade dull red
Till there is left
Just this:
The tremor in your hands;
The beating of your heart;
The wildness in your eyes;
The light that breaks the dark.

"Hishn," she shouted. "Get away. Get Aranur! Go! Now!"

The gray wolf howled, and Dion whirled back, shoving her hand under the boy's scrabbling foot. She flung him toward the rounded top of the boulder as he hauled himself up. She glanced back at the worlags and, jamming her long knife in her belt, leapt after him, the hilt stabbing into her gut as she scrambled. Hishn howled at her, but Dion could not take the wolf onto the boulder. "Go!" she screamed at the wolf. "Get to safety!"

. . . bloodlust, hunger that grips my belly and bunches my legs to sharp motion . . . Blood, bitter in my teeth. Hishn circled, leaping in front of the lead worlag, snapping at the creature's leg. *Lunge—tear the joint, tear the haunch . . .* The beetle-beast dodged deftly, unwrapping one of its middle arms and raking claws across Hishn's flank.

Dion clutched her own side as if burned. "Hishn!"

Fire, the wolf yelped. *The burning in my side!* The image dulled to a searing ache, and Hishn pivoted, lunging back toward the boulder. The rest of the Gray Ones swept into the clearing, onto the flanks of the worlags. The worlags chittered, hesitating, and Hishn skirted their pincers like a twisting snake. The wolf pack snapped and lunged at the worlags. Irritated, the beetle-creatures circled. They wanted the soft, warm prey on the stone, not these wolves with their hairy pelts, gleaming teeth, and hard, black claws. The worlags dropped back to all sixes, scuttling toward the rock. The hard leather of their arms was dull under their sparse, purple-black hair. Their thick, leather carapaces stretched back in a short arc from their faces to the back of their necks. Now on six legs, now on two, they turned and swiped at the Gray Ones who thwarted their path.

Dion knelt on the top of the boulder. She felt the burning of the raw gash in Hishn's side as if her own ribs had been laid open. She tore off her cloak and thrust it back at the boy. Stringing her bow tight, she grabbed an arrow from her quiver and took aim. Luck of the first shot, she thanked the moons: the bolt sank true. The injured worlag screamed and snapped the bolt off at its neck. Dion aimed again—at the same worlag. It would take more than one shot to drop it, and she had but one quiver of arrows. But the wolves lunged in, and the worlag twisted—and Dion's shot bounced off its back. The worlag closest to the stone rose up against the rock and stared at her with its bulbous, red-black eyes. She took an involuntary step back. Its forearms stretched along the boulder. Thick-skinned jaws opened, its inner jaw pincers clacked together, and its thin, middle arms scratched for purchase in the stone.

"Moons damn you to the darkest hell!" she snarled. Its jaws gnashed. She held her aim. It turned its head slightly as it eyed a lower spot on the stones. There—the purple-black leather was thin, soft inside the joint, where the heavy, leather neck met the head. She held her breath. The worlag looked back, then shifted to climb up, and Dion sank her bolt into its neck. It screeched, yanking its head and jerking it up and down against the shaft. Black ichorlike blood seeped out of the wound, then gushed suddenly as the worlag clipped off the arrow, jerking the shaft within its jugular. Dion plunged another arrow into its left eye at point-blank range. The beetle-beast fell back, thrashing as it tried to tear the second bolt out of its skull.

Behind her, the boy cried out. Dion turned to see a black

pincer-hand reaching over the boulder. With her bow still in her left hand, she drew her sword and hacked in one movement. Her sword jarred against stone, and she drew back, trembling. But the limb had sliced through cleanly, leaving only threads to connect the pincer in a grotesque dangling dance. Ichor flushed across the stone as the worlag's other foreleg jerked up.

"Here!" Dion flung her bow across her shoulder and grabbed her long knife, thrusting it at the boy. Then she kicked the bow back into her hands, slashing with her sword at the second limb that crept over the edge of the boulder. The worlag dropped back, chittering angrily. "Keep them from the edge!" She wiped her sword swiftly on her leather jerkin, then jammed it back in its sheath, turned, and grabbed another arrow. "We have a good chance of holding them off until Aranur arrives."

The boy gripped the knife between his fists, unheeding of Dion's words. A knife, he thought blankly. He had a knife. He touched its edge. Sharp. Not dull like Gered's, or broken like Luter's blade. Sharp, he thought, stunned. Sharp enough for any raider's hide. Sharp enough to—to avenge the death of his father. Sharp enough . . . He stared at the blade, then at Dion, then at the worlags circling the stone.

Dion did not see his expression. She was searching the beetle pack with her eyes. Where was the wounded one? The one she had already shot? Dead, it could not harm her. Injured, it would climb through the second hell to kill her. There—it was over there. She judged the wind, then, as the breeze calmed for a second, she drew back and loosed the shot. The worlag screeled and stumbled, twisting, then finally fell on its side. Its legs thrashed like a spider. Dion sank another bolt into its carapace before thrusting the bow at the boy to hold and grabbing her sword again. He was still standing where she had left him. He took the bow automatically, as if he did not really see it. She had no time to wonder. "Give it back—throw it if necessary—when I call for it," she ordered sharply. He nodded, but his eyes were still on the knife. "Do you understand?" she said urgently. "You must not hesitate."

"I understand," he said in a choked voice. He looked at her then, and his face went suddenly calm. Dion nodded curtly.

Surrounding the boulder, the worlags circled. There were

eight now. Two were down, and one of the eight was without its foreclaw, but there were still too many by far. Their claws clicked ominously on the stone as they tapped its sides, looking for holds. They would be climbing even now. Hishn, limping, licking her ribs, looked toward the boulder and howled in frustration.

Hishn, Dion sent urgently, *find Aranur and lead him here.*

The gray beast made a limping run toward one of the worlags. *He cannot hear the Gray Ones as you do. He cannot hear me as you do.*

"No," Dion returned out loud, knowing that Hishn could read her words as images, "but he can hear you well enough, Hishn, if you meet his eyes with your own." Dion glanced at the boy's puzzled expression and pointed with her sword at the wolves, indicating that she spoke to them, not him. "We cannot hold the worlags off forever," she admitted to the wolves, "and I am not sure I can kill them all even from up here. It takes two, sometimes three arrows for each one. I have only ten bolts left. Even if I did not miss—and with the wind, I am sure to—I can take only three, maybe four of them down by bow. That leaves at least four—maybe five for the blade. And if they come more than one at a time, it might be more than I can handle."

Then I will not go. Hishn's voice was stubborn. It faded suddenly as she twisted and dodged a worlag's irritated swipe. She jumped back and circled with the other wolves, gazing toward the boulder.

Dion crouched, turning, twisting constantly in a circle as she eyed the rim of the rock. "We can hold them off for a time," she argued. "Long enough for you to find Aranur. He should be on his way to meet me—you should pick him up four, maybe five kilometers to the north." She stabbed at an eager arm. "Look, Hishn," she said firmly, "the worlags are not certain of us yet. They are still trying to come up one at a time, and I can hold them off for now. But not forever. I need Aranur."

Dion yanked the boy suddenly from the rim, cutting at the pincer-hands that snapped against the boulder where his foot had been. She noted with a narrowing of her eyes that his ankles were bloody and the rags around his feet were red. The stick-grass, she remembered. They had run through the meadow on the way back to the rocks.

Wolfwalker— Hishn howled, and the rest of the pack took up her frustration in its song. The streak of pain in Hishn's side made Dion wince.

"Hishn, go. Let the other Gray Ones help here. You cannot dodge the worlags forever with that wound. If they tire of taunting us, they will turn on you."

It is a shallow wound, the wolf sent angrily. *It will not keep my teeth from your hunters.*

Dion glared across the distance at the gray creature. "Go," she ordered abruptly, no longer asking in her urgency. *Go now! And, hurry,* she added, softening the command. *We cannot hold them off forever, and your fangs, sharp as they are, cannot pierce the thickness of their leather. You cannot keep the beasts from our throats.*

Hishn gave a strange, yelping howl, then turned and raced into the forest. Dion sent her a shaft of approval. Gray Yoshi circled after his mate, splitting from the others so that two remained, and two fled. Hishn and her gray shadow were gone before Dion could blink.

"Will they—will they be back?" the boy asked.

"They have gone for help."

The expression in the boy's eyes shuttered suddenly. She shook her head. "Ariyens. Not raiders." Her face changed, and she lunged at him, snapping, "Get down!" She swung, but her sword glanced off the slick leather casing on the worlag's leg. The creature jerked, but reached back for the boy's arm. As he stabbed awkwardly with the knife, Dion slashed again, over him, cutting into the joint. The pincer-hand rattled across the stone. Grunting with the force of it, Dion swung her sword like a wooden bat against the worlag's carapace, flinging the beast off. Twisting and falling, it landed on its five limbs, chittering in a deafening fury. She turned back to find the boy staring at her. It was her warcap he was staring at—or the silver healer's band that peeked out from under it. Dion tucked the silver circlet back under the cap and tugged the cap in place.

"Yes, I'm a healer, too," she muttered, wondering what he was thinking. Who in their right mind would trust a healer to wield a sword for protection? He was probably thanking the moons that she had given him her knife. She began again her crouching circle of the boulder's top. "What is your name?" she asked abruptly over her shoulder.

The boy regarded her warily. "Tomi."

"I'm Dion." She slashed at another creeping pincer. "Use both hands on that knife. Stab into the joints. The knife won't cut through the casing on their arms or head." Gamon, Aranur's uncle, had told her that once. Gamon, she prayed silently, if you were only here right now . . . As she crouched on the boulder, his words came back to her, and she repeated them to the boy: "Aim for the joints or eyes. If you can puncture the throat, that's best. If not, go for the shoulder and elbow joints. Severing the body joint doesn't stop the arms from moving right away, and their wrists are too strong to break."

In front of her, Tomi clutched the blade. His eyes blazed as he regarded the rim of stone, and this time Dion saw the expression. But then he scrambled to his feet, his eyes hidden again as he widened his stance and rocked onto the balls of his feet in a crude imitation of Dion's feather balance. She nodded grimly in approval.

Below, the worlags clacked their inner jaws in frustration, scrabbling at the stone. They were wary now, cautious of the blade at the top. While they chittered, the severed claw lay on the boulder, opening and closing mindlessly in rhythm to their sounds. Tomi, watching it in fascination, finally used the tip of Dion's bow to shove it off the rock.

Dion examined their retreat with narrowed eyes. The boulder on which they crouched was rounded, with an upward slant behind the boy. It flattened briefly before curving down. On two sides it dropped clear to the ground. On the other side, a small flat stone butted up against the boulder, and next to it squatted the other rounded stones by which Dion and Tomi had clambered up. When the worlags attacked, they would come, as Dion and Tomi had, over those stones. They followed the scent of their prey—Gamon had told her that also. They followed and, like ants, left their own musk behind to lead other worlags to the food. Dion shivered. She would have to listen for them now; the boulder was too steep on its sides for her to look over the edge without putting her feet within reach of the beetle-beasts.

Beyond the rocks, the two wolves paced. Dion did not need a bond with them to hear the disgust of the Gray Ones. With the acrid stink of the worlags in her nose, she understood their growls intimately. She nodded at the lower side of the boulder where she watched. "They will come over this edge," she said to the boy. She was still catching her breath, her heart settling out of her throat and back in her chest. "But watch behind you. They cannot climb this as easily as they can climb trees, but it will not take them long to figure out how to get up."

"Are they—" Tomi ventured. "Are they smart?"

"Clever on the hunt?" Dion nodded curtly, as if by shortening her motions, her own fear would not show. "Yes. They might not use weapons like you and I, but they know how to get at their prey as well as any raider would."

The boy's face blanched at the mention of raiders, and Dion watched him closely. From the side, the scratching sounds shifted, and the warning of the yearling wolf burst in Dion's mind. She whirled. Two worlags crawled up over the edge of the boulder to her side, and she stabbed at their legs, breaking their holds on the rocks. She shouted, lunging wildly, smashing her sword into their carapaces as Gamon had taught her. The thrust of the point would do no good, she remembered—it was as a club that her sword was best now. One worlag tumbled back under her assault, the other slid down, out of sight again. She stared after them, one knee under her, the other leg out, slipping on the edge of the rounded stone where she had skidded with her force. She dragged herself back with a curse, then flung herself at the other side of the boulder, sword ready. But so far, that side was clear.

Tomi eyed her with awe, and she nearly laughed as she identified the emotion. Wariness, distrust, even fear, she expected. But awe?

"They're hungry." She had to struggle to keep her voice even. Could he not hear the fear in her words? "Starved enough to be impatient." Images flashed from her memory of a dark night when a band of worlags tore her trader friends apart. Those beetle-beasts had been patient enough to set a trap. These were too hungry—starved even—to do so. It was not just the chill wind that made Dion shiver.

She thought of Gamon, then Aranur, then the boy with her on the rock. Tomi—who was he? Why was he here? He was from Bilocctar, of that there could be no doubt. His thin frame, the rags . . . She glanced over her shoulder, examining the boy as she turned. He was young. Ten, maybe—or eleven. Dark hair . . . though, with all the dirt in it, it was probably lighter than it now looked. Bruised—like the other refugee that had made it through to Ariye. His legs were marked with weals and cuts only partly caused by the brush he had run through. No wonder the wolves had picked him up so easily: his damp tunic stank of rancid dirt and sweat. He had no leggings to keep his body oils from the brush. No real footgear, either—there were only rags tied around his feet.

"Tomi," she said as she circled, "what are you doing here?" She slashed at a sly leathery hand that ventured over the edge. "Where did you come from?"

The boy opened his mouth, and then his face closed off. He met her glance with a stubborn challenge.

"I am no raider"—she whacked at one side of the boulder—"that you should fear me, Tomi. I am one of the wolfwalkers who sent word to your people of the crossing at Devil's Knee."

Still, he said nothing.

She tried again. "Did you try to ford the Phye?"

An expression of despair crossed the boy's face, and the emotion was so alien on his childish face that she stopped abruptly.

"Tomi," she said slowly, "you do not know me. You do not know if you can trust me. I understand that. But I am partly responsible for the crossing at the Devil's Knee. I must be able to tell my people if it is safe for us, not just for you. If the raiders know of the crossing, they can stake it out and ambush both sides of the river—just as they did at the Sky Bridge. They want our fighters dead as much as they want you. Do you understand that?" She slashed at an eager foreleg that crept over the boulder's edge. She cursed silently as she missed, a scattering of purple-black hair sticking to the blade of her sword where it was tacky with the worlags' blood. At last the leg disappeared.

The boy looked down.

Dion looked at him. "You ran from the workcamps; I know that—your tunic gives you away. You could not have tried to cross the Sky Bridge—the raiders have had that guarded for ninans." Dion bit her lip thoughtfully as she regarded him. "No," she said slowly, "either you made a run for the river—tried to ford it where it seems shallow—or you came down from the

Slot. And I can't believe you came down from the Slot without one of the wolves scenting you.'' Or one of Gamon's scouts—there were three up there, after all, and one of those a wolfwalker like herself. She shook her head. ''You tried the river?'' she asked. She paused, watching him closely, ''You tried to cross the river,'' she repeated, more to herself, ''and the current swept you downstream.'' She hacked at the eager pincer-claws again. ''But you could not have escaped the camps alone,'' she reasoned while she circled the boulder's top. To cross that much forest, filled with raiders and worlags, badgerbears and wolves, without help, without a map?

A sob seemed to catch in the boy's throat, and Dion stared at him through narrowed eyes. ''Tomi . . .'' She stopped. The raiders along the river—the group fleeing along the river since last night . . . Could he be one of that group? But what had they done that might have brought Tomi to this bank? Tried a crossing below the falls, where even a bridge could get swept away by the river's surge, ripped apart by a reaching snag?

Dion was stunned. What other answer was there? The falls pounded stones to sand—no human could survive their ride. If Tomi had crossed the Phye, it had been done between here and the Devil's Knee. She crouched on the edge, turning her head to stare at him. ''You are with that group I saw last night.'' Another thought struck her. Children. Two days from now, the refugees Aranur expected would be mostly children—like Tomi. ''By the moons,'' she whispered. ''It is you. Your group—it is the children coming now. What have you done?'' she said blankly. ''Didn't you know you would be early? Didn't your leader get the map—the message?'' Her expression turned to disbelief, and she burst out, ''Gamon isn't done with the bridge yet—there will be no bridge for two more days. Your people cannot cross today, or tonight, or tomorrow. What did they do?'' She flung the accusation at him, ignoring his expression. ''Use ropes on the lower part of the river? How many did they drown on their first attempt? Are you the only one who made it across?''

He shook his head silently.

''Damn it to the seventh hell,'' she cursed. ''You knew there would be no bridge, and still you came early. So where,'' she demanded ruthlessly, ''are the rest of them waiting? Below the falls? Above them? Now that they have seen the power of the Phye, will they go north—to the Slot?'' Gods, she raged under her breath. They could not hide along the canyon—the raiders were thick as gnats by the river. She glared at the boy. ''How could you do this?'' She tried to control her voice. ''What were you thinking? Did you plan to walk into the raiders' arms and ask for sanctuary until the bridge was ready?''

The boy did not look up.

Dion took a deep breath, shaking in her anger. All Gamon's planning. All Aranur's men at the falls. All that time. And still the lives of the refugees would be wasted, because they could not wait two days. She looked out at the Gray Ones, letting their dim gray threads filter through her mind. Hishn's voice was distant, steady, urgent—a beat that studded Dion's thoughts with the gray wolf's racing steps. Dion looked toward the sky, drawing her anger inside, calming her sudden fury. It was not even all anger, she realized, but fear fed by the worlags below.

''It is not your fault,'' she said finally. ''It is not fair of me to take this out on you.'' They were silent for a long moment, the river mixing its voice with the snarling of the wolves and scratching of the worlags. Hesitantly, Dion reached out and touched the boy's shoulder.

Tomi stiffened. His knuckles were white around the hilt of Dion's knife. He did not look at her. ''The slavers—'' He took a breath. ''The raiders were killing us.'' His voice was low, and Dion had to lean in to hear him. ''We could not wait. They—they were killing everyone. They said we were too skinny, too weak to work. They would get others to take our places.'' His eyes grew unfocused. He did not see her; he was seeing a nightmare in his mind, and his voice cracked as he tried to speak of it. He looked at Dion, and then his eyes widened as he looked suddenly behind her.

Dion whirled instinctively. The worlag was already halfway over the edge, its hairy forearms stretching out for her back, and its middle legs snapping. Dion scrambled to the side, slashing down. The worlag caught her on the shoulder, and she staggered, hacking again and again at its darting claws. It twisted, its bulbous eyes searching her out as she dodged, its pincer jaws clacking as it sought her flesh. She smashed her sword under its arms, against its body joint, and the creature folded. Again, she jammed the point of the blade into the joint and wrenched, slipping and falling as the point burst free. Tomi screamed something behind her, and she smashed the blade against the worlag's body, flinging it from the rock. And then the other eager chittering got through to her, and she turned, gasping for breath, just as two other worlags crept over the bulge of the boulder. She lunged, sweeping one from its perch. Tomi stabbed at the foreleg of the other. And then Dion was on it, hacking and stabbing and jumping back until she rolled it from the rock.

The beetle-beasts fell. Two others were knocked away from the rock by their tumbling bodies. Chittering angrily, they tangled. In a minute, their claw-hands scraped against the boulder again, searching for the holds they now knew were there.

Dion paced the top of the rock like a caged wolf. "Moon-wormed piles of maggot bait." She turned and whirled at each change in the chittering sounds. "Dag-chewing, black-eyed parasites . . ." She dropped the tip of her sword to the ground and bent, panting, leaning against her thighs. Three down. Five left, and of them, two were missing some of their pincers.

"There were to be no refugees for two more days," she said hoarsely. She glanced back at the boy. "What happened?"

He regarded her with a blank expression. "There would have been none left to come."

His flat, emotionless voice left Dion without words. This boy's eyes, so sharp, then so shuttered in their blue-black depths, hid a pain she could only guess at. What had happened back there? What was happening in Bilocctar? The news, the rumors . . . The situation had to be much worse than even Aranur had guessed. And were there others on the border now? Others fleeing? Others dying while Dion and Aranur and the people of Ariye sat safely on their side of the river?

"The others?" she demanded. "There were others with you?"

"They are . . . trying to reach the Devil's Knee."

She shook out her sword hand and gripped her hilt again. "And you?"

"I—I fell in the water." His face paled. "With—with Eren."

Dion said nothing. Circling, turning, she stalked the top of the boulder again, listening to the boy with one ear, straining to catch the worlags' scratching with the other.

"I tried to grab her—" His voice broke. "I tried . . ."

"She drowned," Dion finished abruptly. She hesitated, touching his arm again deliberately. "I'm sorry, Tomi."

He shook her off. "I tried—" A sob caught in his throat, but he saw the sympathy in Dion's gaze.

The boy's face was suddenly a mask—a mask so complete that she wondered if she had seen the despair and pain she could have sworn to only seconds ago.

"Tomi—" she began. A scratching sound made her whip around, and she stabbed at the carapace rising above the edge of the stone. "Moons!" Tomi scrambled back, clumsy as he tried to hold onto Dion's bow. His eyes were wide. Dion cut down and across. The pincers slashed, and she went flying, knocked across the boulder. She fetched up at the edge of the stone, one leg dangling over before she could crawl back up. Something caught her ankle, and she cried out in fear, yanking it out of reach. And then she was on her feet again, her blade darting between the worlag's hairy arms until it found one of those black and bulbous eyes and skewered the beetle-creature through its head.

The nightmare beast thrashed, dragging Dion to the edge of the stone. Its forelegs slashed at her arms, her ribs, ripping through the leather, and she cried out, hanging grimly onto the sword, ducking her face between her sleeves for protection. When the beast dropped to four legs, it smashed her down onto her knees, its claw hands catching her forearms with crushing force. The old female wolf howled. In her head, Hishn skidded to a halt, turning back. Tomi leapt forward, jerking the long knife down into the worlag's hip, wrenching the slim blade sideways as if to separate the beast from its legs. Below, the yearling wolf lunged at the other worlags, trapping them against the base of the boulder.

Clutched by the worlag, Dion rolled, snapping one of its arms beneath her and breaking its hold. Half the arrows spilled from her quiver in her wake. She yanked her blade free and swung it completely around to catch a second worlag as it scrabbled over the edge behind her. Pincers still snapping, the first worlag slipped from the boulder and fell limply. The second, its first set of legs dripping from its previous wounds, dragged itself forward as Dion dragged herself back. Blood mixed with ichor on the stone.

"Tomi!" she shrieked. "Behind you—"

The boy twisted. Dion flung her sword around, smashing against a third worlag's middle pincers. The beast snapped at her, lunging forward. She overreached. By some miracle of the moons, so did the worlag. She sliced right through its body joint. The worlag screeched, chittering and spitting. Tomi screamed as forepincers caught his ankle. There was no pause. Dion grabbed Tomi's arm and jerked him free, flinging him across her body to the other side of the boulder, his thin elbows and knees striking stone as he tumbled with vicious force. The second time the worlag's pincers closed, they closed on air, and Dion shoved the beast off the stone, kicking the third worlag after it. Twisting and rolling, she smashed her sword again and again on the second worlag. She hit its middle claws—and its balance was gone. Chittering, grasping, sliding off her blood-slick blade and grasping futilely at the loose arrows, the worlag slipped, the scrabbling sounds below marking its fall.

"Gods damn you to the seventh hell," she sobbed. She fell back, dragging her legs further up the boulder. "Oh, gods," she gasped. "Oh, moons." Her calves were gashed. She had not even noticed. Now, the blood soaked her leggings, and the burning of the worlag's fluid was already in the wound. "No—stay back!" she snarled at Tomi. "Get away from the edge. There are still three more."

She struggled to sit up, biting her lips and cursing under her breath as her legs shifted. "My bow . . ."

It hung on the edge where it had clattered, and the boy scrambled to reach it, the knife still in his hands. "Here—" He thrust it awkwardly at her.

She reached back, caught her breath, and dragged an arrow from her quiver. Her hands shook. She clenched them, then pulled the bolt back on the string. The next worlag over the edge would have a warbarb in the eye. The next worlag . . .

She swallowed hard as a wave of nausea swept her. The chittering from below had not let up. Soon—maybe minutes, maybe seconds, and they would attack again. Hishn—She felt the wolf turning back, racing toward her again. *Hishn,* she sent desperately. *No! Find Aranur. Bring help—*

Hishn was torn between Dion's pain and the commands.

Dion steeled herself to bluntness. *You will kill me if you return without him . . .* She ignored Hishn's shock. *There are two wolves here, and they cannot get beyond the worlag's claws.* She sagged back on her elbows, and the arrow slipped in her fingers. Her stomach heaved. Retching, she doubled over. Behind her, Tomi swallowed. Crouching, his eyes darting from one side of the boulder to the other, he clenched his fists on the long dirk.

Dion coughed and spat, then retched and spat again. She drew her legs up so that she was kneeling. Grimly, she forced her stomach to settle. *You are with me even now, Hishn. You know I will hang on till you return. Go, now! You have almost reached him—*

The gray bond between Hishn and Dion snapped taut. The wolf howled. *Wolfwalker!*

Hurry— She coughed against her nausea. *You must hurry . . .*

And then the other wolf called Hishn. Through the gray bond, Hishn sent a shaft of strength to Dion, laced with the burning in Hishn's own side, and the wolfwalker staggered up. In her mind, she saw the two wolves race on. On. Yes. On, toward Aranur.

How long before Hishn returned? Before Aranur arrived? The chittering below was subdued, cunning. How long before the worlags gained the top of the rock? They had bodies, not just boulders, to climb on now. And Dion was retching, sick with the poison that had seeped into her blood.

"Dion . . ." Tomi crouched forward.

The wolfwalker did not turn her head. "Get my arrows. Tear strips off my cloak."

The boy hesitated, then crept forward and gathered up the three arrows left on the rock. He slid them into her quiver, then turned and groped for the bundle of cloth. He stabbed it with the knife, dragging the blade through the wool in ragged chunks.

"Tear it with your hands," she said tersely.

Tomi looked up.

"With your hands," she repeated.

Holding the knife in one hand, he tried to pull the cloth apart, but he could not get a good grip. Unwillingly, he laid the blade under his foot. Grabbing the cloth, he ripped as hard as he could, and fell back with the force as the cloth separated easily. The knife slid out from under his foot. With an inarticulate cry, he dropped the cloth and lunged forward, grabbing at the blade, huddling in on himself when it was once again in his hands. Dion, trying to raise her head against the nausea, frowned at him. His face pale, he put the long blade back under his foot and finished ripping the strip. Then he notched another place in the cloak where he could tear the cloth again. Dion, her eyes back on the boulder's edges, listened, not to the sounds of tearing cloth, but to the chittering that marked the worlags' advance.

"How many strips?" His voice was thin, strained.

"Four for me. Two for your ankles." She did not look around. She drew back on the arrow. The worlags should be trying again any time. When the boy scuttled forward and laid the strips at her side, she nodded her thanks.

"I can help," he said hesitantly.

She shook her head. "You're too close to the edge here. Stay back. Watch behind me. Watch the sides."

Dion laid her bow behind her, leaving her sword on the stone in front while she quickly wrapped the strips around her calves. The first layer soaked immediately through, but then the blood-red stain slowed. She clenched her fists suddenly as another wave of nausea clutched at her stomach. "No," she raged at herself. "I must be strong . . ."

She fought her silent battle until the burning faded and her sight cleared. But it was not she who won that struggle; it was Hishn. She felt the gray wolf in her mind. Her eyes saw more yellow now, and the pain was muffled, as if it were cloaked in a fog. The eager strength of the yearling, the steadiness of the old female—through Hishn, the link was strong, and the gray threads between Dion and the wolves grew taut. An hour? A year? How long would the gray threads hold?

Wolfwalker—

Hishn— Dion closed her eyes in relief. The gray wolf had reached Aranur—his scent was unmistakable—and Dion saw the images as clearly as if Hishn were beside her. She felt his shock as Hishn met his eyes. Dimly, she sensed his fear—for Dion—then his anger, then his urgency. He shouted—Hishn's ears rang with the noise. Then he was running for the river. Behind him, another figure sprinted in his wake. And in front of them, the two wolves, one staying back—just ahead of the humans—and the other already out of sight in the brush, racing, running for the wolfwalker trapped on a boulder with a child at her side.

"They are coming," Dion whispered.

"The wolves?"

She pressed her fist to her chest where the tiny gem studded her sternum. "Aranur."

From below, the worlags scratched at the stone. They were climbing again. Dion's hands shook as she thrust the other two rags back at Tomi.

She grabbed her bow. Which side—which way would they come? There were only three left. If she could get just one good shot . . .

They came in a rush, each one on a different side of the boulder. Dion let her arrow fly at the first carapace she saw, but the worlag jerked its head, and the arrow bounced off its sloping jaw. Another crawled up beside Tomi, and the boy, panicked, stabbed at the foreclaws until the creature dropped back in frustration.

Dion kicked the beast in front of her off the boulder, then whirled, smashing her bow against the worlag that rose up behind. It swayed, its pincers locked instantly onto the bow. The tortured wood snapped. Dion ducked, tumbling. She grabbed her blade and swung it up like a scimitar. It met the worlag's claws with a smacking sound, and the creature latched onto the metal, jerking her up. She cried out. She was flung out, in a short arc—off the boulder. The worlag, locked to her by its grip on the sword hilt, tumbled with her through the air. She hit the ground hard. As they landed, the worlag slid off her blood-slick blade. It rolled, its pincer claws digging into the earth a meter away. The wolves dodged toward her, and Dion scrambled up, her breath stuck in her lungs as if her side were caved in. The worlag scuttled forward, its forebody raised up, its pincers reaching out.

Flashes in her head. Hishn, running, tearing through the brush. The worlag, in front, to the right, to the left—images doubled and tripled from the yearling and the old female on its other sides. The worlag chittered, advancing. Dion raised her sword, stabbing at the beast, cutting across its arms. It slapped her blade aside, snicking at her thigh. The yearling lunged at its hindquarters, and the worlag turned. Somehow, the yearling wolf got its jaws locked in the worlag's leathery leg joint. With a howl, the old female slashed in, driving at the creature's other rear leg. Dion turned and fled for the rocks.

From around the boulder, the other worlags scuttled. Lunging forward, Dion stabbed at the bulbous eyes of the one she had wounded before. The creature screeched, blinded. She jumped for the stones. But the other worlag caught her legging and jerked. She screamed. She tumbled back, rolling against the blinded beetle-beast. Pincer legs stomped her body, and she thrashed in panic to get clear.

Wolfwalker— A gray muzzle flashed beside her.

She rolled, crawling, scrambling toward the stones. The wolves tore frantically at the worlags' limbs, their gleaming teeth making little impression on the worlags' casings. The yearling cried out—a claw grabbed and snapped his foreleg. He was flung back, yelping. Dion scrambled to her feet. She hacked at the blinded creature between her and the others. Her sword smashed through its body joint. Screeching, the worlag folded, catching her blade in its hard leather casing. Dion yanked, then jerked it free in panic as the other two beasts closed. Where was Aranur? Where was Hishn? Oh, gods. Oh, moons . . .

Something tugged at her ankle, and she stumbled, smashing down with her heel on the twitching joint of the fallen worlag's leg. Back, she edged. Back to the boulder. Watch the claws—watch the bodies. The beasts were down, not dead. Not dead. Oh, gods. Their pincer-hands could catch her even now. Jerkily, nervously, she jumped across one body onto a clear spot in the earth. The downed beetle-beast rolled as it sensed her over it, and it reached up to snap at her legs. The other worlags crawled after her, mindless of the bodies they scuttled across.

"Tomi," she shouted, "throw me the knife!"

Above, frozen as he watched Dion dodge the worlags' claws, Tomi crouched. His knuckles were white around the hilt of the blade.

"Tomi—the knife!"

He stared at the hands on the hilt.

Below him, the worlags advanced. Behind them, the old female wolf jumped across a body and worried the legs of the live ones. Dion backed against the boulder. The worlags scuttled forward.

"Tomi!" Dion screamed.

The worlags swept in. She whirled her blade like fire slashing across their bodies. The beetle-beasts paused now, swatting and kicking behind them at the wolves, their bulbous eyes intent on Dion's slight form. Panting, she wove the blade before her. The worlags swayed. The flashing wall of blood-slick steel kept them wary, cunning in their attack. Inner jaws clacked. Dion stabbed suddenly at their faces, and their leather carapaces slid forward, flexed over their eyes. She dropped the blade to their bodies, but they knew that tactic now. They arched back, snaking their arms around to her sides until she beat them back. If Tomi dropped the knife, she did not know. Her eyes were only for the worlags.

The snarls of the two wolves matched the cunning chitters of the worlags. The tableau held. A dance—it was a dance. The gray wolves lunged; the worlags swayed. Like a nest of snakes, the five of them shifted one way, then the next. Dion darted her blade between their arms, only to have it slapped away. She stepped back, yanking a boot knife from her leg and throwing it in one motion. It sunk into a joint, and the worlag tried vainly to grip that short, slick hilt. She stepped again and pulled the last arrow from her quiver, holding it in front of her like a fragile blade. Then her foot landed on the limb of a dead worlag.

Dion stumbled to one knee. The worlags darted forward. She twisted up, slashing, bashing one worlag against the other. Her fist plunged the arrow's barb into an eye. There was a shriek. A forearm caught her ribs and slammed her against the boulder. Her sword, jammed desperately into a shoulder joint, was torn from her hands.

Wolfwalker— Hishn's voice deafened her.

Another forearm caught her leggings, tripping her. She kicked free. Frantic, she turned and leapt at the smooth side of the boulder. Her blood-slicked hands found no purchase. In her panic, she was deaf to the snarling and chittering that filled the air. She fell back, landing beside her sword. Without thinking, she grabbed it and swiped across the arms of one of the worlags. The beast reached out. She caught its limb with her bare hand, hooking the sword's hilt across its tendons, and yanked until the joint snapped. A second later, a gray shadow closed on the worlag from behind, and she wrenched her sword up into its neck joint. Something threw her back. Her head cracked on the stone. She turned and flung herself at the boulder's heights again, hanging for an instant on the edge before a burning pain ripped across her back and dragged down. She thought she screamed again. She stabbed out blindly, frantically, and fell.

Chapter 5

Healing skills and healer's band,
Fresh-grown herbs and gentle hands,
Tonics, potions, lotions, pills—
None can cure the mortal ills.
Ovousibas, the healer's skill,
Ovousibas alone can heal.

Only one art can prevent
The death that through our lives must rend.
Only ancient secrets strive
To fight the moons and bring back life.
Ovousibas, the healer's skill,
Ovousibas alone can heal.

The dark smears that stained the sides of the boulder were red-black beneath the sky. The river's voice thundered dully. In the clearing, the yearling wolf whimpered, limping toward the forest on three legs. The old gray female led, then circled behind her cub, growling deep in her throat. Behind them, Hishn and the other adult wolf worried at the pile of worlags, snarling and snapping at each other while they tore grimly at the black-leather limbs.

Even before Aranur burst into the clearing, he glimpsed the boulders standing gray-white between the trees, against the river canyon. "Here—over here," he shouted, changing direction to follow where the wolves had raced ahead. Those shadows—those shapes at the base of those stones . . . Worlags. The beetle-beasts. He drew his sword and sprinted. Running beside him, a tall, silver-haired woman pulled her bow from her shoulder and halted only long enough to string it tight before pelting after him.

"Dion!" Aranur shouted. "Dion!"

He reached the boulder and spun, searching with his eyes. He saw the blood streaks on the boulder; her bow, snapped in two, on the ground. "Oh, moons, please . . ." Her sword—there, still jammed in a beetle-beast's shoulder. "Let her be alive . . ." He grabbed a worlag's carcass, jumping back as its pincer-claws clutched weakly in the air. Viciously, he plunged his sword into its joints, wrenching against its inner skeleton until he severed its spinal cord, leaving it limp. He hauled the carcass away from the stones, then looked up wildly. "Dion!" he screamed.

One of the wolves turned and howled at him, and he lunged through the hardened casings. "Here—over here," he shouted. The older woman reached him and began tearing at the pile, stabbing and dragging first one, then another twitching purple-black corpse away while the others ran to help. "Oh, gods," Aranur sobbed. "Dion!"

He dropped to his knees, ignoring the bloody ichor that stained his leggings. "Dion . . ."

The wolfwalker lay twisted beneath a massive carapace, one pincer still clamped on her torn leg, her torso encircled by the worlag's upper limbs. Gently, Aranur disengaged the pincer from Dion's thigh, his throat catching as blood seeped sluggishly from her leg. "Help me!" he shouted over his shoulder. Hishn leapt on top of another carapace, slipping, then balancing edgily as she snarled at him. The other gray wolf growled, snorting as if to clear his nose of the worlags' stench.

Aranur pulled the beetle-beast's forelegs from around Dion's body. Something shifted, and a boot knife, blackened with blood and ichor, slid out of the worlag's eye socket. Slowly, he straightened Dion's torso. He stared down at her. "Oh, moons." The other woman tugged at the carapace, pulling it away in braced jerks, and he wedged himself under it to lift it with his shoulders and keep its weight from dragging across Dion. Finally the carcass was gone. Hishn jumped down beside him, nudging Dion's body and whining.

"Dion," Aranur whispered. He touched her neck. Moons, but—it was not his imagination—her pulse was there, beating against the bloodstained skin of her neck. He gathered her up, stumbling through the rude path made by the missing carcasses.

"She is alive," he told the other woman. "Quickly, get the dressings."

The woman, Mjau, slung her thin pack off her shoulders and ripped it open, groping for the roll of bandages she carried. With a calm born of long experience, she poured her bota bag out onto the cloth, jamming it into his impatient hands.

Aranur did not take his eyes from Dion. She was slashed across the arms and legs, but her studded mail had protected her. The gashes were raggedly deep only in spots, mostly shallow where the metal studs had deflected some of the worlags' blows. The bruising, though . . . He washed her face and neck, letting his breath out when they came clean. There was only a thin, raw scratch on her cheek which ran across her eye but missed the eyelid. She was not blinded. He closed his own eyes in relief.

Hishn nudged his arm, whining.

"She's all right, Gray One," he said softly. He examined Dion more closely, finding the tear in her jerkin where another claw had pierced her mail. Another ragged, shallow cut had glanced off her ribs, leaving a smeared and bloody trail, but it had already clotted, and her tunic stuck to the wound when he tried to pull it free. Her back was more serious. Her skin was torn across; his hands came away stained red-black. Gently, he wadded cloth and held it against her muscles. The body in his arms stirred. "Dion?" He touched her cheek.

Her eyes fluttered. She choked, coughed, and he raised her up, holding her against his chest. But her eyes opened suddenly, and she screamed. Wild-eyed, she shoved hard against him, swinging with both fists.

"Dion, it's me—" He grabbed her fists. "It's me, Aranur. You're safe now."

She stared at him, then gave a half sob and buried her face in his chest. Beside him, Hishn wormed her gray-furred head into Dion's arms. The wolfwalker gripped the thick fur convulsively, unable to stop herself even when the gray wolf flinched. The thin gash on Hishn's ribs ached, but it was more Dion's pain the wolf felt, not her own.

Behind Aranur, Mjau looked around. "Seven, maybe eight worlags," she reported softly. "Quite a mess."

He looked up then, seeing the bodies he had flung aside a moment before. "It's a miracle," he said grimly.

"If they had not made it to the boulders . . ."

Aranur, his gray eyes like flint, stilled Mjau's words. "Start hauling the carcasses to the edge of the canyon,'' he said curtly. ''We'll let the river take them. They'll draw too many carrion-eaters here.'' He paused with a sudden thought. ''Wait on that. The Sky Bridge is downstream, and the raiders watch it closely. If we dump the bodies in the river, the raiders will see them float through.''

''What about the forest? It will attract the carrion-eaters, but from across the river, it will be more difficult to tell the number of them gathering back in the shadows.''

''Good,'' he agreed. ''Do it.'' He turned his attention back to Dion, who had gripped his neck, trying to pull herself up. She shook herself free of his steely grip, then groaned suddenly. Her body folded, and she put her head down between her knees.

Aranur pulled her hands away from the back of her head, staring at the blood on her fingers. Even though he was suddenly gentle, she cried out as he removed her warcap and the healer's band that circled her forehead. ''It's split the skin,'' he confirmed, probing the wound. ''It's swollen like a melon. You'll have one hell of a headache for the next few days.'' He helped her sit up, this time more slowly. ''How do you feel?''

She touched the back of her head, wincing at both the movement in her arms and the throb of her skull. ''Dizzy.'' Her face paled, and she closed her eyes for a moment. ''Nauseous.''

He watched her narrowly. ''Concussion?''

''Worlag blood,'' she returned shortly. ''It mixed with mine.''

''Are you sure?''

''I felt this way long before I knocked my head on the rock.'' She looked up, a bleak look in her eyes. ''There was a boy with me. Have you—have you found him yet?''

''No.'' Aranur shook his head slowly. ''What boy—from where?''

''Tomi—a refugee. The one who ran into the worlags.''

Aranur called over his shoulder, ''Mjau, there was a boy with her. You had better search for him quickly. He might be hurt.'' He looked back at Dion. ''How old?''

''Ten, maybe eleven?'' She took the cloth he offered and held it to her head, steeling herself against the jagged bursts of pain as he began to wash the blood from her left arm, tearing scabs free no matter how gently he scrubbed. Clenching her teeth, she motioned with her chin toward the top of the boulder. "He was on top when I fell."

Aranur caught Mjau's attention and pointed toward the boulder. "Look up there," he directed.

He turned back to Dion, watching her closely. How much blood had she lost? How much strength? Her color was paler than usual, and her black hair was matted with blood and dirt. He smiled wryly. She would be horrified if she knew what she looked like. He flicked a bug from her tangled braid, waiting until she glanced away before doing it, so that she did not know it had been in her hair. She was not Ariyen, from his own county. She was not used to all the denizens of his forests, though, no doubt, he would be as startled by those that crawled through hers. He smoothed her hair gently. In Ariye, her high cheekbones and creamy skin were an unusual combination—unsettling to some. To him, her looks were arresting, making him want to touch her, to gaze into her violet eyes and guess if the moonwarriors left their seed on this world as the legends said. Her brother, he knew, used to tease her when she sparred in the fighting ring, telling her that she could chill a man's heart in his chest by freezing him with a glance of those deep, violet eyes. She looked little like the myth of a moonwarrior here. In the circle of his arms, she was only a battered, frightened woman who had fought a nightmare. Her breath still came raggedly, and she jerked at the scrabbling sounds of the claws in their death rattles around them. Aranur soothed her as if she were a child, stroking her hair, letting her feel his strength around her. But as his relief waned, his anger began to grow, and he took up his rag again, wiping at the open gash in her arm grimly. It was one thing for her to run the border as a scout, he thought curtly; something else for her to provoke a band of predators to her trail. She was a wolfwalker. She should know better. Even Aranur would not willingly face more than one worlag if he could help it. The beetle-beasts were ruthless and voracious—persistent as the night after a long day. She knew that. If she had not managed to get atop those boulders . . . If they had been able to come at her more than one or two at a time . . . She must have been frightened half out of her mind. Although she had fought worlags once before, he remembered, she had not gained confidence from that. Rather, the experience had given her a terror deep in her memory. She never spoke of what she had seen so long ago, but he could guess. She had been one of only two people to escape that band's hunger. The images she must have taken with her as she fled their feeding frenzy . . . He glared at her as she clutched his arm weakly, stopping him from putting the rag to her wounds again. "What?" he snapped.

"You'll rub my arm off if you do that any harder."

The wound was oozing blood again where he had broken open the forming scab. "Moonworms, Dion, I am sorry." He dabbed at the blood.

"You are almost as bad as a worlag yourself," she teased faintly. "If you are going to snap at me, I would appreciate it if you did it with your words, not your hands."

He wiped the trickle of blood from her arm more gently, cursing himself for his clumsiness. When he pressed the cloth over the gash, she shuddered. There was terror still in her shivers, he realized, not just pain, and he cursed himself again for agreeing to let her work as a scout. Then he laughed at himself. For the most part, Dion could take care of herself. And when she could not, the Gray Ones took care for her. Had it been himself on that rock, Dion would have been just as worried, just as panicked to reach him. He smiled inwardly, feeling a smug sense of possession. Dion, his Dion, had held off the worlags herself. She had faced her fear and proved him right in the face of the other weapons masters. It had not mattered how well she sparred in the fighting rings; she was from a different county, and they wanted proof of her heart. Well, she had given it. He stroked the loose hair from her cheeks. A year ago, Dion had made him swear on the seventh moon, he remembered. Swear to believe in her as she believed in him. To trust her strength as she did his. He wrapped the bandages around her forearms, then gathered her to him, crushing her against his chest so that the rough cloth of his tunic caught on the gemstone that studded his chest. Perhaps, he realized, it was the first time he truly believed in their bargain.

Dion clung to him, reaching up to touch the tiny bump of the gem in his own chest. She rubbed her fingers over it, letting the sense of the stone seep through the cloth.

"You tempted the luck of the moons, Dion," he whispered roughly. "You know that."

"I know."

"To run in front of a band of worlags . . ."

She shrugged, her expression changing to a wince at the movement. "I had little choice."

"Why didn't you use the Gray Ones?"

"I did," she answered slowly. "But the boy was more terrified of them than of the danger he was running into."

"Terrified—of the Gray Ones? Like that other refugee?"

She nodded. "The Gray Ones tried to turn him, send him back towards me, but he panicked when he saw them. He bolted right into the worlags' path. By the time I reached him, the worlags were close enough they could see us both."

Aranur stared at her. "Scared of a wolf . . . This is like one of the old legends, when the wolves used to be predators of people, not partners. How could the boy have such fear?"

"Easy," Dion said grimly. "Raiders." The word was enough to make Aranur's face turn to stone, but, knowing that the anger behind it was not directed at her, Dion went on, "I think it is because of the rumors of wolfwalkers in the hands of the slavers. Remember? We heard those rumors a year ago, and then again last month. I did not believe them—I don't think anyone here did, but now . . ."

"You think it might be true," he finished for her.

She gestured toward the river, her swathed forearms bulky over her jerkin. "What if the raiders really are working with the wolfwalkers? It does not have to be because the wolfwalkers want to. The raiders could beat them, torture them, and the Gray Ones would track anyone, follow any trail, to keep the pain of the partners from their minds. The wolfwalkers could stay mindlinked, reading the trail from a base while the Gray Ones ran the forest and tracked the refugees to their deaths."

"A wolf would never harm a human," he said flatly.

"If it was a choice of tracking a human for me or letting a raider burn my skin, which do you think Hishn would do?"

Aranur regarded her grimly. "I guess that does not require an answer."

She touched his arm. "With so many wolves in Ariye, they could know where we are at all times, too. The graysong is strong lately. Even from the across the river, the echoes are loud.'' Hishn nudged her hand, and she stroked the gray beast's head.

''A mental trail,'' Aranur said softly.

She nodded. ''That is how I knew there was a pack on the west side of the Phye. And how they must know we are here now.''

''And will they know about the crossing we are building under the falls?''

She met his eyes steadily. ''They will know that you go to the place often. Your movements are part of the packsong—you cannot hide them. But what little I picked up from the Gray Ones across the river . . .'' She shrugged. ''The raiders do not suspect enough to ask questions about it, and the wolves do not volunteer the knowledge—at least,'' she added, shooting a quick question to the gray creature at her side, ''not as far as Hishn knows.'' She jerked her head south, downstream. ''The raiders know only about the crossings south of the Sky Bridge and north of the Slot. What we build at the falls is hidden from their minds.''

For several minutes, Mjau had been picking her way through the worlags' bodies, peering reluctantly beneath the casings for the signs of human skin. At last she abandoned her task and clambered up on the pile of boulders. As she hoisted herself up, she froze for an instant. ''Hey!'' she called, startled. ''The boy—he's up here!''

In front of her, huddled against the rise in the boulder, crouched the child. He stared at the thin gray-haired woman, his eyes wide. In his hands, he clutched a knife. Dion's knife, Mjau noted. She stared at him for a long moment. ''Here, boy,'' she said quietly, reaching out.

But the bony child lunged suddenly, sliding past her grip and down the side of the boulder.

''Hey!'' she shouted.

She got a brief glimpse of his white face turned toward her, then he landed in a staggering tangle among the worlags. He bolted.

''Stop him!'' she cried out.

Aranur, looking up at Mjau's shout, left Dion in a lunge, cursing himself at her sharp cry of pain. His long legs caught up with the boy in seconds. But the child turned suddenly, and the knife in his hands swiped across Aranur's reach. Instinctively, Aranur flowed with the movement. He twisted the blade from the boy's hands almost without thinking, sweeping it free. The child screamed, his fingers wrenched. But it was in frustration, not pain, that he cried out. Flinging himself at the man, the boy fought hysterically, screaming that some woman—"the Siker," he called her—would get him; she would get them all. Frantically, Aranur wrapped his arms around the thin body and locked the boy in place, keeping his head back from the boy's thrashing skull, and his arms away from his biting mouth.

Dion scrambled to her knees, ignoring the burning jags of pain that surged in her legs, but Hishn closed her gleaming fangs on Dion's arm, preventing the wolfwalker from running forward, a gesture that Dion appreciated only seconds later when her head spun. "Tomi," she shouted, "stop it—you're safe now. Stop struggling. He's not a raider. He's from Ariye. Ariye!"

The boy stopped kicking slowly, staring at Dion, his chest heaving, and his mouth opened to scream again.

Dion grabbed her head. "It's all right, Tomi," she managed, groaning at the throbbing that racked her thoughts. "These are the people I told you about. None of us are raiders," she repeated. "We are the ones setting up the crossing at the Devil's Knee."

Regarding the boy narrowly, Aranur set him warily on his feet, keeping his hands on the thin shoulders. Beside them, Mjau picked up the knife. Her lined face had a curious expression. Dion had given up her knife when she must have needed every blade against the worlags. Mjau glanced at the boy. She was not sure she would have done the same.

"Come." Dion held out her hand to the child.

The boy did not move. He stared at the wolf by her side.

"It's all right," Aranur said quietly. "You are safe now."

Tomi twisted away, his eyes darting from Dion to Mjau and back. "I want the knife." His voice was flat, and Aranur, startled at the tone, frowned and took a step forward.

Tomi backed away. "I want my knife." He cast a glance toward Dion, and she could not stand the fear she saw in his eyes. "Mjau," she said, "please, return my—his—knife to him."

The gray-haired woman met her gaze over that of the boy. "Of course." She glanced at Tomi. "I would not want to run these woods myself without a weapon."

Tomi's hands trembled as he snatched the blade from the older woman's hands. And then his face was a mask again, and, head held high, he stalked to stand by Dion, defiantly ignoring the wolf.

Aranur gave Dion a questioning look.

She shrugged helplessly.

"Where are his people?" Aranur asked.

"On the border," she returned. She glanced at Tomi to see if he wanted to answer the man, but with his young jaw clenched, he was not yet ready to speak. She added, "Heading north. I think the raiders have been on their trail since they fled."

Aranur frowned. "Can't be. We're not ready for them. No one is supposed to run for the Knee for two more days."

"They could not wait." She started to add another comment, but her stomach asserted itself, and she found herself clutching her gut and shuddering as the nausea hit again. Hishn growled. Finally, Dion straightened. The worst of the nausea seemed to be over. "They got our message about the Sky Bridge," she said tightly, shoving Hishn's nose away. The damp, sweet breath of the wolf was almost more than she could stand. "Just as we told them," she managed, "they are heading for the Devil's Knee."

Aranur, watching her with concern, pursed his lips. "We left the ropes and the rest of our gear when we ran to help you," he said, calculating the distance in his head. "It will take us half an hour to go back, then more time to return to the canyon, but we will need the gear in place for the crossing to be finished later."

Mjau cocked her head. "There are already harnesses and raingear at the site," she offered.

Aranur glanced at her. "If we have no choice," he said slowly, "we could try a crossing today . . ." He frowned, thinking of the scant rigging they would have to trust. He wished for another man to help haul on the lines. Mjau was a clever archer, but not strong enough for what had to be done. Besides, he could not leave Tomi alone on the rim, and he could not subject the boy to the frigid cold of the falls that the others would have to endure.

Dion would need to bring the refugees to the platform up on the cliff and get them into the harnesses. No, he would have to work the ropes alone. Although, if the adult refugees were not in as bad a shape as Tomi, perhaps they could help him once they were down. He turned to Tomi. "How many are in your group?"

The boy looked warily up at the tall man.

Aranur frowned. "How many, Tomi? And how old are they?"

Dion watched the child closely. "Tomi," she said softly, "this man can help you. Look at him. Look at Mjau. At me. Do we act like raiders? Do we act as if we want you dead?"

The boy bit his lip; his knuckles, where they clenched the knife, were white. "You want me to tell you where my . . . people are."

Dion knelt in front of him, and he flinched as Hishn sniffed his face. "Hishn won't hurt you," she said softly. She sent a mental shaft to Hishn to back off, and the gray creature obediently sat back, running her tongue over her teeth and panting. Tomi did not look reassured. Dion tried again. "If we were raiders, Tomi, we would make you tell us about your people by hurting you, not by asking you. Your arms and legs are proof enough of that. If we lifted your tunic, we would find more proof on your ribs. Wouldn't we?" She reached up, pushing back her warcap, though a lance of pain sent a new rush of throbbing to her mind. "Here." She touched the silver circlet that was exposed. "I give you my word as a healer that we are not raiders. Touch it. It is real."

Tomi reached out tentatively, barely fingering the band before he drew his hand back as if burned. "How—how can you be a healer?" he demanded.

She smiled faintly. "Believe me, I worked at it."

"But you use a sword—like the raiders do. You use a sword and bow."

"Yes." She adjusted her warcap, and the silver of the circlet was once again nearly hidden. "I wear both healer's band and blade." Her smile faded.

"Why?"

"I made a vow once." Her voice was soft. "A vow to protect myself and my friends from harm. The healer's band—it reminds me that I am sworn to heal my people. And when I cannot do that, when there are raiders and worlags and threats to face, then the sword is there, to defend myself and my friends."

"Healers can't kill," he said with childish bluntness. "Swordsmen can't heal."

Aranur held his breath. Dion's smile was suddenly stiff.

"I am both. I do both," she said softly. She was suddenly exhausted. Aranur touched her arm, his expression grim. She could almost read his mind, and that faint smile returned to her lips. He would not have this child upsetting her, she read him wryly. Not when she had just risked her life to keep him alive.

The boy met her eyes. "You swear on your healer's band that you are not a raider?"

She nodded.

"You swear by the seventh moon?"

"I would have left you to the worlags if I were a raider. Ask yourself this, Tomi: If I were a raider-rat, why would I risk my neck for a boy I would only have to kill later?"

He struggled with the question. "Then how come you did run after me?"

"Because you needed help."

He thought about that for a moment. "If you could not use a sword, you would not have come, would you?"

"No," she disagreed gently, "I would have come anyway."

"Why?"

"Because I had to."

Aranur's jaw tightened. Yes, she had to. She rarely thought before she acted, and her wounds were proof of that.

"You have a sword," said the boy in a forlorn voice. "We don't have any swords. We don't have anything but a broken knife." He stared at them. "Why didn't you come before now?" he burst out. "My father is dead. Why didn't you come then? Why didn't you stop them?" His voice broke.

Dion tried to hug his stiff body. Aranur closed his eyes, the childish voice echoing in his ears: Why didn't you stop them?

Tomi was crying openly now, his mask gone, great sobs racking his scrawny body. "We can't fight. We don't have any swords. We don't even have sticks. We can't do anything,'' he cried out. ''All we do is die.''

''Shhh,'' Dion crooned, anguished. ''We're here now,'' she whispered. ''We can help now.''

The boy's shoulders shook as if he would break apart, and Dion lifted him, cradling his thin body even as Aranur had held her earlier. The child wrapped his arms around her neck as if he would choke her, the knife draped down her back and his head buried in her shoulder. She rocked him back and forth. Aranur made a gesture, but his image was blurred through her tears, and she could only shake her head helplessly.

When Tomi's sobs turned to hiccups, Dion set him on the ground. He wiped his sleeve across his eyes, smearing dirt in a streak from temple to temple. Dion did not smile. He stared at her, noting the tears where they ran down her cheeks. ''You are crying, too.''

She nodded.

''How come?''

''Because you hurt.''

He regarded her with eyes older than he was. ''Moira does not cry anymore,'' he said with a strange note. ''None of the elders do.''

Over the boy's head, Dion met Aranur's eyes with an agonized look. ''Perhaps,'' she managed, ''they have forgotten how.''

He shook his head. ''No,'' he said matter-of-factly. ''It is because they have cried too much before.''

Dion caught her breath. Tomi looked up at Aranur. His tears were gone, the only trace of them the muddy streak across his eyes. He jerked his head in a nod. ''Eleven,'' he said abruptly. ''There are eleven left, not counting me.''

Aranur gave him a sharp look. ''How many are adults?'' he asked in return. ''How many children?''

''Seven kids.'' He drew himself up. ''But they are younger than me.''

Aranur's gray gaze was sober. ''How young?''

He thought for a moment. ''The littlest one is five.''

''Five?'' Aranur swore under his breath. Five years old, and running from the raiders? Moonworms. How had they managed? No child that young could run or hike more than a few kilometers. He would have to be carried. And if there were more than one that young . . . He ran his hand through his black hair and stared out at the river canyon as if he could discern their trail from where he stood. Children. Enslaved and beaten children. His jaw tightened grimly. "How long before they reach the Devil's Knee?"

The boy looked uncertain. "I don't know. The wolves were getting close, and we had to leave the trail for a while."

"Wolves?" Aranur would come back to that in a moment. "Are they traveling quickly?" he asked. "Running? Or walking?"

"Walking. Our feet hurt."

"Walking . . ." If their feet were shod as Tomi's were, it was no wonder they hurt. Aranur was afraid to find out what was under the rags and bark. Blisters? Open sores? Separated pads? And it was five, maybe six kilometers from where they stood now to the Knee. He turned to Dion. "When did you meet up with him? How long ago? Where?"

"Half a kilometer?" she guessed. "It was into the forest a ways. He said he fell into the Phye and was swept downstream. Judging from the current, he could have been a half kilometer further north than that when he went in."

Aranur turned back to the boy. "You fell in? Where? What did the bank look like where you fell?"

"Flat," Tomi said hesitantly. "But there were rapids just downstream. And the bank was sandy."

Aranur cursed silently. "That describes half the length of the Phye."

The boy glanced up warily. "There was a wide curve . . ."

Dion bit her lip. Aranur gave her a sharp look.

"Four kilometers above the Sky Bridge," she said slowly. "There is an oxtail—a curve with a bank on the far side."

Aranur nodded slowly. "I know it. The current is strong there—the water runs with deep, standing waves as tall as I am."

She agreed. "It is the only place with a wide curve below the falls and above the Sky Bridge."

Mjau glanced at the canyon. "We're about three kilometers north of the Sky Bridge now."

"We almost went to the Sky Bridge," the boy said. "Peyel said it would be safe there for us."

Aranur frowned at him. "The Sky Bridge? Not likely. Dion has been watching the raiders squat on the bridge for two months." He tapped his chin, calculating. "How long ago did you fall in? Can you guess?"

"I—I don't know."

Aranur dropped to his knees, gripping the boy by the shoulders. "Think, Tomi. Your people's lives may depend on it."

Dion nodded encouragingly. Tomi frowned, then jerked his head in a sudden, shaggy nod. "It was midmorning," he said slowly. "We went a long ways since we got up. I don't know when I fell in. I was thirsty, and we stopped to drink. But it has been hours and hours since then."

Mjau and Dion exchanged looks. It might seem like half a day to Tomi, but if he had stopped at midmorning to drink, it had been no more than an hour and a half since he fell into the Phye. Aranur took off his warcap, running his hand through his hair. "How did it happen? Did anyone try to go after you?"

Tomi's face paled.

Dion touched Aranur's arm warningly, and the man halted, regarding the boy thoughtfully.

"Eren fell in first," the boy said tightly. His voice was flat, expressionless. "Moira yelled at me, and I jumped in after her. Moira jumped in after me. Eren was right there—I grabbed her arm. Then it was like something pulled me under. I tried to shout, but the river—I hit the bottom and shoved up. We came back to the surface and it sucked us under again. Eren grabbed me around my neck. I couldn't breathe." The horror of it was with him, and he tried to look away, but something in Aranur's eyes held him. "We kept going under the water," he choked out. "It—it pulled us, like on a rope. I could not get to the shore. And then we went under again, and Eren let go. I could not hold her." His voice broke. "I tried—I couldn't hold on. She did not come up again. And the river just kept pulling me with it. I tried—I really tried . . ."

"Child," Mjau said softly, "you did your best. Even Aranur could not have done more than that. There is nothing to blame yourself for."

"I had her," he said in a small voice. "I let her go."

"Oh, child . . ." Mjau shook her head.

Aranur cleared his throat. "Where did you climb out?"

Tomi looked up. "Up there." He pointed north. "The river pushed me against some rocks. There weren't any waves, so I climbed out. I . . ." His voice trailed off. He looked down, cringing away from them, and Dion caught her breath at his gesture. "I found Eren there," he said in that same, small voice.

Aranur nodded gently. "And you climbed to the rim then?"

"I climbed up the rocks till I got to the top. There was a trail, so I started walking upstream. I thought I could find the crossing place."

Aranur frowned. "If you were on the trail, why did you go into the forest? Dion said she found you in the woods, not on the rim."

Tomi flashed a look at Hishn from under his eyebrows. "I saw a wolf."

Hishn stood, as if mention of the Gray Ones had brought her to her feet, and Dion shook her head. "The Gray Ones are no threat to you on this side of the Phye. They would not have fought worlags for you otherwise."

Tomi said nothing.

Dion gestured back at the forest. "They risked their lives for you, Tomi. Hishn caught a claw on her side, see? And the yearling's leg was broken—for you. They would not have done that if they did not mean you well."

The boy looked down at his feet.

Dion shrugged finally. Aranur glanced at her.

"If he fell in at the oxtail," he said thoughtfully, "he was not in the water long. Climbing out would not have taken much longer—you picked him up only half a kilometer from here?"

She nodded, giving up for the moment on convincing Tomi about the wolves. "We ran back full speed."

Mjau, the lines around her eyes crinkling with humor, said tartly, "With worlags on your tail, who wouldn't?"

Dion agreed. "I'd guess it took him around twenty minutes to climb out of the river and get to the top of the canyon. Ten more minutes to make his way upstream—he was running," she pointed out. "Five minutes back here after I found him. Twenty minutes on the boulder, then I went down. I don't know how long it took for you to get here after that."

"The worlags were barely dead when we got here," Aranur said. "I would say it was an hour total. Maybe more. But Tomi's people will not be traveling fast—not with five-year-olds in their group," he muttered. He glanced at the pale sun. "Mjau," he said to the older woman, "let's get started with the bodies. Dion, get some food into this boy. You've got something in your pack?" He barely waited for her to nod before striding after Mjau. Left behind, Dion opened her pack and fished in it for a package of dried meat and fruit, which she handed to Tomi.

"Aranur, wait. Tomi—" Dion turned to the boy. "The little girl—you pulled her out?"

He nodded reluctantly.

Dion looked at Aranur. "Her body—it will be visible from the other side of the river. It is a sure sign that someone is headed upstream."

"Moonworms," Aranur cursed again. "Tomi, you will have to show us where you climbed out. We'll bring her body up here, then burn her properly when we come back."

Dion closed her pack, swinging it to her shoulders and starting away until Aranur strode back and checked her with his hand. "Where are you going?"

Her eyes flickered toward the forest, and he frowned.

"You are going to work on the wolves, aren't you?"

She nodded reluctantly. "They are just inside the shadows. The yearling's front leg is snapped."

"Dion," he said in a low voice, "no Ovousibas. No internal healing. Hear me?"

She looked at him without speaking.

"No Ovousibas," he repeated.

She shrugged, turning away to the treeline.

"Dion."

She looked over her shoulder.

"I mean it. No healing. You're not up to it right now."

A stubborn look came over her face. "I hear you," she returned shortly.

He snorted. "You are mess enough without adding weakness on top of it. You've lost blood, your head is bruised—possibly concussed—and you limp like a three-legged dog."

"And thank you for the compliment," she retorted dryly. At least he noticed that her nausea was almost gone.

He glanced at her. "Ovousi—" He broke off, glanced at Mjau and the boy, and lowered his voice. "Ovousibas saps you," he asserted. "It leaves you weaker than a day-old pup. We cannot afford that right now. If we are to get the refugees across today, I will man the ropes, but you will have to cross to find them and bring them back. You have to be strong enough for that. And," he added soberly, "you have to be strong enough to resist the pull of the wolves on the other side of the river."

Tomi, catching Aranur's last words, looked up abruptly, his mouth full of dried meat on which he choked. "No—wolves—" He gulped, hiccuping in his haste as he scrambled to his feet. "No," he repeated. The fear in his eyes was palpable. "The wolves—you can't trust them. The Gray Ones there run with the raiders."

"They would not betray me," Dion reassured him. "I am a wolfwalker, too. Betraying me would be like sending a member of the pack into a trap."

"But they do that. They catch people," he stammered. "They beat them and kill them and then they send the wolves out for more. You said yours don't hunt people, but the ones over there do. That's why I knew—I thought you were a raider, too."

Dion shook her head. "The wolves can't hunt a wolfwalker for the raiders, Tomi. It isn't possible."

"But if you speak to them, they will know where we are—they will have to tell. They will bring the rest of the raiders down on us. They'll kill everyone!"

Aranur knelt and grasped the boy's arm. "Dion is a healer. She cannot betray any man, woman, or child to the raiders."

Dion regarded him searchingly. "At the most, all I would do is listen to the packsong," she said reassuringly. "That cannot harm you or your people."

Aranur forced the boy to look at him. "You were on the trail for at least a day, right? Do you really believe the wolves could not find your group within minutes after you fled? There are ways to sidetrack the raiders, to gain time—give your people the hours they need to reach the Devils' Knee. The wolves must have been doing that ever since you fled. So you saw them. Did you also see the raiders with them? No? Then they were helping you as best they could, keeping the raiders back further, losing them in thick brush.''

Tomi looked skeptical.

Mjau grinned suddenly. ''It's actually quite a joke, Tomi. You would have taken the most direct route to the river, but I can just see the Gray Ones doubling back, taking those raiders through the stickgrass and briarbrush, the poison redplant and the stinging grass. I bet the Gray Ones even made them crawl a few times, just for the hell of it.'' She grinned again, her wrinkled cheek dimpling.

Dion reached out to him. ''Trust us, please.''

He looked down at his feet and nodded reluctantly.

''Moonworms, boy. Don't look like we're doing you such a favor.'' Mjau's voice was dry, and he looked up, startled.

Aranur clapped him on his thin shoulder and pointed to the jerky he held in his hand. ''Come. You can chew on that while you help us.''

Aranur found Dion's sword and returned it to her along with one of the boot knives he pulled from a carcass. A moment later, she accepted her other misplaced boot knife from Mjau. It took several minutes to wipe the ichor from the dull metal, but when she finished, they were clean enough to slide back into her calf pouches without sticking to the leather sheaths. After a glance toward Aranur, she left the others and limped with Hishn to the treeline.

Hishn wrinkled her nose at the scents clinging to Dion's leggings. *Acrid ichor,* she sent in disgust. *You smell like a worlag.*

Dion made a face. ''When I can find a bathtub, I'll bathe. Until then, you'll just have to suffer like me.''

The images Hishn returned, of preferable scents—such as well-rotted meat, old garbage, the ripe odor of a peetree's roots, and the mud-slick leather of an old shoe—made Dion give the wolf a shove. Hishn dodged her hand, trotting ahead and looking back with a lazy gleam in her eyes.

''Fine,'' Dion muttered. ''Next time you smell like a wet dog, I'm going to feel great satisfaction in leaving you outside.''

Another pair of yellow eyes gleamed at her, and Dion glanced to the side, noting the gray male, Yoshi, who paralleled them into the wood shadows.

Of the other two wolves who waited in the forest, neither had formed a bond to man or woman. The yearling, who was the old female's last cub, had met only a few humans in his young life. The female was one of those who had crossed into Ariye the previous winter. Dion had met the pair a month ago, when she shared a hunt with them for deer. Now, she opened her mind to the threads of gray that stretched out to Hishn. When she did, the worried tones of the old female were strong, insistent, howling over the pain of the yearling.

"Gray One," Dion said softly.

Wolfwalker, the old female returned. *My cub is lame and cannot run to safety.*

Dion nodded slowly. *He honored me with my life. I would help him now.*

Then come.

The yearling, standing head down in a deep shadow, looked up at her with dull eyes. His foreleg hung, swollen. Opening to him, Dion felt his pain reach into her own leg, and she stumbled. He panted, his breathing filled with discomfort as the motion of his chest lifted his leg slightly.

Dion dropped her pack and knelt beside him. "Gray One," she whispered.

He whined. His nose found her hand, and she let him sniff, touching him in return. *I cannot run,* he said painfully. *I cannot lie down. I cannot fight for myself or my mother.*

Dion bit her lip. She glanced back toward the clearing, where Aranur and the others worked at the bodies. There were no dens or caves nearby. No place of safety for this yearling except a hole between some roots where the first predator that found him could make him into a meal. Splinting his leg would not prevent him from becoming an easy target. And he was injured because of her.

Hishn nudged her arm, whining low in her throat. *His pain beats in my head. It blinds my nose and ears.*

Dion touched the gray fur lightly. "I feel it, too: his leg—and your ribs."

Wolfwalker, the yearling pleaded.

She closed her eyes, clenching her fists for a long moment. "I'm sorry, Aranur," she muttered, "but I cannot leave him like this."

She looked into the yearling's eyes. She spoke aloud, but her mental words were clear. "There are two things I can do to help you," she said finally. "I can splint your leg, and it will heal in time." She built an image of a splint and cast in her head, sending it to the yearling. "But you would have to stay with me or another healer until your leg was strong enough to come out of the cast."

The yearling growled. His leg, swathed in cloth, hampered by sticks? His snarl spread to his dam, and the older female looked at Dion in dismay.

Dion nodded her agreement. "There is one other thing I can do." She took a breath. "I can help you heal yourself with Ovousibas."

Ovousibas. Hishn licked Dion's cheek, pleased. The old female reached across and nudged Dion's hand.

"You understand, Gray One, that I will need you to help me."

The images in the female's mind were clear. *There is no danger I would not risk for my cub.*

Dion nodded. "Hishn will show you how to work with me," she sent quietly. "The greater the strength you focus through me, the better the healing will be."

The female nudged Dion's hand again, then sat back by her cub.

The yearling whimpered. *Will you walk in me?*

If you wish it.

He nudged her arm, and Dion sat back on her heels. Aranur would be furious if he found out. No Ovousibas. His words rang in her ears. But the internal healing—the healing with the body's own force—was the only healing that would let the wolf survive long enough to reach his den: the images of that warm hole were half a day's run away, and his leg would never stand it, not with the shock in his body and the fever just waiting to set in. Hishn's hot, smelly breath puffed over her shoulder, and Dion turned her head, shoving the gray wolf aside. "I cannot heal you completely," she admitted, "but I can give you enough strength to return to your den. I think it will be enough."

The yearling nudged her, agreeing.

Ovousibas would sap her strength even more than the worlag's poison had, making her feel weak and starved, but she did not see that she had a choice. Even Aranur must agree that the young wolf could not be left alone in the forest with a broken leg.

Hishn circled and sat across from Dion as the woman hesitated. Beside her, but back a meter, Gray Yoshi placed himself. The old female seated herself next to her cub. *Run with us, Wolfwalker.*

Dion took a deep breath. *Then take me in, Gray One.* She gazed into Hishn's yellow-slitted eyes and let her mind flow with the wolf's. There was a different consciousness here—a feeling of power, an energy of the body that filled her senses. With Hishn to guide her, her thoughts were channeled into that energy, dropping down, seeming to whirl to the left. Down, deep in the yearling's body, ran the energy trails. Deep in his bloodstream. Pounded, beaten by his heart. Her senses were caught by his pulse, as if she were a blood cell, swept along and through and back to his heart again. Concentrate, she told herself. Think. She must separate herself to feel more than this pulse, this pounding in her ears. She frowned, catching the thread of other energies. The dull pain of the break in her—*his*—foreleg tripped her, stealing her focus. When she faltered, Hishn swept in like a gray blanket, warming her against that cold pain, buffering her against its ache. With that pain in the background, the nerves, the muscles—all the young wolf's systems—seemed open before her, as if she were wandering among them, studying them closely, searching for signs of damage. She let the voices of other wolves in to howl with Hishn, controlling her instant's panic and forcing herself to slow as the gray wall grew thick and peaceful. Follow the plasma—follow the pain like a map. Let the wolves be her shield. Gray, this blanket against the pain. Yes, she could sense it, but it no longer pounded so brutally against her consciousness. Gray shield. Gray strength. She thought her way through the yearling's body. There—the broken leg. There, where fluids gathered sluggishly, pressing against nerves and stretching muscles and skin. Here, the broken ends of bone—sharp and cutting into the muscles. Think, she told herself. She gathered her strength. The Gray Ones, sensing her task, filled her with their own intangible might, and Dion flung her mind forward. Focus . . . This bone, snapped in two, must come together. She latched onto the ends and pulled, eased, inexorably forced them toward each other. The fluid—in the way. She forced it to move, massaging the muscles to filter it away. Now she could work. Gray strength again, and she built a bridge of new cells between the broken ends of bone. Here, she must knit it together . . . She worked quickly, gathering materials from the yearling's blood and forcing the molecules and acids into new shapes. Knit—the bone ends were touching now. Weak, yes, but touching. Would they hold? There was little time. The irregular heartbeat of the yearling was getting stronger in her ears. She was tiring. The gray shield thinned as she sucked strength from the Gray Ones. A little more. Just a little longer, and he could walk on it. Enough to get to safety. Enough to get home. She massaged the muscles one last time, and then the gray strength swept her up, out, beyond the bloodstream, out beyond the yearling to her collapse on the forest floor.

The yearling whined, and the old female nudged him. She licked his face, then his leg. *Wolfwalker,* they sent gratefully.

Dion opened her eyes, drained. "Gray Ones," she whispered, "you honor me."

The old female looked at her. *You run with the pack, Wolfwalker.* She nudged the yearling to take a step, and he did, whining at the weight.

Dion got to her knees, reaching out to touch him gently. "It will hurt, Gray One, but you can walk on it."

The old female nuzzled Dion, then led her young one away.

A minute later, a hand of iron gripped Dion's shoulder. Aranur. Dion steeled herself to face him. Silently, he handed her a compact chunk of honey-soaked bread and a thick piece of dried meat. She did not speak as she took them, though her stomach growled and gnawed at her insides. When she stumbled to her feet, stubbornly shaking off his help, she staggered, his strong arms catching her and leaning her back against him.

Hishn watched the other wolves disappear into the forest, then looked up. *The yearling runs with the pack again.* The satisfaction in her gray voice was almost human; and Dion, while Aranur glared at her, had to hide her smile. So far, he had said nothing, but as he led her silently back to the clearing, she stifled the impulse to cram more food in her mouth. "How—how did you know?" she asked hesitantly.

Aranur swallowed his anger with difficulty. How she thought she could do the internal healing and not show the effects afterward . . . Dammit, just when he thought he could trust her to show some judgment, she went and did something as stupid as this. If the forest was in flames around her, she would be sitting in the middle of the fire, trying to heal some poor creature who had been burned. He just wished that for once, she would look ahead to see what would happen to everyone else before she did Ovousibas on the trail. Now she was already tired, and they still had half a dozen kilometers to run before they reached the Knee and even began to deal with the problem of the refugees. And as for having a few minutes alone with her . . . He snorted to himself. All she would want to do now was sleep.

Dion, flushing at his silence, caught his arm. "I had to do it, Aranur."

"Did you?" he retorted. "Could it not have waited until after we got the refugees across the Phye?"

She shook her head. "The dead worlags are going to draw a lot of predators—he wouldn't stand a chance, even until tonight, of escaping their notice. Do you really think I could have left him with his leg broken, and the fever settling into his blood, just waiting until some badgerbear discovered him and tore him apart?"

Aranur sighed. "No, Dion," he said heavily. From beside him, Hishn nudged his hand, and reluctantly, he scratched her shoulder. "However," he added, "it is also true, that if there had not been three Gray Ones to help, I would not have let you do it."

Dion, in the act of tearing off another bite of dried meat, almost choked. Aranur "let" her do Ovousibas? *"Let"* her? Like she was some sort of child to be ordered around? She stifled her retort with difficulty. Her arms and legs burned, her head ached with every pounding of her pulse, her stomach was cramped with the lack of food, and now Aranur had the audacity to "let" her do the internal healing? She was a healer—a master healer, at that. She made her own decisions about what healing was required and when it would be done.

"I know you're a master healer, Dion," Aranur said sharply, reading her mind with irritating accuracy. "But there are times when even you simply cannot do Ovousibas."

She glared at him.

He chuckled. "The set of your jaw and the expression on your face gives you away," he said dryly. "I would be blind not to see the nasty comments you hide behind those flashing eyes."

Dion snorted.

"There are better times to do Ovousibas than in the middle of a battle, Dion."

"The fighting was long over, Aranur." She pointed with her chin at the boulder and the carcasses still littering the ground. "I left mess enough to prove it." Now it was Dion who stalked on ahead.

He grabbed her shoulders and turned her toward him, glaring. "We have seven kilometers to go, top ropes and rings to connect and test, and eleven refugees to get across the river. Our fight is just beginning, and you are starting it out already exhausted."

"I can make it."

"It is not a question of whether or not you can make it," he retorted grimly. "For the refugees' sake, you now have no choice. And neither do I." He gritted his teeth. "Three days since I've seen you. Before that, we've had only an hour here, one night there . . . I hoped at least for a meal together, a walk—something. And now . . . now this." He gestured helplessly at the clearing. "The worlags, the healing, and now the refugees. By the time we make camp, all we'll do is go to bed. And then Gamon will send me back out to the Knee and you to town to rest, and it will be another ninan before we're together again. It is not," he added vehemently, "the way I envisioned our Waiting Year."

She looked down.

He stared at his clenched hands. "Dion."

"Yes?"

He searched her eyes. "Nothing," he sighed.

Reaching up, she touched his chest. He covered her hand with his own. For a long moment, they stood motionless, the sound of the river drowning the wind in the trees.

* * *

In Bilocctar, far to the east, months before, just past midwinter feast . . .

Conin strode along the corridor purposefully. His guts were churning, and the fire in his stomach had only flared more after breakfast. But he had promised Namina. He would see Longear and force her, just once, to give him something of his own. As he walked, the corridor darkened, went down, and dimmed again. There was light up ahead, but it did nothing to relieve the gloom of this place. He hated it. It was probably why Longear chose it.

He emerged finally into the wide room where Longear held her audiences. There were eight openings into the room; her desk was in the middle. The only other furniture in the room beside it was a single chair. Anyone coming to see Longear, including the Lloroi, must stand.

Conin crossed to the desk, ignoring the archers who lounged alertly in the openings. Longear took no chances with herself. Someday, he thought with bitter promise, he would come down here and slit her throat in spite of them. He would surely die, but, he thought, it would be the one act he could make that would allow him to take his path to the moons with some measure of self-respect.

Longear did not look up from her paper, and Conin's face darkened. "Longear," he said sharply.

"One moment, Lloroi," she said, not quite hiding her insolence. When she finally looked up, she smiled slowly. It was not a pretty smile. "Good morning, Lloroi. I take it you have come to let me know that you agree with my last recommendation?"

"I'm not here about the raiders, Longear."

"Oh?" She sat back. Conin was not man enough to stand up to her on any issue, and he hated the prison center more than any place in Bilocctar. What could bring him down here if it was not the business she gleefully forced him to carry out?

"I'm riding to the east border. Namina wants to visit her family, and I want no trouble from you while we do it."

Longear regarded him thoughtfully until Conin felt like squirming. "What brought about this sudden desire for family?" she inquired pleasantly.

He shrugged. "It has been a year since she saw them. Does she need more reason?"

Longear pushed the papers across her desk. "Look at these, Conin. The Ariyens move along the border in force. If it were not for the raiders we have stationed there, they could have invaded across the Phye months ago. Are you sure she just wants to visit? Or could she perhaps be luring you to Ariye to become a hostage yourself?"

Conin jerked. "Namina is not a hostage here."

"No?" Longear drawled insolently. "She bargained herself in exchange for setting her cousins and brother free over a year ago. What makes you so sure she has not now found a way of revenge?"

"Namina is not a vengeful person."

Longear tapped her fingers together. "Whether she is or is not, is not the question. If you want to go to the border, I will go with you. It is time I put in another two months in the towns. Besides," she added, grinning evilly at him, "we wouldn't want our dear Lloroi to be hurt on the trail, now, would we?"

Conin swallowed his fury, noting Longear's amusement at his emotion. He wanted to strike her, to wipe that smile from her face with his fist. He knew he would do nothing. He would take her tone and her words and swallow his pride again and shrink a little inside each time. He would do this for Namina, he told himself. He might not be able to do anything for himself, but this at least, he could do for her.

Two days later, when they left the city, they rode in a small group. There was no need of a larger one; they could not be attacked by raiders.

Longear rode with them.

Chapter 6

Where the Phye flows down,
The falls blast back.
Water rises; rocks grow black;
The river booms, and snags go slack;
Thunder fills your eyes to see
There is no silencing the Devil's Knee.

Aranur, Mjau, and Tomi hurried silently as they carried the worlags' bodies to the forest edge. The boy, carting a load of hard-cased limbs like firewood, struggled beneath the weight of his burden. In front of him, Aranur and Mjau lifted and carried the whole—or nearly whole—carcasses by the upper arms and hind legs. When they could, the two Ariyens tucked the middle arms across the worlag bellies. Otherwise, the scrawny arms dragged, catching on roots and tearing thin trails through the grass. At the edge of the forest, they did not bother going more than a few meters into the trees, but flung the bodies into the shadows they selected.

Dion sat and watched. Now that the exhaustion from the healing had set in, her arms ached. Her calves pounded. Her head throbbed. Her back felt as if a firebrand had been drawn across it. She shifted, trying to ease the growing discomfort in her back, while each heartbeat thrust a lance of pain in her brain. With her body in this shape, she would not be running scout today—or any day soon. She would be lucky just to keep pace with Aranur.

She watched him enviously for a moment. He moved so smoothly—like a forest cat. Where had her own grace gone? She rubbed her forearms, trying to smooth the bruises out of her muscles. Even when Aranur paused—his head raised, his eyes examining the forest shadows, his energy stilled and dormant—he was quiet only in the way a great cat was motionless before it leapt. His long body was lean and muscular, his hands scarred from many blades, but strong as steel itself. He had black hair, like her own; the cropped fringe on the sides edged out from under the leather-and-metal mesh warcap. Handsome? Perhaps not, she admitted. But the angular strength of his face and the piercing gray of his gaze caught her attention as no other could. She put her head in her hands, letting her mind hold Aranur's image while she closed her aching eyes.

Aranur's image slipped into that of Tomi's, and she thought of the refugees running the borders. Running—and for how long? Since last night? The day before? With young children in their group, they could have been four days on the trail to cover the same ground Dion would travel in one. And they would not have taken a direct trail, either—not with the wolves hounding them all the way up the river. She glanced up the Phye. On her side—the east side—Hishn and her gray mate, though out of sight, were not gone. In spite of the eagerness of the male wolf to return to his own wolfwalker, Hishn's worry for Dion did not let her get more than a few hundred meters from her human partner. Gray Yoshi would have to wait if he wanted Hishn to pace him back to the heights. Hishn would not leave Dion until she was sure Dion ran without pain.

As Dion reached out to the wolf, the gray creature filled Dion's senses with the sweet odor of Aranur's sweat, the bitter stench of the worlags' fluids, and the dust of the morning trail. Dion smiled wryly. Her own images, with the throbbing of her arms and legs, and the nausea still faintly in her stomach, must be suppressed, or Hishn would dog her footsteps like a shadow, complaining at her pain and whining at her stubbornness. As would Aranur, if he guessed how lousy she really felt.

Mjau caught Dion's attention and motioned for her to join them. Reluctantly, Dion rose. She did not get far. Her face paled abruptly as the nausea surged again. Her neck muscles taut, her fists clenched, she struggled with her stomach before swallowing against the acids that rose in her throat. She shuddered. When the nausea lessened, her fists were still clenched. The internal healing must have made her more susceptible to the worlag poison, and with that in her blood, she could not fight the queasiness and stay on the trail at the pace she knew Aranur would set. Hating her weakness as much as the worlags who had caused it, she slung her pack to the ground and dug in it angrily, searching for the herbs so carefully stored in their separate bags. Picking several, she rolled them in her palms until they formed a small, rough ball. As she took a swig from her bota bag, she grimaced and swallowed the dry leaves. Their rough edges rasped against the roof of her mouth, and the bitter taste made her gag before she could swallow. Soon, she knew, the pain would dull and her stomach settle. Until then, she would have to run with the discomfort. Slinging the pack over her shoulder, she took up the water bag's thong and limped over to the others.

Aranur wiped his hands in the grass as she joined him. The purple blood of the worlags had stained his fingers and turned his nails dark. He eyed the color with disgust. "They'll stink for days."

"Better on your skin than under it," Dion returned sourly.

Aranur grinned, though his eyes were concerned. With the nausea so obvious in her face, he wondered that she could still joke with him. "Perhaps that will teach you to think before you leap. Or at least teach you not to take everything on by yourself," he retorted.

She gave him a sly, sideways look. "I don't know. You make a good carcass carrier. It might teach me to let you clean up my messes all the time."

He chuckled evilly. "I'll teach you some things . . ." He sobered. "Dion . . ."

"Do not worry," she said quietly. "I'm fine enough to make the Knee."

He nodded reluctantly. "Then it's back to the trail for both of us."

They exchanged a long look, and then he turned and strode

off, breaking into a loping jog as he set his feet to the path along the river, one hand holding his sword hilt steady against his pace, the other swinging with his stride. Dion fell in behind him, Tomi behind her, and Mjau followed the boy. The older woman noted the youth's clenched fist as he clutched Dion's knife. Not even while running would he loosen his grip.

Dion winced in Aranur's wake. Her stomach rebelled briefly, surging up with the jar of each footstep so that she clenched her jaws to keep from throwing up. The sensation finally faded into dull queasiness, but by then, her calves, which had been tight and cold when she started, were aching with the stretch of the run. Bruises she had not noticed before made themselves known as her pack slapped softly on her back, and the throb of her blood in the cuts on her arms and legs were screams that rose in voice with every stride. With an effort, she closed her mind to her body, enduring that first half kilometer, then the next, letting the rhythm of the pace match her heartbeat. Close-by, Hishn ran through the forest in a long, loping stride. Her gray images, mixed with those of the male wolf, interlaced with Dion's thoughts so that she saw through three pairs of eyes and heard the sounds of the woods through three sets of ears.

Her nose seemed low to the ground. Her arms became feet and padded softly in the dirt with her legs. Damp dirt clogged Dion's mouth, jamming up under her fingertips and catching on her claws before being kicked off. Leaves and wind brushed short hair across her face where her own clear skin had no fur. Aranur, looking back, saw that her eyes were unfocused. He was strangely reassured. Dion would not admit to discomfort or weakness, but he could trust the wolves to gauge her strength for him. Hishn would not let the wolfwalker run in pain—not, anyway, if the wolf could help it. The wolf would cover Dion's senses with her own sharp sight and smell, forcing Dion to think through the mind of the Gray One instead of in human thoughts and pain.

The ache in Dion's calves had barely begun to dull when the group reached the spot where Aranur and Mjau had left their gear. As Aranur drew to a halt, Dion stayed standing, shifting from foot to foot to keep her aching calves loose. Tomi, reaching the clearing a minute after her, collapsed on the ground. His thin chest heaved, and his breath was ragged. Dion unslung her water bag for him. He reached for the bag greedily, but she shook her head.

"Only a sip," she cautioned. "And let it warm in your mouth before you swallow."

He nodded reluctantly, and Dion kept her hand on the bag, pulling it away from him when he swallowed quickly and greedily, sucking the water unthinking.

"One mouthful at a time," she said sharply. "You'll get cramps."

The boy fingered the knife that he still clutched, but Dion ignored the movement.

She took a sip and rolled the water around her mouth before swallowing. She offered him another swallow and, when he was done, one more before slinging the bag back over her shoulder. "When your body cools down," she added gently, "you can drink deeply."

In the meantime, Aranur had found what he was looking for in his pack. It was with an air of satisfaction that he pulled out his extra tunic and moccasins. "Knew I carried these for a reason," he murmured. Kneeling, he did not remove the rags on the boy's feet, but slipped the man-sized moccasins on over the rude footgear, lashing the leather snugly to his calves with thongs. On Aranur, the moccasins would have barely reached his knee; on Tomi, they flopped over. Aranur, regarding them for a moment, folded them back and retied the thongs, leaving the boy's knees bare. "Easier to run in," he said. Tomi stood then, trying out his mock boots. Aranur watched him closely. "Do they slip?"

Tomi shook his head.

"Here." He handed the boy the oversized tunic, and Tomi took it warily. Another thong belted the garment at the boy's waist, and then Aranur motioned to the boy's knife. "The scabbard can hang from the belt. It will leave your hands free, if you need them."

"No!" Tomi scrambled back. "I'll do it," he amended hastily, his face flushing. Then the flush faded and his mask was once more in place. He carefully threaded the loose end of the crude belt through the scabbard so that the knife hung on his left.

Aranur turned and, seeing that Mjau was also ready to go, strode away in a fast-paced walk. Tomi stayed where he was, staring after Aranur, struggling with the wariness that seemed to choke his words. Mjau, regarding him with concern, realized Tomi was trying to say a single word: thanks.

The older woman pointed at the trail, indicating for him to go on after. "He knows," she reassured him gently.

In another half hour, they returned to the riverbank and made their way quickly upriver. When they stopped again, it was at Tomi's gesture. Aranur looked back, and the boy pointed again to the place he had climbed up from the water, his face expressionless. Aranur walked gingerly to the rim, testing the ground before putting his weight where there might be little substance beneath him. His gaze raked across the far bank, searching for movement, for any sign that someone might be watching. He saw nothing and, still uneasy, turned to Dion. "Can you sense anything?"

Dion scanned the river, the forest. Even the graysong was quiet, searching but not close. "Nothing," she returned slowly.

In seconds, he stripped his pack and dropped it among the roots of the silverheart trees. His sword was next, handed to Dion as he slid like a shadow to the cliff's edge. At the rim, erosion had crumbled away the soil so that a network of roots hung out over the steep, rocky slope. The marks where Tomi had climbed up were obvious. Roots were pulled loose and bent. Some of the limbs were naked in patches and weeping sap. Aranur nodded to himself. That would be where the boy had slipped, his hands stripping the thin skin from the roots as he clutched at their fragile security for balance. New slides of earth and stones marked his upward passage, and Aranur regarded them warily. With his weight, he would scar this slide twice as much as the boy had already done. At least there was plenty of loose dirt at the top. If necessary, he could roll a large boulder down, hiding the marks of his passage with a more-natural slide once he regained the top.

Dion, watching him, could almost hear his thoughts. Then his shoulders tightened slightly, and the tiny muscle in his jaw tensed and relaxed. So, she thought, he has found the little girl. She glanced at Tomi, but the boy's mask was in place.

When Aranur reappeared, his outer tunic was gone, and he was carrying a small bundle in his arms. He was sweating as he regained the top, but neither Dion nor Mjau stepped forward to help him as he clambered over the roots. He wedged his burden up in the branches of the silverheart, where it would be difficult for the ground predators to get at it. When he lowered his arms, he turned without a word and strode up the trail.

As the others fell in behind him, Dion stretched her senses to the wolves on both sides of the Phye. The gray creatures to the west still did not welcome her, but she listened to their song through Hishn, and they could not refuse her that.

There was time. The western wolves were not yet close to the refugees. They wandered the game trails, leading first one way, then another, into root caves and rock overhangs where the refugees might have stayed. By the time the Bilocctar wolfwalker and the wolves tramped up the ground, there would be little for the raiders to see. Besides, raiders did not waste trackers on a trail when they could rely on the Gray Ones to find their quarry for them. For that oversight, Dion sent a prayer of thanks to the moons.

Three kilometers farther, the temperature rose to a muggy warmth, occasionally cut through by the chill wind that gusted off the canyon. By then, the clarity of Dion's thoughts had faded to a jumble of painful sensations.

The ground, once fairly even, rose sharply to rocky inclines. They did not jog here. They hiked along the twisted path, leaning into the trail when the steepness stole their strength. Tomi's breath came hoarsely. Dion stumbled more than once. Aranur, his legs like iron, said nothing until he turned his ankle on a loose rock and swore a blue streak while the pain subsided. He refused the wrap Dion offered, relacing his boots instead and walking gingerly until he could ignore the shooting pain that crept up his calf. Behind them, Mjau walked steadily, her short-cropped silvered hair ruffing only slightly in the wind, and her blue-veined skin barely showing her perspiration. Dion, glancing back, met Mjau's eyes, and the older woman smiled wryly, acknowledging the wolfwalker's envy with amused apology.

A low-hanging branch slapped back awkwardly, and Dion let out a stifled curse as it caught on one of her forearms. "Moon-wormed misbegotten branch of a blackroot," she muttered, thrusting the branch aside and warning Tomi of its arc.

Constantly, Dion's wary gaze swept the far bank of the Phye, though it could hardly be called a bank anymore. With the cliffs rising over a hundred meters above the river, the channel was steep enough to keep all but the noon sun's rays from its depth. She stumbled again as she looked toward the canyon's edge. The voice of the river was muted here, its rush trapped in the canyon. It had not risen with the trail, and now its waters were far below, speckled with white as if to spite the shadow of the rock walls. The sun, though higher than before, had not yet broken through the cloud cover; its light was indirect and dull. On all sides, the forest thinned with altitude; the trees were short and their trunks scrawny. The canopy overhead was more skimpy, letting the dim light through in patches and allowing new brush to grow thickly around the trunks. But for Dion, each shadow seemed to hold the small bundled shape that Aranur had left behind them on the cliff. She had to struggle to see only the ground beneath the trees.

Aranur slowed again. The path they were following led to a scattering of tall stones, and he eyed them warily. This place was a favorite hunting ground for a family of watercats who lived nearby. A ninan earlier, he had discovered their perches when he ran this trail to help bring up the supports for the crossing. He glanced over his shoulder questioningly.

Dion, her eyes unfocused, shook her head. "It is safe." She spoke reluctantly, as if the silence had been a tribute to the dead child behind them. "Nothing hides among them."

Tomi looked at her, startled. "How can you tell?"

Dion shrugged.

From behind, it was Mjau who answered him. "The nose and ears of a wolf are ten times more sensitive than those of a human," she explained. "Dion looks through Gray Hishn's eyes, not her own."

Tomi eyed Dion warily. "I do not see any wolf."

Mjau grinned without humor, a twisted tooth coming into view and contrasting oddly with the nearly straight row of her other teeth. "Seen not," she answered, "but they are there."

As they climbed toward the rocks, the sounds around them changed strangely. Their ears were coaxed, then deafened, by noise. Thunder burst, then faded strangely between the stones.

"It's the river," Dion explained to the boy. "Its sound echoes off the rocks, bouncing from one to another." Around them, the sounds grew until they became one dull roar. A strangely irregular beat seemed to punctuate the thunder, but it was not until they stepped out from the rocks into the dull sun that the sound became a booming, crashing beat, and the sight of the canyon brought them to a halt.

"By the moons," Mjau said reverently. Surreptitiously, she made the sign of the blessing of the wolves.

Aranur stepped to the edge of the canyon. The chill air was damp and biting with the wind. The cloud of mist that clung to the falls and climbed the cliff walls did not reach above the rim of the canyon, and Aranur let his gaze roam the length of the Knee below it and above, as if to catalog every rock and pattern in the mist and water.

Dion joined him, seeing his shoulders relax their wary set when he could find no sign of danger. She looked back at Tomi. "There," she yelled above the thunder, pointing up the river. "It is power. The spirit of the moons poured out for us. For the little girl. They grieve and give their anger for her so that we can let her go."

Tomi stared at her. Mjau grabbed his arm, pulling him back from the edge. He stiffened at her touch, only his eyes alive in his dull, bruised face.

Dion turned back to the river. From where she stood with Aranur, the rim curved away under their feet and eroded into an overhang barely an arm's length thick. Their gaze trapped by the view, the two dark-haired figures exulted in the crack of the river as it exploded from air pockets and slammed the spring snags onto the rocks.

Abruptly, sharply, the river canyon dropped with the falls. Moisture, which clung to the walls of the cliffs, turned the rock faces green and orange. In front, the Devil's Knee bent the river like a straw in a woman's hand. Over the cliff, rushing out, then down, the rocks twisted the water into a double fall, a blasting inferno that sprayed back up on itself as it drilled into the rock.

Two snags spun over, tilting at the edge before being sucked down, then followed by the debris of their branches. With wonder, Dion watched the cloud of white that hid the base of the cascade toward which they plunged. The water of the top falls sheeted down, exploding out where air was trapped in a pocket in the pool below. Dion breathed in, her lungs expanding. The wind tasted like the river. In her sight, there was nothing but this—this white cascade flinging itself down the cliff and smashing into the pool below. In her ears, no sound but the crashing thunder of the Phye.

Two dozen times? Thrice a dozen? How many times had she stood at the Knee and let its power invade her soul? And each time, the river was new. The upper falls; the lower; they grew and faded and changed, and repeated not at all.

The upper cascade was a sheet of power. It threw itself off the lip of the river and slammed into the rocks below, splintering and bursting into a thick cloud of mist that climbed halfway back up as if determined for another chance to ride that torrent down. It was a cloud that held rainbows by day and pale moonbows by night. In the dull, midday light, a faint rainbow floated in the midst of the cloud, hanging over the middle pool and the lower falls like the ghost of a moonmaid. The lower fall itself could not be called a single entity. It was a twisted, plunging, bucking thing that blasted across rocks and arched agonizingly through the stones, demonically destroying and creating its shape each second of its life. Dion flung out her arms suddenly, screaming at the river. She did not know what she screamed, just that she had to add her voice to that of the Phye or she would explode with its power. And suddenly, her mind was full of a gray storm screaming and howling with her. She reeled, blind. She did not notice when Aranur grabbed her arm in his steely grip. Her eyes were sightless. The impression of the falls was burned into her mind, and the gray voices of the wolves rang in her brain with their response. She arched back, lifting her voice with them, and the sound that burst from her lips was not human.

Aranur held her on the canyon's rim. He had been shocked when he touched her—the echoes of the wolves had passed into his own mind, filled his ears. He looked down at the woman in his hands, feeling her muscles taut and shivering, staring into her sightless violet eyes, unable to keep himself from memorizing the feral expression on her face. The bond of the wolves . . .

If it was strong enough for him to feel, what had the wolfwalkers in Bilocctar picked up?

Dion shuddered, her voice fading. Slowly, the sight came back to her eyes. Her lips relaxed over her teeth. The thunder of the gray storm in her head blended and became the thunder of the falls. The joyous chill of the racing pack on the heights became the cutting cold of the canyon wind. The young teeth wrestling, chewing happily on her tolerant arms, became the steely hands of her Promised.

Aranur. Her gaze focused. He looked at her searchingly. Shivering suddenly, she leaned against him, and his hands soothed her. Aranur's eyes were worried as he moved back with her, away from the edge. Dion was one of those people sensitive to other forms of life—a talent that the ancients had recognized and bred into both humans and wolves. Aranur himself was not empathic enough to bond with a wolf, but even he could feel the shattering power of these falls. For Dion, with this power focused through the Gray Ones . . . He had known that their mental power caught her up when she was tired, but he had forgotten how incredibly strong that bond could be. He turned and glared at the waterfall. He needed Dion, he thought savagely, not a woman who was half-wolf in her mind. He needed her here, strong, concentrating on what had to be done. Mjau was too old to make this crossing with him. The boy—Tomi—was too young. So it had to be Dion. And Dion was only half there. Somewhere, the Gray Ones called to her with a power like the falls. Somewhere, they held her, as tightly as he did now.

Mjau and Tomi watched them curiously. When Dion's eyes refocused, Aranur motioned toward the path, and Mjau gently pushed the boy ahead of her, following the tall, gray-eyed man and the slender wolfwalker without a word.

Chapter 7

Revel, sang the moonwarriors, in the chilling stream.
Let your skin grow cold and so discard it.
Hunger for our moonlit path.
We lead your feet
  so softly,
  so gently from your world to ours.
In our stars, your death, your future is waiting.
Run from your hunters now.
Soon, your sleep will be peaceful.
Soon, you will be home.

The trail that Aranur followed curved away from the edge of the falls and wound back into the forest, avoiding the massive boulders that formed the top of the Knee and made riding difficult. This was the traders' trail—the Silver Trail—or it had been, when crossing the border had been a profitable venture, not a lethal challenge. Except for a few hardy caravans that risked the border raiders, the traders in Ariye rode only the Valley Road now, down to the coast towns. Better a thin skin in Sidisport than no skin at all, so they said.

Dion filed after Aranur, stumbling when her gaze was drawn back to the waterfall instead of to the ground under her feet. When at last Aranur halted, Dion, glancing, then looking sharply at the area, gave him a puzzled look. He grinned, nodding at the pile of boulders on the river side of the trail.

"We disguised the chimney," he shouted over the river's din. He motioned at the rocks. Following him, Dion realized why she felt so baffled by the trail. The boulders were new—they had not been there when she had last passed the falls. She stared at them in pleased surprise. There was an opening in them that led between two of the taller boulders. The narrow path went only a meter before it seemed to end in another haphazard pile of rocks, but, as Dion stepped past Aranur and explored the way, she saw that the channel had merely turned, hiding its true direction from curious eyes. The rocks were cleverly placed. Since they pressed out along the very rim of the canyon, beyond the lip of the chimney which plunged down to the falls, the stones would hide the cleft from both sides of the river. Anyone who climbed the cut would be able to rest at the top, out of view of the path.

Aranur nodded smugly at her pleasure. He had argued with his uncle Gamon over placing the boulders, but once they had been moved, even Gamon admitted that the idea had been a good one.

Dion made her way back out of the rocks. Examining the ground, she could guess where the burden dnu had hauled their loads of stone, but the faint limpness of the grass that patched the ground was not from the hooves of the six-legged creatures, but from turf that had been laid down over the tracks and was just now catching its roots back into soil. She looked back and forth along the trail. Had she not known the path at that point, she would not have guessed how it had changed.

Aranur glanced toward Mjau. His gesture was short, decisive. Neither Dion nor the archer argued. The older woman had the endurance to run long distances, to judge wind, to make knots, to shoot arrows, but not to haul bodies up and down ropes. Asking her to climb a cliff, jump into glacial water, and come out ready to fight was like asking a dnu to be a bird—it wasn't possible. Dion, in spite of her weakness, was still the better choice.

As he glanced her way, Dion took off her pack and tossed it in the woods against the thick bore of a tree. Aranur followed suit, removing his sword and other weapons until he kept only two knives. Dion kept her sword, but dropped her empty quiver beside his blade. While Mjau and Tomi carried the gear to a dry spot off the ground, Dion stripped off her jerkin and tunic, replacing only the former. The tunic she offered the boy, who took it gratefully, layering it on under Aranur's shirt. She wanted something dry to come back to, and in the meantime, Tomi might as well be as comfortable as possible. Aranur agreed. They would be as wet as the fifth hell when they went behind the falls. While the archer, anticipating his needs, took the ropes and rings from his pack, he changed, too.

They would take the ropes and rings down with them, but they would not place them in the rock. With the refugees here now, it was pointless to rush a job no longer needed. Aranur could send someone else to finish the job later—perhaps tomorrow night, when the next load of timber was brought from the base camp.

From where Dion waited, the crossing could not be seen. It was hidden behind the Devil's Knee, sheltered by that plunging fall in a narrow cavern that stretched from one side of the canyon to the other. The wolfwalker rubbed her muscles, wincing involuntarily at their complaint. She would have to steel herself for the climb on the other side of the Knee. This side was steep, but not very exposed—the chimney had three sides, making it seem more like a channel than an open cliff. The only real danger here was that the motion of the falls could make it seem as if one were falling, changing one's balance and making it easy to slip. No, it was the other side of the falls that made her breath catch in her throat. The cliff was open and exposed there. She would feel like an ant. Something familiar gripped her stomach, and she swallowed, wishing, in spite of her hunger, that she had not eaten.

Then Hishn stretched into her mind, the gray voice a soothing blanket against her fear. The wolf crept out of the forest and laid a warm muzzle on Dion's thigh, and the wolfwalker hugged her, mindless of the smell. She got a lick in the face for her trouble, and Aranur wrinkled his nose at that. Gingerly wiping her cheeks and chin with her sleeve, Dion made a face at both of them.

"You'll stay here," she told Tomi as the boy started to follow her toward the cliff. "You can pick a spot back there to wait with Mjau." She gestured toward the stand of silverheart, and the boy followed the archer reluctantly. Then the wolfwalker turned to Hishn. "Stay with Mjau and the boy?" she asked the wolf.

Hishn butted Dion with her head, growling.

"I'll be back soon." She rubbed the Gray One's ears persuasively. "You cannot cross the falls with us. The rocks are slick and wet, and you cannot walk the ropes like Aranur and I."

The wolf's eyes gleamed. *You are tired like an elder after running the ridge. There is no strength in your limbs.*

"I can rest once the refugees are across."

You need my fangs to sharpen your hands for the hunters on the other side.

"My sword and knife are enough."

You no longer have your short fang.

"I will take Mjau's."

Hishn growled again, her teeth closing on Dion's arm ungently, and the wolfwalker hissed out her breath. It was a long moment before Hishn gave way to Dion's gaze. When she let go of the wolfwalker's arm, the wolf lay down with an angry thump. Her yellow eyes gleamed balefully.

Aranur touched her arm to get her attention, and Dion hauled herself to her feet. She glanced at Tomi, at the way his hand rested tensely on the hilt of her knife at his belt, then asked Mjau with a gesture for the other woman's knife. Mjau handed it over without comment, and Dion belted it on.

Tomi, exhausted, watched them dully. His eyes went to the canyon rim. There, both banks of the Phye were rocky, plunging steeply into the rapids below. It was easy to see where the boulders for the chimney guise came from: where the boy huddled, the ground was hard beneath the moss. Trees clutched the stones between their roots as if gathering them up. The boulders between the trunks were massive, twice as tall as Aranur, and seamed and cracked like an old man's face. The fissures where the ice formed each winter held spring moss, tempting Tomi to put his fingers inside the cracks.

Mjau stopped him. "Don't."

His hand froze, and Mjau, her mouth open to caution him against gellbugs and redbugs, frowned at him, watching him hold his body still, until she realized what he reminded her of: a dog that had been kicked too often. An animal that had been beaten until it sat patiently, waiting for the punishment to end. Suddenly furious, she looked up and met Aranur's eyes. He had seen it, too. He gestured abruptly for her to remove the boy further into the forest.

"Come." She jerked her head. "We wait back here."

Standing at the top of the falls, Dion frowned at the canyon. The water, rushing through standing waves and rocks, still pulled her gaze. A log passed, followed by the tangled branches of another snag. She watched them hesitate on the edge of the falls. Their plunge below was marked by no more thunder than that of the river. Her herbs had worn off, she realized. Her headache had returned. Either that, or they had not been strong enough to dull the pain in the first place.

Aranur was studying the far bank of the river.

"Can you see them?" She had to shout to make herself heard, and the effort made her wince.

Aranur shook his head slowly.

Nodding her understanding, she moved to stand beside one of the boulders so that her line of sight with the opposite bank was not distracted, then closed her eyes against the mesmerizing pull of the river. The strength of the wolves had not faded completely from her mind, and their voices rushed back in as she called out to Hishn. A second later, a warm muzzle nudged her thigh, and she smiled faintly, her hand going automatically to the gray wolf's scruff.

Hishn ignored Gray Yoshi. *Wolfwalker,* she sent, pleased at Dion's call for help.

"Gray One," Dion said, "you honor me."

The river boomed, and both Hishn and Yoshi's ears flickered. The two opened their minds together to the packsong, blending their voices in a lonely howl. Images ranged into pictures of trails and hunting and the scent of the opposite bank. For Dion, whose fatigue lowered her will as it stole her strength, the depth of the two voices pulled steadily. Resisting, she finally closed her mind to all but Hishn's voice. *The hunt?* she asked.

The hunt is near, the wolf returned. *It grows eager and loud.*

A chill struck Dion, and this time, it had nothing to do with her fear of heights. "How near?" she demanded urgently. "How loud?"

The wolf touched her muzzle to Gray Yoshi's, and his images joined with hers. Together, their voices blended into a medley of sensation. Dion's senses stretched. Yoshi howled, expressing his wish to return to his own wolfwalker, and Hishn bit his shoulder. The two wolves reached into the songs of the packs on both sides of the river. Concentrating on their images, Dion stood silent, unmoving. On the other side, the song was still dark, overshadowed, and closed. Not far, though; Hishn was right. Their song was full of briarbrush and clumpbush, dust and the droppings of deer; and Dion knew that they were not following the river exactly, but were coming through the game trails instead. Time, she realized—the Gray Ones were giving the refugees time. She broke her contact. When she turned to Aranur, she pointed across the falls. "They are there. The raiders"—she motioned to the south—"are there, too: close, but not yet on them."

Aranur nodded. Slinging the ropes over his shoulder, he waited for Dion to do the same with her matching burden. The metal rings he had clipped onto his coil of rope slapped hard against his jerkin with every movement. He grimaced.

He led the way through the rocks to stop at the top of the chimney. The steep, rocky channel dropped clumsily down to the waterfall. Dion peered below, but could not see the bottom. Halfway down, where it met the middle part of the waterfall, it was obscured by the rising mist and a spattering channel of the cascade. Slick footing. Slippery holds. She paused and drew on her gauntlets. Aranur did the same. He gestured at the doubled rope, then eased himself over the rim until he could wrap his legs around one of the lines. Then he was gone, sliding steadily down into the mist as the other line fed up from below.

When she could no longer see him, Dion shifted her rope coil and watched the rope slide smoothly through the pulley. When it stopped, she reached out to grab it and repeat Aranur's move. Her hands shook. She closed her eyes, clenching her fists. Grimly cautious, she used her arms to lower her body until her legs could wrap around the line. And then she was sliding down, her weight pulling the rope through the pulley above.

Ten meters down, her front was soaked from the wind-driven shafts of spray. Twenty meters down, her face was whipped to a burning chill. Her leather leggings were an icy skin on her thighs. The din of the falls drummed the inside of her skull until she thought even her heartbeat was deafened by the sound. Thirty meters down, a blast of water sprayed out, catching her full in the chest and swinging her toward the chimney. The sudden cessation of water was icier than the spray. And then she was into the cloud of mist. Blind, frigid water dripped from her eyelashes and ran off her nose. Her bangs were flooded, and the runnels that swept down her cheeks to her chin to her chest froze the purple gemstone in her sternum with a cold that reached deep into the bone.

Light was only a cloud of white. Black shadows burst out as the falls subsided, then flared beside her. The thunder pounded her bones. And then her feet hit stone, and she stumbled to gain purchase in the puddle in which she landed. The torrent of water rushed past at an almost-vertical angle, drawing her eyes and making her sway with its motion. An arm reached out of the blackness behind the fall, and Aranur drew her in.

Black; frigid cold. The underside of the waterfall was a slick, rocky cave. Sharply rounded boulders tumbled haphazardly near the base of the fall, rising in a tiered wall behind it. A fierce wind blasted back, the convection currents carrying a chill spray up in sheets. Dion gasped, her icy body shuddering. She stumbled, feeling little in her bloodless feet. Aranur led her on, and she stared about the cave in wonder.

She had never been behind the falls. She had only heard about it a ninan ago—nine days—when Aranur's uncle, Gamon, had chosen the site for the crossing. With the tremendous boulders in the double falls, it had not occurred to her to guess the upper fall was hollow behind its cascade. But Gamon had remembered a legend about the falls—a story of the ancients, who had mapped the world so deeply and accurately that mining deposits no larger than a child's shoe were pinpointed. He sent a group of people to the Ancients' Library immediately, and it had taken them only a few hours to locate the map he wanted. Another several hours had been spent designing and carving the message ring that would represent that map for his men. But with the message ring, it had been easy to locate the cavern. The wooden ring had been so vivid—blue and black and carved with the fast fall of water and the abrupt chasm of rocks—that now, when Dion stared at the cavern, she still saw the ring's design. She remembered the cold she had felt when she first viewed that ring, the shiver that had clung to her back, as if the carver had somehow captured a piece of the Phye and wrapped the wooden column with it. The place was exactly as she had viewed it from the ring. Moons, what she would give to have a talent like that . . .

She stood huddled in Aranur's arms, their bodies clinging to the memory of heat in each other that was now absent. Her glance darted from one dark corner in the cave to the next, cataloging the shape and comparing it to the image in her mind. The cavern was narrow and jagged behind the falls. Its wet surfaces were slick with glacial cold, glistening in the faint light that dared to cut through the falls. It was as if the torrent that pounded below stole the light from their eyes as well as the sound from their ears. Aranur's lips moved, and she knew he was shouting. She shook her head, and he pointed again. This time, she saw what he pointed at. There was a rope slung along the rock wall, providing a handhold across the slick stones. Hewn beams were jammed in new frameworks on which the walking platforms would rest and from which the rope bridge would be suspended. She followed Aranur, edging along a tier where a rut gouged down the center from the water running down from the fall's outside edge. When the tier ended, Dion stepped across onto a wooden platform and slid immediately onto her knees. Aranur grinned wryly as he helped her up. The wood in this cavern had not taken a day to slick up with mold.

They crossed the platform carefully, then stepped onto another tier along the cave's back wall. This one was wide, but shallow, the overhang of the cavern's roof closing at shoulder height. Twice Dion almost banged her head on the protrusions. The water that gathered on her skin and ran from her bangs down her cheeks blinded her so that she ducked the slick blackness of the stones by instinct more than sight. Although the cavern blackness swallowed the light, she could see the pale wood of another platform to the fore. It was bulky, strangely shaped. She was almost on it before she realized what it was: a large pulley system installed between the roof of the cavern and the platform. Clever, she thought. The double lines that led up and out made a clothesline hauling system that a single person could operate. One more person, to go up on the rope, find the refugees, and help them back . . .

Neither Aranur nor Dion bothered to try hiding their shivering. They scrambled up on the second platform, where Aranur unlocked the ropes and gave them a jerk. They slid easily through the pulleys and he nodded toward the corner of the platform. Two bales of material squatted there, and Dion explored the first one, finding—with relief, for the refugees would not be well-clothed—boots and raingear. The other was a mess of straps, hooks, cleats, and pulleys; boxes of nails, tubes of bioglue, coral starters, and a tangle of rags and used-up clothes. She pulled the straps apart to find six climbing harnesses. Five of these she slung over her shoulder. The sixth she stepped into, drawing the straps up around her thighs and buttocks. The design was as simple as it was ancient. To the front, she clipped several of the metal rings, then turned back to Aranur.

He pointed at a third line that was tied to the end of a flag. He made a jerking motion. She nodded. When she was at the top, she would pull on that line. The flag would twitch, and Aranur would know that the first refugees were ready to come down. He checked her harness, then pointed at a thick spot in the dripping rope. The two eye splices that marked the two ends of the line fit into each other, forming a low-profile loop and making the long rope one massive circle that stretched from behind the falls out through the water, and up the cliff on the west side of the Phye. Where the double eye splice hung, Dion clipped in. Her carabiner hung from the top eye splice, and she clipped another in reverse next to the first. The water that fled down the rope from the falls found a second channel to run off with her 'biners. She hissed at the chill, shuddering. Then she grabbed awkwardly at the rope as Aranur hefted her up. She twisted, hanging in midair, glaring at him for not giving her warning.

He grinned. Better get used to it, his gleaming eyes said. He hauled at the rope, and Dion spiraled up, her right leg wrapping around the rope to stabilize her body. The torrent of the Devil's Knee blasted Aranur's image from her mind. The rope made a straight line into the wall of water, and as she lifted within five meters, the freezing wind coming off the falls sucked at her strength. And then she was suspended beside the Devil's Knee, hesitating. She knew dimly what would come next. She caught a breath, ducked her head, wrapped her arms, and drew her body in on itself.

Fists of steel slammed her head. Legs of iron kicked her neck. Massive hands of water forced her head down, down against the river's plunge. Her shoulders shuddered, blasted in their nerves by downward spears of ice. And then she was through, and the fists slammed the last time on her neck, and she was out and merely blind in the blistering white mist of the falls. Something cut across her ears, thin and weak, and she realized that she had screamed coming through the cascade.

Her body shuddered uncontrollably. She was dizzy, disoriented by the falls. No, she could not have climbed the rope herself. She doubted that even Aranur, had he gone through the falls, could have done so. The mist thinned, and the falls drew back, and she realized that the rope was still hauling her up. She could almost see the cliff. Wiping her face with a frigid sleeve, she peered toward the canyon, seeing finally its slick surface as surely as she saw the cloud of mist below her. The ropes ran up the cliff and stopped along a darker line—the line of the trail, she realized. So they had not strung it to the top. No matter. There should be ropes strung along the length of the trail for the refugees to hold on to. And for her, she reminded herself in disgust. Here, suspended between water and sky, she found she could no longer unwrap her hands from the line. The moisture dripping from her nose could not be wiped away. The line cut into her fingers: they could not be shifted. Her heart began to beat louder than the falls, pounding up into her throat.

She stared at the cliff, willing it closer. She had no control over her slow, inexorable pace. She could not loosen her 'biners and climb the rope herself. She could not even draw a deep breath because of the fists of fear that clutched her lungs.

The rope lifted. The other side of the line slid by. Something scraped above her, and she tried to lift her head to look. Then a wooden beam passed her eyes, and a shelf caught on her shoulders. She twisted, panicking, and then the rope jerked, and her body slid up and halted.

She was at the base of the pulley, her feet dangling just at the level of the shelf, a wooden platform that had been built into a cleft. It was partially suspended, along with the ropes and pulleys, from a series of pitons hammered in above. Two beams beneath it were wedged into the cliff side to provide stability. Dion loosed her leg from the rope and stretched until her feet gained the precious stability of the platform. Her hands, the knuckles white around the line, did not immediately let go, but had to be coaxed off the line. Finally unclipping her 'biners, she shrank to the back of the platform where the rock wall of the cliff rose up and ended above in an overhang.

In front of her, the vista of the canyon swept away. The thunder of the falls was natural now, deafening her as if she had never known sound. But there was something she had to do. Her body, shaking, shuddering with chill and fear, could only crawl toward the trail. Refugees. Yes, that was it. The refugees were waiting on the rim. Close—how close? Hishn's gray voice was dim in her head, and Dion reached out, drawing the gray thread of their bond taut across the canyon. Move. It was time to move. Something caught and jerked her back, and she looked over her shoulder slowly. The canyon spun away.

Don't look, she snarled at herself. The harnesses—that was what had caught. Best to leave them here.

She shrugged the straps from her shoulders, unclipping the extra 'biners and clipping them back on the harnesses. She left the clump of gear clipped onto the line that ran along the platform edge.

Shocked cold. Her mind was not clear. She shook her head, but the canyon spun again, and she shrank back against the wall. Hishn's senses swept in. Behind the graysong, another pack ran, and the view through Hishn's eyes was twofold. She saw the falls from a distance, from the other side. She saw the pack that ran the raiders' trail. She saw herself on the canyon wall, trembling like a twig.

"Moonworms!" she shouted against her weakness. "Moons damn you."

She hauled herself up, forcing her eyes to stare at the trail at her feet. A meter, that was all she had to do at a time. One meter, three steps. She glared at the trail. Her hands clutched at the outcroppings on the wall beside her. There was a rope—yes, strung tightly along its length. Her left hand dropped to its security, her fingers wrapping around it as if it were life itself. Another meter. Another three steps. The falls thundered down. She wondered dully what the refugees would think. If she really looked the way she suspected she did, they might think the people of Ariye would give them a worse haven than their own raiders.

The falls blasted less noisily now; the trail climbed steadily.

The cliff was a series of angled protrusions, the layers of the earth shoved up and worn away, with massive streaks of red and brown along its wall. On this protrusion, the trail was wide, tilting down into the cliff face, instead of away toward the open falls. Dion was in light, then in shadow as the rocks sheltered her from the sun. What warmth she imagined from the day was rudely stripped away by the wind. She could not stop shivering, even with Hishn's heat in her mind. Her bones were cold. She started to run, afraid to stay longer on the cliff, her feet padding lightly on the windswept rock as if she were half-wolf herself.

The song of the pack drew her on, up. She was still running when she hit the top of the rim. The rocks broke suddenly, the wind spanning out across the rim, as she scrambled up. Her nails were crammed with mud, her cheeks smeared where the dust mixed with the river's legacy on her face. Her leggings, once a smooth brown, then stained with blood and ichor, were now black with wetness and stretched with the weight of the water. The brown leather fringe spattered drops on the trail, and the smooth soles of her boots rubbed against the blisters that swelled on her feet. She glanced up and down the trail. She could see herself, Hishn, and the raiders in her triple sight. Raiders, yes—and close. Downriver still. But the refugees—which way? Above or below the Knee? She reached out, stretched her sight, and Hishn howled in answer. The wind lifted the scents, and the Gray One read the packsong on the other side of the river. Downriver. Downriver still. Dion chose her trail and ran.

Moisture spattered off her jerkin. Water dripped from her braid down her spine like an icicle. Wind stripped the river's touch from her face and chafed the skin it found beneath. Raiders. Refugees. Which? Where? Her feet ran three trails with each step. Boulders grazed her shoulders, and trees slapped her haunches, and the air around her was clear of both. The wolves howled. Dulled terror ate at Dion's nostrils, and it was the sweat scent of the refugees in her nose. She leapt over a rock, landing and stumbling on the rough dirt before regaining her gait. Her gait? Were there four feet beneath her or two? And which had faltered? And which waited beyond those rocks?

Raiders ran beside her. Slaver scent filled her nose. Their leather stank of dry sweat; their boots, of dung and mud. A man laughed. Another snapped. The trail was steep; the branches low. The trail led upriver, and, with vengeful satisfaction, their feet quickened in their run, and their sword hilts hung, half-drawn.

Slaves ran before her. Their feet bled out on dusty ground. Their legs burned sweat in rancid oils. They grabbed the branches. They brushed the leaves. And one of them left drops of blood, a trail of blood, a trail of heat, a gallows line around their necks as they fled to the Devil's Knee.

Dion ran. Her breath was gasping. Her body shivered, from cold and heat alike. Her leggings, stretched by the river, dragged from her crotch and slapped against her legs like a skin of ice. Within her boots, her feet slid forward with her pace and back with her lift, and the leather rubbed her ankles raw. And in her mind and in her sight, Hishn paced, the yellow eyes piercing the forest on the far bank while the wolves on the west side lunged through the brush and faded between the trees.

Faster. She must be faster. She sucked at the air as if there were none around her. She leapt on a boulder and down to the dirt, and her thighs screamed at the lunge. Close. Closer. The sweat in her nose could choke her. Run, damn you. Run like the moons. She leapt round the boulders and—

Raiders! Moons, but she had missed the trail. She was among them! To the fore—a man, a woman. She skidded to a stop and lunged back, yanking her sword from its sheath and grabbing a knife in the same movement. Steel flashed. Eyes, startled, gaped. She swung—

They were close. There was steel at Moira's back even if it was an hour away. And if not, the cliffs were high enough to give them some release. Please, by the nine moons . . .

Moira was to the front. Had Luter the strength, he would have led the trail, but his leg was gone. Gellbugs had set in. How long would he last? She did not know. He could go at any moment. When the gellbugs spun enough webs in his veins, the clots would form, and then he would die. Was it cruel to keep him with them? No, better the slow agony of the trail than the torture of the raider's steel.

Pray moons she was right.

The trail was wide. Steep. She dragged two children up. Jered and the others dragged the rest. Close. The river's voice was a thunder. She could not hear the raiders, and she knew they were behind. How close? How far away? How soon? How much time? How much life? How much death?

"Moons help me." She did not know she spoke. Close. They were close. The riverbank was up ahead. The Devil's Knee. The crossing they were promised. The death they would have to take instead. There were boulders now, rising beyond her shoulders, hiding the trail. Were the raiders behind or ahead? Dammit—behind or ahead? The trail? Keep to the trail? Or take to the shadows?

"Help me," she screamed futilely at the river's power. "Help us—"

It was too late.

The first raider rounded the rocks. Moira drew her knife. Jered grabbed the children in front of him and spun, throwing them behind to the other elders. His broken knife thrust out—

—Dion drew her sword and swung.

And stopped.

And caught her tongue between her teeth, her chest heaving, her breath coming in great gasps.

The raiders ran beside her. Gray images filled her mind. But these were—refugees?—standing before her. No gray tint to their scent. Their rancid filth and ragged clothes were real. Were here.

Here.

Dion's eyes flickered from one to the other. So many . . . One of the old women, her face bruised and her lip split, favored her ribs, her hand pressed against them as if to hold her side from falling away from her. Her legs—moons alive, but all their legs—were blackened in stripes. One of the children scratched at a scab that covered half her forearm, and as Dion gazed at her in a strange, objective fascination, the girl froze, dropping her hand to her side and staring suddenly at the ground. Dion stepped forward. Her violet eyes, unfocused with the bond of the wolves, still saw double, and she had trouble separating the images of these frozen people with the vision of the raiders running in place in her mind.

Jered met her blank gaze and froze, his knife hanging in the air before him, a shudder carrying itself from his shoulders to his toes. Violet eyes. The Devil's Knee. Gods, it was to be now after all. "Moonwarrior—" he gasped.

Moira was still as a stone. Violet eyes, she realized.

The figure before them was motionless. Its blade shone dully in the midday light. The thunder of the river blasted reason from Moira's mind. A moonwarrior, she thought. If anyone had told her she would see the legend take her from this world to the next, she would have laughed. And now she knew its truth, and she could only wonder.

They were already dead.

She laughed, and could not hear herself. She motioned with the knife.

The moonwarrior gestured for them to follow. Black hair. Violet eyes. Wet as if it had risen from the Devil's Knee itself, the figure beckoned.

They were dead, and now no one could touch them.

Moira laughed again, and Jered eyed her strangely. The moonwarrior looked up at her and spoke. Moira could hear nothing. The moonwarrior was shorter than she, and she thought it funny. A moonwarrior looked up to her—to Moira, ex-elder of the council, slave of the Bilocctar raiders. The figure spoke again, and Moira laughed. The river stole her senses like a thief. She heard nothing. She smelled nothing but the cold wetness of the river on the rim. And something crossed the moonwarrior's face—did the legends feel compassion as their people did?—and the sword lowered, the knife returned to its sheath. And as Moira watched, uncaring, unfeeling, unaware even of the agony of her body, the moonwarrior showed a graceful concern as it gave her death. In slow motion, as if time itself had slowed and ceased—which, did it not make sense, since the moonwarriors brought death, guided those gone on the path to the moons—it reached up and touched her face.

Moira blinked.

Fingers brushed her skin and withdrew.

Fingers, chilled and gentle.

A hand that shivered in the wind like hers.

A hand so scarred it made her look away, back to those violet eyes. Those eyes of . . . death? Of life? Hope flared in her heart.

"Who are you?" she whispered.

The river stole her voice.

The figure before her beckoned. "This way!"

This way? A voice—a scream that rose above the river's din. A sound as full of desperation as Moira's heart? Was this—was this person real?

". . . Ariye . . ."

Moira stared down. Her legs did not move. The chill wind and mist stripped her strength. It had been so long. So far to run. She could not go further. They were dead. This moonwarrior would give them to the moons. But why then was it so hard to move? To step? Was not death peace? Was not peace a painless rest?

She gazed at the figure blankly.

"Come on!"

This moonwarrior's hands were scarred. And its face was cut—a full, ragged line across from temple to chin—and though its skin was pale with chill, its cheeks were colored in spots, as if it had run uphill. Run? Moira wondered dully. Run from where? Why would a moonwarrior have to run anywhere? There was nothing but the Knee to beckon. Nothing but the icy water of the mountains to call them now. She regarded the moonwarrior with curiosity, surprised to see impatience on its face.

"Now! Come on!"

Jered took Moira's arm, and she did not argue. She laughed again, letting him lead her like a child. There was something about a child . . .

Oh, yes. Children. There were children to set on the path to the moons. Moira reached out and touched the moonwarrior, and the figure turned. Moira pointed behind her at the little ones. "Children," she struggled to say the word carefully, as if the river could strip her articulation as it did her mind.

The moonwarrior nodded. ". . . can get . . . through the Knee . . ."

Words. It spoke in words. Somehow, Moira had thought it would not need to use human expression. Slender, it was, too, Moira noticed. And strangely dressed—its arms and legs were swathed in rags above the ankles, below the elbows. Rags? Like hers. As if it had engaged in battle, too. Man or woman? Its face was too pretty for a man, she thought, though there was a weariness in its expression. Could a moonwarrior be tired? As tired as Moira herself? She laughed softly. Did the moons send those most like the ones to die? If so, this was a fitting creature to set them on the path to the moons. Wounded. Tired. And there was fear in its eyes. Moira smiled, and followed unquestioningly. A moonwarrior. Would that she could tell those back at the workcamp. No fear, she thought. No more pain to endure. The legends were true. The moonwarriors would guide them, take them to safety. Take them back to the stars. The stars of the ancients—the First World: Earth.

Jered shouted something in her ear, and Moira frowned. Why did he bother her now? Here was the moonwarrior. Here were the violet eyes of myth. She shoved him away. "Give me peace." She did not know she shouted, but suddenly, the moonwarrior turned.

"Come."

Moira nodded impatiently. She knew the way. No raider could touch her now. But there was something about this figure . . .

"This way."

She turned obediently, gesturing for the others to follow. Jered did not loose her arm, and she tugged against him.

". . . close."

Of course they were close. One did not see a moonwarrior unless one was already on the path to the moons. Moira shrugged impatiently, but Jered did not let her go. His fingers were sharp, digging into the gauntness of her muscles, and Moira writhed as his nails scraped her.

"Where?" he shouted.

"Down here—" The moonwarrior gestured, and Moira nodded her passive acceptance.

Down to the Devil's Knee. She wondered if it would be cold, like the water itself. If one was dead, did one still feel?

The moonwarrior moved, and Moira decided it must be a female moonwarrior: a moonmaid. That was right, she thought. A moonmaid for Moira. A moonmaid of death. She smiled faintly.

"Down here—" The moonwarrior grabbed her hand, and

Moira glanced at it uncuriously. No raider's torch had caused such scars . . .

And then she stepped below the canyon rim and found herself on a shelf of rock. And the river dragged her sight below, and the mist rose up and choked her throat, and she closed her eyes and swayed.

"This way!" Dion screamed at the woman. What in hell was wrong? Did she understand? There was no time to wait, to explain. The old man shoved a child at her, and Dion grabbed the boy by the arm and dragged him along, muttering her apologies as the child flinched from her touch and writhed until she shifted her grip. With the way they had been beaten, it was a wonder she could touch him at all without him screaming at the pressure. She looked back, cursing under her breath. Would they not hurry? There, now, the tall woman had a child in each hand. She was moving at least. "Down here." She shouted, but she wondered if the woman heard. The refugees' eyes were dull with exhaustion. How long had they been running? She glanced at their feet and blanched. The rags of their footgear were held on only by the thongs tied to their ankles. The soles of their feet were blistered raw.

Dear moons, she thought desperately.

. . . wind across the nose; mud flicked back from feet before her. Heavy boots, thick pants, and the rasp of a raider's breath . . . Through the wolves, Dion blinked, struggling with her vision.

Her gaze caught the elders and children before her.

The raiders—they were close. But they were not here. The refugees—they *were* here. She could not see the line that she knew cut through the upper falls. She could not see Aranur waiting in the frigid chill of the cave. But he was there. The lines were there. If she could only get these people to the cliff.

Raiders, running.

Raiders on the trail.

Howl, wolfwalker, the Gray Ones sent. *Sing the song of the hunt.*

No—she was what they hunted. *Go back—go around!* She tried to shout that mental plea above the thunder that filled her head. *Give us time!* She was close—too close to the wolves. She had not the strength to fight them. Hishn was in her head, in her mind. The gray bond stretched taut like a thick line between them, and Dion saw the cliff above her and the path beneath her as two views superimposed on each other.

"Hishn—"

Wolfwalker . . .

Thirty meters—that was all. Just another bend. The chimney—it was there. She could see it now. The harnesses were waiting. The lines were ready. Moons, would this woman not hurry?

She turned back, screaming above the river's din. "This way!"

The tall woman nodded calmly.

Dion gnashed her teeth. She pointed toward the rocks that hid the rim from the trail, and the old man nodded, pulling the others in his wake. Dion scrambled aside, letting them pass her. She watched them to make sure they continued, then raced back along the trail. A fern, broken off at the ground, became a trail twitch, and she brushed it across the damp dirt, rubbing at the impressions of the feet that had marked its soft surface when they slid off the stones she told them to walk on. She got down on her belly and blew across the loose dirt then, shifting the tiny dirt nodules that lay in the fern's brushmarks. As she crept back, she roughed up the grass. In time—in minutes, pray the moons—it would spring back, so that from the trail, it would not appear that they had left the path and headed straight for the river's edge.

The raiders were close. The packsong had grown loud enough in her head to drown Hishn's voice. Between the sounds of the wolves and the Devil's Knee, Dion felt deaf. Making her way to the edge of the cliff after the refugees, she jumped from stone to stone as she had had the children do before her.

. . . deep rhythms of breath, heads thrown back in a howl. Dodging into a darkened trail, the insects blurring in a cloud, then settling on the brush-ruffled fur . . .

Dion shook herself. The children—where were they? Had they gone on? Or had they waited with the blank patience of the woman who led them on? That the older woman had been beyond exhaustion was plain, but exhaustion would not save their lives. Gods help them if they tarried. They must get below the river's rim if they were to escape the eyes of the slavers.

The song of the wolves was loud. Their panting filled her ears as if it were part of the river's rhythm. Hurry. She jumped and slipped and slid behind a boulder that sat on the edge of the canyon, and her short, sharp shriek was cut off abruptly as she grabbed for the rim. She caught it, her nails digging in the soil, her fingers driving through the softened earth to catch on a buried stone. The fern fluttered away, down the cliff, disappearing in the cloud of white that marked the base of the falls. She dragged her feet up. Away from the edge, away from that thin, deadly edge. Shaking, she grasped the boulder and swung herself around, catching sight then of the refugees. They were climbing down the path. Relief swept over her.

She joined them, guarding their backsides. Was it fear or cold that made her shiver? She gripped the rope handline as they did, clutching that thin safety in a desperate grip. Down, onward to the platform. The trail widened as it had before, and she shouted at them to wait, swinging herself around first one of their gaunt bodies, then another. She forced herself to walk near the edge to pass them. Their faces were white as they stared at the falls. Two of the children could not tear their eyes from the sight. Dion touched each gently, forcing her cold fingers to bring their horrified gazes back to the trail. When she reached the head of the line, she motioned for them to follow again and led on down.

They reached the platform in minutes. Quickly, Dion pulled the first two children forward. She freed the clump of harnesses that still hung from the rope and selected two, instructing the children by touch to step into them and stand quietly while she snugged the straps tight around their scrawny thighs and buttocks. Two at a time—they could hold on to each other. The old man glanced at the lines sharply, noting where they cut into the waterfall itself. He gave her a considering look, his eyes traveling up and down her still-wet body, and she nodded curtly. She turned and shoved the two children out over the cleft, steadying the rope with one hand. The little boy clutched wildly at the rope. He started screaming, and the little girl, dully, joined in.

"No!" Dion hauled him back, her hand clamped across his mouth. "No screaming." The children stopped abruptly, the boy freezing into motionlessness at her touch. "It will be cold," she shouted over the noise of the falls, "but there is a cave on the other side. A man will catch you there." She pried his fingers loose from the girl and placed one of his hands above him on the rope, the other around the waist of the girl. She did the same for the other child, to allow them to cling to the line and to each other at the same time. She pressed their heads together so that their upraised arms would shield them from the force of the falling water when they went through the Knee. "Stay like this," she told them sternly. "Do not move until you see the man in the cavern." She yanked the flagline. Then the long loop with the children loosed and began to slide away. The little girl raised her head slowly, staring at Dion until she dropped below the edge of the platform. When the girl could no longer see the violet-eyed woman, she tucked her face again into her partner's shoulder. Dion motioned for the next two to come forward.

Two more bodies. Two more harnesses. Another set of eye splices came up on the clothesline-rigged ropes, and to them, Dion hooked the next two boys. This time, as they went down, the first pair of harnesses she had used returned on the other end of the eye splices. There was a wait. The harnesses were adjusted. The next two children—two girls almost the same size—hooked on. And their terrified faces disappeared down the cliff and into the Devil's Knee.

Once more she sent two children down, then an old woman who cradled the last boy in her arms as they slid away down the rope. Next went an old man whose leg was useless and his arms hardly better. He would have dangled helplessly like baggage except that the tall bruised woman stepped into one of the harnesses herself and held him gently, as if she cradled a child, not a man twenty years her senior. Dion made to swing them off the platform, but the woman stopped her, reaching out to touch her face.

". . . to you . . . moonwarrior." The woman's words were whipped away by the thunder.

Dion jerked her head at the falls. "Go. Now."

The woman nodded, then turned her attention back to the man she held. And then they were gone, sliding down the rope. There were only the two of them left, and Dion helped the last old man into his harness, clipped him onto the rope, slung the extra harnesses and 'biners on her shoulders, and clipped herself on next to him.

He clutched her instinctively as she swung away from the platform. His body was bony, hard and sharp. He tried not to show his fear, but his hands trembled, and his face was taut and pale. He did not notice Dion's own terror. There was that instant of stepping off that solid, safe platform into air—three seconds of blank, mindless void in which the old man clung to her while the rope swung, then steadied with her weight. A moment of blinding terror when she looked down and saw the thunder of the falls crushing the rocks below . . . Moons let me do this just once more, she prayed.

Her fear made her shake no more than the cold, and the chill of her body was excuse enough for the catch in her breath and the sob of terror drowned out by the falls. The old man's lips moved soundlessly as he clung. His eyes were squeezed shut. Dion's were open, staring into the gulf, staring mindlessly at the endless void into which they dropped. Talonlike fingers dug into her arms. Her own fingers wrapped around the rope until her fingernails were white and her skin stretched taut around her fist. Down. The thunder pounded. The spray reached up. The mist engulfed them. Frigid water whipped in a convection wind, then streamed from their bodies, running from their noses, blinding their eyes with the algid wind. And then they were sliding into the Devil's Knee itself. Dion cried out, unable to help herself as the river's fists slammed into her head and the cascade smashed her hands off the rope.

Wolfwalker!

"Hishn!" she cried out, gasping, as their bodies hurtled through the falls. The thunder slammed her senses back to numbness, and her body, caught finally in Aranur's arms, swayed.

"Dion!" He shouted her name. "Get them out to the chimney. I'll follow."

She clutched his shoulders. Why did he shiver when he was so warm? Or was she so much colder even than he? He felt hot to her. Was that a bad sign? It was hard to tell. She was a healer—she ought to know that . . . Hishn paced somewhere out in the light, and the packsong swept in, engulfing her. . . .

sweating heat, sweating stench. Shouts and the hoarse breathing of the humans who ran behind. Dust. Dust and the taste of rabbit dung. Hunger—the hunt. Dion could not tell if her fur was on or off. Fur—no, she had no fur. Just wet leather and cold cloth and frigid, freezing skin.

Aranur shoved her toward the line of children, and she nodded dully. Yes, a little farther. She crept toward the head of the line, grasping the lead child and pulling him inexorably in her wake. He was shaking soundlessly, his skin tinged a dangerous blue from the icy water. He had footgear finally—the oversized boots had been thrust on each child's feet and lashed over their rags. The raingear afforded no warmth, but at least it would keep the fresh water from icing their skin; the rest of the clothing was not to be delivered until tomorrow.

Behind her, Aranur fitted the rest of them with the raingear and boots. As he finished one, he shoved that one after Dion, so that the adults trailed the children, while Aranur, in the end, dragged the crippled man. Shaking, shuddering in the thunder-filled cavern, enduring the icy rocks, the haggard group followed Dion along the back-wall tier. If the children cried out, she could not hear them. If they stared in wonder at the cavern or the back-sheeting of the falls, she did not see. She crept on, slithering across the second platform, finally reaching the outer edge of the Devil's Knee. When she wiped her eyes and saw the ropes leading up the chimney, she turned and pointed up the rocky cleft.

Where she and Aranur had slid down earlier, scraping by the rocks, those same stones now made a crude staircase. Up the trail; up like ants on the rocks. "Up," she shouted. "Climb."

And they climbed—scrambling, bleeding on the stones as they slipped, hauling themselves by rote. Dion pushed them on. Somewhere behind her, Aranur brought up the rear, carrying the old man now as the starved, bony body shuddered with the same chill that shook the children. Somewhere above, Hishn sang the graysong strongly in Dion's head. The scent of the wolf caught her nose and made it wrinkle. She grabbed a sharp protrusion and hauled herself up, her fingers numb, the water running off her nose unheeded. She gripped the nearest child and shoved the girl above to the next foothold. Up. Ever up. If there was still fear in her gut from the height, it did not matter. There was so little warmth, so little energy, that even terror could not take hold.

And then they were at the top. It took an eternity to drag them through the rocks and to the treeline before Hishn skidded up beside her and Mjau took the children from her hands. Tomi was crying out, shouting something and running past her to fling himself into the arms of one of the elders. Dion did not look. She shook her head as if to clear it of the thunder. Trembling, her muscles would no longer hold her up, and she sank down, her head against the wolf, her gasping breath muffled in the burning, burning, gray fur.

Chapter 8

Fire warms your skin;
The Gray Ones warm your soul.

Fire. They had to have warmth. Aranur set his unconscious burden down in the moss with the others, catching the old man's head before it flopped back against the ground. The wound in the elder's leg was gory. It was no wonder he had passed out. Aranur stretched back, rolling his shoulders to rid them of the strained cramps his burden had caused. His chest heaved, and his sweat ran down his spine and from under his arms. It was cold, like the water, and he stifled his shiver with difficulty. If he was as cold as this himself, how did these others, with their starved bellies and ill-clad legs, fare? Moonworms, but he had never seen such a condition in a group of people. With their blue-white shudders and chilled, dull wits, they would succumb to hypothermia before he ever got them on the trail. And Dion—where was she? With the strain of the battle, then the healing, and finally the rescue, she must be at the end of her endurance. Sure, she was stubborn enough to keep going if he said she must, but if he pushed her too hard, she would end up little better than these refugees. He searched the group until he located her not far from the rock pile that guarded the chimney's opening. She was huddled against the wolf, her shoulders shaking. When he touched her shoulder, he saw the fear still in her eyes.

Gods, he berated himself, how could he have forgotten her fear of heights? He had just sent her down one cliff and up another, and she had gone without a word of protest. He cursed himself like an idiot. He reached for her, to draw her into his arms, but Hishn bared her teeth. Damn it all to the seventh hell, he swore at the gray wolf's growl. Was it not enough that he blamed himself for her fear, but that Hishn must curse him, as well?

He looked back at the rest of the group. The children crouched like bats, their small bodies lost in the oversized gear, their arms wrapped around their chests as they rocked and shivered and said nothing. Their lack of response puzzled him. He frowned, looking more carefully. There was only a dull acceptance in their faces as they watched the adults surrounding Tomi, gripping his arms, and shouting words that remained unheard in the thunder of the falls. One of the women—the tall one with the bruised face—was shaking the boy, and Mjau finally took him away from her, leading Tomi to the other children and letting them touch him tentatively with their wet, icy hands.

Mjau met Aranur's eyes, and he nodded toward the trail. They were exhausted, but they could not stop here to rest. So near the river's edge, they could be spotted by the raiders, who would search until they found the narrow path down the cliff. It would be the end of their cavern crossing. No matter how tired they were, they would have to move.

He touched the nearest elder, a woman, on her arm. "You've got to strip," he shouted at her over the thunder of the falls. "Your tunic will continue to strip away your body heat."

The older woman stared at him blankly, her shudders uncontrollable. Heat? There was no heat left to strip away. The wind shifted an icy-wet clump of hair onto her cheek, and she pushed it behind her ear. It was so hard to concentrate. She shook her head, not understanding his gesture.

Aranur stared at her face, noting the bruises that darkened her scalp beneath the thin gray hair. Was she deaf? With an oath, he stripped her raincoat off clumsily, batting away her hands when she tried to cling to the garment. He motioned at the tunic. Still she stared at him, her hands on the hem of the raincoat, and, taking advantage of her grip on the garment, he let her have the coat while he took the edge of her tunic and tried to pull it up. The woman's eyes flared in fear. Suddenly wild, she struggled against him, his determination making her panic even more. "Mjau!" he shouted.

Quickly, Mjau took the woman's hands, soothing, persuading the elder woman to let her lift the tunic over her head. When she stripped it from those bony arms, Mjau smiled, wringing the icy cloth out, then shaking it and using it as a damp towel to rub the worst of the water and mud from the woman's body. The elder just watched Mjau as if in a trance, standing like a doll while Mjau knelt and rubbed the circulation back into her shaking legs. The elder woman did not even wince when the archer wiped away the blood that ran from the gash in her left knee. When Mjau was done, she wrung the tunic out again, folded it into a neat bundle, and tucked it inside the crumpled coat, handing the package back. The elder stared at her. When Mjau turned away, the woman reached out and touched her on the shoulder, mouthing her hesitant thanks. Mjau smiled, but the expression did not reach her eyes.

Aranur moved to the next elder, an old man who began shedding his own coat and tunic. Seeing that he was not needed there, Aranur turned to the children, and then they were all stripping, wringing out their tunics, wiping blood and water from their bodies, and shaking as they tried to warm each other with the friction of their contact. When they were done, they stood, near-naked and shivering, in the shade of the forest, several of them still touching Tomi furtively. Mjau gave up her own tunic to one of the little girls, stripping down and then pulling her jerkin back on over her bare torso. Tomi had given both Dion's and Aranur's tunics to other children. From the packs, Mjau pulled her own spare and Aranur's stashed shirts, passing them along to the ones who were shivering the most. She had to grit her teeth to smile at them. When one of the little boys took Dion's shirt and then turned to help another little boy put it on, Mjau turned away abruptly, her jaws clenched.

It took only ten minutes to get the group ready. Even so, by the time the dry clothing was parceled out, Aranur was practically shoving them onto the trail. He and Dion remained in their wet leggings and jerkins; if they had to fight off any forest hunters, they would need the protection more than they needed warmth now. With their extra clothes, there had been six tunics to share. Tomi and one of the smallest girls were the only children without. The elders who took the children's hands kept their elbows in to their sides, hoping for that little warmth as they led the children after the archer. The only difference between the women and the last old man was that the emaciated breasts of the women sagged in loose skin, while the old man's skin was shrunken across his bones. The withered arm of the old man was hardly different from his good one. Aranur tried not to stare. In the darkness behind the falls, the marks on their bodies had not been more than shadows. In the light of day, the blackened welts were zebra stripes on their filthy skins.

"This way," Aranur ordered grimly. "Follow Mjau." The archer had two children by the hands and led them onto the path back to the woods. Tomi followed her, leading two younger children. The others trailed after, except for the one tall woman, who stood staring at the river.

"We have to go," Aranur shouted over the falls. She did not respond, and he took her arm, pulling her from the bank. She shook him off. He tightened his grip, and then stopped. There was something about her eyes . . . Images flashed in his head, and he remembered a day, long ago, when he was a child. A hot sun, a half-filled berry basket—and the bodies of his parents, writhing and kicking as they died with the war bolts piercing their chests. The look on his sister's face . . .

He blinked. The body of the little girl back on the trail, the one who had drowned. He touched the woman gently. When she finally turned her head, he pointed to the river, and then held his hand above the ground at the height the drowned girl would have been had she stood. He shook his head slowly. An expression passed over the woman and was gone as quickly as a gust of wind, and then her shoulders sagged. She would have fallen had Aranur not been quick. As he steadied her, he set her back on her feet. She nodded blankly. When he pointed at the path, she stumbled in its direction, her feet, still clad in the boots, dragging across the dirt.

As she followed the children, Aranur turned to Dion, kneeling beside her. The wolfwalker's face was still buried in Hishn's fur. The wolf's eyes gleamed at Aranur, challenging him to disturb the woman, and he glared back. "I have rights, too," he stated flatly. He met those yellow eyes with a shock of gray awareness. The echo swept into his head, and Hishn's images drowned his thoughts. *Cold chill, the bones shivering. Wet skin slick like water on glass. Eyes burning, nostrils dripping. Fear gripping her belly like a hunger nine days old.*

Aranur shook himself, breaking that contact. "Dion," he told her instead, shouting over the falls, "there's a broadleaf meadow barely half a kilometer from here." She looked up blearily, and he was shocked at how pale and haggard her face looked. He took her arm, shivering as her icy hands clutched his. "Come on. Just a few minutes. You can make that much more."

Caught in Hishn's images, Dion let him haul her to her feet. Were they still in the cavern? No, it was light here. And Hishn was here: the dusty hair of the wolf was gritty against her skin. They were on top of the rim, then. She stared around dully, not noticing as Aranur dragged her toward the forest and shoved her after the others. She was so cold. The sun split through the overcast sky, and its momentary warmth left her colder inside than before.

Aranur swore under his breath. "Dammit, Dion, walk. I haven't the strength to carry you and this one." He gestured toward the unconscious elder he had carried before.

She nodded blankly, her feet stumbling beside him until a massive furry shoulder pushed its way under her hand.

Aranur hauled the old man's limp body up over his shoulder like a sack of redroot palms. "Go, Dion," he repeated.

She obeyed. Staggering, her free hand found itself in another thick pelt. Yoshi. His strong voice joined Hishn's, and Dion shuddered and nearly dropped to all fours. Hishn snapped at the other wolf, driving him from Dion's mind.

Dion barely noticed. Her body was beyond exhaustion. She walked the trail now because they led; she had not the energy to lie down. Her vision blurred. Still there were wolves running beside her, running on the ridge, running with raiders, as Hishn picked up the song on both sides of the river. One of the songs was different. Which one? Dion wondered absently. Ah, the one across the Phye: there was less bitter betrayal there now, less frustrated sorrow. The hunger that underlay the other emotions had not weakened, and Dion wondered when the wolves would eat. It was dangerous to run so long without food. That they hunted still, there could be no doubt. But, she thought, now that the refugees were no longer on the trail, perhaps they would turn to deer instead.

Wolfwalker, they howled.

She heard them this time, pleased that they had allowed her to listen. They sang her name into their pack, and she stumbled against the wolves at her side. The protectiveness of Hishn versus the hunger of the other wolves; the tolerant strength of Yoshi against the bitterness of the pack . . . How could she sing with those wolves? She did not even understand their howl. Her hands tangled in Hishn's scruff, and her lips pulled back from her teeth unconsciously.

Yes, they welcomed her. *Sing with us, Wolfwalker.*

You honor me, she returned through Hishn. Then the wind cut across beneath her dripping jerkin and froze her skin. She closed her mind again to all but the gray shadows at her side.

Behind her, Aranur struggled with the weight of his burden as the unconscious body shuddered with the cold. His wet clothes pressed against his shoulders and chest, rasping rawly on his skin. The laces of his jerkin brushed across the gemstone in his sternum, catching and tugging at his shirt.

Watching Dion stumble ahead of him, Aranur cursed silently. If only he had a carrier bird, he could contact their camp, have his uncle Gamon meet them on the trail. If there were more wolfwalkers, he could send word through the pack that help was needed. He snorted sourly. If he could talk to the moons . . . Dion was too exhausted to control the link through Hishn. Even if the wolf would listen to him, she would be caught up in Dion's aches so that she would not think in words, but more primitive images, which would gain him nothing.

The body in his arms shuddered again, and a sudden warmth seeped through his jerkin. He smelled something acrid.

It was not shivering he had felt. The man was dead.

He dropped the body as if burned, the shivers catching his

body and shaking it. He had been carrying a dead man. The release of the elder's bladder had sent the hot urine onto his jerkin, and he winced at the faint fumes. He steadied himself. He had carried dead men before. There was no less honor in this man's death because he had died in flight—the running had been to save the children, not himself. Aranur steeled himself, bent, and rearranged the elder's limbs. He stared at the bony face, the scraggly gray stubble, the hollows of the cheeks. At least the man had not died in a raider's fire. At least he had died in Ariye.

Ahead, Dion felt Aranur's presence fade. She glanced back dully, to see him catching up at a jog. His face was pinched, grim, and she wished she had the strength to ask him why. He merely touched her shoulder in passing, striding past to sling two of the smallest children into his arms instead.

With the two youngest off the trail, the pace quickened. At first, he told himself that the heat of the trail would warm them. But he saw, glancing back, that they had no reserves to sweat out. Gods, what he would give for even two riding beasts. Making a decision quickly, he changed direction, pushing them off the trail toward a place where the broadleaves grew.

Dion watched their path change. Warmth—Aranur was taking them to the broadleaf meadow. But even if they stopped to warm themselves, the plants would not be enough. These people were too chilled. They had run too long. Already three of the children had fevers raging in their bodies. By the time Gamon or the others knew something was wrong, they could lose several to death. Her mind clearing with purpose, she tightened her grip in Hishn's fur. "Gray One," she whispered. "Can you call the pack? There are so many here, running the ridges above us. Will they help us, lend us strength?"

Wolfwalker, you are of the pack. Hishn's tone was joyful. *You howl with them. They run as you wish.*

Dion struggled to concentrate. "We need riding beasts, Hishn—warm clothes for the children. And food. Could a Gray One go to the camp? Speak to Gamon?"

Hishn growled low in her throat, and the song in Dion's head changed. A driving beat entered the rhythm. An urgency fed into their song. *Yes,* the pack answered. *Wolfwalker,* they called.

"You honor me," she managed.

We run, we hunt with you.

"Gray Ones, I—" Her relief was palpable. "I am grateful," she said simply.

Her answer was a tide of gray that swept down from the ridge. She did not have to see them: their silent howls rang in her head, passed on through Hishn so that she would understand their song. A single wolf dropped out on the trail, speeding east, toward the camp.

And then there were gray shadows sweeping through the forest, and one of the refugees cried out. Someone screamed. Dion cried out for them to be calm. Aranur turned. He saw the wolf pack flashing through the trees. Dion must have called them. He cursed her timing even as he blessed her thought. She would have sent one ahead to the camp, to warn them of the refugees' coming. But the refugees were already scattering. Terrified, their shrieks warned each other of the hunt, of the raiders.

"No!" Aranur lunged, grabbing a boy and one of the women. Hauling them back to the trail, he shouted again. "They are here to help. They run free in Ariye—not with the raiders."

"Stay," Dion cried out. "They are friends—"

It was Tomi who ended the panic. The boy jumped up on a stump and screamed, halting the fleeing bodies. "Hear me!" He waved his arms. "Don't run. They are not raider-spawn. I've seen them. The Gray Ones are good. They saved me from the worlags." Moira and the others stopped, holding the children close to their naked bodies, and he went on. "They fought for me. *For* me. Not to kill me."

Aranur stopped struggling with the child and woman. A meter away, Moira gave a low cry, pointing her naked, bony arm at Dion. "Look," she called. "Tomi is right. The moonwarriors and the wolves." The others murmured. "As it was for the ancients," she said in a strange chanting voice, "let them now lead us to haven."

"Moonwarriors," the children cried.

Dion shook her head. "I am no moonwarrior to lead you. I am just a healer. Aranur is the one to lead."

"Violet eyes. Wolves . . ." Moira swayed with exhaustion.

Aranur shouted. "Listen to me. We are people, nothing more. Please—believe in the wolves. They are here to help, not hunt you. I give you my word as a weapons master of the Ramaj Ariye."

Dion pulled her warcap from her head, letting the silver circlet shine against her wet, black hair. "And I give you mine as a healer."

One of the other elders looked uncertainly back at Dion. "A healer who carries a sword?" he asked, gripping his own broken blade with one arm, while the other, withered from some nameless disease, dangled uselessly. "A weapons master who waits for us under a waterfall?" he added. "How do we know? How do we believe you?"

Moira's shoulders drooped. "We have no more trust in us," she said in a low voice.

"You do not have to trust us," Dion returned quietly. "You only have to let us help."

Moira drew herself up, ignoring her unclothed body and her bony frame. "I am Moira, council leader," she said firmly. She stepped forward. "I ask refuge for these children."

Aranur nodded, extending his arm for her to grip in greeting. "We got your message. As did you ours."

She could not hide the shudder that clung to her body. "We could not wait." She paused and looked at Dion, then Mjau, then Aranur, wonderingly. "It was the Devil's Knee, after all."

He smiled wryly. "And now that we know it works, we can use it again."

Moira closed her eyes, realizing what he had said.

"We had no time to try it before you used the crossing today," he explained.

Moira nodded soberly. She had brought the children too early. They had not known if the crossing would work. If it had not been for the moonwarrior—that healer, who stood so exhausted, clinging to the wolves as if they gave her strength itself . . . What she had done for them, what she had risked to fling herself through the falls before she knew if the ropes would hold for her to return . . . Moira closed her eyes, swaying again.

Jered reached for Aranur's arm, gripping it and releasing it quickly, as if not quite sure of that contact. "I am Jered, second elder." He glanced at Moira and offered her his arm as he asked, "How far to reach your camp?"

"Too far for you," Aranur returned bluntly. "But there is a

broadleaf meadow through those trees. We can wait there. Dion sent a wolf to our camp to bring back help, so we should see food and clothing arrive within the hour.'' He glanced down the line. ''Through here—'' He raised his voice as he pointed. ''Just another few meters and we can stop. You can warm yourselves against the wolves.'' He turned to Moira, leading the way through the brush. ''We are still too close to the Phye to risk a fire. Until my uncle arrives, the Gray Ones can give you the warmth of their skin.''

Moira regarded him slowly. Finally she nodded, and when he pushed his way through the brush, pointing to a small clearing, she stumbled after him.

''Over here,'' he said, gesturing.

The sea of green that wound between the open stretch of trees was shoulder height, its smooth green waves molding itself to the rise and fall of the ground. The shadows beneath the leaves seemed dark and warm, like a den, Moira thought suddenly. And under the leaves, the gleaming eyes of the wolves looked back. Aranur moved forward slowly, tapping the leaves to dislodge the leafy residents before reaching beneath to grope for the stems. The fuzzy coat that protected the leaves through winter had not been completely shed. At least the loose clumps did not come off in his face, he thought wryly, bending the plants down into a makeshift shelter. The downy filaments could tickle one's nose for days. He stood back and motioned for the nearest elder to deposit two of the children and herself in the shelter. It was not much, what he had made, but at least their pitiful body heat could be contained. He nodded encouragingly at the two boys who were holding hands so tightly, and the woman with the thin hair and scalp marks knelt with them, murmuring to them and folding her skinny frame around theirs so that she could give them what little warmth she had.

Moira watched them curl up, then glanced back at the line. ''Where is Luter?'' she asked with a frown.

The old man? Aranur straightened, his voice curt and apologetic when he answered. ''He is dead.''

''Was he—did he . . .''

''He died as I carried him. I do not know from what.'' He bent another broadleaf down, gesturing for Moira to crawl under it.

She stared at the tiny shelter. "Moons bless him with quick passage," she said automatically. Aranur looked at her in surprise. Except for the fatigued hoarseness of her voice, she could have been saying grace at supper for all the emotion she showed. She guessed he expected some greater response. But there was no grief left in her, she realized. When the river took her little girl, her heart had emptied at last, quietly, without her knowing it. "Here," she told the children with her. "Huddle together."

Not knowing what to say, Aranur pulled the plant stems down so she could tuck them around her. She was startled to realize that the fuzz on the leaves radiated a soft warmth. Aranur, seeing her surprise, nodded. "They radiate heat in spring only—it is what makes the fuzz drop off. When you harvest them in early winter," he explained, "they are conserving energy, and you cannot feel any warmth on their surface." The two children with her, one girl and one boy, just looked at him, and, uncomfortable under their solemn eyes, he finally nodded curtly, then moved away.

Moira pulled the two children close. The girl put her arms around the boy, but flinched away from Moira's icy skin until the woman tucked the oversized tunic the girl wore more fully between them. She had just finished doing the same with the little boy when the soft, whuffing breath of a wolf made her freeze. She caught her breath as the creature wormed up between the leaves to lie down beside her. Its fur touched her bare skin. She flinched. Moons above them . . . Trembling, she curled around the small chilled bodies in her arms, praying that the wolf would not bite, that the rasp of its tongue as it tasted her would not be lethal.

Ignoring her response, the wolf snugged up against her back, and she held herself rigid, tense. There was no growl. No attack. Warily, she leaned back, pulling the broadleaves over her legs. The warmth that radiated from the lupine fur was almost hot against her skin. The warmth that seeped from the winter fuzz of the broadleaves was tiny in comparison. Moons, but she had almost forgotten what warmth was. She had to force herself to give up that lick of lupine heat to the children, twisting so that their bodies were between hers and the wolf's and her back was pressed against the cooler broadleaves instead. But another Gray One slunk in, pushing itself against her back. She stiffened for a moment—and then she was cocooned. She caught her breath in a sob. That the Gray Ones—the hunters of the raiders—gave them warmth . . .

Dion dragged in with the last of the elders. For once, she was grateful that Aranur was taking charge. She nodded to him when he looked around, and, when all the others but Tomi were bedded down like rabbits in a warren, she stumbled over to him. Tomi, still dogging her heels, followed her toward Aranur. The tall man scowled at the youth. When Dion gestured for the boy to curl up in the leaves, he hesitated, then obeyed. A moment later, Aranur and Dion dropped to their knees and crawled into the last shelter. Aranur held the leaves aside for Gray Hishn and Yoshi, so that the two wolves could worm their way on either side of them. With Yoshi's heat seeping through his jerkin, he put his arms around Dion, shivered from the touch of her skin, and held her close.

It was the rustling in the leaves that warned him they were not alone. He stiffened, but the wolves did not react except to flick their ears, so, when Tomi cautiously eased one of the giant leaves aside, he was not surprised. The boy met his eyes and crouched for a moment without moving. Dion barely stirred. Aranur sighed. When he said nothing, the boy moved into the opening of their shelter, then shifted so that the enticing warmth of the wolves was next to his thighs. Finally, hesitantly, he eased between Dion and Hishn, curling his small body up behind the wolfwalker's legs. Aranur tried not to grit his teeth. One hour, he said silently. Just one hour alone with Dion—was that too much to ask? He looked at the dark form of the child. Then he shifted once more so that the leafy shelter closed around them, cocooning the boy as it did themselves.

Dion barely noticed. Aranur's and Tomi's scents were in the noses of the wolves. The boy's body was neither cold nor warm next to hers. She identified him absently, too tired to lift her head to protest. With two children curled up to each adult, Tomi was the only one without someone to warm him. It was probably just the loneliness . . . It did not matter. Dion was too tired to care. The back of her head pounded steadily, and her stomach cramped, but those were distant discomforts. When the gray images filtered in with tiny patches of daylight, she drifted off, knowing she was safe with Aranur, safe among the wolves. Did the boy know that? Did any of them understand? They were safe now. They were in Ariye.

But in Bilocctar, late last winter, when the snows of the heights pulled back from the fields . . .

Conin stared at the villager. "I am your Lloroi," he repeated. "Have you nothing to say to me? No opinions ? No questions? No complaints?" The middle-aged man continued to stare at his feet, shifting his weight from one foot to the other, and Conin swore in disgust.

Longear glanced sideways at him. "He is an old soldier who fought in the resistance—what pitiful little there was," she said, bored with Conin's attempted inquisition. There were faster ways to get information than to ask as he did. She glanced at her nails, grimacing at the dirt that clung to their undersides. Another day, and she would be back in town, playing the spy for the raiders while she sought out the man who had been making her plans a mess. Soon, she thought, smiling to herself, the resistance fighters would be identified, caught, and burned—a long and slow death, with perhaps a few nightspider bites thrown in for amusement. The lesson would be a good one for the rest of these rabbits on the border. She glanced at Conin. He tried so hard, he did. She almost laughed. He was such a fool.

She tired of the game. "Don't waste any more of my time," she said sharply to the Lloroi. "The man won't answer. He is hardly more fond of your Bilocctar breeding than you are yourself."

Conin gave her a wary look. Was she mocking him publicly now? He met Namina's eyes and saw the frightened warning there. He held onto his temper with difficulty. "Whether I am fond of my breeding is moot," he said quietly. "I had little say in the matter." He stared down at the villager.

The man was still watching his feet, gazing in apparent raptness at their clumsy shapes, and after a moment, Conin wheeled his riding beast away in frustration. The six-legged dnu broke into a slow trot, and he rode out on the trail, knowing that Namina's dnu was behind him, and that Longear was riding behind both of them like a dark shadow. What was he supposed to do? He had been out here for two ninans now, and still he had yet to get one person to talk with him openly. That it was Longear's doing, he had no doubt. But how she had managed it was beyond him. He had seen both towns and workcamps. He had heard councils that discussed such petty problems as which family would move in with which other one. He had watched raiders standing beside villagers as if the raiders willingly worked the fields and mines. The townsfolk were filled with fear—he had seen enough of that emotion in Namina's eyes to recognize it easily—and yet, when he asked and queried and questioned the people, he had yet to find one person who spoke the truth. Damn them to the moons and back, he cursed under his breath. Namina's mother was right; these people were scared. Their eyes, their words—they spoke by rote when he was around. He was not blind to their relief when he dismissed them from his questioning. He could not be, not when they hurried from his presence as if he carried the ancient plague with his words. It was beyond him to reason it out. Gods, but Longear would laugh to hear him admit that. It was what she was waiting for. He could sense her even now, smiling and savoring his frustration like dessert.

By the moons, but he would have the truth, and have it soon. He might have been a bastard child. He might be naive to rule. He might be blind to what Longear was doing here. But he was still a man and still Lloroi. He would call Longear to task for what she had done—even if it cost him his life.

Namina, watching the expressions play across his face, felt a chill creep down her back.

Longear regarded the two of them with barely hidden pleasure. They were far out on the borders now. Only two more villages between here and her base. And then . . .

Chapter 9

The death of a life; the birth of a curse.
Only the Siker knows which is worse.

Dion did not notice when Aranur eased away from her and left the shelter. It was not until he pulled the leaves from her curled body and shook her shoulder that she swam out of the depths of exhaustion. "Get up, earth child," he said with a tired grin. "You've slept three days."

"What?" She started up. "Hishn—Yoshi, I'm sorry—" she muttered quickly as the Gray Ones snarled their complaints, scrambling up and out of her way.

Aranur gave her a hand up. "I'm teasing. It's only been an hour."

She would have retorted, but a blast of pain caught up with her head. With a groan, she let go of his hand to grab at her temples. An hour? It felt like less than a minute. Even so, her entire body had stiffened up. Her legs were tight, her arms bruised and sore. Her back twinged and throbbed, as did her calves. The sole of one of her feet made her gasp when she shifted, and she gripped Hishn's fur automatically, while the Gray One shoved herself back under Dion's hand when she swayed. She must have stepped on a branch or rock on the trail.

Either that, or something had bitten her through her boot. She ached like an old woman.

Aranur watched her closely. As if reading her mind, he said, "Soon, Dion. We'll be back in camp in an hour."

She glanced up. "Aranur . . ."

He touched her chest briefly, the gentle pressure of his long fingers brushing against the gemstone beneath her jerkin. Slowly, she raised her hand to touch his sternum in the same place, his other hand covering hers. When he stepped back, his gray eyes were unsmiling. He watched her pale face, her violet eyes clouded with exhaustion, her muscles twinging and burning with dull pain. "Soon, Dion," he repeated. Then he turned and strode away.

Dion looked around. Her stomach was still knotting up—she needed more food, she realized, glancing around to find her pack and dig in it. A moment later, she abandoned her search with a heavy scowl. What meager supply had been left had gone to Tomi while she was under the falls. At least there were edible plants here—the broadleaves hid a dozen types of tubers and at least two varieties of shadow lily. She could pull out a few roots and munch them on the way back to camp. She stretched her arms, groaning with the motion. Beside her, Hishn whined, and Dion nodded wryly. The other two healers who knew Ovousibas did not even have the bond with the wolves to sustain them after the healing. One of them was a master healer, old beyond time, and the other a young intern. They used Hishn in their link—both were sensitive enough, though neither had bonded with a wolf—but, once the healing was over, those other two healers were cut off from the gray strength and left to the exhaustion of their own bodies—just as Dion would be, were Hishn not here. She glanced down, a tender smile crossing her face.

The smile collapsed into a massive yawn. Then she doubled over, the gnawing pangs of her stomach becoming cramps. Hishn nudged her impatiently, and this time, Gray Yoshi echoed his own dissatisfaction. Dion gave them a wry look. "It is not your hunger, but mine, which you feel," she said dryly. "And I would bet on the second moon that the stiffness of your muscles is mine, as well."

Experimentally, she shook out her limbs, reading the exhaustion in them. Ovousibas. Had it been only hours ago? It seemed like days. Days of lassitude. Days of hunger. She dragged up the broadleaves into which she had been tucked, and the activity made her feel even more tired. At least she felt a little better for closing her eyes a few minutes. Being a wolfwalker had its advantages: she healed faster than most, and the bruised gashes in her arms and legs were already scabbed. As long as she did not stretch herself too far beyond her body's reserves, she could tap into the Gray Ones for strength. Hishn, sensing the thought, shoved up against her, and Dion tousled the gray beast's ears. The shoulder that arched in response almost tumbled her over.

"If you push me back down," she admonished sourly, "I won't be able to get up for a ninan."

Your den was warm enough, the wolf returned, her head cocked and her eyes gleaming. *Yoshi and I were comfortable against you. Why leave?*

Dion glanced down at the broadleaves already springing back into their chest-high platform. She sighed. Gray Yoshi's yellow eyes were a bright spot beneath one of the plants. She shrugged. "I must."

For the forest was crowded with people. Aranur had let her sleep while the other Ariyens arrived. Now, only Hishn and Yoshi remained of the Gray Ones who had come to help, the others having slipped away through the meadow, the ripples of their passing indistinguishable from the green waves of wind. It was easy to spot the refugees among the Ariyens—they were bundled in an odd assortment of clothes, their borrowed tunics not removed but simply layered over. Half of them were already seated on six-legged riding dnu, while the other half waited patiently to be hoisted up. Clutching each other for balance in the saddles, or gripping food which they stuffed greedily into their mouths, they did not speak except when spoken to. Even the children were inordinately quiet. They no longer had on the ill-fitting boots they had put on in the cavern. The boots were still wet and cold and had been replaced with dry socks—the only thing Gamon, Aranur's uncle, had been able to get his hands on quickly.

The dnu stamped impatiently. Their spindly legs did not look as if they could hold up their thick bodies, but their flexible hooves made them more surefooted than goats on strange terrain. Dion, watching Gamon direct the refugees and mounts, waved when he looked around and saw her. She tried to hide her wince at the motion. Aranur was already making his way over to Gamon, so Dion followed, limping across as swiftly as she could without groaning outright.

Gamon looked as solid as ever, his shoulders nearly as broad as Aranur's and his aged muscles still hard as steel. His nose had suffered throughout his life and now bent noticeably to the left, while his left cheek was lined with a series of pale, straight scars that ran crossways across to his battered nose. With his silver hair close-cropped in the front and long in the back, his warcap fitted snugly, framing his seamed face and making it even more similar to Aranur's. Dion thought him immeasurably handsome.

"Dion!" Gamon grabbed her in a bear hug. He held her away from him, turning her from side to side as he examined her closely. "And looking worse for the wear, too."

"Between you and Aranur, I always do," she retorted wryly, surviving the hug and waiting patiently for him to let her feet touch ground again. Behind her, Hishn lunged playfully at the gray-haired man.

"Come here, you mutt," he laughed. "Get your belly scratched." He looked up at Dion critically. "You did the healing again, Aranur said."

She nodded noncommittally.

"On a wolf?"

She nodded again.

He grunted. If she had done the healing, she needed food and sleep—and lots of the latter. The shadows under her eyes spoke of an exhaustion that no single hour of rest could kill. "Brought a dnu for you, too. Figured you would be wanting the lazy way back."

Dion grinned in spite of herself. Trust Gamon to know what was needed. She touched his arm gently.

He glanced at her, his pleasure at her simple thanks coloring his seamed face. "I know, woman," he said gruffly. "Get on up so we can get going."

She glanced over at Moira and sobered. "Gamon, the body of a little girl is back along the river a few kilometers, in a stand of silverheart."

His large hands took one of hers. "Aranur told us," he said quietly. "I sent a rider back to get her."

She nodded, and Gamon tactfully said nothing. He tapped the dnu on its forelegs. It bent obediently, so that Dion could mount more easily. From beside Gamon, Hishn growled lightly, and Dion glanced at the wolf. The gray beast's ears were pointed at the meadow, and the image of the male wolf in the thread of their bond was unmistakable. She smiled faintly. "Go on," she encouraged. "Gray Yoshi won't wait forever."

The yellow eyes gleamed. In an instant, the gray wolf had threaded through the people and, fading into the broadleaves, was gone.

Dion looked after her.

"Saw the mark on her flank," Gamon said obliquely, swinging into his own saddle beside her. "That from the worlags?"

She nodded. He noticed her involuntary shudder. She would be having nightmares again, then. He glanced back at his nephew, noting the tall, broad frame of his shoulders and the set of his face. At least this time, he told himself, Aranur would be there to comfort her.

In Bilocctar, in the late winter months . . .

With a tightened jaw, Conin stared at what was left of the village. Behind him, Longear laughed. Longear. His thoughts crystallized with frustration. A woman who held him in her cruel hands like a lepa plays with a rat. Just that morning, she had put bugs in Namina's hair, laughing as his mate screamed and shook her head and tore at her braid to get them off. There was a rage building in him—a determination to strike that laugh from Longear's lips and treat her as she treated his mate. As she treated these people. This—he looked around—this was her doing. He had not authorized any such squalor, and only Longear could tell the troops or raiders what to do. To bring such a rich land to such poverty . . . It was not confined to the towns, either—the fields themselves lay fallow, drowning in winter weeds. The sap farms were barely cared for. The mining pens were empty. Behind one shed, a pile of breeder worms rotted, waiting to be burned, and behind another barn lay strewn the broken sacks of seed that should have been distributed to the farms for plowing by now.

The contrasts confused him. The town before this one had been clean and neat, the people politely distant, with their "Yes, sirs, it is a decent living" and their "No, sirs, no trouble with the raiders, not to speak of, anyway." And when they saw him coming, they had retired to their little, neat houses and hurried out to their long, neat fields and left him wondering what they hid.

The town before that last one had been crowded, with two families sharing each house, but just as neat and clean, and he couldn't put his finger on why it bothered him so. The people had been just as polite with their "Yes, sirs" and "No, sirs." Well-enough off, they were, they said. Plenty to eat, crops to tend. Mining worms breeding like flies this time of year.

The town before that? Sure, they said, they had a curfew, and a good thing it was to keep trouble from brewing between the soldiers and the farmers and craftsmen and council members. He shook his head, baffled. Like the others, they were clean and polite, their houses neat, their farms well-kept. Polite and distant and crowded together as if they lived in a city, not a town. And then he would come on the villages like this—abandoned workcamps, Longear called them. Filthy. Fallow. If there had ever been workers in them, they had done little in the fields. He had seen two of Longear's "modern" workcamps. They were as clean and neat as the villages. But the air there was just as strange. Workers "Yes, sirred," and "No, sirred," and turned away before he could ask them more than their names. Children were supposedly in school. When he insisted on seeing them in their classes, it was as if the schools had been set up for him alone. There was dust on some of the desks, and the children studying were nervous, jittery, their faces as carefully blank as if they had been memory-wiped. And then on to more villages. Neat. Prim. Nothing to question. Which made him even more warily curious.

It had not taken long to realize that there were few raiders in any one of these villages. When he asked which men and women were raiders, they were pointed out reluctantly. And the men turned and grinned at him, and the women smiled, and he felt like a roasting fowl looking at the knife. Namina, riding beside him, was jumpy as a hen. If she felt as he did, she said nothing, but Conin thought it was so. Why else would she look over her shoulder so often? Why else did she insist on bolting their doors when they stopped at inns to stay the night in comfort, out of the winter winds? They rode with Longear. What danger was worse than the one beside them each day?

He gestured now at the fields that lay to his right. Already the fields were overgrown with cold-weather weeds. "Why are they fallow?" he demanded.

Longear shrugged. "Careers change. People leave."

Conin glared about them. "And the mining worms? Why were they not carted off to the mining colonies? Why were they bred and left to die behind the barns? That was not done years ago. That is recent."

Longear laughed softly. "Recent? Yes, I suppose it is."

A chill crawled down his spine. "What happened?" he repeated.

"I do not know," she said silkily, "but I am sure I can straighten it out. Gribey, stay behind and see what happened here, as Conin suggests. If anyone wants to know who gave you authority, you can tell them it was their own Lloroi."

Conin gritted his teeth until they hurt.

"Good to see you actively ordering your people, Lloroi." She said the title as if it was an insult. "It is so difficult to get people to cooperate when it is only your representatives that they see."

Namina shivered. Conin, seeing her fear, hoped his own eyes were not as expressive. "How difficult has it been, Longear?" he questioned quietly.

She glanced sideways at him. "Difficult enough to give me some amusement." She smiled without humor. "But since you put the boundaries of the county in my hands, it has become somewhat less so."

Conin stared blindly at the fields. Was this the kind of Lloroi he was to be? One who thrust his power into the hands of bullies? One who overlooked what he could not control, and one who could not even control his own boundaries? "Where do we go now?" he asked dully.

Longear glanced down the trail. "Only a little farther. We are quite near the border now, you know—perhaps only twenty kilometers away. You *could*"—she emphasized the word strangely—"be in Ariye by this evening." She watched him closely, but he did not meet her eyes.

Gamon's camp was a set of caves overhung by a stand of owlbark trees and small wooden buildings built in between the tree trunks. The trunks themselves were smooth, spreading out and down into large tentlike canopies that provided the supports for the odd-shaped cabins. It was too dark for roottrees to grow, so the floors were cut wood, supported by the upper curves of the owlbark roots. Above the cabins, where the tree branches split and spread, there were hollows which gave the birds their nests. The clumps of droppings and disgorged remains of the birds gave the roofs a spotted texture. In camp, it was always the youngest boy's chore to clean the roofs of the cabins; the youngest here, not counting the refugees, was fourteen. He was training with Gamon to become a swordsman. His latest growth spurt had made him skinny as a pole, but his lanky form could not be compared to the bony figures who now rode into camp.

The wolfwalker glanced back at Tomi. The small girl clinging to him was still asleep, her head resting between his thin shoulder blades and her arms linked loosely around his waist. "This way," Dion said to him over her shoulder. He should have been up with the rest of the refugees, she admitted, but he had lagged on the trail, dropping back so that he dogged her mount like a shadow. With her fatigue still heavy on her mind, Dion had not argued.

She glanced sideways at Aranur, meeting his eyes wryly. This crowded but quiet companionship would probably be the only real moments they had together for a long time. Once in camp, there would be a thousand things for Aranur to do. Dion would not escape her tasks, either. Gamon would want her scouting report, then would probably send her off to town with the other scouts to take her news to the council. She let her gaze wander around the camp, searching for Sobovi, the wolfwalker who ran the north trail for Gamon. With his sprained ankle, he was either in one of the caves or cabins, or else he was at the firepit, stuffing his face with one of the shepherd's pies being served. At the thought of the other wolfwalker, the gray thread of the pack pulled at her mind, and Dion let herself drift, enjoying Hishn's senses until the dnu tugged at the reins and reminded her that it, too, was hungry. She sighed. Reluctantly, she closed her mind to the wolves.

The arriving refugees had been swept off the dnu, bundled in more blankets, and led off to huddle around the fire and eat, or stagger into the drowsy warmth of the cave and sleep. By the time Aranur and Dion rode in on their slower-paced dnu, most of the refugees were already settled, and it was only the Ariyens who were still corralling their mounts and carting gear around.

Not bothering to speak softly, Dion directed Tomi and his younger charge toward the corral. The smaller child had not awakened from the lurching of the dnu; if the pounding of the hooves and noise of the camp did not open the child's eyes, Dion doubted that mere words would do it now. She nodded toward the corral that had been grown between three of the trees. Cleverly, the branching canopy had been bent and guided into a fence. Only the gate was man-made. "It is a permanent camp," she explained to Tomi, "used every fall during the sap run."

He looked around curiously. "We don't have sap runs. We have sap farms," he said.

"I know," she returned cheerfully. In her own county, she had once had the task of tending the sap trees. It was not a job she wanted to repeat. "Sap trees do not grow so well on this side of the Phye. The ground is different. Too rocky." She shrugged. "We have enough to harvest for the supply of the village, but not enough to farm."

"Aranur," a man called from the other side of the firepit. "Can we see you a moment?"

Aranur, swinging off the dnu, gave Dion a grimace. "Not even unsaddled, and already at work." He loosed the cinch and caught the saddle as it slipped off. The dnu's skin rippled in delight as it was relieved of the weight. No matter how comfortable the saddle was, the creature preferred its fur free for scratching. It bent its head around, nipping daintily at its hide until Aranur took the bridle as well, leaving it free to sidestep into the corral and join the rest of the herd. "Won't be a moment," he promised.

Dion regarded his back wryly. No, it would not be a moment, she agreed silently. It would be at least an hour—maybe two, if she knew Aranur. She swung to the ground, motioning for the boy to wait a minute, and took her dnu to the corral. A moment to relieve it of its saddle and bridle, and another to carry her own gear to the saddle log, and then she turned to the boy.

"Hold onto her," she said, gesturing at the little girl loosely clinging to the boy. She tapped the dnu behind its forelegs, and it knelt obediently, its middle legs tucking under as it dropped closer to the ground. When the children were within reach, Dion took the little girl gently. Moons, but she weighed nothing, even to Dion's tired arms. She frowned at the feel of bone under her hands. Tomi, sliding down from the saddle, looked at her uncertainly. She smoothed her face. "Can you get the gear?" she asked, keeping one hand on the dnu's head to hold it in place. "I'll wait."

He nodded. The saddle was heavy for him, but he managed, staggering under its weight as he hauled it to the saddle log. He could not sling it all the way over, and it took him several minutes to straighten out the cinch and other straps. When he returned and took the bridle off, Dion let the dnu rise. It needed little urging to join the herd in the corral. As she shut the gate, the dnu was already making its way toward the feeding bin, reminding Dion yet again that even though she had emptied Aranur's pack of his own lunch—and Gamon's, too—she was still hungry enough to eat a badgerbear. And that reminded her of the refugees. She glanced toward the fire, catching the eye of one of the men who hovered over the newcomers. He nodded warmly, striding to greet her.

"Hi, Dion, another couple of feet for the fire, eh?"

She grinned. "This one," she said, indicating the lolling head of the small girl in her arms, "is more interested in sleep, I think. But Tomi could probably be convinced to sit by the blaze."

The burly man cocked his head at the boy's scrawny frame. "And to take a few more meals, I should think." He took the little girl gently from Dion's arms, his thick muscles hefting the tiny child with surprise as he, too, realized how little she weighed. He gave Dion a sober look. Jerking his head at the fire, he indicated that the boy should follow him. "Come, Tomi. Before you know it, we'll have you warm as a winter coat in the summer."

Tomi stared at the man's muscles, then at the worn sword

hanging from his shoulder strap. He balked. The thickset man paused. "Huh. What is it, boy?"

Tomi glanced uncertainly at Dion.

"It's all right," she said gently. "Some of your elders are there, see? And I will join you in a little while."

He nodded reluctantly.

Dion looked after them, a frown creasing her brow. The packsong that echoed deep in her mind caught her attention now that she could think again, and she reached for it. Strange notes . . . The bony images of the boy and the others made a disturbing picture in the memories of the wolves. But when she would have stretched further to read the echoes, she was interrupted. From her right, inside the cave, a woman had come to the entrance and called her twice already.

"Dion," the woman called again, finally catching her attention. "Can we see you for a moment?" Her body, silhouetted by the light inside the cave, turned for a moment, as if she were listening over her shoulder, then glanced back toward the wolfwalker. Dion sighed. This was one of the intern healers. One of the less-confident interns, she reminded herself. No doubt, she thought uncharitably, the woman wanted to discuss everything she had done since she had visited the peetrees that morning. Dion grinned sourly. She could guess where the other healer was. Probably, as soon as he heard Dion was returning, he had ridden back to the village—anything to escape this woman's run-on tongue.

Dion waved her acknowledgment, making her way slowly toward the cave. If she was lucky, someone would have set up bedding enough for her to sleep, too. Several people stopped her on the way to the cavern, greeting her and gripping her arms—painfully—as they traded comments on the rescue. So she had been the one to bring in the refugees? And early, too? What had happened to cause this? How had it been, going through the falls—it was like her not to wait until it was set up and tested. Or had it been Aranur who insisted on being first? That was one way to get a shower—clever of her to do it this morning instead of waiting till now, when she would be sharing the stalls with a dozen others. Good to see her back, yes it was . . . Before she got through to the cave entrance, and back to the warm corner where the few wounded refugees huddled, she felt as though her weary smile was frozen on her face. She had no energy to change it for each person. She had little energy for this intern, either, she realized, as the woman ran on at length about the condition of the children she had tucked into the bedding in the cave. It was not until Dion yawned mightily that the woman faltered.

"Oh, Dion, I'm sorry. I thought—I just wanted you to know—"

"It's all right," Dion cut in. She started to speak, but yawned again, opening her eyes afterward reluctantly. The burning that closing them had relieved so briefly was hedonistic agony. "You're doing fine," she reassured. "Their wounds are minor. And, as you already realized, they are just very hungry and very run down."

"I only wanted you to see—"

Dion cut her off gently. "You are doing very well with them," she repeated. "You do not need me here, so I think, if there is an extra space where I can throw my blankets, that I will just lie down with the rest of them and sleep awhile."

"Oh, gods." The woman was instantly contrite. "I'm really sorry. Moonworms, I don't know why I did not think. Going through the falls yourself after days of scouting—you must be exhausted. Here—" She grabbed Dion's arm and pulled her toward a quiet corner. "We have more than enough beds set up—we are sleeping in shifts anyway, what with the work behind the falls going on at night. Leave your pack there—no, don't bother to bring out your blankets—the beds are much more comfortable. Take my bed. No, I insist. You can sleep as long as you like here."

Dion smiled faintly. "Thanks. But, Cheya?" she added. "Don't wake me until dinner."

The other woman turned and hurried back to her charges, and Dion sank down on the soft bedding. She was too tired to strip. She would drag her own sleeping bag from her gear bag later. This bed was good enough for now.

Her damp clothes were warm with her body heat, but turned clammy when she stopped moving, so she got up to grab a dry shirt and pair of pants from the bag at the back wall that had her design on it. Wearily, she set her sword and other gear between the head of the mattress and the wall of the cave. It was another matter, however, to fight the knots in the wet leather laces of her jerkin, and she almost gave up, her fingers trembling with weariness over the task. By the time she leaned back on the sleeping bag, she was already half-asleep. She did not even cover her shoulders before she slept.

Dreams of gray threads. A spiderweb of bonds in her head . . . The song of the wolves was distant, but it pounded like a group of dancers, running, leaping, as they raced from meadow to log to rocky path. She twisted restlessly. In her ears, the distant snorting came softly as the wolves dug in the ground for rodents. In her nose, the sweet, thick scent of damp earth where their black claws tore out the burrows. On her lips, the sweet, hot taste of blood and meat still pulsing from the last bit of life . . . And then the taste changed. Bitter threads were caught in the blood. Red, now purple, the ichor seeped from the meat she had killed. And then the prey began to twitch and rise, and it was no rabbit, no rodent of the fields. Gods, it was a worlag. She tried to scream, searching her body for her knife and finding none to hand. "My knife—throw me my knife!" The worlag raked its claw across her face . . .

She tossed restlessly, her arm flung out of the covers, and her loose, fuzzy braid trailing across her shoulder. Her fist clenched, twitching. Aranur, looking down, knelt and touched her face, calming her from her dreams. Still sleeping, she made an inarticulate sound, brushing at her cheek and catching his hand. He lay down then, easing into the sleeping bag beside her and pillowing his head on his arms until he, too, slept.

In Bilocctar, still in the late winter months . . .

The afternoon was dark with clouds, and Namina huddled in her saddle as the rain rushed suddenly upon them. Conin wrapped her in a poncho, but she was miserable, and he cursed himself for not realizing that the weather might turn. If he had not been so damned anxious to get out of those polite towns, they could have been under a dry roof, having hot soup for lunch and waiting for the rains to stop before they rode out again. But no, he cursed himself, he had had to push. And Longear was probably laughing her head off at Namina's misery.

Ten minutes later, the downpour drizzled out, blowing on to the north. The forest glistened around them, the roottree roads hard and shiny with the rain. The sky was still overcast, so that neither sun nor moons shone upon them, and Conin shivered. Beneath him, the wet warmth of the dnu streamed like a demon's breath.

But then, Longear brought them to a halt and stared expectantly at Conin.

"What is it?" he snapped. "You said twenty kilometers. We have gone barely five."

"We have," she acknowledged. "But this is as far as you go."

"I don't understand."

"I know." She chuckled, and the sound grated on his nerves until he wanted to scream. "But look at your mate. She knows what I mean."

Conin glanced at Namina. She was staring at Longear, the fear stark in her pale face. Her blue eyes were huge, like a nightbird caught in the light, and her hands trembled as they held the reins.

"No games, Longear," he said sharply. "What do you want now? Another agreement? You already control the county. What more can you take from me?"

"Why, Conin," she said softly, leaning forward in the saddle, "you still have so much to give."

Two of the raiders bunched up beside him, cutting him off from his wife. "Wha—" It was the only sound he got out. They slugged him, clubbed him across the neck and head when his raingear tangled their hands, and dragged him from the saddle. Something was flung in his face, and he screamed, digging at his eyes, clawing them while they burned yellow, then red, then black, until his hands were clamped in iron grips. Somewhere in the background, Namina was shrieking. He struggled blindly. The screaming—gods, would it never stop? He beat his head against the ground as the screams rose to an insane pitch and then were choked to a mindless animal whimper. Someone laughed. Namina's voice strangled, cutting off her sudden shriek. Why couldn't they just kill her and let her be? He would tear them limb from limb. He would rip their souls out through their lungs when he got free. He shouted and cried and writhed against the hands that held him, choking on the gag that was stuffed in his mouth. It tasted sickly sweet. It was soaked in blood. Namina . . . He retched. Someone grabbed his hair, and then he felt a woman's fingers digging into his scalp. Namina . . .

Longear looked on her handiwork with a slight smile. ''There, now,'' she said soothingly. ''That wasn't so bad, was it?'' She leered at Namina. The woman's hands were tied into Conin's hair, her mouth and lower body soaked in blood. Three siker barbs were still stuck in her cheek where she had accidentally butted one of Longear's men in her panic, and Longear leaned over and pulled them out distastefully. Namina stared at her, cowering and whimpering away from those small, delicate hands. Longear gestured. Conin's arms were tied around Namina's waist.

''Say you love each other,'' she suggested.

Namina's whimpers rose into a scream as the raider approached. He swung. Conin's head was severed from behind. The body dropped without a spasm. Blood spurted into Namina's face, then her chest, then her thighs, as his body slid down hers, locked around her by his bound arms. His head hung from her hands, staring at her sightlessly, her fingers still tangled into his hair. The bloody cloth torn from her own trousers was still crammed in his mouth. The rain puddle at her feet filled with blood. The surface turned from brown to red. The ripples from his futile pulse spread to her toes, and she hyperventilated.

Longear laughed. As she rode away, she looked back only once. Namina was still screaming, but her voice was going. Longear laughed again. And rode on.

Chapter 10

When your children die,
When your county burns,
When your tears are thin with grief;
When you can see no further, and
When there is nothing left,
There is one thing still:
The gift of death.

The noise of the dinner crew was not enough to wake Dion or Aranur. It was not until a stern hand shook their shoulders that they opened their eyes.

"Come on, wake up, you two. Dinner's getting cold, and there is much to talk about." It was Aranur's uncle, Gamon, his gray hair gleaming like a pale halo in the dim light of the cave.

Dion roused groggily. Aranur's warmth curled around her body, and she felt lethargic, unwilling to move. The dark images of her dreams still caught her, and it took Aranur's sitting up to waken her completely, the sudden rush of cool air shocking where it stripped the sleep heat away. She growled.

Aranur, looking down, grinned. "Hungry?"

She growled again, nodding emphatically. "Enough to eat two dnu all by myself."

"In that case . . ." He tossed back the covers, rolling free and extending his arm to help her up.

Dion winced as she rose, glaring at Gamon's chuckle. Now that Aranur's uncle was old enough to have a weatherwise ache in one of his own legs, he found too much humor in the stiffness of younger folks. Her glare turned to a snort when he chucked her under her chin. Shoving his hand away, she reached out to slap his face playfully, grinning when he withdrew like lightning, blocking her move and giving her his own wrinkled grin. He was a gnarled figure, his face seamed and lined with scars and age. His gray hair was half-silvered, half dull gray, and it gave him a grizzled look. He had been like a father to her this last year. Dion, glancing from Aranur to Gamon, rubbed the sleepsand from her eyes and leaned down to pick up her sword and buckle it back on. Her stomach cramped, growling noisily, and both men looked at her and laughed. "Hush," she said haughtily. "My stomach is merely making a statement about the time of day. Dinner time." She glared at their stifled chuckles. Why did not other womens' guts growl at embarrassing moments? She yanked at her braid and tugged her tunic into some sense of respectability. Her own jerkin was still damp, so she left it where it lay, scrounging in one of the clothing piles near the back of the cave for an extra. Catching a glimpse of herself in one of the mirrors that had been hung, she made a face. Aranur and Gamon glanced back.

Gamon knew instantly what peeved her. "We set up a shower a couple days ago," he said soothingly. "You should use it tonight if you want your turn. Tomorrow, you will be riding back to town."

"Tomorrow?" She frowned, but let Aranur pull her forward to the food tables. She took the plate she was offered, accepting the pile of meat and steamed vegetables eagerly, sneaking a piece of blackroot with her fingers and popping it in her mouth. She sighed with the flavor as Gamon answered, "You, Aranur, some of the elders you brought in today—you will all need to go back and speak to the Lloroi."

She frowned. "Why include me in that group?" She popped another bite in her mouth, unable to wait till they seated themselves near the fire. The heat reached out like a toasty blanket as they walked up, though the fire to the fore made her back feel cold in comparison.

Gamon gave her a sharp look. "Aranur said something about the wolves."

The Gray Ones? Moonworms, she had almost forgotten. She

nodded slowly. "Yes," she returned. "That is something the Lloroi should hear from me—or one of the other wolfwalkers."

Gamon nodded. "Sobovi just got in a few hours ago. Talk with him and decide which of you should go. Although," the old man added, pointing his fork at her, "since he came in with a sprained ankle, it will probably be you."

She gave a sideways look to the tall man at her side. "As long as Aranur rides, too," she said teasingly, "I don't think I'll argue."

Gamon watched the way their eyes met and grinned to himself. He settled on the seating stones, warm from the radiant heat of the blaze, and began to eat with single-minded determination. An old man, he told himself righteously, has to appreciate every meal—in case it is his last. He chuckled silently. His sword arm was still stronger than those of the younger men—except Aranur, he admitted generously—and his aim still as true. The only difference was that age had turned his skin into a wrinkled cloth. He glanced at his nephew; two sets of gray eyes met with quiet complacency until Dion, stuffing the first hot mouthfuls of roast rabbit in her mouth, gave a sensuous groan. Aranur grinned. He raised a forkful of potatoes in salute.

Tomi found his way to Dion's side before they finished their meal. She and Aranur scooted sideways on their warm seats to make room for him. He did not interrupt, sitting upright as though he were wide awake, but his head tilted within minutes, and he leaned slowly onto Aranur's shoulder. The tall man glanced down in surprise. Dion hid her smile. "Now you are stuck," she teased.

"Not as stuck as you're going to be in a month," he returned slyly.

She laughed, reaching across to touch the place on his chest with the gemstone. "And you think I'm going to argue?" she returned softly.

He shook his head. "If you even open your mouth to protest . . ." He left the mock threat hanging.

Dion grinned. "You'll do what?"

He glanced down at the boy and shook his head mutely.

She laughed. "Want me to take him?"

"I want someone else to take him. I want to take you for a walk," he said pointedly.

Dion looked at him coyly. "I thought you would never ask," she said, blushing in spite of herself.

Aranur started to his feet, lifting the boy with him. He would take the child to the cave, put him to bed, he thought, and then he and Dion could . . . talk. But Gamon, returning from the washing tables, gestured for him to sit again. Dion raised her eyebrows.

"Stay and listen," Gamon returned. "It's getting interesting." Dion sat back unhappily, meeting Aranur's look with a grimace. If Gamon had his way, she and Aranur would not have a moment alone until they were mated.

With frustration, Aranur deposited himself back on the seat.

Dion almost smiled at his petulance. "Might as well hear their story now as later," she reasoned wryly.

"Might as well hear it later," he muttered, "since you're going back to the town and it will be repeated there for the council."

She reached out for the hand that held Tomi loosely against him, and he tightened his fingers on hers. With the moisture in the air, the evening was chilly, cutting through their clothes when the fire's heat waves shifted in the wind.

Moira, the tall refugee who had led the children, had been answering questions for the group. "Look at me," the elder said. "I was a large woman, once. Tall as my mate, and broad across the shoulders. I stood my turn on the council, as my father did before me, and his mother before him. For fourteen years, I worked the fields with my mate. For two years, during the resistance and the war, I drew bow with him, as well. And then—" Her gaze swept the group. "Then the war was over, and I worked the fields again. But this time, my mate guided the plow so he could hold himself up while he dragged his mangled legs behind him in the furrows. And what we reaped from our bloody ground fed Lloroi Conin's men—fed his raiders and slavers and soldier men—not my children."

She let her bitter gaze go from one face to the next. "You want to know why we did not fight back more vehemently? We were not badly treated, at first," she explained wearily. "We were the conquered county, and were only taxed, not browbeaten, with the change. The soldiers who came, stayed. They were no trouble to us. The exports to the Lloroi helped support them, too. After two years—'' She paused. ''—they became our neighbors. Two years . . .'' Her voice drifted off. She shivered, and resumed. ''Two years, and they became the husbands of our daughters, the wives of our sons, and the parents of our grandchildren. They became council members. Guild members. Family. It was gradual. It was slow.'' She grasped a handful of dirt and ash and let it slip between her fingers. ''It was invisible because it was right in front of us.'' She looked up, around the fire. ''And because, at that point, they were part of us, we did not even know how to fight them.''

She stared at her hands, her long callused fingers thin and marred with pitch that would not wash clean. ''For two years, we lived with those men and women of the old Lloroi. For two years, we paid taxes that grew heavier, but we managed. But then, the third year, things changed. We sent our goods out on caravans as before, but they were raided. Industries were not restocked from other parts of the county. Our mining worms were stolen from the breeder pens. Our sap crops were burned in flash fires. Stored food rotted from water damage in dry barns.

''Last summer, the old Lloroi died. His son took over. We created a resistance group, poor enough though it was. We had a plan. We were going to fight back.'' Her face took on a hollow look. ''We raided a guardhouse and stole weapons. We took a commander hostage and demanded that they withdraw the soldiers from one of the towns. When the soldiers complied, we were stunned. Had it been that easy all along?'' She gazed into the fire. ''And then the other soldiers left, and we realized that the new Lloroi had ordered them all to withdraw. He sent word that we could rebuild our land as we saw fit. And we cheered, and we came out of our houses and offered thanks to the moons.''

Moira's voice was suddenly flat. ''And then the raiders came.'' She looked up. ''We thought the soldiers had been bad. We thought the loss of a few freedoms intolerable. We thought we won a great battle against them, even though no blood was shed.'' She closed her eyes, rocking softly back and forth. ''We were wrong.'' Her voice was anguished, and the Ariyens winced at her expression. ''We won no battle. We merely opened the door for the raiders to sweep on us like the lepa who flock over a herd of goats. And suddenly we were dying. Those who left town did not come back. Those who led the resistance disappeared. Those who sat on the council died. In—accidents.'' She spat the word.

She ignored the murmur that swept the ring of faces. ''After the first few months, there were fewer deaths. But always leaders. Always speakers. Some of us thought that age would protect us, but even the older elders died in the beating circles or were burned in the fires. We had almost no council left. And the raiders, laughing at us, stepped into the empty positions. The positions they had emptied with their own swords. And by our own laws, we had to accept them.'' Her voice shook with outrage. ''They used our laws against us.'' She ground her teeth, the man sitting next to her wincing at the sound. ''They took our homes,'' she added. ''They took our children. We had nothing left.'' Her voice dropped into a hoarse whisper. ''Not even our dignity.''

''The children,'' Dion said. ''What happened to the children?''

Moira stared at her, taking in the shadows under Dion's eyes, noting the bandages that swathed her arms and legs, the jagged scratch that marred her face. It was for Moira that this woman, this healer, had risked such injuries. For elders, for children Dion did not even know. Moira realized that her mind was too tired. The food, the fire—it was a dream from which she could only awaken. Greeted like friends. Coddled. Defended as if they were precious things . . . There was no sense in it. Not in a world where raiders could beat children to death and laugh as they watched them die. ''Our children,'' she said softly. She looked up. ''Our sons and daughters, our babies, were taken and—held for us—in case we made mistakes in thinking we owned ourselves. In case we rebelled again.'' Her voice broke suddenly. ''My sons . . .''

There was a murmur around the fire.

''You had to leave your other children behind?'' a gentle voice asked.

Moira stared dully at the questioner. ''I left no children behind.'' She picked up another handful of ashes. ''I left only graves.'' She released the particles, the dark swirl casting itself along the ground with the wind.

There was silence. The fire burned hot. The light, which glowed off their faces, showed anger and grim expressions. ''We grieve for your daughter,'' the man who had spoken last said. ''We grieve for your sons.'' Around the fire, the words were echoed.

Moira shuddered slowly. ''Grief?'' she broke in. ''Death has no power over me anymore. Only time,'' she whispered.

''Time,'' she said again. She looked up, and those who met her eyes had to look away. There was a fury deep in her hollow expression that burned bright with violence. ''You want to know what happened? It was not the war that happened, or the soldiers who came, or the raiders who ruined us. It was time. Time changed us. Time gave us complacency. And time—'' Her voice choked. ''Time took away our lives.''

The fire glowed, the bed of coals dancing with the gases.

One of the other refugees stirred. ''Some still resist,'' the older man said. ''There is a group of fighters in the forest, living off the shrubs and roots, grubbing in the dirt for what they eat and stealing what they wear from the raiders themselves. They are led by a woman they call the Siker.'' He grinned revengefully. ''She marks them all—the bodies they leave behind for their comrades to find. Cuts their throats and punctures their cheeks with a siker barb. You say that name—the Siker—in a raider's camp, and the lot of them will shiver like the chill of death was on them already. It drives them crazy.'' He nodded with grim satisfaction. ''The Siker's fighters use the same tactics against the raiders that the raiders used on us—hit and run, hide, and hit again.'' He sobered. ''There aren't many who give the Siker's men help. There is Josh, who tends the mining worms—he scouts the trails when he delivers them to the mining camps, and checks for how often the raiders use the trails. The raiders are beginning to suspect him, though. He'll have to cut and run to the Siker's group before too much longer. There is Peyel, too—the woman who runs the tavern. She sends word to them through the elders. Moons bless her, if it had not been for her advice, we would never have escaped.''

Dion, watching Moira closely from across the fire, glanced sideways at Aranur.

"That was the woman who told you to try for the Sky Bridge?" he asked Moira. The elder nodded, and Aranur sat back, considering.

The others argued then, the murmur of their voices drowning the occasional crackle of the fire. Finally, one of the women stood. "We need to send word of this to our own council," she said, gesturing strongly.

Another fighter nodded. "We should send several riders back—with Moira's group gone from under the raiders' hands, no telling if they will push across the border themselves to see what we are up to here."

Gamon nodded, standing. "We have stirred a nest of lepas here. Now we must make sure we stay far from their claws."

One of the other men turned to him. "Gamon, you are riding in the morning for the town?"

The gray-haired man nodded. "Was planning on it."

Moira glanced his way. Then she frowned, and her tired gaze rested on Dion for a long moment before she slowly recognized the wolfwalker. She rose at once, crossing the firepit in a stumbling walk and halting in front of Aranur while she looked down at the boy who slept so soundly on his shoulder. She regarded him unsmiling. Aranur wondered grimly if her daughter's body had been recovered from the canyon yet. To be so close to Ariye, so close to freedom, and then to lose her last child in sight of the border . . .

As if she could read his mind, Moira spoke abruptly. "Tomi has attached himself to you."

Aranur glanced down at the sleeping head. "Only because my shoulder was more comfortable than the rocks to sleep on."

"Take care of him." She turned then to Dion, staring long into the wolfwalker's violet eyes. "Healer Dione."

Dion nodded. She had gotten so used to her nickname that the full "Dione" sounded strange in her ears.

Moira gazed down at Dion. She was a full head taller than the slim wolfwalker—as tall as Aranur himself—and her steady gaze made Dion shift uncomfortably. "Moonwarrior," she said finally, softly. "You gave us life."

Dion flushed. "I am no moonwarrior," she protested automatically. "And I did nothing that any one of these people would not also have done."

Moira ignored her. ''When we were on the rim,'' she said, ''and you appeared before us, you looked as if you had fallen from the sky to the river and had only just climbed out of the Devil's Knee. I no longer felt my body. I no longer felt the cold. I believed we were already dead. And you were the moonwarrior, come to lead us to the stars. I followed you willingly. Had I known . . .'' She gazed at Dion. ''Had I not been so cold that I could not think even beyond the next step, had I guessed what you really wanted us to do, I would not have followed you even one more meter. A crossing above the falls—it had been marked on the map. And, moons know why, but I trusted it to be true. But a crossing through the falls themselves? The river had already taken two of our children. You wanted us to give to it all of them.''

Dion shook her head helplessly. ''But the crossing was there. You saw it. You used it. It was cold, yes, and dark, but it was safe.''

Safe. Yes. Moira's mind was exhausted, but she recognized that, at least. This—this was real. This food, this fire . . . The children were safe. Safe. And now that they were safe, surely she could let go of the life that had sustained her so long. There was nothing left for her here. Surely she would be allowed to go to the moons now, to cross the sky where her mate, her own children, waited. ''Wolfwalker,'' she whispered, ''Moonwarrior. Give me peace. Take me now, to the moons.''

Aranur stared at the woman, and Dion stood, shocked. ''Moira—I—''

Moira dropped to her knees. ''Moonwarrior, I beg you.''

''Get up,'' Dion said in a strangled voice. She hauled ineffectually at Moira's limp arm. ''Get up. Do not kneel to me. Do not call me that.'' From around the fire, two of the other refugees hurried to the woman at Dion's feet. Gamon stepped forward and pulled at Moira's other arm.

Moira shook him off. ''I have done enough,'' she pleaded. ''I have brought the children to your safety. Please, you have the eyes, the sword, of the moonwarriors. You have the voice of the wolves. You are legend. I beg you—it is my right—let me die now.''

''No!'' Dion was trembling. Aranur was standing now, too, and the boy was waking blearily. ''I am not a moonwarrior.''

Dion shoved the older woman away sharply. "I cannot give you death, nor can you ask it of me. For moonsakes, I am a healer."

"Violet eyes." Moira resisted Gamon's strength with limpness, and he made a helpless gesture at Dion. "I am ready to die," she said gently. "Please."

And then the other elders were around her, raising her to her stumbling feet, soothing her blank gaze, leading her away from Dion, even though she turned her haggard head and said again, her tired voice pleading softly, "Please."

Aranur touched Dion's arm. She shuddered. "Gods," she whispered. "What have they done to her?"

Tomi watched Moira led away impassively. He glanced at Dion. "Why did she call you a moonwarrior?"

Dion looked down at him. "Because my eyes are violet, I suppose," she returned unhappily. "It is not normal—they should be gray or blue or brown. But I am no moonwarrior," she said abruptly. "Believe that, if nothing else."

"But Moira said you were, and she is the senior elder on the council." He regarded her with childish curiosity. "She trusted you."

Gamon, glancing at the expression of dismay on Dion's face, chucked the boy on his shoulder. "It's why we sent Dion to greet you," he said lightly. "Aranur looks grim enough to scare you right back to the raiders."

Meeting Gamon's eyes over the boy's head, Aranur snorted. "I've hardly the face to frighten children," he retorted. "Just old men with big mouths who should know better."

Dion was still watching Moira. "She should ride with us, tomorrow," she said, more to herself than to the others. "She should not be left here."

Gamon nodded slowly. "I will arrange for the dnu."

He looked down, a small hand tugging on his sleeve. "I want to go, too," Tomi said firmly.

Aranur regarded the boy with surprise.

"I want to go," Tomi repeated. "I can fight." His face flushed suddenly.

Aranur hesitated, as if considering the idea. "It is a brave offer, Tomi," he said thoughtfully, "but"—he searched for a reason—"you have only one knife. Since we are riding in an area where the raiders could attack again, we need fighters who can carry two blades. Besides,'' he added, ''the others need you here. There is much we must know about your side of the border, and you are one of the few people who can describe it to us. Most of the others are too young to remember the trails, and the elders will be riding to town tomorrow with us.''

''Oh.'' Tomi stared at his feet.

Gamon nodded. ''It's nothing against your fighting ability, boy. You did well against the worlags. We will need your courage here more than we need another voice back in the village.''

The boy's flush darkened. ''No,'' he said in a low voice.

Aranur looked at him with a frown.

''No,'' he repeated. ''I did not do well.''

Gamon scowled at him. ''Do not be shy, boy. Dion said you fought as well as Aranur could have done.''

The boy flushed more darkly, and then he said furiously, ''I did not. She lied. I did not fight at all.''

Dion shook her head at Gamon, kneeling in front of the boy. ''I spoke the truth,'' she said quietly. ''Why do you deny it?''

The boy twisted away from her, and she grabbed his shoulders to stop him and force him to face her. ''When we were on the boulders,'' Dion said, ''you used the knife against the worlags as much as I did my sword. You did not flinch away from them then. I would call that as courageous as any act I have seen.''

''No.'' The boy looked up then. ''When you fell off the boulder, you called for the knife. You shouted to me to give it to you. I couldn't. I could see the worlags—I saw them grab you—tear you—You screamed,''—his voice was rising—''and I couldn't let go of it. You were screaming, and I couldn't give it up . . .''

Aranur knelt beside Dion. ''But Dion is here, Tomi. Look. She is whole and sound and can still run with the wolves as she is meant to do. And you are here and safe, and you have a knife, and Dion has a knife.'' He put his hand under the boy's chin, forcing Tomi to look at him. ''You made a mistake, Tomi, that's all. You put Dion in danger, yes. But it happens—it can happen often when two people have to trust each other in battle. I make mistakes, too,'' he added at the boy's disbelieving look. ''The second time I led a venge against a group of three raiders,'' he said, ''I walked right into a trap. My first venge had gone so well that I was cocky. Two men were badly injured. I walked away with this—'' He pulled up his sleeve to show Tomi the wide white scar where he had taken a sword stroke on his bare arm. ''That taught me to think.'' He pulled his sleeve down. ''Three months later, I led another venge, and I froze when a swordswoman needed me.'' His eyes grew hard. ''She died. And that,'' he said vehemently, ''taught me to act. But here''—and he nodded at the wolfwalker—''you are now safe, and Dion is fine.''

Dion smiled wryly. ''Don't blame yourself, Tomi. Like Aranur said, everyone makes mistakes.''

The boy stared at her. Dion was a healer. What mistakes could she make? He did not realize that the question was obvious as his eyes flickered from Dion to the silver circlet on her brow.

''Yes,'' she said, her face softening, ''me, too. I—I don't always have the best judgment,'' she admitted. ''I have risked both Aranur's and Gamon's lives more than once by healing others at a bad time or in a poor place. I make mistakes in fighting, too. I did not always have the experience to know what to do and in what order. Once, as with Aranur, a woman died because of my haste.'' She stared at her hands, then looked up at the boy. ''Being asked to give up your one weapon during a battle is a hard choice. I don't blame you for what you did.'' She touched his arm. ''Be sure you do not blame yourself.''

''But you screamed,'' he whispered. ''You didn't stop.''

''I was scared,'' she said softly. ''Like you.''

The boy looked at her unwillingly.

From beside her, Aranur nodded. ''It is true. Dion is frightened more of a worlag a hundred meters away than a firespider on her hand. I'll tell you a secret.'' He dropped his voice, leaning close, and Tomi listened intently in spite of himself. ''All night long,'' he whispered, ''Dion wakes me up with her dreams, hitting me as if I was a worlag myself.''

A chuckle escaped Gamon, and Dion made a face at the older man. ''Maybe it is the thought that I might have to run trail with the both of you again,'' she retorted, ''not my dreams of worlags, that make me strike out so.''

Gamon laughed outright. ''If you are confusing me with worlags''—he rubbed his grizzled chin where his beard was scruffy as the hair on a beetle-beast's face—''perhaps I should look to my shaving.''

Tomi looked up at Dion. "I'm sorry I did not help you."

She smiled faintly. "You do not have to be sorry anymore."

He hesitated, then nodded jerkily.

Aranur got to his feet. "Now that you are no longer sorry, you can look at the experience objectively and figure out what you learned from it."

Tomi gave him a puzzled look.

"What you have learned about carrying a knife," the tall man prompted.

"What I learned?" The boy blinked. He thought for a moment. "To carry two knives," he said soberly. "Not one."

Gamon slapped Aranur's back and made him choke on his chuckle. "Then," he said finally, "you shall have two knives." He took one of his long knives from his own belt and handed it to the boy.

Tomi stared at the blade. He frowned, then looked up at the tall gray-eyed man. He belted the knife on carefully, sliding it around next to the other one, and looked down at them for a moment. "If I have two knives," he said slowly. "I can ride with you tomorrow. Then, when Dion loses her knife again, I can loan her one of mine."

Dion choked on a laugh. Aranur, finding his own logic turned against him, glanced helplessly at his uncle.

Gamon shrugged. "Would it really hurt to have him with us?" he asked.

Aranur opened his mouth and shut it again. He had not meant to give the boy a reason for coming along—and Gamon did not appreciate how difficult it was to get some privacy in this camp—or out of it. He and Dion would not be able to lag behind the other scouts and elders if this boy shadowed them tomorrow as he had done this entire day. But Dion was looking at Aranur expectantly, and Gamon was grinning slyly, guessing the reason for his discomfiture, and so he said reluctantly, "I guess not."

Tomi, satisfied, yawned. Dion glanced at him. "Time to sleep," she suggested.

Gamon nodded. "This way," the older man said firmly, taking the boy by the shoulders. He pushed him toward the cave, where he would be more comfortable than in one of the musty cabins. The trees sheltered the cabins from the wind, so that the muggy spring weather made the insides damp, holding the wet-mud smell like a sponge. The cave, on the other hand, was warm from the reflected fires, and well-aired where the chimneys cut through the stone and sucked out smoke and odors.

Aranur watched the two head toward the cave, his expression sobering as he took Dion's arm and led her from the fire. Dion winced, feeling his hand tighten. Here it comes, she thought. He is remembering Tomi's confession about her fear. Now she would get the what-the-hell-did-you-think-you-were-doing-you-could-have-been-hurt lecture. She steeled herself as they strode toward the shadows of the corral. But the angry words did not come. Instead, Aranur turned her toward him and searched her face with his gray eyes. "You did not tell me about that, Dion," he whispered. "That you fell off into the pack. That you screamed."

She shivered. "I was scared," she admitted in a low voice.

Suddenly she was in his arms, her face ground against his jerkin, and the sharp edge of the gemstone in his sternum rasped against her cheek. "Moons, Dion, I was terrified," he whispered in her hair.

She looked up, touching his cheek gently, a question in her eyes.

He whispered, as if unwilling to say the words aloud: "Terrified of losing you."

"You've never said that before."

"I did not have the confidence to say it before." It was the truth. Not until he had dragged her from under the body of that beetle-beast and found her still alive, crying out for him when she came to, had he known, or truly believed, that he might someday lose her to the forest. Moons, the panic that had hit him when he thought she was dead . . . He trembled, hiding it in a shiver when Dion looked up with worry. He touched her face, tracing the scratch that marred her cheeks. There was a wildness about this woman that drew him to her and trapped him in her violet gaze like a nightbug drawn to a fire. She moved like a shadow in the forest, gliding between the trees like the wolves with which she ran. She was not even aware of her grace, or the way she caught his gaze when she turned her shoulder just so, or tossed her hair back like that. Gods, but he wanted to steal away into the woods with her right now, take her hair from that braid, and spread its glossy blackness across the whiteferns that shone under the moons . . . He gritted his teeth. That he had to share her with the wolves—trust them with her safety—he was finally beginning to accept. Dion would never be able to live completely in his town—the pull of the graysong was too strong, taking her from her bed at night sometimes, urging her feet to the ridges where the Gray Ones ran. He could not take that away from her, nor, he realized, did he want to change that any longer. And he had grown used to running the forest with her. Half in town, and half without . . . He was a weapons master, but there were other options for his skills. Here, with Dion in his arms, it seemed as if there was nothing as important as crushing her to him, smelling the smoke in her hair and tasting the musky scent of the wolves on her skin.

"I've learned to live with our bargain," he said slowly.

She smiled, looking up and rubbing her cheek to his. "I, too," she admitted.

He pushed her back, surprised. "You had doubts? You were the one who insisted I keep my orders to myself."

"I meant it." She smiled to take the sting out of her words. "But I also know that it is your job to understand and weigh the risks of any fighting. It is why you are a weapons master even though you are so young that the other fighters think of you as an infant fresh from the cradle," she teased. She sobered, her voice suddenly quiet. "I knew you would come for me. I knew all I had to do was hold on."

"I would not have left you to face seven worlags by yourself—"

"Eight."

He chuckled, and she knew he was teasing her. "—if only because it would hurt my pride."

"Aranur . . ."

He shrugged. "You are a wolfwalker. Your life is different from mine. I will never truly understand it, but I can believe in it. And I can believe in you."

It was much later when they made their way to the cave where their sleeping gear was spread. They unrolled their bags, turning them toward each other so they could touch hands together as they fell asleep. As the warmth of the cave lulled Dion's thoughts, she heard a faint stirring behind her and rolled drowsily over. It was Tomi again, dragging his bag beside hers, half-asleep as he crawled back in and curled up. Dion smiled faintly, dozing off. Surrounded as she was by so many people, no nightmares would dare disturb her sleep that night.

Chapter 11

Coerce the hunt and speed the feet
Battles rage in distant streets
  How to get there—
  how to stop it?
Plead to stop the blood from spilling?
Race to stop the raiders' killing?
Your words alone, could prevent the theft
of life; prevent the death.

When Dion slid out from under the blankets, Aranur grunted, his hand searching for her body before tucking himself in a smaller curl at her absence. He woke some time later, rousing and scrounging breakfast at the fires before looking for her again. When he spotted her, she was in the middle of a knot of people in heated discussion. That alone should warn him, he thought wryly. What task would she be talked into this time? He grabbed an apple from the bin and made his way around the banked fire pit to greet his uncle before joining the group that was now trying to convince Dion of their plan. He smiled wryly. Dion could fight worlags or raiders and not blink an eye, but when it came to denying a half-starved woman or a child with bruised eyes, she could neither speak nor fight her way to the word "no."

". . . a few days, maybe less," coaxed one of the elders they had rescued yesterday.

Dion shook her head. "I disagree. We should delay at least a ninan, maybe more.'' Sobovi, the other wolfwalker, stood beside her, nodding emphatically, his gray hair shaking with the movement.

Moonworms, Aranur thought, she had already agreed to the task. They were now just persuading her of the time frame.

''But we must act *now,*'' one of the men repeated.

Dion waved her arms toward the west, toward the river. ''It will take time to scout the area. Time to trace the paths, locate the people to contact. Those of you who crossed the border yesterday''—she gestured at Moira and an older man—''cannot be used as scouts: you are elders. The rest are mere children. Not one of you is strong enough to run trail to the Slot and back.''

''If you used the falls as the crossing instead of the Slot, you would cut two days from the run.''

''And if the raiders began to realize that our tracks appeared and ended at the falls,'' Sobovi retorted irritably, ''we might as well forget about using it for anyone else who escapes to the border.''

The old man jutted his face forward, silencing the others. ''We are not ungrateful for what you have already done,'' he said persuasively. ''But we cannot just sit and do nothing while more of us die.''

Dion sighed. ''Neither can we run in, snatch people, and race back to the border like rabbits scurrying in front of a pack of worlags.'' Aranur edged through, catching her eye. She nodded in acknowledgment, her attention on the argument.

One of the other women suggested, ''We could at least get food and clothing to them—''

''After they reach Ariye,'' Sobovi cut in, ''surely. But what about before then? Do you expect Dion and I to cart gear enough for two dozen on our own backs?''

''Sobovi, you saw the condition of those who crossed yesterday. They could barely stagger by the time they reached the Knee. They need the food, the clothing—the hope,'' the other woman insisted.

Beside her, a man scowled. ''Moira said that the Sky Bridge was free of the raiders sometimes. What about using that crossing instead? Divert the raiders' attention, bring the refugees across there—it would save seven or eight kilometers of trail.

We could afford to send supplies across if we used the Sky Bridge instead.''

Dion made a helpless gesture. ''Can you guarantee that the Sky Bridge is clear? And if not, do you want me to lead a group of children straight into the raiders' hands and, when facing them, say, 'Oh, I'm sorry, I must have made a mistake trying this pass. Could you let us cross anyway?' ''

''But Moira said—''

''I said,'' Moira interrupted evenly, ''that Peyel told us the way was clear at the Sky Bridge. That she heard it from the raiders in her tavern.''

''But I saw the raiders at the Sky Bridge myself,'' Dion protested. ''Either the way was never safe to begin with, or they beat you to the crossing.''

The elder standing beside her shrugged, puzzled. ''So Peyel might be wrong. Had we run for the bridge, we would be dead by now. Or dying,'' he added, the images of dead children clouding his sight. ''As usual,'' he said, nodding to the tall elder woman, ''Moira judged right. We made it to the falls, and now we are here. Safe. But should we now sit here in this safety, eating your food, warmed by your fire, and coveting this haven while our people''—his voice took on a dangerous tone—''the ones left behind, suffer, starve, and die?''

Moira sighed. ''Although it is true that the raiders had the Sky Bridge closed off for our escape, it does not mean that others would suffer the same fate. Peyel works closely with our resistance group to help us escape. She helped five other groups flee, and they must have made it free, or we would have seen them dragged back by the raiders and burned to teach us all a lesson.''

Aranur frowned. ''Then why,'' he asked slowly, ''have none of them but one sent word back to you?'' His voice was clear above the murmurs, and the group fell silent.

Moira met his eyes steadily. ''What courier would risk death to tell us that our friends were finally safe? Had your own messenger not used the wolf to give me the map, he would have been dead himself. As it was, the raiders knew someone had been there—they searched the forest for two days afterwards. They gave up just before we made our break.''

His expression was grim. ''Yet you are asking Dion to run

the border anyway, knowing that the raiders will be watching for just such a move."

The healer was safe enough, Moira thought wearily, her frail energy drained by this argument—an argument that had little point. After all, the wolfwalker was protected by the moons. Dion's words might protest, but her violet eyes gave her away. She was a moonwarrior, and the moons took care of their own.

Rafe, one of the other scouts, gave Aranur a sideways look. "Dion would not be going in alone, Aranur. You could trust her with me." He nudged Dion in the ribs, and, in spite of her bruises, she grinned at Aranur's expression. As with most couples, it was a private matter that they were Promised, but the other scout had seen the gemstone in Aranur's chest during a sparring match, and, watching the two, realized who it was that had captured Aranur's heart. He had congratulated the weapons master long ago. He also never lost a chance to tease the tall man about it.

Aranur raised his eyebrows. "I can trust her with you, Rafe, but I would not tempt the moons the other way around. Whether you run with her or not," he said, grinning to reduce the threat in his words, "keep your hands to yourself."

Dion rolled her eyes. "Boys," she said sarcastically, "behave."

"Dion," Aranur responded sternly, "why do you have to go at all? Rafe is a good enough scout to go alone."

Moira shook her head. "Rafe is no wolfwalker. Dion can speak to the wolves. She can keep Rafe and herself unseen better than Rafe alone."

Sobovi ran his hand through his once-black hair, ruffling it in the morning breeze. After a sleepless night trying to keep from tossing and bumping his swollen ankle, he was irritable, and it was difficult to keep his voice from snapping. "There is no argument that we need to know the layout on the other side of the river," he said finally. "Dion and Rafe will be in less danger together than Rafe or any other scout we could send alone. I would go, but—" He gestured at his ankle. "—it will be a while before I can hike at any useful speed."

Aranur glanced at him. "Then why not wait till you are better? What harm can come from waiting at least a ninan, like Dion says?''

''Raiders won't be looking for us to start in so soon—'' The voices began arguing.

''. . . can't wait. Everyone will be dead by the time we scout—''

''. . . Dion runs like a wolf. She would be safe enough.''

Finally, Moira stepped forward. Gaunt though she was, with her tall figure and calm voice she was imposing, and the others fell silent. ''In a ninan, more of my people will die,'' she said to him. ''They will be punished for our escape. They helped us; they pushed as hard as we did to get these children out of Bilocctar. Right now, they will be praying that we send help back to them in time to save them from the wrath of the raiders.''

Aranur met her gaze steadily. They stood eye to eye, and he felt a strange chill in his heart at the expression in the tall woman's eyes. Where Dion's violet eyes seemed to flash and darken and ice over with emotion, Moira's eyes were flat. As if the surface of her gaze was as much a mask as the blankness of her face. As if she had built a wall across her sight to keep her heart from being known.

It was Dion who broke the silence. ''Moira, I'm sorry, but I need a ninan, at least, before I am ready to run trail on your side of the Phye.''

Sobovi agreed. ''And I also. We both need time to heal, to rest.''

''But you are wolfwalkers,'' one of the other rescued elders protested. ''You should heal faster than that.''

Aranur rounded on the speaker angrily. ''Sobovi has a sprained ankle and is so thin from running the Slot that I can almost see through him. Dion has a concussion; gashes in her back, her arms, and her legs. She is bruised up one side and down the other. Her feet are blistered raw in more than three places. Less than a ninan to heal, and you would send either of them out with no endurance to return. Do you even understand what you are asking of them? Do you want to take the burden of their deaths to the moons when you yourself go?''

The speaker looked down guiltily.

''There are other scouts that can be sent,'' Sobovi said gently.

''No.'' Moira tore her gaze from Aranur's and shook her head violently. "If you cannot speak to the wolves, you will be hunted blindly."

"We must get word to the rest of our people." One of the other refugee elders stood forward. "Your crossing is almost ready. If one of the wolfwalkers ran with this scout, you could cross the river, make your way to our village, send word in through the Gray Ones, then return without the raiders any the wiser. You do not have to court danger by scouting each path. With the wolves telling you what to avoid, you can run fast enough to stay far from the raiders' blades."

Both wolfwalkers started to speak, but Aranur raised his hand for attention. "So soon after Moira's group escaped, the raiders will be wary—and doubly cautious. Anyone who runs there now runs straight into a lepa's den. And, as the ancients said, you cannot court a lepa without catching some of its claws."

Sobovi glanced around the group. "That is the real issue, then, isn't it? That we do not know if even I, a wolfwalker, can run trail safely over there? If Dion, a wolfwalker twice as young as I, has the endurance to survive, evade, and return from the raider's camps? To send Dion or I without knowing more," he added soberly, "is to risk our deaths or the capture of our wolves as surely as we know the raiders wait for us."

One of the Ariyen women scowled, gesturing at the three scouts. "But how are we going to find out if someone does not cross the Phye to scout?"

"Give us a ninan," Sobovi insisted. "A ninan to heal, to rest. Then we will go, and gladly."

Rafe nodded, his scraggling brown braid squiggling like a snake across his back. "If we wait a ninan, Dion will be able to run trail to the Slot and back twice. And with her beside me, we would be protected by the wolves. They could not hunt her without her knowing it."

Sobovi looked at him irritably. Did no one understand what being a wolfwalker was about?

Dion motioned sharply at the scout. "No," she protested, "that is not true."

"It is not that simple," added Sobovi.

"I can hear the wolves only through Gray Hishn," Dion said. "If the pack is not talking among themselves, there is no way for me to know what the other wolves are doing."

Aranur turned, surprised. Even he had thought she and Sobovi heard all the wolves all the time.

Sobovi sighed. "We cannot know who hunts us if the wolves don't sing. After they cut me off days ago, I could not even hear the packsong on the west bank. Were I still on that side of the river, they could have been within meters of me, and I would not have known it till I saw them with my own eyes."

Dion turned to him, picking up on his words. "They cut you off? Me, also. They rejected me as if I were a worlag sniffing near their den."

Sobovi regarded Dion thoughtfully. "The song—it changed yesterday—just after noon. That was you, then?"

"I think so. It was just after we got the last of these people off the rim and under the falls. Hishn sang to them that the refugees were safe. The tones—they were not so bitter then, though they still were strange . . ." Her voice trailed off.

"Yes." Sobovi's eyes became unfocused, and he listened to his wolf in the distance for a moment. When he focused again, he turned back to the group. "Like me, Gray Yoshi, my wolf," he added, "was cut off from the packsong until their hunt changed. After that, we could listen again."

Aranur frowned heavily. "Why would the wolves cut you off in the first place? Don't they think of you as part of the pack?"

Dion nodded slowly. "Yes, but the Gray Ones over there, they are haunted. Their song is filled with . . . sorrow. Something has changed them, and, because of that, has changed their song. Even through Hishn, I was not one of their number."

"Changed them with sorrow?" Aranur picked up on that quickly. "I thought the Gray Ones did not carry grief in the packsong."

Moira glanced at her, and Dion bit her lip thoughtfully. "I thought so, too. But the packsong over there is odd." She met Moira's gaze. "Isn't it?" she asked softly.

The group turned, glancing as one at the gaunt woman.

Moira sighed softly. "The Gray Ones run with the raiders. If that is not enough to bring sorrow to their song, I do not know what is."

Aranur gestured grimly. "What we are discussing here needs

to be brought up before the council. The Gray Ones tracked you, yes, we believe that was so. But that they run with the raiders? That is not a charge lightly made.''

Jered, the old elder, shook his head. ''I am loath to say it, Aranur, but the wolves in our county do run with the raiders.''

''It is true.'' Moira spread her hands. ''They were trapped with their wolfwalkers, and now the wolfwalkers, to save their lives, direct the Gray Ones as minions of the raiders.''

Aranur gestured sharply, cutting off the discussion. ''Dion, you were already riding to the Lloroi's town this morning, but Sobovi, you, too, must go to speak of this to the Lloroi.''

Dion looked at him in surprise. ''That will not leave anyone here who can speak to the wolves.''

Aranur shrugged. ''The council will need to question both of you. There are more wolves here than ever before—enough so that three, maybe more, of our people bonded with the Gray Ones in the past three months alone. You know that. Whatever is happening with the wolves—the grief you sense across the river . . .'' He shook his head. ''You must both be there to help explain these things. Perhaps you could ask some of the wolves to come, too.''

The scout called Rafe glanced at Dion. ''You think they would show up at a council—especially with so many people there?''

''I don't know. But there are so many now in Ariye . . .'' Dion's voice trailed off. ''They have been . . . coming,'' she said slowly, finding the word she was looking for, ''for a year already.''

Moira looked at her, surprise showing even on her masklike face. ''Coming—to Ariye? What do you mean?''

''Just that.'' Dion motioned at the forest. ''You spoke of the last year in your county—a year under the reign of the raiders. Well, the Gray Ones were under that reign, too. For a year, they have been leaving Bilocctar, crossing into Ariye and moving north, east, west, all away from your—the county of Bilocctar. We—Sobovi and I—thought it was in response to the aftermath of your war, that the game had been driven away by all the people hunting, by the increase of worlags. But now . . .''

''Now, we are not so sure,'' the other wolfwalker finished. He ran his hand through his gray-speckled hair. ''Hishn, Yoshi—

our wolves have been hearing a call in the packsong. And the wolves are calling us to follow, or are leaving us behind.''

Moira looked startled. ''They cannot leave. They are bonded with you.''

The other elder agreed vehemently. ''Where would they go? What would you do without them?''

Sobovi shrugged. ''I don't know.''

''But they are massing in Ariye,'' Dion added, ''and moving north.''

''What we heard is faint,'' Sobovi said. ''But it is growing louder.''

Dion nodded. ''The Gray Ones . . .'' She shook her head. ''There is bitterness there. Betrayal.''

The other wolfwalker nodded at Moira. ''What is happening in Bilocctar—that is the key. We need time, Moira. Time to listen to their words, time to hear their song. We must do that first, before we cross to Bilocctar. Or we might be running into more than our deaths.''

Aranur glanced around the group. ''We ride in twenty minutes, Sobovi.''

The older wolfwalker inclined his head. ''I will be ready.''

Chapter 12

Sing the hunt on the ridges;
Run with the elk on the trails;
Where the wind rises against your fur,
Where the call of the pack is strong,
Run with us!
Hunt with us,
Wolfwalker!

By the time Aranur and Dion reached the outskirts of town, Dion was nodding in the saddle. The pounding gait of the dnu had driven her bruises into one massive ache. Her buttocks had long since forgotten the feel of the saddle beneath them. Where the damp, sweat-warmed sides of the riding beast pressed against her thighs, her muscles were locked in place. The bruise on the bottom of her one foot had molded itself around the stirrup so that she knew it was there only when she shifted and the movement sent a dull pain up through her ankle. It was not until they left the forest trails for the firm smoothness of the rootroads that she felt any relief from the ride.

She smiled wryly to herself—as if it was the most common thing in the world to travel on roads made out of living trees. And to Ariyens, it was. The main rootroads had been grown centuries earlier, when the ancients first came to this world. Wide and flat, the specially bred roots thickened themselves with each strike of hoof or foot or wheel, so that they remained strong and cultured as long as they were used. That was why the rootroads were not used for the forest paths—soft, unevenly spongy trails made sprained ankles a certainty. There was a new rootroad in Ariye, one being grown toward the homesite she and Aranur had chosen the previous fall. They would live with the earth, Aranur told her, not on it. She had smiled when he said it. She had heard those words often enough from her father when she was growing up in Randonnen and learning the ways of the forests. She fingered the gemstone on her chest. It took a year for the plants to stretch and harden enough for use. A Waiting Year. Theirs was almost over. By then, not only the road, but the floors of their house, would be grown and their home ready for its walls.

How strange, she thought, to grow a street or house like a row of herbs in a garden. Before coming to Ariye, she had never seen a rootroad. In her own home, the mountain soil was too thin for the trees—the roads were made of stone. She herself had set the flat-mining worms to smooth the surface of the road being stretched beyond her father's house. She gazed at the yellow-white surface beneath the hooves of the dnu. In her county, the roads were patterns of white and gray and red—ribbons of rock, unsoftened by grass or growth. In her mountains, patches of quartz and sparkles of crystal lit the roads both day and night. Worm-carved columns guarded the entrances to towns, standing in the passes like moonwarriors watching the way of the travelers. Obsidian flows swept down where lava and ash cones mixed, and glinted in the moonlight like the hidden paths to the stars. Land of the shining roads, people called Randonnen. Land of glass and stone. She closed her eyes against a sudden pang of homesickness. The trees that swept overhead were thick with green, but not the stubborn, toughened leaves that fought their way through icy springs and clutched back their sap so greedily in fall. She had wanted so badly to leave her tiny village, to run with the wolves to her own border, to the mountains across the desert, to the ocean she had never seen . . .

But always knowing she would return to her home—to Ramaj Randonnen. Not to Ramaj Ariye. She gazed into the distance, seeing, not the forest before her, but the rocky heights of Randonnen, seeing her father and her brother. Seeing her home. She sighed. The people here were kind. Gamon was like a second father. Even the Lloroi and his mate welcomed her like family so that she did not feel so lonely. And she had Aranur.

But sometimes, when she was alone in the woods with Hishn, she stood on the top of a ridge and reached out her arms as if to touch the mountains of her home. Stretched, as if to feel the Gray Ones whose voices she had known as well as her own. Had they bonded with others since she had been gone? Did they remember her steps on their trails as well as she?

The gray thread between herself and Hishn tautened, and she opened to it, letting the Gray One comfort her. There were wolves in Ariye as there were back home, she reminded herself—even more now that they were crossing the border to flee Bilocctar. So many wolves . . .

The cool shade of the leafy arbors became chill as Dion rode, her face thoughtful. She sensed the wolves in the forest like an echo deep in her mind. The packsong rolled in like a tide: closer, deeper, stronger in its pull. And still they came on to Ariye. Like the refugees, the Gray Ones came like vagrants. Wolves on the canyon rim . . . Bonds of trust, of loyalty, of love. Bonds that would not allow her to step away. Away? She queried the echo, uncertain if it was her subconscious or the wolves that put the thought in her head. Away from what? She could not turn her back on the howl that haunted her nights—the howl that was not Hishn alone. Even if she wanted to, she was locked to Hishn by the gray threads that tightened like cables when they were threatened. She felt them, breathed with them, sang her voice into their packsong. Aranur might have her heart, but, as sure as the nine moons rode the sky, the wolves had her soul. She was as caught in their joys and sorrows as any other member of the pack; so that now, when the grief and anger of the pack across the river rasped its way into the full echo of the mental packsong, Dion reacted as a member of the pack—unable to see beyond it, unable to act; able only to feel and reflect their grief, to sense their anger building deep within herself.

It was not Dion, or Sobovi, or any of the other wolfwalkers, who would be able to see beyond the betrayal of that echo. She knew, not with rancor, but with relief, that it would be Aranur, or one of the strategists, or the Lloroi himself, who would see beyond, think through that echo. That there was someone to analyze, not just to feel, the Gray Ones gave her hope. Aranur would find the way to help the wolves. He must.

"Thinking?" a voice asked softly, and she glanced up to see him.

She nodded slowly.

"About the wolves?"

She bit her lip. "Tonight, at the council . . ."

He leaned across and touched her hand. "You must be there," he said, recognizing her hesitation. She had never gotten used to crowds, even the small ones of his town, but tonight would be important—the entire village would be there to hear the news. He met her eyes, smiling slightly as he watched her body sway so gracefully in the saddle. She must be feeling as lousy as if she had a nine-day hangover, but as usual, she neither complained nor fussed. She would not waste time with it. No, instead, she was thinking ahead, ignoring her own discomfort for the sake of the wolves, trying to think of ways to tell him what to say, to describe what she had felt through them. She was not relaxed in large groups, and especially not comfortable speaking in front of them. It never failed to amaze him how this woman, who had such a gift with the words she did speak, was so afraid to use it with more than one person. Give her a broken body, and she could heal it. Give her a sword or staff, and she could wield it. But ask her to speak before a room of elders, and she was as awkward as a boy in puberty. Sometimes, he thought fondly, she preferred trees to people. "It will be short," he reassured her. "News like this always is. Then everyone goes home to talk and argue. We do not have to stay beyond that."

She nodded reluctantly. "It's just that—"

"What?"

She hesitated. "I keep thinking," she said finally, "that the problem with the wolves is greater than I can see. I go round and round and I cannot think anything new, but I still worry at it, like a dog on a bone."

"You mean what you hear across the river?"

She nodded. "They call me as if they think I can help, but it's as if I am . . . caught."

Aranur frowned. "By what?"

She looked forward, out at the forest, her eyes unfocused as she slipped back into the echoes that rolled across her brain through Hishn's link to the wolves on the other side of the canyon; their song, caught, held tight by their own bonds. Their grief reached out, changing the howl so that it hung on a precipice of pain. "Caught," she whispered slowly, "in threads of gray." She looked at him then. "I cannot see clearly, cannot separate my reason from their howls."

"Dion," he said slowly, "don't get so caught up in the bond that you forget what we have to do."

"But that is just it," she protested. "I know what you and I want to do; I don't know what it is I *should* do. I hear the wolves, I sense them. They are part of me, and they are hurting, and I do nothing."

He shook his head. "You cannot decide, alone, how to help them. It is not your job to do so—nor your obligation." He stopped her automatic protest. "What *is* your obligation is helping the council understand what is going on so that the resources of our county can be used to help."

"But I do not even know what is needed," she burst out. "I cannot reach the wolves myself—not those on the other side of the river. Sobovi has had no more luck than I. And their pain is growing, Aranur."

"One ninan, Dion, that is all we need."

"Nine days? How much more pain will they suffer in that time?"

"Have we a choice? No, we do not," he stated, answering his own question. "You are not ready to run trail again, and neither is Sobovi. The only other wolfwalkers that have bonded this year are neither scouts nor fighters—they could not do this even if they wanted to. Give yourself a ninan to heal. Give us a ninan to plan."

"What if one of the wolves dies? What if they have already died for the raiders?"

"You sound like Moira talking about her people," he returned wryly.

She gave him a strange look. "The Gray Ones are as much my people as the Randonnens of my own county."

He regarded her for a long moment. "Yes," he acknowledged. "But what would you do for them? How do you want us to proceed?"

She shrugged helplessly. ''I know you are right, Aranur; I just feel that we have to do something—anything—now.''

''Something—anything—could get us killed,'' he said shortly. ''It could also do more harm to the wolves than good. We need to think about this, Dion. And you need time to rest before you can act.''

She bit her lip. ''Perhaps not . . .'' Her violet eyes grew dark with her frown.

Aranur watched her through narrowed eyes. ''What is it?''

''Sobovi and I are in town tonight, but what about the other wolfwalkers?'' she asked.

''One lives in the town; the other two live north and east of here—too far to travel in time to the meeting at such short notice.''

She chewed thoughtfully at her lower lip. ''What if . . .''

''Yes?'' he prompted.

''What if we Called the wolves to us?''

''Hishn and Gray Yoshi? You said you could not find your answers through them.''

She shook her head. ''I don't mean just those two. I meant, Call the pack.''

Puzzlement etched his features. ''But why? Hishn runs with a pack, and you said just yesterday that a few more wolves did not make a difference in the lack of an answer. What will change just because they come to the town?''

Dion licked her lips hesitantly. ''I do not mean call just one pack, Aranur. I mean, Call all the packs. Call them as the ancients did, and read their images as if it were plain as a painting.''

''Call them to council?'' Aranur was startled.

She nodded. ''When there are so many in one place, their images are stronger, and we could read their memories as if they were our own.''

Aranur shook his head. ''A Call has not been made for hundreds of years. No one knows how.''

''Eight hundred years,'' she agreed. ''But, Aranur, it was never a matter of not knowing how. Moonworms, there is little enough to it.'' She almost laughed at his expression. ''All it takes to Call the wolves,'' she explained, ''is a strong voice, a strong identity to hold against the weight of their senses. It has not been done because there was no need. The wolves have their freedom as they always did; nothing threatened them that they needed our help." She sobered. "Until now."

But Aranur shook his head. "Dion, a Calling such as this—you are talking about the weight of all the wolves in the county. The energy of all of them—focused in Ariye, focused in one county—what will it do to you? To Sobovi? To the other wolfwalkers? You go deep in the wolves when there are only ten or twelve of them. What would you do if there were more?"

"I was not myself then. I was weak, tired. I will be rested and strong when we call them."

"I don't like it," he said flatly.

She gave him a helpless look. "How else can we reach them? Close as I am to Hishn, I could not get her to understand what I asked about when I questioned her at the rim. But if we Called the wolves, brought them to the council, asked them to speak for themselves . . ."

Aranur glanced at the forest, wondering if there were wolves even now listening to them talk. "You think they would come?"

"I don't know."

They fell silent, the impassive expression on Aranur's face hiding a deep worry that, the more he thought about, began to gnaw more hungrily at his peace of mind.

In Bilocctar, when the winter ice still stretched its fingers between the roots and weeds . . .

When they found the woman, the resistance fighter called Usu threw up at the sight. She stood in the clearing with a head in her hands. She stared down at it while its body lay at her feet, limp arms making a circle in which she stood as if bound. Her front was covered in blood. Her face was disfigured—her left cheek swollen out as far as her nose, and the one eye unseen in the folds of flesh. The siker barbs strewn on the ground explained what had happened. If she was lucky, he told himself objectively, trying not to heave again, she would keep her eye. She was breathing strangely. It was not until he dismounted and looked into her eyes that he realized she was screaming. They tried to soothe her, but she cringed and breathed her noiseless screams until everyone but Blein left the clearing. Blein untied the woman's hands from the hair on the head and laid the . . .

thing beside its body. The woman did not step away, just stood like a doll, staring at the two pieces of the man and screaming silently as if it were her mind, not her voice, that was gone.

It took two hours for Blein to wash away enough blood to find her wounds and treat her. By the time Usu and the others came back, the woman was no longer cringing. She looked at them dully, as if she did not really see them, and turned and walked and sat obediently, ignoring the pain that must have racked her body. She did not even wince at the crude stitches that Blein used to close her wounds. They had no healers to fix what was wrong—Blein had barely been apprenticed to the healers when she had been bundled from her home and sent to Usu for safety. Blein was young for what she did, but she had seen enough in the seven months she had been running with Usu to know how to treat a gash. This woman, though . . . Blein watched her with worry. Blein had seen that look before. The shock was on this woman deeply. She took the food they gave her, but did not eat until they put it in her mouth. She did not drink until they held the bota bags to her lips. The group Usu led was the resistance—they did not dare bring this woman close to a town to get better help. Neither would she be able to go by herself. If they left her, she would simply stand in the trail until some predator discovered her. Which might be the best thing they could do for her, Usu thought bitterly as he watched young Blein at work. Raiders had done this to the woman—there were no others in this county who knew such barbarity. But to bind two mates together and then kill one was a monstrosity he would have thought beyond even them. He cursed silently, motioning for one of the men to help him drag the decapitated body to the brush. One of the women followed with the head.

Usu came back to stand in front of the silent, battered woman. "Come," he told her gently, nodding at the dnu they had brought forward and offering his hand to help her mount. She obeyed unresistingly. Her filthy clothes had been traded for some like his own, but where his men and women stood straight and wary, this woman was stooped and blank. His people looked like the fighters they were. This woman looked like a beggar.

"We are taking her with us?" Blein's question was more of a statement.

"We cannot leave her here."

Blein nodded. "What about . . ." Her words trailed off. The woman they had found had no voice left. Even when she saw what Usu's group was up to, she could not scream to give them away.

Usu touched her gently on the shoulder. "She would not warn them even if she could."

They mounted and rode forward, Usu far ahead of the others, his eyes watchful and wary beneath the trees. It took them two hours and three rainstorms to reach their destination, and when they did, they dismounted carefully, leading their dnu far back into the brush and covering their traces with moss pulled from underneath the ferns far back from the trail. There were small gullies all along here, and the riding beasts were led to one of these. They were too precious to risk the raiders' warbolts.

"Hei-chu-chu, hei-chu," one of the watchers called in the cry of the chunko bird. The cry was passed down the road, and on all sides, dark figures bellied down or crouched in the brush, their bows taut and their arrows steady between their fingers.

Closer rode the raiders. Eight, then ten of them in view. Usu was tense. This was a larger group than he had expected. Wait, he told his people silently. Wait . . . He could smell the dnu, hear the creak of the saddles, the soft slapping of the reins on the dnus' neck as they stretched their heads toward the fresh greens on the side of the road. Wait . . .

Now! The lepa cry startled the raiders, but the warbolts were already flying. The two raiders across from Usu toppled from their dnu. The one ahead of those two crumpled over his saddle but stayed mounted, his dnu panicking and racing ahead. A woman screamed. Someone fell and was kicked by his own dnu as he writhed from the arrow sticking in his kidney.

Usu ran out of the brush, his sword in hand. He stabbed the raider who was crawling to flee into the forest, cutting through his kidney and wrenching his blade free again. The raider's dnu stomped, shying its middle legs away from its rider's body. Usu dodged its nervous kick, grabbing the reins and running it forward, away from the blood, where he could calm it. Behind him, others did the same. It was short, fast, and the only noises were the grunts and screams of dying men. Usu looped the dnu's reins to a tree and looked back.

"By the moons . . ." He stared. Moving among the writhing bodies like a sleepwalker, was the woman they had rescued. She had a knife in her hands. A raider weakly raised an arrow-pierced arm to cut at her legs with his sword, but one of Usu's men sliced his own blade across the raider's back. The woman did not notice. Instead, she knelt beside the still-writhing body of another raider and, before Usu could shout, slit the man's throat with two quick strokes.

She looked up, stood, and moved on to the next raider, and Usu began to run. Her hands dripped red, and her tunic was wet where the raider's blood had spurted. She was oblivious to the fighting. Another raider was down, and the knife was slicing across the throat; and Usu dodged the body that still kicked the earth in its throes. She moved on. A dnu, stampeding past, shouldered her aside and knocked her to her knees. She did not rise, but crawled to the next raider, who, his spine severed and his arms paralyzed, watched her with rising horror. She took his hair in her hands and stared at it for a moment, then cut again.

Usu slowed to a halt. The fighting was over. His people were gathering the dnu, stripping the weapons from the bodies, stealing the boots and jerkins where they were not too torn, and there this woman moved, unaware of her surroundings, going from body to body and slitting throats. Even the raiders already dead did not escape her blade. And when she was done, she stood and walked back through the bodies, stooping and marking each face with the siker barb she pulled from her pocket.

Blein came up beside Usu. He said nothing, and Usu shook his head. "Look at her," he said softly. "She is death."

Blein shuddered. "That siker barb . . ."

He nodded. "She is marked with it herself." He tried to ignore his chill as the woman moved closer, pressing the barb into the dead raiders' cheeks. Three movements, three holes. Usu frowned. There was something about this systematic mutilation . . . He leaned forward, regarding the woman with a new expression. "Blein," he said softly, "we will keep her with us." He nodded, growing more certain with every second.

The younger woman looked at him in surprise. "Is that wise? We know nothing about her."

"She hates raiders." He gestured with his chin. "And what

she does here will send a message to them. We have used their own tactics against them in the battles; now we use their terror. That woman, for us, will be a symbol—a figure that will strike fear back in the hearts of the raiders themselves.''

Blein stared at her, watching the woman puncture another cheek. ''And her name?'' she asked harshly. ''What will we call her?''

''She is fragile, like a flower,'' he said softly. ''She is venomous as a snake. We will call her after what she does. We will name her . . . the Siker.''

When Aranur and the others reached the center of town, the sky was still overcast, the sun a pale shadow of what it would become in summer. The afternoon shadows were long, and evening had already begun to chill the air around them. When they swung down, Dion's legs refused to work for a moment, and she clung to the saddle, waiting for the circulation to return. She grimaced. With circulation came the ache of muscles too long in one position. She snagged her gear from the back of the saddle, letting it slide into her hands as the stablegirl took the reins and led the mount away. She glanced wearily toward the council circle.

''Dinner first,'' Aranur said from behind. ''The meeting starts at the second moonrise.''

Tomi straggled after Dion, his blanket roll awkwardly in his arms, and Dion glanced back, taking pity on him. ''Tomi, you look worse than I do. You are asleep on your feet.'' She started to help him, but Aranur checked her, taking the boy's gear so that he could stumble after them without losing anything in the twilight.

Food—hot food and warm drinks. Dion's mouth watered at the smells coming from the home toward which they made their way. Ahead of them, Aranur's uncle had already entered, greeting his boarders and telling them that they would have another guest for the meal, albeit a young one.

The meal was short. Gamon followed his nose to the kitchen, where he found plates for himself and the boy. It took only a minute to fill them with slabs of roast pig and the crusty, black-edged roots that made the boy's mouth water. Tomi burned his fingers, then his tongue, on the roots. ''It will be here when it cools,'' Gamon said gently, seeing Tomi's eyes water with the burn. The boy stiffened and dropped his hands from the plate. Gamon frowned at him, but said nothing more.

Dion did not sit while she ate, her buttocks still feeling warped by the saddle, and her legs stiff. She stood, pacing back and forth with her plate in her hands, until Aranur put his arms around her and drew her onto his lap. ''Relax,'' he whispered in her ear. ''You make me tired just watching you.''

She made a face at him. ''Your thighs are hard as my saddle. I can hardly relax on your lap when my behind feels like it has been dented by that dnu.''

''If you want tougher buttocks, do more riding and less running.'' He grinned at her indignation. ''Besides, if you scouted from the back of a dnu, you would cover the same ground in twice the time. We could see each other every day instead of every other.''

She leaned across him and set her plate on the table. ''Fat chance of that,'' she retorted, struggling to free herself. ''If I rode a dnu on the trails, you would just have me cover twice as much ground.''

His gray eyes crinkled as he shrugged elaborately. ''Would you have me let you grow lazy? I would never survive the ribbing from the other scouts. A weapons master of my stature cannot be giving special privileges to a lowly scout like yourself—'' He broke off with a laugh as she shoved hard against him and scrambled to her feet. She put her hands on her hips.

''Lowly scout?'' She glared at him.

''Did I say lowly? I meant lovely,'' he returned with a grin.

She raised her eyebrows.

''Truly. Lovely. You are.''

Dion would have retorted, but there was a knock on the outer door. They sobered abruptly as a woman named herself politely, then poked her head inside and called them to council. A few minutes later, wrapped in her cloak and settling her healer's band firmly on her brow, Dion walked out between Aranur and Gamon. Tomi trailed their shadows without a word.

The council circle was an outdoor amphitheater. It sat in the center of town, worm-carved out of bedrock so that it dipped deeply below the surface of the earth. Copying the design of the ancient domes, gas vents from the mountains had been channeled beneath the carved tiers so that the stone seats were hot and the circle radiated warmth. In the summer, the channels were closed. Since this was spring, and a wet chill was in the air, the channels had been left open. The rain that had fallen earlier had not lingered on the seats, but dried with the mountain's heat as if it were summer. Had it still been raining, they would have met in the covered theater that was worm-carved out of one side of the cliff that bordered the town on the northwest side.

There was already a crowd in the amphitheater when they arrived. Looking down, Dion saw that the Lloroi was seated with the other elders, and that the refugees were seated near them. Except for the elders, the people took whichever seats they preferred, looking for spots near friends or family. It did not matter where they sat; the acoustics were perfect. One could hear a child's whisper from one end to the other, and a dropped coin was a sharp sound that could not be ignored.

The crowd gathered and settled, shifting as children clambered and fidgeted to be near their mothers or fathers or friends. Parents looked worriedly for their young ones while the small, quick bodies flashed in and out of sight in the bobbing mass of taller heads and shoulders. While they settled, the elders spoke to people in greeting, waving at some, gesturing for others to join them for a short discussion. Dion and Aranur hung back, but the Lloroi caught sight of them and motioned for them to come down to the center. Aranur shrugged at Dion, then made his way down the stairs. Reluctantly, Dion followed. Tomi trailed doggedly after, his thin hand gripping the edge of her cloak when the mass of people shifted thickly around them. The Lloroi, who regarded them as he spoke to the elder beside him, almost smiled at the wariness Dion projected. Her steps were lighter even than Aranur's, and her movements as soft in the shadows as if she were a wolf herself. Where others climbed the stairs, she glided; where his people sat, she faded into the stone. But the moons were rising, and the people waiting. With an imperceptible sigh, the Lloroi stood. Council had begun.

The elder who had lived longest rose. "We, of Ariye," she began, asking the question formally of the Lloroi, "why are we here?"

The Lloroi inclined his head at her, but looked around the amphitheater slowly before he answered with his own ritual words. He was a tall man, very like Aranur in stature. His eyes were old and gray, like his hair, and his face was lined with the heaviness of leadership. There was about him an air of thoughtfulness, of duty, that seemed to give his body more weight than it physically carried. Dion, knowing that she would add to the weight of his worries, bit her lip until she caught a concerned glance from the Lloroi's mate. Dion's face softened, and the Lloroi's wife nodded with a reassuring smile.

Before them, the Lloroi let his gaze return across the tiers until each man felt he had been acknowledged, each woman greeted, each child noticed and weighed. "We, of Ariye," he said quietly, "come forth beneath these moons to hear the words which guide our wisdom."

The oldest female elder nodded her head regally. "Guide this discussion, then, Lloroi, and may the moons weigh our decisions and find them just." She sat down gingerly, easing her bones to the cushion on the tier behind her.

The Lloroi remained standing while the silence grew expectant. "There is news," he said shortly. "News come to us from those on the rim. Word that can bring with it both hope and pain. Gamon"—he turned to his brother—"led the group working at the Devil's Knee. He will describe what he is doing and what he knows now of the border."

Gamon stood and stepped out a few meters so that he could turn and face the tiers. "You all know of the project at the Devil's Knee—that of building a bridge beneath the falls to bring people across from the county of Bilocctar." There were encouraging nods from around the theater. "We are not yet finished, but our work is on schedule. That was fine because there were to be no refugees until tomorrow. But the moons rise when they wish, not when we will it. So there were refugees on the border yesterday." There was a concerned murmur, and he nodded. Most of the people here had seen the strangers, and the news of the crossing had gone round the town quickly. "Even though the crossing was not ready, we had no choice but to use it. So Healer Dione"—he nodded toward Dion—"went through the falls and led them back to the crossing. She and Aranur got them through the Devil's Knee. Mjau," he went on, indicating the archer seated to his left, "led them to safety in the meadows, which was where we found them and brought them back to camp." He glanced at Moira, who was seated near the Ariyen elders. "Of the eighteen who started out, only four elders and seven children made it to Ariye."

At the mention of the children, Dion glanced down at Tomi. He sat so still that except for his eyes—which darted from one face to the next—he could have been a statue. She slid her arm around him. He stiffened against her touch, but she ignored it, letting the light weight of her arm relax him slowly.

"Eleven out of eighteen." Gamon ran a gnarled hand through his short-cropped hair. "The number of raiders on our border is growing. That alone is going to make it more difficult to get others out of Bilocctar."

An elder man stood. "You say the number of raiders is growing, but where are they staying? There are no towns to the north in Bilocctar. And we have had reports only of temporary camps from the Sky Bridge to the Slot."

Gamon nodded. "That was true even four ninans ago, but things have been changing quickly. The wolfwalker Sobovi," he said, with a nod at the man, "who was scouting up north, was the runner who crossed into Bilocctar to get word of the Devil's Knee to Moira and her people. Sobovi will explain what he saw."

The gray-haired wolfwalker stood up. The contrast between the two men and the Lloroi made Dion smile faintly. Sobovi looked like a thin copy of Gamon, who himself looked like a lean copy of the Lloroi. It was as if each person who spoke got smaller in the moonlight.

Sobovi nodded his greeting silently to the elders as he said, "I was scouting with Ervia and Breen"—he indicated the other two scouts—"when I got word of the need for a runner." The other two had returned to the town one and two days earlier, reporting in shifts at the end of their scouting assignment, as was their habit. Their break would last a ninan, and then the three would return to the Slot, relieving the other team who watched the border while they rested.

"I crossed into Bilocctar at the Slot," he continued. "As I made my way down toward the camp where these people"—he tipped his head toward the refugees—"waited for word, I watched the raiders' movements as closely as I dared, but my visit there was discovered, and my path back to the Slot a hurried one." People nodded with concern, appreciating his understated danger. "It was closer than I expected," he admitted at the Lloroi's raised eyebrow—a hurried hike was not what had been described when the haggard, exhausted, and injured Sobovi had been picked up by Gamon's people. Sobovi shrugged. "The raiders are moving much of their gear north. I could not use the roads to return below the Slot—I took the cliff trail instead." He turned and spoke directly to the elders then. "You can't see it from the cliff trail or the top of the Slot, but the camp they set up is far beyond temporary. It looks to be turning into a permanent base. They are planting roottrees all along the trails, and placing more in the clearings. Hells, they could be building a town. Within a year . . ." He let his voice trail off. Within a year, the rootroads would be firm. The raiders could have their jumping-off place to Ariye. In the spring, the raiders could flood into Ariye with the force of the Phye, massing comfortably in their barracks while the Ariyens slogged through mud to meet them.

At Sobovi's words, the assembly's shocked murmur rose, but the Lloroi listened impassively. Gamon, sitting beside him, glanced at his face and wondered how his younger brother could show such calmness to the town. He knew that when the Lloroi returned home, he would pace all night, thinking over the options, calling for Gamon at three or four in the morning when he needed to talk. The night hid the Lloroi's worry from most of the people, but to Gamon, it was a palpable thing, and the older man regarded his brother with concern. The Lloroi's face was too long, the lines on it deeper than Gamon's, and the forced relaxation a sign of stress. He had a right to be worried, but then, Gamon admitted, so did they all. If the raiders moved north to the Slot, they could cross into the one flat corner of Ariye with impunity. Once in the county, they could not be stopped even by the Black Ravines. The raiders would control the north corner from Dog Pocket to the Slot, forcing the Ariyens—if they wanted to flank the raiders—to cross into Bilocctar on the other side of the Slot, days away from the fighting they would have to do. And what if the raiders moved onto the border now? What would stop them? There were only three scouts north; it had not seemed necessary to assign more. But now he would have to persuade this council to station even more men and women where the cold winter weather still ate at the ground, and where the place of the ancients was like a predator, lurking in the earth, humming its threat to any who ventured close. It was not so much the risk of plague that concerned him—Dion had been to the Slot three times, and she reassured him after each journey that the ancient disease no longer clung to the place. Rather, it was the difficulty of supporting a base in spite of the awe and fear that such a looming place of the ancients inspired. For the Slot was not a picturesque peak. It squatted over the Black Ravines like a badgerbear, never catching the sunset colors, remaining dark where other peaks, farther east, burst into flame at dusk. The place was intimidating—even he would admit that fear gripped him when he saw it. And neither dnu nor other beasts would venture near. Whether the Ariyens used the cliff trail or the Slot road itself to gain height for the lookouts who would watch for the raiders, their travel would have to be on foot.

Gamon tilted his head, regarding the night sky absently as he chewed on a new idea. Did the raiders realize the impact the Slot would have—on them and on their dnu? Their new root-roads would lead them to the Slot, but not beyond it. The cliff trail was simply a rocky ledge that eased along the sheer wall of the mountain above Dog Pocket; the Slot trail ran up and over the flattened mountain, but it twisted around in the broken rock of the mountaintop like a fish in one's hand. No one would be planting roottrees on the Slot—nothing taller than a man's waist grew there; the soil was thin, and the winds stripped away anything that tried to gain a foothold. The strange magnetics of the place prevented anyone from taking steel tools there. Those who rode the Slot Trail found their swords and knives glued to each other, the studs of their jerkins folding the cloth together, and even the cooking gear in their packs smashing anything stored between pots and pans suddenly drawn to each other. The only creatures that lived on the cliffs were the predator lepa and the rock rodents.

The only real road in the north was an old one, and it led all the way around the Slot, far away enough that it saw barely a dozen people a year. No, if the raiders wanted to build a road into Ariye, they would do it at Dog Pocket, the short plains near the headwaters of the Phye. If Ariye was not wary, the raiders could take the Black Ravines quickly, and once dug in, they would not be ousted from the rocky gullies with ease. From there, they could sweep down the Ariyen border just as they had surged up the border on the other side of the river. Gamon ran his hand through his silvered hair again. He wondered . . . If the raiders controlled Dog Pocket, perhaps the problem with the dnu could be turned to an advantage. He could set up several camps in the last ravine—Digger's Gully, it was called. That would give the Ariyens a position from which they could repel any raiders who tried to leave the pocket. It would also force the raiders to use the Slot rather than the low trail, and if the raiders tried to take their dnu up the mountain, the beasts would refuse to go. They would be reduced to traveling on foot . . . He tapped his grizzled chin. It would not be easy. Supporting so large a force in the north would tax the villages already sending supplies to the central and southern camps. The central and southern villages would have to support their own camps, and the northern towns, like this one, would redirect their resources solely to the Slot.

He wondered briefly how much of Sobovi's information had come through the wolves, and how much from his own eyes. He knew that the wolfwalkers gathered images from the Gray Ones—Dion had tried to explain it to him, and he had been honored to speak with the wolves himself several times, but still he could only dimly understand what a full conversation between wolf and wolfwalker was like. He glanced at Dion, his gaze softening. Aranur was like a son to him, and Dion like a daughter. Dion, with her dark violet eyes and her odd set of skills, was stubborn enough to stand up to his nephew, and independent enough to keep him on his toes. If Aranur had once thought to control her as he controlled his archers and swordsmen, the young weapons master had been surprised. Dion had a mind of her own. Gamon regarded her fondly. The bond of the wolves was strong, but so was love. When she settled into the house being grown on the ridge, he would see more of both her and Aranur.

". . . perhaps as many as forty people in the camp now, with more arriving each day,'' Sobovi continued as Gamon dragged his attention back to the discussion.

One of the elders raised her hand. ''All raiders?''

''It looked like a mix: soldiers and raiders together. There was tension between them, but even if they hated it, they did work together.''

The elder's face turned thoughtful. ''It would take a strong leader to pull that off.'' She glanced at the tier of scouts, then back at the wolfwalker. ''What did you think of the layout of their camps?''

Sobovi did not hesitate. ''Designed to intimidate.''

The woman raised her eyebrow. ''Hmm. Intimidate us or them?'' She indicated Moira and the other refugees.

''Both, I would say.''

The woman gestured for him to continue, but he shook his head. ''I have seen nothing else of importance. Dion, Rafe, and the others have reports for the central and southern parts of the border.''

Dion stood reluctantly and took her place before the assembly. ''I scout the area from the Devil's Knee to the second camp, ten kilometers below the Sky Bridge,'' she said. The elders nodded, and she continued. ''As long as I have been running that length of trail, the raiders have guarded the Sky Bridge completely. It is useless as a crossing. From what I have seen, they travel the river road between the bridge and the Knee, but not regularly, and not in numbers. If they are moving supplies and people to the north, it is on one of the trade roads that runs through the woods, back from the canyons, not along the Phye.''

''It is so,'' Sobovi agreed. ''They use the river road only when they want to track someone along the rim.''

''Along the Phye itself, there are far more raiders south of the Sky Bridge than north of it,'' she continued. ''Plus, they do not seem to care that their night camps can be seen from Ariye.'' Her voice sounded puzzled, and the Lloroi's eyes sharpened. This he had not heard. He watched Dion narrowly as she chose her words with care. ''It is almost as if,'' she said hesitantly, ''they challenge us to see them, to cross the river to deal with them directly.''

Gamon frowned. If the raiders were more bold to the south, it was probably a ruse to catch Ariye's attention and pull it away from the Slot. Moonworms, but if the first refugee had not himself crossed and made contact with them, the Ariyens would never have sent a scout across the border to the north. The Bilocctar camp could have been a breeding ground for raiders before Ariye even noticed what had happened. His frown deepened suddenly. The escape of the refugees into thin air . . . The raiders must be incensed, but also wary. If they guessed that Ariye knew of their camp . . . Did Dion realize she had intimated that the raiders were toying with the Ariyen scouts? She must, he told himself. She was a careful speaker, astute and thoughtful; she would have thought deeply about the implication before she was willing to put it into words. It was one of the reasons he himself listened more often to the guarded opinions of this healer than he did to some of the elders. The other reason, he reminded himself, was that Dion had seen more of the raiders than most people in his county, and she understood what she had seen. He smiled faintly. She might think she was asked to speak so often before the council only because she held the station of a healer and wolfwalker; she did not realize that she would have the respect of the council whether or not she carried the weight of the silver circlet or the bond of the wolves. Even the Lloroi asked her opinion as if she were an elder herself.

One of those gray-haired people had been thinking along the same lines as Gamon, and now the elder stopped Dion with a question. "How many camps are we talking about?" he asked. "And how large are they on average?"

She shook her head. "Three camps? Five? Depends on the night and the stretch of river you look along. The further south you go, the more there are—sometimes half a dozen in one place. And I, too, have seen some signs of them to the north. As far as numbers at each camp, that is difficult for me to tell."

"But you have the ear of the wolves. Can you not sense their numbers that way?"

A strange expression crossed her face, and Gamon's gaze narrowed as Dion shook her head. "The wolves on the west side of the river have closed their song to me. I cannot read them except as a distant echo, so what I guess now is only what my eyes and ears can tell me." Gamon filed the comment away; he would ask her about it later.

"Numbers at each camp?" Dion continued. "At the Sky

Bridge, perhaps ten, maybe more. South of the bridge, increasing numbers until there are as many as twenty at the camps on the lowest border of my run. Ruskic," she said, motioning toward another woman, "can tell you of the next section of the border."

The next scout rose, and so it went, report after report filling in the descriptions of the county boundary along the river and down to the lower regions of Ariye, where the foothills faded into Wyrenia Valley. Gamon was called back to speak then, giving a summary, which he did grimly. He knew of the movements to the north and, like the Lloroi, understood their implications. There were patterns in the raiders' plans—shifting purposes that confused the eye like a feint being laid out before them. So many raiders in arrogant sight on the lower Phye, while a hidden town was being built up north . . .

The Lloroi glanced at him, noting his thoughtful look. "The north?" he asked in a low voice.

Gamon nodded. "We'll have to send more people up there than three scouts," he murmured.

The Lloroi grunted his agreement softly. "Another camp will be difficult to accept."

"Just one?" Gamon asked. "From what Sobovi says, we might do better to think of three or four."

"Hmm." The Lloroi did not comment, and Gamon sat back, letting his shoulders rest against the stone tier. He did not envy his brother. The task of leading the Ariyens to support another camp—or more than that—to the north was not an easy one. Ariye could bear the weight of the supplies—each family supported the camps as best they could with their skills and goods. But this was spring, and the farms had to be tended, the mining worms retrieved and bred, and the yearly crop of winter wool gathered from the mountain goats and sorted for export. Giving up more men and women to watch the raiders could cripple those activities. He shook his head. The thinned numbers of this council was a constant reminder of the three hundred people already guarding the borders to the south. Another fifty placed north, and the supplies to get them started so that they could begin supporting themselves . . . And then there was the question of who would go. War—which, until the raiders appeared, had been a theory studied only in school—was not as easy to organize as the old tales of the ancients would have it. This conflict with the raiders was draining Ariye like a plague. Gamon, his thoughts grim, stood and said as much, grimacing with the elders at the realization of what it would mean to call more families from the villages to guard the border.

"Gamon," one of the elders said finally, "what would you say are the raiders' strengths?"

"And their weaknesses?" another elder added.

Gamon frowned. "I would rather you heard that from Aranur."

Aranur stood and stepped forward. "I have spoken with the scouts, the wolfwalkers, and with Gamon at length," he began. "What we have agreed is that the greatest strength of the raiders is that they have cowed the people into accepting their presence. Their second greatest strength—" he paused "—is that they have somehow coerced the wolves to run trail for them."

There was a shocked murmur. Heads turned, looking from the two wolfwalkers to the refugees and back. Questions burst out: "Is this true?" and the skeptical, "Not possible," and, "Dion, what do you say about this?"

Dion frowned. "It is true that the Gray Ones run for the raiders. The refugees themselves were hunted by the wolves all the way to the Devil's Knee. But," she said quickly, "I do not think it is by choice."

One of the old women stood. "How could the wolves run and hunt and say they do not do what they want?"

Dion glanced at Gamon, getting his unspoken approval before answering the elder herself. "The packsong of the wolves across the river," she answered, "is not a song that has the love of the hunt in it, but a howl of grief, of frustration—even anger against humans."

"How can this be?" The voices rose in consternation. "What does it mean?"

The Lloroi stood up, demanding quiet. "How is this?" He looked searchingly from Dion, to Sobovi, to the refugee elders. "No wolfwalker can coerce a Gray One. It is love that commands their bonds."

"And if the bonds are in the hands of the raiders?"

It had been Moira who answered him, not Dion, and the Ariyen elder met the woman's eyes with skepticism. "How could the raiders tell the wolfwalkers what to do?'' the Lloroi demanded.

''Yes, how?'' Drawing attention from the tense stare between Moira and the Lloroi, Aranur pulled Dion to him. ''We all know that wolfwalkers are not easy to control.'' There were telltale chuckles at Dion's sudden discomfiture, and a smattering of answering laughter that broke the tension. He sobered, asking, ''So if the raiders control the wolves or the wolfwalkers, how do they do it? Have they bonded with the wolves themselves? Sobovi says it is not possible. Have they captured the wolfwalkers or their wolves? Dion says there is a shame in the song of the wolves that underlies their sorrow, but that she does not know for certain—and does not know if she would even be able to tell—if the bonds of the wolves are in the hands of the raiders.''

''Wolves cannot run with raiders,'' one of the Ariyen elders stated.

Aranur turned to give the man a searching stare. ''Are you sure? Dion sensed more than sorrow in the packsong. There is betrayal there, she says—a breaking of the trust they have in us.''

''We have not dishonored the wolves,'' the elder protested. ''The four new wolfwalkers in our county prove that.''

Dion raised her hands. ''It is not that the Gray Ones break their trust with those of us in Ariye, but that they break their trust of humans in general. Something is happening in Bilocctar—something that affects the Gray Ones deeply. To them, we are simply men and women, as are those across the river. How can a wolf tell the difference between us? Their memories are strong, and are passed from one wolf to the next. What is done in Bilocctar is also done, in their minds, in Ariye.''

The Lloroi regarded her grimly. ''And what is being done to the wolves in Bilocctar?'' he asked quietly.

''I don't know.'' She made a helpless gesture. ''I only know that I cannot reach the wolves over there, and that whatever it is that brings them such grief, it is forcing them to flee to Ariye and the other counties that surround Bilocctar. Look around,'' she said over the growing murmur in the assembly. ''Look to the forests. Watch your pastures in the early dawn. In your generation—in three generations—have you ever seen the Gray Ones come so boldly to hunt the mice in the fields? To run the deer and elk down in your back woods? They are coming through Ariye like a storm, calling all the wolves to withdraw, to go north, to leave us behind."

"But they can't leave us," the elder protested.

"Oh, yes," she returned quietly, her voice ringing in the sudden silence. "They can." She looked around the assembly, meeting the startled gazes of the elders. "The wolves are not bound to us by cords of steel or chains of iron. They are tied to us and we to them by love alone. Betray that love, and they, like winds caught in your hand, are gone." She gestured at the people. "They are doing it now—leaving. You want to stop them—you want to know why they flee? So do I. But I cannot tell by looking into the eyes of only a few gray wolves. This betrayal is not a word or speech to which I can listen. It is couched in images I do not understand, buried already in memories that have been passed from pack to pack into our county."

The Lloroi met her eyes. "Then how will you find out?"

Dion met his gaze reluctantly. "If we want to know why the wolves in Bilocctar hunt the refugees, we must ask them," she said simply.

Realizing that she was asking for the help of the other wolfwalkers, he nodded. "Then do so, Healer Dione."

But she shook her head, surprising him. "All of them," she said more strongly.

The Lloroi frowned, and Aranur, standing beside her, glanced around the council. "What she means, Lloroi," he said steadily, "is that it is time to Call the wolves to council."

There was stunned silence. A murmur rose into a din as people turned to their neighbors, eyes wide, heads shaking, voices both wary and excited. The Lloroi sat impassively, his head tilted back, his eyes on the sky above them. When he finally stood, the amphitheater grew silent.

"By the law of the ancients, we are bound to the wolves by our honor, as they are bound to us by trust." Calm and steady, the rhythm of his words were like a chant, soothing the assembly. "In the centuries through which we have taken this world as our own, we have not broken our honor, nor have they broken their trust. Not even raiders have abused those ancient ties." He looked slowly around the ring, his gaze coming to rest on Sobovi, then Dion. "Now," he said, "there comes a time for thought, a time for decision, a time for action, and a time for judgment. Winds that once were ours alone no longer bide within our boundaries. They blow across the borders and blow back with other scents. Now come to us these people." He nodded at Moira and the other refugee elders who sat with her. "Aid, shelter, homes—these we can give them. Families for their children. Industry for their skills. Does the council agree?"

Voices joined in a single murmur. "Aye."

The pause lengthened like a sigh, but no one dissented. "So be it." He turned to Moira's group. "You are welcome in our midst," he said quietly. "You are welcome as our family. Ride and eat and fight with us, and your children shall be as our own."

A haunted look crossed Moira's face. Her eyes were filled with despair as she saw, not the Lloroi before her, but a tiny, cloak-bundled body in the moonlight. Jered touched her arm. "We join you," she said by rote, "and take your burdens as our own."

The Lloroi inclined his head at one of his own elders. "Gleya, you are charged with this task. You know the vacant homes that are open and in good condition for newcomers. You also know the families who want children. Take what help you need from the stores, and ask for what you cannot find." The woman nodded.

The Lloroi was silent for a long moment, thinking. "With these people," he said finally, "there comes also to us a choice. So far, we have kept the raiders from our borders for almost a year. Like a storm rising and pushing against us, we hold them back, while they settle in Bilocctar like a winter fog. Look well at these people who are now your neighbors." He waited, and the Ariyens glanced from one to another. "Look well," he repeated. "and think of your own mates, your own children. For now comes to us this choice: Do we guard our borders and wait for the raiders to take their time, move against us when they are ready and we are not? Or do we rise to their challenge and take up the fight we have been handed? Know," he said, "that if our choice is the latter, it is not just homes, but hope we can give to our neighbors. Hope, courage, and belief. And what we take from the raiders in payment will be blood—blood and the fear-won power they so boast. But—" He paused, and his voice warned them then. "Realize also that as we take blood, so do we give it back." He looked slowly across the assembly. "When we take the raiders' lives by the blade, we give ours in return. Do we risk this? Will we pay this price to keep Ariye free of their stench?" He looked at the elders. "What is our choice? We can give these raiders blood, but we can also force on them the fury of Ariye. Does the council agree?"

His question rang out, and a thin woman stood slowly. "Were it my children in Bilocctar," she said into the silence, "I could have only one answer. Let it be known that I, Bitlia, agree with this choice."

From beside her, two men nodded and rose together. "Let it be known," one of them said, "that I, Eddon, agree with this choice." And, "Let it be known that I, Gacic, agree . . ."

There were eighteen elders; only six dissented, although they agreed to work with the others. When the vote was finished, the Lloroi nodded. "Gamon, meet with the strategists and come back to us with a plan. Take whomever you need from the other camps if you cannot find those you want here."

Gamon inclined his head reluctantly, accepting the burden. "I will need Loube and Tehena immediately," he said, gesturing at the two strategists. The former, a paunchy man with a rotund belly, had a mind that could worm around any obstacle; the latter, a scrawny woman with a tough, hard face in strange contrast to those near whom she sat, had the bitter cunning of a starved wolf. "I would also like the scouts and weapons masters to stay in town for the next several days during the discussion." He pointed at the left side of the amphitheater. "Gather with me over there, after council, to figure out when you will be called to the discussions." He nodded to the elders, then made his way to the edge of the amphitheater.

The Lloroi waited patiently while the crowd shifted and the weapons masters and scouts followed Gamon to the indicated area. After a few minutes, when the murmuring died down, the Lloroi raised his arms.

"We make choices. We promise justice." He had their attention again as surely as if he had shouted those quiet words. "With justice"—he spread his arms—"comes judgment. The bond of the wolves could be broken. Do we know?" There was silence in answer. "The wolfwalkers hear grief in the song of the wolves. Anger. Pain.'' He paused. ''Who brought these things to the packsong? Do we know?'' He waited. ''The wolves flee Bilocctar. Their packs roam our county in numbers we have not seen for centuries. They are here, calling to us as loud as if they stood in this ring and shouted—calling to us when they have been silent for so long. Why? Do we know?''

When he looked this time around the crowd, it was as if he were gazing into each person's eyes, and each man and woman, each child that stood at her parent's side, each youth that watched in wonder, felt transfixed by that gaze. ''Do we know?'' the Lloroi repeated softly. ''And if we do not, are we not bound to Call the wolves to us, to ask what they need, to give ourselves to them as they gave themselves to the ancients? By the law of blood, the law of love, we are bound to them as they are to us. To us comes this judgment, then: We must Call the wolves to speak. Does the council agree?''

A slender woman rose. ''A Calling has not been done in centuries. How do we know they will come?''

The Lloroi inclined his head toward Dion. ''They are here already, in the shape of the wolfwalkers.''

''Dion and Sobovi are only two. Even with the others to help, there will be no more than six wolfwalkers here. The ancients Called the Gray Ones when they were hundreds strong.''

The Lloroi nodded. ''That is true. The ancients are long gone; the wolves are fewer, and time has dulled all memories. But there is this: Never has a Calling been ignored.'' He glanced slowly around the ring. ''Again I say, we must Call the wolves to speak. Does the council agree?''

There was a second of silence. Then, ''Aye,'' rose the answer.

''So be it.'' The Lloroi nodded. ''Healer Dione, Sobovi,'' he commanded.

Slowly, as if drawn forward, Dion and the other wolfwalker stepped into the moonlit circle. Under seven of the nine moons, it was almost light as day; a few clouds scudded across the sky, yet the light was not dimmed. Sobovi's gray hair was silvered by the moonlight like a halo around his head. Dion's black hair was a glossy piece of night, the silver healer's circlet gleaming like a beam of the moons themselves.

''Call them,'' the Lloroi said. ''Call them here to us. When they come, we will listen." He touched Sobovi formally, on his chest, then Dion. With his eyes shadowed and a strange wistful twist to his lips, he turned and strode from the circle.

Behind him, men and women rose and followed quietly. Questions raised by childish voices were hushed, as if they might jinx what would be done. Then there were only Dion and Sobovi on the moonlit stones to stare at each other and wonder . . .

Aranur waited at the edge of the arena with Tomi. The boy neither fussed nor fidgeted, and Aranur glanced at him before returning his gaze to the arena's floor. A strange child—one with the air of a fighter who had seen too many ghosts follow his blade. Aranur wondered at the age behind his shadowed eyes. In some ways, Tomi reminded him of his uncle, Gamon, his youth a mockery of what he had survived. He glanced at the boy again, seeing the mask of his face in the moonlight. If he had had a son who had suffered thus . . .

Something sparked deep within him, turning his gray eyes to ice. What had Tomi suffered that others did not still endure? Aranur stared at the boy, noting the thin face, the bones pronounced in his cheeks. Had the hunger that ate at this child's guts been assuaged by a few simple meals? Had this boy's nightmares been stilled by two simple nights of safety? What did he dream, this child who had seen and lived with death? For Aranur did not doubt that he survived his family alone—it would not have taken Moira's words to tell him that. Tomi's manner was too silent, too still when a voice was raised, even in greeting; his face a mask that showed no fear, no weakness, though his eyes were bruised and hollow as a dark drum when a hand was raised or a crop tapped lightly against a dnu. It was that which made Aranur burn. The fear in this child begged to be touched, to be reassured that the nightmare would not begin anew; that the raiders would not come; that he would not be left to face his horror again . . .

Tomi turned his head and met Aranur's eyes. The boy regarded him warily, then returned his gaze to the ring. Aranur, his lips tightened, told himself that those who had hounded the childhood from this boy would pay a price that sent them to the moons and back.

Overhead, the seventh moon slipped out from behind a cloud, its crescent casting a glow in the sky near the other six orbs that hid the starlight. As usual, the second moon raced across; the fourth moon was sluggish. The fifth moon was near the treeline, caught in the branches that stretched along the streets of the town.

In the amphitheater below, Dion and the other wolfwalker stood and stared at each other without speaking. A Calling. Aranur could almost hear their silent questions. Did they dare to do it? How many years—centuries—had it been since the last Calling? And how many wolves had answered that summons? There were more Gray Ones in Ariye this year than could be remembered in human records. But how many were there compared to the time of the ancients? Were there enough to bring the depth to the Call that Dion needed?

Once, long ago, he had seen a small Calling: In a dark night filled with ice and snow, a dozen wolves had answered. There had been more wolves there than he had seen in his lifetime. What Dion had told him in the last few months—that there were more than a hundred wolves now in Ariye—made him clench his jaw and narrow his eyes in concern. Such a small Calling he had seen before, and yet it had affected him so strongly that when he strode among the Gray Ones, he had wondered if he stood on four feet or two. It had taken all his strength to resist their pull. He stared down at the two wolfwalkers, so still, so silent in the moonlight. Could he—could the Lloroi himself—judge if there was enough at stake to tell Dion and Sobovi to do this thing? The Lloroi—his uncle, his guardian along with Gamon since he was a boy—since the day his father died; the Lloroi who must weigh and sentence each act of the council—he had looked into Gray Hishn's eyes himself, and the pull of the wolves had not been light upon him, and yet he had told Dion to go ahead and Call the wolves, to summon the Gray Ones to this council. The Lloroi did not guess—did not know, as Aranur did—what the pull of the Gray Ones did to Dion. Aranur had seen with his own eyes how a pack drowned her senses and swept reason from her mind. He had seen her gaze unfocused, her lips pulled back, the snarl deep in her throat; he had seen her hands extended as if they were pointed with the black claws of the wolves, her nostrils flared as if to catch his scent more deeply, her throat rigid as she strained to break that immutably gray hold and found herself lost within their song. He had known since he met her that Dion could speak to Gray Ones other than Hishn. But could she Call them as easily as she said and still remain herself? How strong was her will compared to the weight of the wolves?

He stared at the two figures. They had not moved—had they Called the wolves already? Would the Gray Ones answer? And if the wolves did answer, how many would come? Four or five? One dozen? Two? Aranur did not claim to have the empathy that Dion felt, but he had been caught in the gray song himself. Now, watching the wolfwalkers, he strained his ears for a hint of the gray howl he knew they heard in their heads, his eyes squinting for a glimpse of the dark trails they sought.

Dion saw neither him nor the small boy at his side. Where she stood with Sobovi, she was still as a statue herself, letting the sense of the amphitheater fill her nose and seep into her skin. This council circle was a centering of power. Over centuries, so many people had stood and spoken, argued, cried, and convinced in this place. So much emotion to settle in these stones. She did not have to look to see the moonlight split the terracing. Her eyes, wide, were filled with the afterimage it left, their unfocused gaze letting the gray threads gather in her mind.

She reached out physically, and Sobovi's arms met hers. They braced each other. There was an unspoken question. To stay here, in this place of human history, this arena with its human signature? Or to run, quickly, silently, to the forest, where the shadows slid between the trees and the yellow eyes gleamed in the brush? Dion shivered. There was too much hunger in the woods—once they opened themselves, the forest itself could pull them away, lose them in the Gray Ones' power. No, the Lloroi's words still rang off these stones. They must bring the wolves here. Dion caught the thread of Hishn's sleep and called the wolf gently. Far away, Hishn stirred. The gray thread between them grew taut, then stronger as the creature sensed Dion's need. Before her, Sobovi, and in the distance Gray Yoshi, bound their own senses as strongly.

Wolfwalker . . . Hishn's howl sang in Dion's ears as if the wolf were standing beside her.

Gray One, she returned. *You honor me.*

Their minds stretched into each other, and Dion swayed. Gripping her arms, Sobovi was drawn into his own link. Their heads tilted back. They arched their backs, their fingers clutching each other, flexing muscles that neither had. Their lips pulled back, and they bared their teeth.

Wolfwalker, each wolf howled.

You honor me, the two humans returned. *Come, sing to us, howl with us.*

Run with us, they Called.

Sobovi shifted, his feet urged away from his stance as if he would break into a run. Dion clutched him blindly. *Run with us,* she returned. *Speak to us of your sorrow, of your grief. Bind us with your trust.*

The gray threads thickened as the wolves were brought up against the song of the pack. From across the ridges, wolves stopped, halted their hunt. *Wolfwalkers!* they howled.

Come, Dion shouted among them joyfully. *We run with you. Now run with us.*

The packsong swept in, gathering weight, catching Dion as if she were a leaf before an autumn wind. *Wolfwalker!*

Come!

The pack pulled. Gray senses swelled. Winds swept Dion's hair, and damp earth filled her nose. Fur hugged her body as winter hair loosened, matted, and was scratched away. Her pads toughened as she ran. Ridges swept across her sight. Shadows beckoned. Hunger ached in her belly, and bloodlust clashed with the drowsy warmth of the den. Dens, close and dark. Heat, curled and tender. Belly motion. Cubs against her teats . . .

Dion howled, an inhuman sound. *Come!*

Wolfwalker!

The gray tide shifted. Toward her. Toward their bond. Toward the moonlit circle where she stood. From den to ridge, the summons swept. Wolves roused, stretched, cocked their heads, listened to the silent wind. Voices joined. Packs merged. Across Ariye, the gray threads wove into a solid sheet of song. Deep in the earth, deep in the forest, that howl grew, rising to the wind and carrying across the canyon, east to the desert, north to the mountains, south to the sea.

Howl with the wind, Wolfwalker! We come!

Chapter 13

Calling, howling;
singing, running;
Bringing tension;
Bringing heat;
Bringing the lust of the hunt—
Honoring the ancient bond:
What do you ask for,
Men of Ariye?
What do you want of the wolves?

A day passed, then another. Wolves gathered in the hills, hunting in packs that swelled and grew with the weight of their numbers. A gray tide swept across Ariye, and with it, the Gray Ones' howls filled the air like a thunder on the ridge. Above the town, the pack padded through the forest like a thick shadow. It was not only Dion and Sobovi who felt their presence; a dozen people in the town found themselves drawn to the ridge, hiking the steep trail as if in a dream, searching for the packsong that whispered, then rang, in their heads. A metalsmith apprentice put her tools away when she saw that she wrought only lupine shapes; a thickset man fled his books for the woods. A boy only eight years old started singing a chant that was more a soft howl than a human song. At dawn, the Gray Ones gathered in the fields, ignoring the livestock and hunting out rodents that dodged into burrows not nearly deep enough. Their hunger stretched across the cultured ground and into minds that found themselves snapping and snarling at their families.

Dion could not remain and work in the hospital—she was

swimming in the gray senses. She no longer saw Aranur as human, but as the wolf-spawned image that accompanied his scent, which, through Dion, was passed on to the Gray Ones she had called. Three days passed. Four. Dion found herself vaulting into the saddle of a dnu and racing for the hills when a wolf howled for help against a badgerbear that trapped it against a cliff. A wild ride—not alone—as there were others summoned by that cry—and a brutally short battle against the badgerbear; and then the carcass shredded by the wolves who gathered to share the kill. Snarling, tearing at the hot muscles, gutting the creature and dragging the meat across the ground, they fed, licking away the dirt and leaves that stuck to the bloody mass, while Dion and those caught in their senses fought to keep from digging their own hands into the carcass.

Six days fled beyond the moons. A female wolf, heavy with cubs, curled in a den and birthed, and across Ariyc, people cramped, clutching their bellies and writhing in their sleep. Dreams changed, filling with an intensity that did not come from human perception alone. The fields were haunted with wolves. Day and night, the yellow eyes gleamed in the thick spring grasses, slunk between the growing grains. When the rains came on the seventh day, wolves curled up in barns and tucked themselves under wagons, welcome to what dry comfort they could find. And they haunted those who could feel them. In one home, two brothers slept on the porch with the wolves who would not leave their home. A young mother planted her spring garden while three Gray Ones routed out the rodents who carved their tunnels beneath the bulbs. A talk-painter propped open his doors so that the wolves who watched him design the Lloroi's messages could come and go at ease.

The song of the pack was loud, and the rotting, musty smell of the Gray Ones wrinkled noses while the acrid scent of their piss in the dirt grew with the rain. There was not enough game to support such a tide of predators near the town. On the eighth day, the Lloroi sacrificed his own livestock and spread it among the wolves. On the ninth day, two males tore each other apart, fighting over a female in heat who flirted with both. The packs watched impassively. When it was over, Gamon and Aranur carried the loser to Dion, who closed its gashes and soothed its wounded pride.

That night, as the sun dragged itself behind the western peaks and evening fell, the council gathered. Mingled human and lupine feet made their way to the amphitheater, while voices and snarls were mixed to create a din that ate at Dion's nerves and chewed at her thin control. In the center of the arena, she stood, clustered with a dozen others who felt the pull of the Gray Ones. Hishn leaned against her. Dion tightened her fingers in the creature's shaggy scruff. Hishn was only one of a dozen wolves that paced and snarled deep in their throats as they watched the people collect their seats and the elders find their wary way to the lower tier.

Aranur stood behind Dion, his hands on her shoulders as if to connect her to his world by touch alone. On the second tier, Tomi sat beside Gamon, his small form dwarfed by the lean, elder man.

The Lloroi stepped forward with one of the elders, and they faced each other. "We of Ariye," the elder woman asked, "why are we here?"

A roar answered her. She stood stock-still, frozen in place by the deafening shock of that concerted howl. Around the edge of the amphitheater, gray shadows appeared, their heads thrown back as they raised their voices to the moons. In the center of the arena, Dion and the others screamed their inhuman sounds, caught by the cry.

When the howl died, Dion's body shuddered from the echoes. Her eyes were unfocused, and Aranur felt her tremble beneath his hands. He tightened his grip, trying to close his thoughts to the weight of the senses that swept across from Dion to his own mind.

Dion opened her mouth and shouted across that lingering echo, "I speak for the wolves!" The voices of those clustered with her rose identically, their words a thunder like the howl of the wolves. "Why do you Call us, people of Ariye?"

The woman elder who had asked the formal question stumbled back, feeling behind her for her seat before she trusted her legs to let her down. The Lloroi was left alone, but his voice, when he spoke, rang out over the low murmur of the lupine growl that still clung to the stones. "You honor us, Gray Ones."

"We honor the Calling, as we honor your kind," the wolfwalkers voiced the words of the Gray Ones in a deep chorus.

Around them, above them, the Gray Ones seethed and settled on the outer ring of the arena. "But again, we ask," they voiced, "why do you Call us?"

The Lloroi inclined his head. "There is a burden in your packsong. We feel that weight as if it is our own, but we do not understand it. We ask what we can do to take it from you."

The speakers of the wolves were silent for a moment. Then a snarl rose and became a howl. The sound swelled and beat against the stones of the amphitheater until the people inside swayed and clutched at their ears. But it was not in their ears that they were assaulted. Images burst in their minds, splitting out, fraying into memories of the wolves. Pictures of a wolf dying from an arrow. Hot pain from a lash across a flank. The fury when a wolfwalker, whipped, was beaten again and the wolves, flinging themselves at the walls within which the man was held, could do nothing but howl. The shafted agony, then the death hole of a wolfwalker killed by a sword, leaving a blankness in the packsong. The burning shame of sniffing the ground for the scent of bare and wounded feet . . .

The images rolled, burning into Dion's sight, pressing in on Aranur's mind. Did she howl, too? She was lost in the tide of the memories.

Dion did not know when they faded. She took a breath and choked. Moonworms, what had happened to her throat? It was swollen and sore and so dried out that it stuck to itself, causing her to swallow urgently against its parched tissues. She looked around and saw that the assembly did not seem changed. The people were still sitting in the theater as if made of stone. The ring of yellow eyes on the upper tier burned into her sight. The clump of people and wolves who reeked of damp fur and skin still surrounded her, and Aranur's hands still dug into her shoulders as if they were pitons. Then she realized what was different: the wolves had withdrawn from her mind.

"Hishn," she whispered.

Wolfwalker, the Gray Ones returned soberly.

"You honor me."

She let her gaze cross the crowd. Had they seen what she had? Had they felt the power behind those memories? She reached out to the threads of gray that now only echoed in her mind, but the Gray Ones did not answer. Even Hishn, beside her, was silent. They were waiting.

The Lloroi stood still, his face still rigid with the weight of the senses that had poured through his mind. Around him, people shivered, and gathered their identities back as a cold woman clutches a cloak. It was not until Gamon stood that the silence was broken. The old fighter made his way to face Dion. He looked at her for a long moment, then gazed into the yellow eyes of her wolf. "As the wind blows in both counties," he said softly, "so does blood flow."

Hishn cocked her head at him, her ears out to the side as she listened intently.

"Not your blood; not our blood; not the blood of Ariye alone, but the blood of us all." He raised his head, meeting the yellow gaze of the wolves on the rim. "What is done in Bilocctar is carried across this county like a storm. The spirit of the earth, of the water, of fire and wind, of rock and tree and star—these are bound with us and us with them." He gestured at Hishn, then at Dion. "Your burdens are ours," he said quietly. "We will free you even though we must give our lives to do it."

Hishn growled at him, the sound not threatening, but an acknowledgment of the promise. The growl swept through the crowd, growing again as each wolf picked it up and carried it on. On the rim, the shadowed forms took their snarls with them, fading into the streets and out of town, letting their feet carry them past the outskirts and into the night forest where the moons dared only peek beneath the spring canopy. The Gray Ones in the arena stared at the people in the tiers, until, knowing that none would move, they slunk up the stairs, followed by those with whom they had bonded. With her hand in Hishn's scruff, Dion climbed the stairs in a dream. The weight of the Gray Ones' senses was subdued, and she could almost see the stairs in front of her with her human sight. It was not until she was at the edge of the forest herself that she stopped.

"Dion?" Aranur said softly. He had followed her. His hands rested lightly on her arm, reminding her of her identity. "Dion?" he repeated.

Tomi, haunting his footsteps, gazed at Dion with wary awe. She shuddered. "It—it is not so strong now," she whispered. "They are moving on, leaving us. The sense of them is fading."

From the edge of the forest, Hishn turned and gave her a long look before loping into the shadows of the blackheart trees. Gray Yoshi followed silently. Without the weight of the other wolves, Hishn's song was merely the thick gray thread it had been before.

The cool earth against her boots was wet, and when Dion stretched her toes, it was only Hishn's feet that she felt. Moons, she breathed. She swayed with the joy of it. It was as if a tremendous pressure had been released from her heart. She flung her head back and laughed out loud. "Gray One," she shouted joyfully.

Wolfwalker! Hishn howled.

And then Aranur pulled her, unresisting, away from the edge of the forest. The other Gray Ones might disperse to the outer mountains, but Hishn and she—they were still bound by their love. Dion reached once more for that gray thread. Her violet eyes were sane again, she knew. Their clarity was focused, and the haggard stress of holding herself against the weight of the wolves gone. In the moonlight, she looked younger, almost vibrant.

"Dion?" Aranur said slowly.

She turned to face him. "The forest is alive with shadows. Can you feel it?"

He nodded. He hesitated. "Come, now," he said firmly.

She searched his face for a long moment, then, with her hand in his, and Tomi dogging their footsteps, walked back to town.

Dion slept two hours past dawn. When Aranur finally went looking for her, he found her still in bed. He watched her for a long moment, reluctant to break her sleep. For the first time in a ninan, her face was peaceful, her dreams not restless. He traced a line with his fingers from her shoulder down her arm, then knelt and brushed her hair from her face.

She stirred sleepily. "Aranur?"

"I'm here," he said softly, a strand of that glossy black hair sliding through his fingers like water. He sat back on his heels. "Time to wake up, sleepy. The Gray Ones are gone, and it is your turn to find something for Tomi to do."

She stretched lazily. "Moonworms, you look serious."

"I am." He made a face at her skepticism. "The boy follows

me around like a puppy when you are not here. Every time I turn around, he is there on my heels. I cannot get anything done.''

She reached for her clothes. ''What about the elder responsible for the refugees? Ask her to assign him something to do.''

Aranur grimaced. ''Moira got to her before I did. She told her that since Tomi was already comfortable with us, it is better for him to stay, rather than send him from home to home, until we find him a family.'' Dion tugged her boots on, glancing around for the boy as they spoke, and Aranur pointed to the door. ''He's outside. I told him to follow Gamon around for a while.''

Dion smiled faintly. ''I bet he loved that.''

''Actually,'' Aranur returned, his voice sounding peevish, ''Gamon found more things for the boy to do in one hour than I did all yesterday.''

Dion laughed. ''You want the boy out of your hair, and yet you get mad when someone else handles him better than you.'' She found her comb and plaited her hair into its usual thick braid, tossing it over her shoulder when she was done. The scratch across her face was now only a long white line running from temple to chin. By autumn, the line would have tanned back to the color of the rest of her skin.

Aranur caught her eyes in the mirror. ''Very rakish,'' he teased.

She snorted. ''Scars are the sign of someone who can't duck fast enough.''

''Did I say anything about that?'' He grinned. ''Just because you haven't learned a thing Gamon or I have taught you . . .'' He ducked her mock punch, heading for the door before she swung at him for real.

When they left the house, they headed for the fighting rings, where Gamon waited. ''Yesterday,'' Aranur said absently, ''I brought Tomi down here and showed him how to start using that knife.'' He shook his head. ''I don't generally teach the children, but I thought I was doing fine until Gamon came up. In two minutes, he had gotten more out of that boy than I got in half an hour.'' He made a face. ''I thought I was better at handling people than that.''

''Tomi isn't a 'people,' '' she corrected, settling her sword against her hip. "He's a child. Give him the respect you give anyone else, but allow him to explore. He is smart enough to keep out of trouble."

Aranur frowned. "I think that is part of the problem," he returned slowly.

"You mean that he does not explore because he is afraid of our reactions."

He nodded. "He does not trust us yet."

She glanced at him with a frown. "How could he? Look what he has been through. He has no family, no friends. He is lost here, and the other children are the same. We have taken them from their home and told them everything is better now, that they are safe. And all the while we openly admit that the raiders are on our borders—they could sweep into Ariye at any moment. Do you wonder that Tomi still feels fear? What if he were to trust us, come to like—or even love us—and then lose us to the raiders, too?"

Aranur scowled. He did not speak as they continued, and Dion put her hand on his arm. "Give him time," she said softly.

"That is what you always say," he retorted.

She smiled faintly at him. "Must mean there is something to it."

He glanced at her sourly. "There's our ghost now," he said under his breath.

Dion looked toward the armory. Near the doorway, standing quietly, was the boy. He did not move until they were close, then he fell into step behind them. Aranur quelled his urge to turn and shoo the boy away.

As they entered the training building, Gamon looked up and waved. Dion nodded a greeting, taking the arm squeeze from the older man with a wince. "What wild ride have you planned for me now?" she asked curiously, glancing over his maps.

He grinned, the seams deepening around his mouth and eyes with the expression. "Why, nothing daring, fast, or dangerous, Dion. You know I would not put you in such a position—or let you volunteer for such."

She snorted. "I would bet on the speed of the fourth moon before I would believe that."

He chuckled. "Here—" He indicated the map carved into the

surface of the table. "Sobovi's sprain is not yet healed, so it will be you and Rafe who ride to the Slot and down." She raised an eyebrow, and he nodded. "Even with the raiders moving north, you still have a better chance of crossing unseen there than anywhere south. Besides, if you cross to the north, you can scout their camp as Sobovi did. We would then have a good idea of how fast they are expanding."

She nodded.

Beside Gamon, a gaunt woman looked up: Tehena, whom Dion had first met in a Bilocctar prison. After the escape, she had followed the wolfwalker to Ariye, where she was rapidly proving her worth as a brilliant strategist, despite her youth. "Here," she said, pointing. "When you return from Bilocctar with the wolves, head for Digger's Gully. It is the last of the Black Ravines, and we can wait for you there. If you lead the wolves into the opening, we can ambush the raiders who follow."

Aranur glanced at the map. "The only problem is communicating. We will have to have scouts out at all times to be sure to be ready when you come across."

The skinny woman shook her head. "Not if Dion's Gray One stays with us." She held up her hand, her white-scarred forearm stalling Aranur's automatic protest. "The healer should not take the wolf into Bilocctar in the first place unless she is prepared for it to be captured and used against her. Besides, it would give us a clear picture of where she is at all times."

Dion nodded slowly. "Aranur, you can hear Gray Hishn."

He shook his head. "And how well would you run trail without her? I am not about to let you and Rafe risk crossing the border with only your own ears against the raiders' wolves."

Gamon gave him a sharp look. "There is more to Dion than a wolfwalker's skills," he reminded his nephew.

Dion, irritated, nodded curtly. "I was trained as a scout long before I bonded with Hishn. I am perfectly capable of running trail without her."

"As for the raiders' wolves," Tehena added, "Hishn can let Dion listen to them even if the Gray One is with you, Aranur."

Aranur looked surprised, but Dion nodded. Aranur could hear Gray Hishn easily when he looked into those yellow, lupine eyes, but he still did not fully understand what the wolf could do.

"If you get in trouble . . ." His voice trailed off, and Dion touched his arm.

"If I get in trouble, Hishn will stay with you still. I will not," she said vehemently, "let her cross the border to me, no matter what happens."

Tehena nodded as if it was settled, and Gamon called in the rest of the fighters, going over the general plan, and discussing their gear. Aranur listened with half an ear. Many of the faces were new to him—at least ten of the men and six of the women had ridden in from a town farther east—but his mind was on Dion. Such a tenuous bond to stretch across a river. Dion would be near the other wolves, but she had already admitted that they could hunt her and she would be able to do nothing about it. He was not sure he trusted Hishn to keep her safe. If the raiders had several wolves, the packsong there would be as loud in Dion's mind as Hishn's voice from the distance. When Dion linked in, she could be drawn to them as they hunted her, and Aranur would not be able to do anything about it.

Two days later, Dion stood at the stable and lashed her gear onto the back of her saddle. Rafe, a man not much older than Aranur, checked his own pack, then patted his riding beast on the neck and mounted. Beside him, Dion gave her dnu's cinch a last tug.

Aranur handed her the reins. "Ride safe," he said.

"With the moons," she replied soberly, swinging into the saddle. Hishn made a low, growling sound, and Dion made a face. "We will be fine," she reassured. "Just make sure you are there to meet us when we return. I don't mind running like rabbits before the wolves, but I have no desire to become dinner."

He nodded reluctantly, hiding his uneasiness until she cantered off. But he could not hide his concern from Gamon.

The gray-haired man watched Dion and the other scout speculatively. "Someone walk on your path to the moons?"

Aranur raised his hand as Dion turned and waved at him before entering the forest. "I do not care how safe their plan seems," he said shortly. "I don't have a good feeling about this."

The older man glanced after Dion and the other scout. "Then

it is best,'' he returned slowly, ''that we prepare for everything.''

Aranur nodded. They made their way back to the armory with purpose.

Chapter 14

When the ancients landed,
The domes arose,
The Sky Hooks descended,
The satellites glowed,
The roads were planted,
The animals freed,
And what was left to do
But spread human seed?

Dion reined in at the top of the lower ridge, crossing her wrists on the double horns of the saddle as she leaned forward to view the flattened mountain. Beside her, Rafe brought his dnu to a halt and removed his warcap, wiping the sweat from his brow with a dirty sleeve and ignoring the smears it created. Dion hid her smile. Dirt was hardly a consideration at this point. Soon, they would both be smearing mud and leaf dyes into their clothes, covering their skins with streaks to break up their shapes and hide the pale color of their faces. Rafe, his forehead already dark brown and an earthy mustache above his lips, had a head start on his disguise.

Ahead of them were the Black Ravines. Shadowed by the steepness of their sides and hidden by their trees, the Black Ravines cut the land into ragged slices. In early spring, the storm torrents washed the bottoms clean; later rains clogged them again with debris. In this shadowed gully, the clear, cold creek splashed on rocks and bounced over dozens of fallen logs. All along the race, white curves hid air pockets beneath the water's path and rushed south, to give the Phye its swollen strength. At least they were far enough north, Dion thought in relief. They could ford these creeks by dnu, and later, when she and Rafe were on foot, they could wade or cross by stepping on the debris that cluttered the fluid paths.

Dion studied the two trails that ran up and across the ravine. If they took the trail that led down and up again, they would stay in the ravines until they reached Sobovi's camp. If they took the other trail, they would approach the Slot from the northeast. Dion frowned. The northeast trail would take twice as long as the steep one. It was also more open to the sky. With the shadows of hungry lepa spiraling overhead, Dion had little desire to leave the shelter of the ravines, even for an easier ride. Glancing at the sun, she bit her lip, then pointed toward the skinny trail that led into the draw and back up the other side.

Rafe grunted. "That the short cut?"

She nodded. "It should take us only two hours from here to reach the top of the ridge. The main road is at least six kilometers longer, but," she added, "it is smoother."

Rafe shook his head. "I'd as soon get this over with as you would."

Without comment, Dion urged her dnu off the wide path and onto the narrow trail. Its once-smooth gait became ragged as it humped over the buried rocks that broke the surface of the dirt. As they approached a stand of redwood on their right, Dion threw her right leg up over the saddle horns so that she rode sidesaddle, hoping to avoid being stung by the sharp barbs on the tree bark. The hairlike needles contained parasites, which injected with the tree's sap into the bloodstream and made life a burning hell for ninans. Dion was not concerned about the dnu; their fur was thick enough that the needles would get caught in it, and the parasites squirted onto their hair died when exposed to air. Neither did she have to warn Rafe. The other scout, seeing what lined the trail, was quick to swing his leg across the saddle, too.

The trail did not flatten at the bottom of the gully. Instead, it barely acknowledged the ravine, crossing the stream at a narrow point and climbing abruptly again on the opposite slope. Lurching across the creek, the dnu clambered up the far side, unsettling Dion's warcap against a twiggy branch. When she reseated it, her hands automatically brushed over its surface, dislodging the two ticks that had dropped onto its enticing leather-and-metal mesh. She wondered sourly how many had already managed to crawl down her cap and inside her collar.

Leaning low across the saddle, she avoided the overhung branches that spread out from the steep side of the hill. Under most of them, the trail was bare, but some spots showed signs of digging. These she regarded carefully. If the digging was from a rodent hunter, it would be harmless enough, but if there was a breathing hole nearby, the disturbed earth could indicate a badgerbear trap instead. She had seen badgerbears erupt out of the ground before, and being unseated from the dnu on as steep a slope as this was to court a broken arm or leg from the fall.

The trail switched back along the side of the hill, and they shifted in the saddle to compensate. They were a full kilometer up the trail before they caught another glimpse of the top. By the time the trees opened enough to let them see their goal, they were sweating even though the dark ravine was cool. There always was a chill in the Black Ravines, Dion reminded herself. Even in summer, the heat never quite seemed to break the coolness free. Here, the chill of melted ice still clung to the ground, and she noted the patches absently. By the end of the ninan, though, even they would be gone.

Rafe gave her a wry look as she glanced back over her shoulder. "When you said this trail was steep," he called ahead, "I did not think you meant vertical."

Dion grinned, the expression disappearing as a branch snapped across her ear. She ducked, flinching instinctively, and gave the offending bough a dirty look. "I did not think so, either," she returned dryly. "Gray Hishn has different ideas of trail conditions than I do."

"You can still sense her?"

Dion nodded. "The distance makes it harder, but since Aranur is only a day behind us, it is not too bad." She shrugged. "If I need to ask her about details for this path, I can still remember through her."

Rafe twisted after her. "I've always wanted to ask you about this remembering you do."

Dion ducked another branch. "It isn't my remembering–it's the wolves'. I just listen in."

Rafe grunted noncommittally.

"They have racial memories," she explained. "Nothing they do is ever really lost. The details of their trails, their hunts, their births, their deaths—all these are kept in each mind. They share memories through the packsong. So when I want to know about a particular place, I ask Hishn to remember it for me."

"Sounds simple."

"It would be," she admitted, "if I did not get more than one memory at a time. The only problem with going through the Gray Ones is that since their memories are shared, I have to read more than one wolf. Like this trail—" She gestured at the path. "When I asked Hishn about the shortcut, I got not only the memories of the last time she ran this trail, but also the memories of the other wolves."

Rafe ducked a branch and guided his dnu around a rock. "Can you tell them apart?"

"Sort of. It's going to take me years to figure out what all the differences are between Hishn and the others. Sobovi and Gray Yoshi have been bonded for over a decade, and Sobovi still has trouble distinguishing the memories from each other."

"I take back anything I said about simple," Rafe said with feeling. "I have enough trouble with my own memory—as my mother told me often enough when I was a kid."

Dion laughed. "See the spot coming up? Last year it washed out—you can see the slide that took those trees down. But the washout this year exposed enough bedrock to make the trail passable again. Hishn ran this trail a month ago; the memories of the other wolves told me of the slide last year."

"Which are stronger?"

She shrugged. "The memories of the last wolf at the site are always strongest. But the packsong itself is like a group of voices in the background—like an echo in your mind. Since I am bonded with Hishn, not them, Hishn's are the only ones that really catch my attention. With Hishn, I just let her flow into my mind. With the other wolves, I have to concentrate. It's only when I look one in the eye or when there are many of them around that I can read them easily. Then, like Sobovi, I get sucked in to their song."

"Like at the council."

"It can be confusing," she admitted. "That is why, even

when Gray Hishn is on the trail with me, I sometimes look only through my eyes, not hers and mine together."

He nodded. They fell silent again, twisting up one ravine, dropping down into another, and rising ever higher against the Slot. They were perhaps an hour from the main trail on top of Digger's Gully, the last of the Black Ravines. At that point, Dion thought, they could take the low trail into Dog Pocket and cross the Phye at the ford, or climb the high trail above Lepa Wall and hike over the ancient Slot itself. The high trail was strenuous, but they would gain the vantage point of the Slot. The only real danger on the Slot Trail was from the lepa. Dion chewed her lip thoughtfully. Lepa were huge birds—some wingspans were over three and a half meters in length. They were feathered, but their legs were covered with scalelike skin. Their mouths were sharp, serrated beaks with inner teeth that tore flesh apart in seconds. Their talons were long, the tips sharp as broken glass. They could spot movement kilometers away, swooping down from their cliffs like lightning. When they flocked, the skies turned black. They swept across the land like night, gathering in a thunderhead of death that attacked anything that moved. Dion glanced up, watching that circling figure against the sun. It was spring, and lepa flocked in spring . . . No, she told herself, it was past time for their migration. The lone birds circling above could only be parents of the young ones hatched out of season. Still, she shivered. Even four or five could be a mortal threat.

As she rode, the north side of the mountain fell away more steeply, exposing the basalt columns that made up the underlying rock. When they reached the last ravine, they could see up along Lepa Cliffs and all the way down to the Phye. The green expanse of Dog Pocket spread from the base of the cliffs out to the darker lines of green that bounded the river. Though the river itself was hidden by the line of trees along its twisted length, Dion raked her gaze across it anyway. She was not studying the lushness of its green, but searching for something different—the smoke of a raider's camp, the flash of color that did not belong, the sparkle of metal in the pale spring sun. If they were there, their smoke would not be seen as a thin tendril or straight column up; instead, it would be as a barely discernible cloud—like a tiny patch of fog clinging to the upper branches along the bank. The wood they used burned clean, and the canopy near the river spread what little smoke there was like a filter. By the time the smoke reached the height above the trees, it would be nearly invisible to her eyes. Rafe, letting Dion scan the trees, stared north and south, letting his peripheral vision catch what movement there was. He shrugged at her questioning look. Nothing. Reluctantly then, Dion turned to the wolves' song, opening her mind to Hishn and, through that dim link, tasting the senses of the Gray Ones who ran the ridge around them.

Hishn howled joyfully at her mental touch. *Wolfwalker!* Her cry swept out, calling the other wolves to join her, and faint echoes rang in Dion's head.

She smiled involuntarily at the happy welcome to the pack. *You honor me, Gray Ones.* The images carried no taint of men that could be raiders—or refugees.

Wolfwalker, one of the wolves sang. *Hurry—the winds are up and the scent of deer is strong.*

Dion touched her cheek. The faint sensation of cold air blew there, but it was not real. She was on the lee side of the mountain, still sheltered from the downdraft of the slope by the lower branches of the trees under which she rode. The senses that filled her mind were on the ridge. *I thank you,* she sent back, *but I must ride. Hunt fully.*

The Gray Ones' disappointment was strong, but hunger was foremost in their images. The wolf who had called hesitated only before racing away to join the rest of the pack already heading up the trail. Dion closed her thoughts to the images. The trace that slashed across the mountainside was easy to see, but difficult to climb, and she needed to keep her senses on its rough surface, not on the loping run of the wolves. The dnu was bred for the mountain steppes, and it could be trusted to keep its footing, but there were other hazards she had to guide it from—and redwoods not the least of those.

Far away, the gray wolves' hunger-lust grew. Even though she had closed her mind to the other wolves, the link through Hishn was still open, and Dion let herself revel in the feel of muscles bunching and stretching. For a moment, she was caught in the hunt. An old buck was cut from the herd, forced toward a thick, tangling stand of silverheart trees. Raking, slashing, at the haunches of the deer, the wolves lunged in. A female wolf leapt forward, dodging under the antlers and catching the deer on the throat. The buck screamed, staggering with her weight, and instantly, the other wolves were on his haunches, dragging him down. Dion blinked. She shuddered, closing her mind more firmly.

A kilometer later, they wound their way up the last switchback, urging the dnu over the branches that had fallen across the trail. It was obvious they were near the top. The treeline thinned; the sky opened. Dion was not sure how close they were to the main Slot Trail, but they would be within at least a hundred meters. One of the Gray Ones sniffed its way to the main trail before running off with the pack, and Dion, with the linked images still echoing in her head, knew she could find the main trail within minutes of achieving the ridgetop. From there, she should be able to see the Slot itself.

When they topped the rise, they halted, gazing at the entrance to the Slot. From where they stood, they could see the wide, open flange that marked the ancient place. The bermed mountain on either side rose up until it was cut off abruptly in a smooth plateau on top. Flattened like a trapezoid, the mountain was then split in two, with a wide opening that tapered into a narrow channel. It was as if the ancients had taken a knife and first topped the mountain, then cut down through it to make a smooth conduit to the other side. The channel's opening had rounded lips that funneled into the three-sided cut, and in the center of it, a shallow groove deepened and narrowed as if to provide a guide for the ancients' knife.

The Slot was old—as old as the first days of the ancients on this world. It was not unique; there were Slots in all the counties. Their flat tops were a constant reminder of the skyhooks the ancients had used to come down from the sky and return again to the stars. Unlike the domed buildings of the ancients, the Slot was not cursed with plague, but people still avoided the area as if just being near it would put one on the path to the moons.

Still, Dion gazed at it in wonder. Three times, she had seen the entrance to the Slot. Each time, seeing its scale against the mountain, she felt like a gnat. The opening in the mountainside did not look large until one remembered that it was a third as wide as the mountain itself. As they drew near, the sides of the Slot would begin to tower, stretching up along the mountain with a vertical rise impossible to comprehend in its sheerness.

The ancient road that wound up the bermed mountainside would take her two hours to climb. When she reached the top, she could crawl to the edge and look down and stare into the depths of that straight, smooth channel with the hair rising on the back of her neck and arms, and her braid like a spiked snake as the loose ends strove to push each other away. She could lie on that smooth, cool lip and gaze at the groove that sliced the floor of the Slot, and the hum of the ground would tickle her bones and bring an anxious shiver to her gut.

As she stared at the outer lips of the Slot, she calmed her stomach. Unlike the others who made the sign of the moons' blessing surreptitiously near the Slot Trail, she had no fear of plague. She was herself immune. The inoculations she was developing would someday, she hoped, make all of Ariye safe from the deadly ancient plague. No, it was not sickness that brought such fear to her belly. It was the scale of the thing. Who could comprehend such might as it would take to shear the top off a mountain off? Who could imagine a channel through solid stone? This Slot was not worm-carved—it would have taken millennia to do it that way. The ancients had built their installations with the power of the stars, not the slow and solid strength of the earth.

"All right?" It was Rafe, his voice concerned, and Dion shook herself, glancing wryly at the other scout.

"It gets to me," she admitted.

He nodded. "I've seen it a dozen times, and each time I swear I'll never take the Slot Trail again, and each time I find myself drawn back." He indicated the entrance with his head. "There is a power here that you find only around the sites of the ancients."

Dion forced her gaze away from the view. With a sharp word, she urged her dnu on.

They wound their way up the side of the mountain, working along the cliff when it was bared by erosion, and plodding back on the earth trails in relief when the rocks were once again behind. A half hour passed, then an hour until they reached the entrance to the Slot, and they had to soothe the increasingly skittish dnu to force them onto the high trail. This close, the lip of the Slot extended half a kilometer down and three kilometers across. The road on which they traveled ran up to the very edge, where the bedrock suddenly ended and the smooth Slot began.

Up, and up again, they directed their dnu. Dion stood in the saddle, leaning forward so that she almost lay along the dnu's neck, clicking and chirruping to urge it on. Another half hour, and she sighted the trail marker that indicated the turnoff for the other scouts' camp. It was not quite at the top of the Slot. Instead, tucked below an overhung section of the cliff, it could not be easily seen from above, the rocks and canopy of trees hiding the corral.

Dion dismounted. As she glanced around, she felt a pang of worry cut into her guts. Sobovi or one of the others was supposed to meet them so that the dnu were cared for while they were gone. So where were they? She looked more carefully at the camp. To the right, along the side of the mountain, a line of tiny caves held waterproof packages. Ahead of her, the corral was tucked against the cliff and formed, as the other forest corrals, out of the owlbark-tree branches. This camp had been used years earlier, when people still traveled between the counties. In the last several years, it had become overgrown, so that now, as Dion regarded the corral dubiously, it was more jungle than clearing. Still, she and Rafe had to leave their dnu somewhere. At least here there was grass enough in the corral to feed them for a day. By then Aranur would arrive.

Leading her mount by the reins, she found the corral opening and urged the dnu inside. Once there, she removed the saddle and blanket, took the bridle, and slapped the creature on its rump to indicate that it could feed at leisure. When she finished, Rafe moved his mount up and duplicated her motions.

The two looked around warily. "Nobody home," Rafe said softly.

She picked at one of the caves, noting that the package inside had not been disturbed. "No sign of a struggle. They were not forced away."

"Then where are they?"

She shrugged. "We haven't time to wait. Leave a ring message at the corral. They will see it when they return."

He nodded. Pulling out a small cylinder of wood from one of his belt pouches, he began carving a design. In the meantime, Dion took their scant packs from the backs of the saddles. Since they were not planning to spend much time in Bilocctar, they would travel light: enough dried food to last the first day, and then only an emergency ration; no sleeping bag—rather, a thin blanket that could double as a cloak if the weather turned foul; one bota bag apiece for water; Dion's herb pouches; and Rafe's trail gear. They did not need more; they would sleep little, and eat on the run on their way back. By the time she finished, Rafe's message was carved, and he was staining the wood with the tiny package of oil crayons he carried. He glanced at her, holding it up for examination.

"Nice," Dion commented. The design was simple and bold, with quick slashes to indicate travel along the trails—such as the shortcut to the Slot—and smooth lines for the ease of the trip so far. The colors he added spoke of the weather, blending over the carving so that the whole stick, no longer than Dion's middle finger, was an eloquent statement of the journey.

He held it up. "Bet you wish you could make a message ring like this."

She grinned, touching her healer's band. "The only carving I'm good at is body carving, and you should be glad that I'm not needed here for that."

"Amen." Rafe got to his feet, picked two flexible blades of grass, and tied the message ring onto the upper corral post by the gate. When Sobovi and the other scouts returned, they would read the message and, if necessary, contact Dion through Hishn. The contact would be weak, Dion had warned, since it would go through two wolves and cross far too many kilometers, but in an emergency, it would do. Satisfied, the scout regarded his handiwork, then slung his pack on and followed Dion out of the camp again. They scrambled up where the dnu had taken long steps and, when they reached the main path, turned back onto it, making their way on toward the top of the Slot.

In Bilocctar, a few ninans before . . .

Usu stared at the aftermath of the battle. Another raid. Six more slavers dead. A goodly store of cloth and wood for buildings, but little food.

The woman he had named the Siker was still bent among the bodies, moving from one raider to the next while some of the resistance fighters held down the struggling forms, waiting for her to kill them. She had been with them for—what? Four ninans? Five? She never spoke. Sometimes Usu forgot she was there, but the raiders did not, he reminded himself with grim satisfaction. Already her name was feared among them. It had been a good strategy to keep her with his group. He did not worry about losing her in the battles—unable to fight, she stayed back until the first volleys flew. When she did walk out, it was as if the moons kept the blades from her skin. The only time he had seen her wounded was when one of Usu's men could not hold back the raider who snatched a knife and sliced shallowly across her ribs. The Siker did not seem to notice. She just waited patiently for Usu's man to disarm the raider, then cut his throat as calmly as if she were sitting down to tea.

Usu did not think the Siker was dumb—she crooned at night sometimes, rocking herself back and forth, her hands clenching air as if they were still tied in the hair of that head. Her eyes were no longer blank, but her face was still. No emotion played there.

It had taken days for the swelling to go down from her face after they found her. Blein said that the siker barbs that had punctured her face had missed the eye pouch, and that the woman had the use of the sight in that eye. Blue eyes. Beautiful, Usu would have said, but blank like a mooksim stone in the light.

A kinee bird called, and Usu started, shutting off his wanderings at the bird's irritated warble. He gestured for the supplies to be sorted. What they could not themselves use, they carted back to the caves and cached. Nothing was burned or thrown away. Everything they took from the raiders represented work that someone—their brothers, their daughters—had suffered for. Everything would be saved.

One of the men who had been a trader checked the lashings of the supplies on one of the wagons. He looked over his shoulder, catching Usu's attention. "Which cache?"

Usu bit his lip. "Gray Rocks," he decided. "It is dryest, and we will want to keep the moisture from this load. If it soaks, it will take a year to dry out again, and we will need it to rebuild."

The other man nodded. He climbed up to the driver's seat and took the reins, clucking to the dnu, urging them to turn around. Usu stared after him. When the moons gave their lands back from the raiders, when they began to rebuild their homes, they would do it from these tools, these woods. When they were free . . .

It took a full twenty minutes for Dion and Rafe to reach the summit. The sudden exit from the trees took the wolfwalker's breath away, and she gazed out at the expanse below her. There was no fear here. The height was not exposed the way a cliff was: at her feet, the treetops stretched out like a gentle green slope. The lepa that circled the sky had disappeared, and, catching her breath, Dion glanced toward the Slot. With the raptors no longer hunting, she and Rafe would not need to worry about an attack from above. Instead, she thought wryly, they could worry about the place of the ancients.

A kilometer away, the edge of the Slot severed the mountain in half. It was barely visible, but she could feel her hair prickling on her skin. She walked slowly toward the dropoff, dodging the loose rocks and clumps of shrubs. The wind, cold and cutting across the flattened mountain, reached into her bones with the hum of the Slot, and she shivered. Her sword and knife edged slowly toward each other on her belt. Beside her, Rafe grimaced. Both of them pulled their jerkins closed as another gust blasted across the plateau and brought a pale color to their once-flushed cheeks.

"Cold as a digger's hell," he muttered.

Dion did not ask if he wanted to skip looking at the Slot. Like the waterfall at the Devil's Knee, one could not help being drawn to the spot.

"Moons make my passage safe and sure," she whispered as the far wall of the Slot came into view. Her sword and knife were pressed against each other as if lightly glued. They tugged toward the ground, making Dion sway in the wind until she dropped to her knees. When she reached the place where the soil and growth gave way to the smooth material of the ancients, the tip of her scabbard was drawn to the smooth, magnetic lip like a moth to the flame. In her quiver, her arrows bunched together, their steel points an awkward bulge against her back. She would have to crawl from here to the rim. Rafe was already easing forward, but Dion did not hurry. As the expanse of the Slot became visible, the fist that gripped her gut tightened, and she quelled her shiver with difficulty. She crawled forward another body length, closing her eyes for a moment as she centered herself on the cliff. In her bones, the hum grew until it seemed to vibrate the very air around her. Where her tunic rasped against her arms, the hairs tickled, rising against the cloth, and Dion caught her breath, forcing herself closer. When she reached Rafe, she dropped to her belly and wormed forward until the channel lay open before her. She had to fight the tendency of her blades to remain vertical.

"Gods," she breathed.

"And more gods," Rafe added. "Look at it. Think of the minds that created this."

She nodded, staring down. From where they lay, the distance to the other side of the Slot was almost three kilometers. It was four wide at the outer lip, and it tapered to no more than forty meters across at its narrowmost point. The two sides of the taper blended into a single box, glistening in the daylight, with only a thin line of light—where it opened to the other side of the mountain—splitting it vertically.

Eventually, she shook herself out of her reverie and eased her way back. When they were well away, they exchanged a long, wondering look, shaking their heads at the massive channel. It was not easy to put its vision from their minds. As they gathered their packs and shook out their tangled arrows, they found their gazes drawn back. Finally, they hiked away, the hum in Dion's bones fading so that only the itchy sense of her hairs on her arms reminded her that she stood on a place of the ancients.

She crossed to the edge of the cliff, standing on its rim. The clutch of her vertigo swayed her for a second, then settled into a tight grip on her guts. She fought it, stepping up on a rock ledge that hung out into space.

"You look like a goat," Rafe said with a chuckle, "who is viewing his favorite weed on a far-distant slope."

"If I look like a goat," she laughed, "then you—" Her voice broke off, her eyes widened, and she cursed. "Moonworms!" She flung herself on her belly, crawling forward until she could see over the edge. Rafe was instantly down beside her.

"My gods . . ."

She nodded. "Look at that camp. Right below us—a hundred meters."

"Raiders," he breathed, staring at the sight. "Moons, but

we could spit on them if the wind would not carry it away before it hit.''

''You can throw spit,'' Dion muttered. ''I'd rather throw a rock.''

''Or several rocks,'' Rafe agreed. ''How many do you think there are?''

She shook her head. ''Fifty-five? Sixty? A hundred or more?''

''Did they see you?''

''I don't know.''

They were silent for a moment. ''There—to the west.'' Rafe pointed. ''A wagon is rolling in. Maybe supplies?'' he guessed.

''Or more building materials. Those are serious cabins. If they were any more sturdy,'' she added slowly, ''they would be forts.''

Rafe let his breath out. ''Forts. And look at their location.''

''Right on the ford of the Phye.'' She scanned the river. ''No one can cross without them knowing about it. That one camp just closed off the north border like a cork in a bottle.''

''Except for the Slot itself.''

''The Slot . . .'' Her voice trailed away, and as one, she and Rafe glanced behind them.

There was no one there. With slightly embarrassed smiles, they returned their gaze to the camp.

''So how,'' Dion voiced her worry slowly, ''do we bring the Bilocctar wolves and their wolfwalkers across?''

''Over the Slot?'' Rafe sounded dubious.

Dion shook her head. ''I can't see myself running full-tilt up this trail, can you? And even if we did take the Slot Trail, the raiders would know it. It wouldn't take them more than a few hours to set up an ambush on the other side where we would have to come down. We would walk right into their arms again.''

''Moonworms,'' he muttered. ''It was not a complicated plan. How could this one thing—this camp—make it impossible?''

Dion laughed softly. ''Maybe it doesn't.'' She pointed at a snag that was bobbing down the river; it ground to a halt a hundred meters south of the ford, turning slowly as its rootball stuck and its trunk fetched up between two large rocks. There was other debris cluttering that part of the river, but this one was larger, and its bulk made a bridge that stretched three-quarters of the way across the race.

Rafe grinned. "Do the moons always bless you this way?"

"Can't you see my ancestry in my eyes?" She batted limpid violet eyes at him, and he chuckled.

"If you are a moonwarrior, I am a dnu." He shook his head. "But that snag is luck itself. If it holds . . ."

They watched it anxiously. The Phye surged underneath the snag, lifting it so that most of its length was above the water. One of the smaller logs broke free, sweeping away slowly, then gathering speed as the river's pace caught and carried it on. The other debris held.

Rafe pursed his lips, regarding the makeshift crossing as he would a three-legged bird. "How long will it take to get down to Moira's workcamp and back?"

"With the raiders along the trails—one day. It's about twenty-six kilometers."

"And we have no way of knowing if that dam will hold until we get back."

"Nope. We also," she said softly, "don't know if the wolves can cross the open water at the end."

"There are boulders."

"They are far apart."

He sighed. "This whole thing is a risk."

"We knew it would be so."

He nodded. "But this . . ."

Dion shook her head. "Do we have a choice? I don't see another option. If we use the ford, the raiders would see us for sure. If we cross on the near side of the Slot, the raiders will be waiting for us when we come down. If we go as far as the north side of the Slot, we are not only out for days, but we are in greater danger from the predators and the mudslides than we ever would be from the raiders here. Given the choices, I would rather risk the logs."

"I know. But dammit," he said vehemently, "what if they are not there when we come back?"

After a last glance at the river, Dion wormed her way back from the edge. "I don't think," she said slowly, "that I want to contemplate that."

Chapter 15

A graying storm; a prison planned;
Betrayal sweeps across the land.
The pack runs through the Black Ravines;
Betrayal makes the howling keen.
The Gray Ones call; the pack flees by;
Wolfwalker, come with us or die.

On the southern edge of the Black Ravines, Aranur paced the clearing restlessly. They had stopped for a break barely five minutes earlier, but he was already irritable, anxious to get going. It would be at least another five minutes—the dnu were still watering at the stream. He glanced at the sun, then swept his gaze over the group. Ten archers, five swordsmen, himself, Tehena, and Gamon. He had wanted more archers because it would be an ambush, not a ground fight, but he had insisted on the swordsmen just in case—they had no idea how many raiders would follow Dion and the other scout back across the border. He brought the strategist, Tehena, along only on Gamon's insistence. His uncle said she could use the experience, and this ambush would be a good testing ground. With Dion—and the other scout—as the bait, Aranur was not so sure he agreed. If he was honest, he thought sourly, he would admit the other reason he did not enjoy Tehena's company: she was a hard woman. There was no softness in her—not even for Dion, the one person to whom she gave unconditional loyalty. She rarely spoke, and when she did, there was a bite to her words that could make even Gamon wince. Why his uncle insisted . . .

He sighed. Gamon insisted because, despite Tehena's shortfalls, she was a damned good strategist. Not having studied tactics in the schools had not hurt her thinking. She had the kind of mind that could worm her way around any obstacle, adapting the Ariyens to the terrain when she could, and changing the terrain when she could not shift the fighters. It was easy to forget her youth. She was seventeen and looked to be thirty. Her thin hair hung limply, and her scrawny frame had picked up no meat on her bones even after a year of good eating. The dator drug that had addicted her, then aged her, had left her thus, and even the best that Dion could do for her had not regained a month of her youth. Looking at her now, seeing her stillness, her wary distrust, he wondered if she had ever been a child.

They had gone only a kilometer farther when he grew uneasy. He was last in the line, letting Gamon take the lead, and he had been watching their backtrail closely. He could swear there was someone on the trail behind them. Twice now, perhaps a kilometer back, a shadow had passed behind the trees when he looked. He glanced around, but Hishn had disappeared. Moonworms. "Jans," he called softly ahead. "Watch the forest. Pass the word. There is something behind us."

Quickly, the message swept up the line. As soon as they passed beneath the next stand of trees, Aranur stopped and reined around. The other riders stopped by his signal. He stared at the trail behind them. Waited. Patiently. Waited.

There—he was right. "Look," he called softly. Two of the men and one of the women dismounted, coming to stand beside his dnu, their bodies carefully half behind the trees. At the distance of the rider behind them and with their browns and striped greens, they could not be easily seen. The movement came again. Someone was climbing the trail after them.

"What . . ." Aranur's eyes narrowed.

"That isn't a man," the woman archer said slowly. "Nor a woman, unless it is a small one."

Aranur swore vehemently. "Dag-chewing, worlag-spawned rastin-baited worms." He dismounted. "Take my dnu." He handed the reins to one of the men. "I'll catch up to you later."

The man hesitated. "I'm not sure I like that."

Aranur grinned without humor. "I'm damned sure I don't like it, but if I want to catch that boy, I'd better be able to step out from behind one of these trees like a ghost, or I'll spook him."

"Boy?" The woman was incredulous. She glanced back along the trail. Comprehension dawned. "You mean Tomi? He was following you and Dion around like a dog . . ."

Aranur nodded. He took an emergency pack from the back of his saddle and set it into a hollow in the tree roots. Tomi would not notice it there, and if things did not go well, Aranur himself might need it.

The man holding his dnu shook his head. "You mean that boy has been following us all the way from town?"

Aranur nodded shortly. "And probably no one even knows he's missing."

"You want help? What if you run into trouble catching up to us?"

"It's not necessary. Gray Hishn will warn us of any danger."

The burly fighter nodded slowly. "The Gray One left you and went back to him?"

"Dion must have realized Tomi was following us. She is still linked to Hishn, even though the distance must be as great as it ever has been. If Hishn smelled the boy, Dion would know. She would have been worried out of her mind about him riding alone." He shook his head in disgust. "She would have asked Hishn to go back. I can't see any other reason for a Gray One to run with a boy who is afraid of wolves."

"Why not have Hishn tell you that the boy is behind us?"

Aranur smiled grimly. "I cannot speak to the wolves myself. Unless Hishn caught my attention, I would not know there was anything to say between us. Later, both Hishn and I will be waiting for her contact—with the ambush, we will need it—but that will be when she is close to both of us. At this distance, Dion's link must be pretty weak. Besides—" He shrugged. "Dion knows we would not get far without noticing that we were being followed."

The woman mounted her dnu. "We'll stop at the bottom of the next ridge. If you aren't caught up to us by then . . ."

"Thanks. Better get going." Aranur glanced back. "He will be able to see these trees soon enough."

They called word along the line, and the riders chirruped, urging their dnu on. They wound along the trail and passed out of sight within minutes. Aranur leaned against the tree and waited.

Eight, perhaps ten minutes later, he heard the faint chip of a hoof against stone. A minute after that, he heard the sound again, followed by a soft rattle where other rocks were knocked loose. When the sound was closing in, he risked a glance around the tree.

It was Tomi, all right. The boy looked nervous, though Aranur could not tell if it was because of the wolf who trotted in front of him or the wavering shadows of the forest. Hishn must know Aranur was there: the wolf could not help but scent him. He could not ask her to ignore him—he had no way of contacting her unless she first looked into his eyes. Damn, but he would have to chance making the boy bolt.

The wolf loped ahead and faded through the brush, coming toward him. Aranur stiffened. He turned and saw her yellow eyes, and her voice was a gray shock in his head.

Aranur.

Gray One, he thought silently, as clearly as he could. *You honor me.*

The cub is afraid of me.

Hishn sounded disappointed, and Aranur almost smiled. *He might be afraid*—he formed the words carefully—*but he is as obviously determined. Let me handle this.*

The wolf turned and trotted on, as if she had no more than a passing interest in a burrow, and Aranur let his breath out quietly. Tomi was getting closer. He could almost hear the dnu's breath snorting softly . . . He waited, judged the steps, then—

He stepped out, grabbing the creature's reins. "Whoa," he commanded the dnu.

Tomi screamed, seeing only a dark figure step out of the trees. He hauled back on the reins, and the dnu reared its forelegs. Frightened, it struck with its hooves at Aranur's shoulders.

"Down!" Aranur's voice cracked like a whip. "Tomi, it's me, Aranur. Stop it."

The boy froze, huddling on the saddle, and Aranur, his mouth open to shout at him again, stared instead. He had forgotten. Tomi's face was blank, his shoulders cringing against the blow he knew would fall. "It's all right," Aranur soothed the dnu, speaking to the creature rather than the boy so that Tomi could get used to his presence. "Shhh. You are fine."

The fear was masked again in the small boy's eyes when Aranur spoke again. "Tomi, why did you leave the camp?"

The boy's lips clamped shut, and his shoulders hunched again.

Aranur made an exasperated noise. "I am not going to hit you, boy. But do you not realize the danger in which you've put yourself?"

Tomi gave a tiny nod.

"Then by all the moonworms in Ariye, why did you follow us?"

The boy said nothing. Aranur, with a silent curse, gestured for him to move back in the saddle, then swung up in front of him, taking the boy's skinny arms and wrapping them around his waist. Gray Hishn watched in silence. The yellow eyes of the wolf gleamed dully, and Tomi clamped his mouth shut, fearful that Aranur would feel him tremble at the gray wolf's gaze.

Within half an hour, Aranur caught up with the rest of the group. Gamon had seen him on the trail behind them and stopped the line at the top of the ridge. The trail was too narrow to allow him to pass back along it and speak to his nephew, so the older man just waved when they joined up, starting the line forward again and riding on.

It took Dion and Rafe the better part of an hour to cross the top of the Slot and make their way down. It took another three hours to circle the secondary camp of the raiders and move south. By then, it was growing late, and the chill spring air was eating at their sweat, making them shiver. Crouched in the shrubs along the lower side of the Slot, Dion pointed at one of the trails that led south. Rafe nodded, moving like a ghost onto the path, his leather leggings brushing quietly against the branches that dipped onto the trail. A moment later, he was gone. Dion rose to follow, her senses stretched to hear Rafe's quiet breathing and smell his lingering scent.

They moved along the trail until they were deep within the tree shadows, twisting, easing through the darkening brush when the trails petered out, finally locating the main trail and staying on it, but farther, ever farther, south. They did not stop until they were two kilometers from the raiders' camp and the evening light made the trail they followed little more than guesswork.

Rafe pulled up, taking deep breaths and stretching out his legs until they cooled without cramping. He glanced around. "Seems like a good enough spot to stop here," he suggested.

Dion nodded. She was busy stretching her own muscles, rolling her shoulders and raising her arms high as she calmed her breathing. Her calves ached, and her feet felt bruised. She had not planned on doing so much running until the way back, and she had more than once stepped on sharp rocks that left her feet throbbing. Dion grimaced at the sudden sensation of heat and acrid stomach acids. She was closer to Hishn than she guessed. At this distance, Hishn's hunger was more than she wanted to experience.

The night was quiet, but the sleep Dion's body craved did not come. Legs aching and eyes burning with weariness, she stared at the canopy instead. The overcast sky hid much of the moons' light, so that beneath the trees, very little of it punctured the canopy and shone on the wet leaves. Somewhere to her left, a night creature crawled along the trail, the swishing of its tail reassuring Dion that it was no snake to worry about curling up with. Dion eyed Rafe's dark bulk with envy. He had barely lain down before he fell asleep. Dion, with her soft sleeping blanket and aching eyes, could only stare at the night.

In the morning, it was Rafe who woke first. He did not have to call to Dion; the subtle scraping sounds of his leather against the roots caused her to open her eyes immediately. With a smooth motion, she rolled out of the pocket in which she had been lying, and stood. Rafe gave her a grin. "And a good morning it is to you, Healer."

She stretched. "Good enough," she agreed. It would have been better if she had not been so nervous sleeping. She rarely spent the night in the forest without Hishn, and she had not realized how heavily she depended on the wolf to warn her of the night denizens.

Rafe, glancing at her tired eyes, dug in his pack. "Breakfast hot or breakfast cold?"

"Cold," Dion decided reluctantly. "The wind is up, and the raiders have the Gray Ones to smell any fire we make."

Rafe grimaced. He pulled the dried fruit and meat from his

pack, while Dion did her morning duty at a peetree she had located last night. The ancients had scattered the trees across the continent when they first landed. With the hollows beneath their roots and the growth of the bacteria within, the peetrees remained sweetly scented, not rancid with the waste they processed. She was several minutes later coming back than Rafe expected, but when she returned, her hands were full of sweet, white, lily bulbs.

"I was getting worried," he said calmly, eyeing the bounty.

Dion handed him half the bulbs. "This was too good a chance to pass up. They were hidden in a dip where a seep flowed out—you can't see it from the trail, so, unless the wolves draw the raiders' attention there, no one will notice where I dug."

"You'll find no argument here," he returned gratefully. One of the better things about scouting with one of the wolfwalkers was the way they always seemed to locate the choicer foods. Not that there was any worry of going hungry, he mused. Even in spring, there was plenty to eat: the tender spring shoots of many plants were edible. Those that were poisonous could be cooked with the extractor plants developed by the ancients. Extractors leached poison from native plants so that normally inedible leaves and berries could be eaten. Throw away the water and the swollen pulp from the extractors, and he could have a filling meal from a burrberry bush or a hot soup of kisacac.

While Rafe made his own trip to the peetree, Dion slipped the slick outer skins off the bulbs. By the time he returned, the tubers were clean and ready to eat, and the stalks of fiddler fern she had gathered in the meantime were cleaned of the bugs that hid in their tendrils.

They ate quickly. Within minutes, they were on the trail again. It took an entire kilometer for Dion's muscles to warm up, and by then, she was hot enough to start peeling down to her lighter clothes. They hiked steadily. It would be around evening, Dion suspected, that they would run into the first of the raiders' camps that Moira had described. The refugee elder told them that the wolfwalkers were quartered in a separate location, not far from the main camp. The elder had never questioned the wolfwalkers' quarters, as if their separate housing had been a privilege, but Dion wondered: if the wolfwalkers were being held hostage, separate quarters would allow the raiders to use the wolves and their partners without the villagers seeing the conditions of that use. The end result would be that the villagers would think, as Moira had, the wolves were definitely working with the raiders.

The wind blew strongly along the trail, and the scent it brought made Dion freeze midstep. Seeing her, Rafe went motionless.

"Smell that," she breathed so silently that Rafe had to strain to hear her words.

He frowned, closing his eyes to make the smells less distracted. Urine, blood, the acids of spilled guts—there was death ahead. Old death, too, from the smell of it.

Dion was stalking now, slinking forward and keeping her body low in the brush, below the height of the plants that waved in that rancid wind. She motioned for Rafe to stay back at a distance. He nodded, stringing his bow silently and creeping forward only when she moved out of his line of fire. She could not hear him behind her, but his presence gave her a confidence she would not otherwise have had. She breathed carefully, controlling the sound as much as possible. Her heart pounded in her chest. In the distance, Hishn reached out for her, a long, low howl distracting her from the noises up ahead. She closed her mind, straining her ears. A meter more, and she could almost see that clearing up ahead. That sound—there were forest cats here . . . Dion slowed her advance, moving less than a foot's length at a time. She eased forward, froze, breathed, and eased forward again. Near her, a pod of burburs sat on their haunches like a group of wrinkled old men, watching the cats with wary patience. When the cats were done, the burburs would race forward, tearing what pieces they could find of the carrion and stuffing their hollow cheeks to return to their burrows. Unlike the wolves—who ate and then regurgitated for their young—the burburs merely stored their meals in their faces, letting their saliva soften the meat they spit out for their pups. Dion bit her lip as she saw them. Unless she wanted to risk enraging the eating cats, she would not be able to get closer than a distant view of the clearing. Just one more bush . . .

She crouched behind the briarbush, far enough back to avoid its sharp thorns and lowered two of the brambles carefully.

She stared—and bit back her shocked exclamation. The forest cats were eating voraciously, but what they had dragged in the dirt and grass was still human enough to recognize. Insect trails were already thick across the small clearing, and the bodies were strewn about it like the fallen branches after an autumn storm. Six, seven . . . she counted with a shudder. The bodies were nearly naked, filthy, and torn apart by the cats. Broken arrows poked from the limbs and torsos she could see—those that were not being worked into meaty strips. Other than the broken shafts, there were no weapons left on or around the trail. No swords, no arrows, no bows. Not even a boot knife. Hells, with the boots and jerkins stripped away, there was hardly a place to hide such an object. The only parts of the bodies that were not marred by battle were the heads. Of the three facing her, the only marks on them seemed to be the three punctures along each left cheek. As she forced herself to view the bodies objectively, stingers whipped by her in the air, hurrying to the feast. Largons, the antlike crawlers that could strip a body to bones, fought the stingers off for the juicy meat at the slit throats and carved their way inside, taking their booty out along their bloody trail.

These were not refugees. Dion eased her way back. The only clothes—leather jerkins, thick leggings—that remained, although torn and stained, had told her that. No, this had been a band of raiders. Attacked—by whom? And how long ago? With the forest cats at work, she could not tell. When this group did not check in where they were expected, another group would surely track them back. And her prints, as well as Rafe's, were clearly along the ground.

A thread of panic touched her chest, and Dion forced herself to move cautiously. Hishn reached out, insistently now, and she let the gray wolf into her mind, reassuring the creature but holding herself at a distance until she was far enough from the scene. Rafe glanced once at her face. His eyes narrowed, flicking toward the sounds, but Dion motioned urgently for him to follow her away from the trail. She brushed their tracks from the path as best she could; Rafe did likewise. A moment later, they hurried onto a side trail, walking quickly with many a glance over their shoulders. Not until they were half a kilometer away and had rounded a hill that would soak up their voices did Dion speak.

"Battle scene," she said shortly, gesturing with her chin back toward the other trail. "Crawling with predators."

"Refugees?" Rafe asked cautiously. The death of more refugees would have turned Dion's stomach, but would not have put the paleness into her face or the fear in her eyes.

"Raiders." She nodded at Rafe's look. "Half of them died by arrows or by the sword—even after the cats got hold of them, I could tell that. The others' throats were cut."

"And they have been there long enough to be half-eaten," he voiced her concern. "So the other raiders will be wondering where they are."

"There were marks on their cheeks," Dion added thoughtfully, as if she had not heard him. "Three punctures."

Rafe cast her a puzzled look. "From darts?" he guessed.

She shook her head. "The marks were made after the raiders died. There was no blood from the wounds, and they looked deliberate—all evenly spaced, all slightly conical in shape—at least, that's what they looked like from where I sat."

"Three punctures . . ." Rafe's voice trailed off. "That reminds me of something, but hell if I can figure out what right now." He paused. "Gamon would have told us if he was sending anyone across the river to fight raiders. In any case, Aranur and he are leading our fighters up to the Slot to meet us when we come back, so it could not be them. That leaves only the soldiers—who Sobovi said were working well with the raiders—or the resistance group that Moira described."

"I would put my money on the resisters." Dion fingered her sword hilt. "Those cut throats—I've seen such things before, but this time, it was . . . eerie."

The other scout said nothing, his mind picturing the bodies, gutted and torn by the cats, their cheeks raked by fingernails with the three-clawed mark of the lepa. When Dion turned and strode hurriedly along the trail, he did not argue. There might be no chill in the wind that blew beneath the trees, but one clung to his spine anyway.

They hiked quickly. Once, they froze halfway across a creek while a nest of spotted adders floated past. One swirled briefly around Rafe's leg, and he stared at it, wishing it away, praying to the moons that it did not decide to climb the soft leather of his legging to look for a place to roost. Barely a kilometer later, they flattened themselves against a tree while a badgerbear slunk past. Its sightless head swung across the trail ahead of them, picking the scent of possible prey out of the dust and circling an open spot as it tried to decide if it should dig its trap there or not . . .

They covered one kilometer, then another. Except for a few pauses, their pace was grueling. It would have been easier to take the road that the raiders had used, but that would have invited trouble faster than walking into a camp at noon. Which left them with the secondary trails—steeper and rockier and half again as long. By the time the sun was three hours past dawn, Dion caught her second wind, her long legs stretching along the trail without soreness or pain. This time it was Rafe who called the halt, unslinging his pack and rocking back and forth on his feet, easing his weight from one to the other before dropping to sit in the dirt. "Ahh . . ." he breathed in relief.

Dion glanced at him. Hishn's voice was a faint echo in her mind, and she listened to it, letting the gray threads twine around her thoughts like tangled yarn. There was a growing strength in the echo. Even though the wolves on this side of the river closed her out of their song, they could not hide their proximity from another of their kind. They were close; she knew it. Like a haunting breeze, the threads blew through her mind, growing into a wind with every passing moment.

Hishn, Dion called, *can you tell how far they are from us?*

The Gray One howled, her nose filled with the scents of men and dnu. Aranur was close—Dion could almost taste his sweat, and her lips curled back from her teeth. Hishn stretched into the packsong. Close, yes, and running hard. Hunting, scenting the oils that drifted down to the ground from the hunteds' heads. An image . . . Dion stiffened. A scent that felt like her own; an image of wolves that was strangely familiar. But Dion had not seen these creatures before—she was sure of it. So why . . .

"By the moons," she exclaimed, whirling to look back along the trail.

Rafe, half drawing his sword, shot her a sharp look. "What?"

"The Gray Ones—"

"They are hunting?"

Dion shot him an agonized look. "Us!"

Rafe grabbed his pack and slung it on. "Where do we go? Which way?"

Dion was already racing ahead, her mind split between her own images and those of the wolf. "Here," she cried. "This way." They were upwind—the wind was in their faces. "Hurry!"

They ran in earnest. When the trail dipped awkwardly into a muddy seep, Dion was already jumping the shallow puddle, her feet landing solidly on the rock that cut into the other side. From there, to the stones along the path, and then back into the dust, her bootprints soft and smudged among the older tracks in the path. They circled a ravine and ran now with the wind at their backs. *Hishn,* Dion sent urgently, *Call them. Tell them to pass us by.*

Your scent is strong in their noses. Your taste is on the ground. Hishn's reply was unhappy. *They cannot let you go.*

They must. They cannot hunt a wolfwalker.

They will be punished.

Dion threw a glance over her shoulder. The wolves had not yet reached the ravine where she and Rafe turned. With luck, they could keep ahead by speed, if not by guile. *We can free them,* she sent desperately. *Tell them that.*

Hishn's voice grew dim, and in her mental howl, she passed on the images that Dion sent. Freedom . . . The three Gray Ones behind them howled so loudly that Dion's ears rang. "Rafe," she gasped, "through here—" On her heels, Rafe had to slow, then whirl back so that his soft boots did not dig into the soil.

She froze, and Rafe went motionless. She could almost sense the wolves from across the draw herself. Would they listen? She and Rafe were crossways in the wind to them. Their scent would be lost in a moment.

"Where are they?" Rafe asked under his breath.

Dion pointed silently across the gully. Something howled. Rafe stiffened. "They will find us anyway," he whispered.

Wolfwalker . . .

Hishn—where are they? They were close—they were there—they must be. But she could not see them.

Quiet, the wolf snapped.

Dion clamped her hand on Rafe's arm.

Wait.

Dion held her breath. The wolves howled. Dion did not have to listen through Hishn's ears any longer; the song of the pack was loud enough to raise the hair on the back of her neck. Rafe scrunched his shoulders further into the shrubbery. Not fifty meters away, on the other side of the draw, the gray shadows passed, howling, racing by. The raiders who followed were breathing hard, running after a lean figure on a long lead. A wolfwalker . . .

Hishn, tell them we follow them—that we are coming.

No! The gray wolf's voice was adamant. *Go back. They must follow your trail. Loop back and lose them in your tracks like a wounded deer when it knows it is hunted.* The Gray One growled in Dion's mind, and the image was drowned out by an echoing howl of the wolves to her left. Gods—they were already coming around the draw.

Dion scrambled to her feet. "Come on," she barked at Rafe. "Run."

They sprinted, one hand out to ward off the branches that whipped in their faces. They circled the gully, sliding down a patch of loose humus with little regard for the tracks they left behind. The wolves knew where they were anyway. "This way," Dion cried out, reaching the trail and running along it again in the direction they had originally taken.

"No—this way." Rafe turned and would have sprinted north.

"Rafe—I know the wolves. They will miss us, but we have to help them do it. Circle"—she whipped the words out—"so that we lead our tracks back to the draw again."

He hesitated.

"There's no time," she snapped. "Come on."

He nodded curtly, and sprinted after her.

She could not see the raiders or the wolves. *Hishn,* she called. *We are halfway along the draw.*

The gray wolf howled, and the answering chorus across the gully, to the south, was frightening. Dion pulled up.

"Here," she said sharply. She stepped under a fern, the moss at its base compressing, then springing back when her weight was gone. From fern to fern, she stepped carefully into the forest, letting only her legs touch the plants and her feet brush the ferns aside to clear her path. Some of these were old ferns.

The oils of her hands would have browned the leaves, and their path would have been as obvious as if they had painted their way along.

Rafe followed suit, crouching as the wolves howled again. "Over there—" He pointed. "The dip is big enough for both of us."

She nodded, changing direction.

Wolfwalker . . .

Hishn, I hear you. I hear them all. Dropping to her knees, she pressed her body into the soil, rolling under the ferns as far as possible so that their leaves broke up the shape of her body. Seconds later, Rafe pressed down beside her. Their breathing was harsh, and they fought to control their lungs. Shadows, shapes, swept through in the forest, and they relaxed against the earth. The cool dampness seeped into Dion's leggings, and something wriggled against her thigh. She dared not move. Spiders from the ferns dropped onto Rafe's shoulder, and she reassured him with her eyes—they were not the bright green of the deadly Chao, but the duller tone of one of the harmless insect-eaters.

The gray wolves howled. Dion arched her back involuntarily, the sound filling her ears and bringing a snarl to her lips. Rafe clamped his hand on her forearm, holding her down. Moonworms . . .

The Gray Ones raced forward. The raiders followed, cursing. They hauled on the lines tethering the wolfwalker to them, and the man stumbled, going to his knees. One of the raiders backhanded him, and the wolves milled suddenly, snarling at the raiders, who laughed, holding the wolfwalker by his arm and yanking him to his feet. Dion could not catch what they said. They kicked at the brush, looking desultorily for tracks and signs, then cursed the wolves again, directing the pack back along the trail.

Where do they go now? Dion asked the gray creature across the river. Hishn's tension was palpable, and Dion wondered if Aranur, beside the wolf, could read it, too. For a Gray One to allow his wolfwalker to be hurt . . .

Hishn, when she answered, was calm, her mental voice hiding its rage in an undertone of images that showed the raiders torn apart by the Gray One's fangs. *They run till they come to their camp,* she sent. *They have lost you for the hunt.* The fading howls of the other wolves almost overrode Hishn's words, and Dion closed her eyes, concentrating on that single, faint voice.

"How far?" she asked.

A few minutes' run. They are hungry.

"They will eat then?"

Hishn's denial was firm. *They cannot eat. They earned no food for them or their wolfwalkers.*

Dion got to her feet, her face set grimly. *We will free them tonight, Hishn,* she sent, staring after them on the trail. *Tell them that.*

Rafe, glancing at her, got his knees under him before he froze again in place. Dion was already watching the trail warily. On the path so recently vacated by the raiders, staring at them with his yellow eyes gleaming, was one more wolf. He met Dion's gaze, his tired voice melting through her thoughts like a chinook.

"Gray One," she whispered. "You honor me."

The wolf did not greet her in return. Instead, it panted hungrily, its lean sides showing its ribs, and the half-healed marks of a whip on its back. *Freedom,* it sent. *Freedom for my mate—for my brothers—you promise this by the bond of the pack?*

Rafe stayed still. Dion did not glance at him. "We go to the camp now. If we can, we will free them ourselves—now. If we cannot fight the raiders there, we will let ourselves be seen, and allow you to chase us back to Ariye."

The wolfwalkers would still be in pain.

"Gray One," she said softly, "Can you help me speak to them? I don't know what is best to do. I need their thoughts on this."

The wolf regarded her for a long moment. *Wolfwalker, can you howl my song with the pack?* His question brought with it an image of a whip dropping across his back, bruising, then slicing through his fur. Of a collar so tight he could not breathe except in gasps. Of a hunger that still roiled in his belly like worms. He stepped forward so that they were barely a meter apart. *Do you carry the shame in you that fills my nose like dirt?*

Dion dropped to her knees. "Gray One," she whispered, "I, too, have felt the shame." He gazed at her, and she opened her mind, Hishn sweeping in and guiding the other Gray One to her own memories. There was a time when Dion, too, had felt the chains and the whip . . . "Reach out," she whispered. "Stretch to hear the wolves in Ariye—can you hear them? We listened to your song. We took it for our own. Look back, look back six days to the council that was called in Ariye. We gave our word to help you. I swear by the bond this is so."

The Gray One touched her lightly with his nose. *Then howl with me,* he said softly. *Wolfwalker.* As it came closer, the voice in Dion's head gained strength. Anger, frustration, hunger, pain—the emotions swamped her like a flash flood. She reeled, putting her hand out to the dirt. She was nose to nose with the wolf now, and its sweet, rancid breath puffed in her face.

Wolfwalker?

It was a distant call, like a voice almost lost in a wind. Dion frowned. It was not a Gray One. She closed her ears to the forest, staring deeply into the gray wolf's eyes. "Wolfwalker?" she asked hesitantly. "Can you read me?"

I do not know where you came from, but you must go back—leave this county now. Don't wait. The raiders . . .

Dion nodded, sending an image of reassurance. "I know. It is why I am here."

No . . . The gray voice grew faint, and Dion realized that the pain underlying the voice was that of the wolfwalker, not the Gray One who passed the words along. Pain, and cold. Her hand went to her ribs. Cracked, yes—and two of his bones were broken. She could feel the agony of the man's breath rasping in his chest.

"I must," she said. "Listen. If we let ourselves be seen, will the raiders use all the wolves to track us?"

There was a faint agreement in the gray tone that echoed back, but underneath it was uncertainty.

"How many of you are imprisoned? And how many run trail with the wolves when they are tracking?"

Three wolves, one wolfwalker run trail. Two more of us are held here, hostage against the other's escape.

Dion bit her lip. "Is there any way to free all of you at the same time?"

No. But I am dying anyway, and Occan is weak enough that he will not last many more runs.

She hesitated.

Do what you have to do, he returned with a surge of determination. *We have decided. Wilse will run with the wolves; Occan and I will die anyway. We are willing, if you will free our Gray Ones.*

Dion had to choke her words out. "I swear I will try," she returned. "Tell your wolves what to do. We will be at your camp soon. When we let ourselves be seen, chase us, keeping close enough to tantalize the raiders so that they do not give up. We are only five kilometers from the river. There is a log crossing a kilometer below the ford—we will run for that. I think the wolves can make it across."

I understand.

"There will be an ambush when we reach the other side. Gray Hishn will tell the other wolves when to flee. Your wolfwalker must drop to the ground immediately. Our fighters will know who he is."

There was a pause, and Dion felt the racking cough that brought a blinding pain to the other man's voice. *Take care of our wolves, Dione.*

"You know me?"

You cannot hide your voice from the pack, the other man returned gently. *Run safe.*

"May your path to the moons be gentle," she whispered.

The faint voice faded, and then there were only the yellow, gleaming eyes of the wolf, gazing at her and running its tongue over its white, glinting teeth.

Chapter 16

A single eye
Isolated in time:
Seeing nothing,
Seeing only dark,
Since the dreams
Died

To the north, the woman called the Siker crawled out on the ledge with the others, resting her chin on her forearms as she edged her head over that precipitous drop. Without a word, the ragged group studied the treetops far below. The sun was high over the Slot behind them; anyone looking their way would see no detail, just the bright, burning light that watered their eyes and made them squint uselessly up. They had found body prints from two other people lying at the edge just as Namina's group was now doing, but since they had certainly been watching the raiders' camp as well, they were not those she hunted, but Ariyens.

Namina scanned the forest ceaselessly. She searched for movement—any movement—that would betray the steady, snakelike trail of raiders working their way through the forest, heading north. The camp the raiders had set up in Dog Pocket was in the strongest position possible, but the trails that led to it were still open to attack.

While Namina stared at the treeline, the man next to her studied the scene below. His forearm was over his brow, shielding his view from the sun as he catalogued the raiders' wagons, their positioning, and their strength. He had not been wrong when he told the others that the camp was a goal beyond them. Backed up against the mountain on one side, it was guarded by the river on the west and south, while the fireweed meadow on the east kept even the worlags from nosing in. The river could be crossed only at the southmost corner of their camp; above and below their position, the Phye ran too swiftly for even a dnu to keep its footing. A man would be swept away as if he were a leaf. Usu could not help his scowl. If only he had more men . . .

One of the men grunted, and both Namina and Usu glanced over, following the direction of the other man's finger. Namina saw nothing, but she waited patiently until the metal that had first caught the other man's eyes flashed again. It was almost hidden beneath the thinned tops of the trees, winking out of sight immediately, but it was there, and it could not be mistaken for the white underside of a swallow or the bright reflection of water.

Beside her, Usu nodded. So, he thought, the raiders are running their supplies along the old road. He would not have guessed it. It was a stroke of luck for him, though—the rootroad they were using would still be spongy from a winter of disuse, and the dnu would not be able to respond quickly when attacked.

One of the women on the other side of him gestured abruptly, and he nodded. They eased back from their vantage point silently. Not until the rim of the rock hid them from below did they stand and jog down the trail.

Dion and Rafe jogged after the wolves cautiously. The raiders kept a good pace, and she and Rafe would have been left far behind had they walked. Now, close enough to see the buildings in the clearing, she dropped to her hands and knees. Rafe was ahead of her, lying on his belly and worming forward to the edge of the treeline, his knees and hands wet with the damp earth. The moist dirt brought a welcome coolness to their warm, sweating bodies.

The clearing they approached was big enough to include three houses, a barn, and several outbuildings. Two of the outbuildings were greenhouses; the other three were sheds, one of those being a storage unit. It was to the storage shed that Dion directed Rafe's gaze. He followed her finger, nodding as he saw the heavy bar across the door and the lock that dangled from the outside. From shoulder height down, the finish of the door was gone, scratched away. The deep grooves that remained tore the wood into long vertical lines. There were no such marks on the other sheds or barns; the wolfwalkers had to be in that one. As she watched, a group of raiders stomped out of one of the houses, and Dion and Rafe shrank back into the brush. There were three wolves with them. Moons—if they looked this way, the raiders would know . . .

Hishn, Dion called softly in her mind, *I see your brothers and sister. Can you reach them from there—let them know we are here?*

I howl with the wind, Wolfwalker, Hishn sent. *Their song is mine.*

As Hishn reached across to the packsong, all three wolves cocked their ears. The tide of grief and anger that swept back through Hishn left Dion frozen in the brush, her eyes wide and unfocused, while Rafe, unaware, frowned. A moment later, the wolves turned away, disinterested. Rafe let his breath out as two of them were shoved into the wire run. The third wolf was kept out, one of the raiders taking down a training loop and placing it over its snarling head. He tightened the loop, holding the stick between him and the suddenly choking creature. Dion's hands went to her throat. She caught her breath, coughing. "No," she whispered.

Rafe frowned. "What are they doing?"

The wolfwalker near the shed grabbed the raider's arm, shouting at him, trying to loosen the grip. He was shoved away, his shoulders, then his head, striking the wall of the shed. He got groggily to his feet.

"No," Dion whispered again. Rafe looked at her, his eyes narrowed. Her violet gaze was unfocused, and her lips pulled back in that rictus snarl. One of the raiders pulled a whip from a hook in the shed and uncoiled it. Rafe tensed. The whip snapped, and Dion jerked. Rafe clamped his hand over her mouth as she cried out. He dragged her body to his, muffling her face in his shoulder, staring at the scene. The other wolves flung themselves on the wire walls of their cage. The whip snapped again, and the gray wolf yelped, cringing and snarling. Dion struggled wildly against Rafe. He rolled on top of her, his hand still over her mouth. The whip lashed again, striking the wolfwalker, then the wolf. Dion tore free. She screamed, scrambling away, springing to her feet. "No!" she shouted.

Rafe gave a choked-back cry. "Dion—"

The raiders turned.

Blasts of fire scorched her back. Dion's ears were deaf with the howl that rang in her head. She flung herself at the raiders, her sword leaping into her hand and her knife stabbing indiscriminately at the bodies before her. Behind her, Rafe cringed in the brush, moving back, away from where she had leapt out.

"Get her!" one of the raiders yelled. "Watch out!"

The raiders' shouts made no sense to her. The wolves lunged and flung themselves, snarling, at the wire walls of their cage, and Dion screamed, striking out, whirling her sword so that the raiders got in each other's way trying to reach her. She beat one attack aside, leapt back, stumbled, and brought her sword up with a clang against another raider's blade. Something hit her in the back. She staggered forward, her lips pulled back in a snarl. Hands of iron closed on her forearms. The gray howl in her head surged, and she screamed in fury, struggling wildly. The raider slammed the hilt of his knife into the back of her hand, and her sword dropped with a thud. She slashed back with her knife, but he stepped in. She overreached. Her knife went harmlessly under his arm. Someone grabbed the blade and wrenched it from her grasp. She pulled the raider off-balance, bringing her knee up. When he turned his body, twisting her around, she used his weight as her leverage, dropping the woman who risked grabbing her other arm, and then smashing the knee of the man who tried to grapple her from behind. Screams . . . Her braid was yanked back. A fist slammed across her cheek. Once, twice . . . The fourth time, the gray howl was a dull rage. She struggled weakly. Her lips were smashed against her teeth. She snarled with a choking sound. Two more blows. She sagged, her nose streaming blood, her lips cut and dribbling red. When the beating stopped, she hung limply, moving only weakly, in jerks, as the raiders watched.

"Moonworms in a worlag's den," one of the women cursed,

clutching her slashed arm to her chest. "I'll cut her eyes out for this." The man whose knee was broken dragged himself to the side, two of the others pulling him ungently up on the porch. He would never walk again. Not because of his knee, but because of his throat, which was slit before he could protest: raiders did not waste food or drink on any cripple. The wounded woman watched the raider die with a sneer on her face. But when she reached Dion, one of the men stopped her.

"She's mine," the woman snarled.

"Not yet." The other raider stepped forward and grabbed Dion's chin, lifting her head so that he could look into her face. Dirt and blood made an ugly mud on her cheeks, dripping down across her mouth to mark her tunic. Eyes narrowed, he stared at her. "This one is no worker from the camps," he said slowly.

"One of the resistance fighters?" one of the others suggested.

"Maybe." He turned her face from side to side, noting the way her lips still pulled back from her teeth.

"Cut her and hang her up with the rest of them," the woman returned crudely. "Show them what happens when they get too close."

"I don't know ..." The first raider tilted his head, glancing down the length of her body. "Her mail—it is not from this county. Look at the tone. This is finely tooled—worked in the old way."

"Let me have it," one of the smaller men suggested. "It's about my size." The first raider raised his eyebrows, and the other man grinned. "When she's dead, she won't care."

"Not this one," the first man said thoughtfully. "This one we keep."

"What the hell is wrong with you?" the woman whose arm was slashed burst out. "Since when do we keep worm-spawn like this alive? There's a little matter of payment for this"—she gestured at her arm—"which this one owes me. Not to mention our men dead on the trail back there." She pointed north.

"Yeah, she owes you and us," the first man agreed, "but we keep her alive. You can have her to mark, but not maim."

The woman gave him a venomous look. "I'll have her to kill, as is my right." She stepped forward, her good fist clenched on her knife.

The first man thrust out a massive forearm, stopping her in

her tracks. "Uh-uh." He stared her down, forcing her to step back as he pushed against her wounded arm. "Look at her eyes. She's one of them." He gestured at the other wolfwalker.

"Another wolfwalker?" one of the other raiders breathed. "But we have all the ones from this county right here."

"So maybe she's not from this county." He regarded her with a frown. There was something about this one . . . He could not put his finger on it, but he would bet on the second moon that Longear would give him a bonus if he kept this one for her.

Dion stared at them. Blood dribbled from her lip, and she tasted it absently. Hishn raged in her head, and she was having trouble seeing. Her jerkin was stripped down, then off, leaving only her tunic to cling to her body. Behind her, one of the raiders wrenched her arms back and lashed them at the elbows and wrists, her shoulders jutting back with the strain. Her tunic did not even pretend to protect her from the lines that cut cruelly into her skin. But she made no sound, her eyes filled with the bloodlust of the wolves, and her nose wrinkling to the rancid sweat of the raiders. They jerked her around, and her warcap slipped, revealing the silver circlet.

The first raider stared. He reached up and stripped the cap from her head. Glossy black hair was clean beneath the cap. The silver circlet shone on it like water in the moonlight. "Look," he said urgently. The other raiders stared. "A healer." He grabbed her chin, ignoring her weak jerk to get away from him. Forcing her face up, he stared into her eyes. "A wolfwalker and a healer. You know what this means?" He grinned evilly. "This is not just another wolfwalker. This is Ember Dione."

The other raiders eyed Dion warily. One of the women walked around her, examining her as if she would find Dion's name cut into the design of her mail. "They would not risk Dione in this place," she said slowly.

The first man shook his head. "They would if they had no others to send."

"But as a scout?"

"She is like wind itself on the trail—passing, yet leaving no tracks. Longear gave us those lists, remember? This Dione was one of the names on it." He turned her face roughly to them, ignoring the blood that stained his fingers from her split lip. Dion threw her head back, but he ground his fingers into her jaw, making her writhe. "Look at her eyes," he said softly. "She could be any wolfwalker, except for the color: violet. And the healer's band and the sword? There is only one wolfwalker who carries both. No." He shook his head. "This is Ember Dione." He let Dion jerk her head away, noting the still-unfocused eyes with satisfaction. To have captured another wolf-walker alone would bring a bonus. But to have taken Ember Dione, the healer from Ariye . . . What would Longear reward him with for this? He glanced toward the woods, his thoughts crystallizing abruptly. "We tracked two people this morning," he said curtly. "What do you want to bet this is one of them?"

A man's eyes narrowed. "If it was Dione we chased, it would explain why we did not catch them."

The first man nodded. "While we ran in circles, she was talking with the wolves, telling them to skip past her on the trail." He spat in disgust. One of the women turned and stared at the other ragged wolfwalker, who huddled, still groaning, against the shed. "Stupid worm." She kicked him viciously in the gut, then the kidney. "Did you think we would not catch on?" The wolves barked, growling and surging at the fence again, and Dion, caught in their emotions, kicked out until the raiders slammed her down to her knees. The first raider watched with a smile. Behind her, on the ground, the other wolfwalker groaned, unable to curl against the blows. Finally, staring at the moaning figure, the woman spat on his haggard face, her spittle running down the man's cheek in a slow, disgusting stain.

The first raider watched them impassively. "You know what this means?" he said thoughtfully. "There is still one more of them to catch. Bring her," he said shortly, gesturing at Dion. "And him," he added pointing at the huddled wolfwalker near the shed.

He turned and grinned wolfishly at the forest. "You! Ariyen!" He hauled on Dion's arm, and she swung a kick instinctively at him. He blocked her easily, slugged her in the stomach, and laughed as she doubled over. Behind him, the wolves howled.

"Ariyen!" he shouted. "Come out, and I promise not to kill this one. I have two wolfwalkers, after all. I can spare one of them, and yours is in much better shape than mine."

In the shrubs, pressed against the knotted roots of the silverheart trees, Rafe clenched his fists.

The raider motioned for the wolfwalkers to be dragged forward. "See what your reluctance does to this poor man," he called. He nodded at the raiders who held the male wolfwalker's sagging body, and with a grin, one of them took his knife and gouged it into the wolfwalker's arm. The man screamed, struggling against the pain, and the air was filled with the barks and snarls of the wolves. "Again," the first raider ordered. The knife dug in. Dion screamed with the other wolfwalker, writhing as he did. The first raider scanned the forest. There was no movement as he said calmly, "Again." Blood poured from the mangled flesh of the wolfwalker, soaking the other raider's hand so that he wiped it on the wolfwalker's ragged tunic. The tip of the knife ground against bone, and the raider twisted it, scraping along the length of the arm bone until the wolfwalker, his voice screamed into a hoarse whisper, sagged. His eyes fluttered, then closed, and he slipped down to the ground, his jaws working, rattling with his ragged breath. His leggings stained wetly in the front.

Dion, feeling a blackness, a void, invade her soul, screamed an inhuman noise, and the raider holding her arm felt a chill crawl down his spine. "Shut up!" he snarled, backhanding her in the jaw. Her voice subsided into a strangled growl. He stared at her unfocused eyes, the violet of their gaze searching him, looking through him, seeing him not. There was something eerie about it, and the raider jerked her arm, cursing her to silence.

And suddenly the silence screamed as loudly as the wolves had howled a moment before. No growls, no human voices, cut through the air. The raiders glanced at each other uneasily. The raider who had cut the wolfwalker dropped the limp body to the ground and shrugged. "He's dead."

The raider holding Dion nodded. "All right," he said calmly. "We start in on her."

Dion's mind was whirling. The absence of the Gray Ones was shocking in the hollow emptiness of their thoughts. A wolfwalker had died. The words were her own, not those of the wolves. A wolfwalker was dead. She stared at the body on the ground beside her. The stain of blood that crawled across his chest was soaking through his tunic, spreading as if a red shroud were slowly being pulled across. She choked. The raider grunted warningly as she struggled to stand erect, but since she swayed, her balance still shot with the blinding ache of her battered face, he ignored her movements.

He turned to the forest again. "Do you see, Ariyen? One wolfwalker killed because of you. You want this one dead, too?" He jerked his own knife from its sheath. "I promise not to kill her if you come out. I need her—and you—alive now. You don't need a word of honor to know that," he shouted with grim humor. He scanned the treeline. "Not coming?" He raised the knife. "Don't be stupid," he called. "I can cripple her and still use her." He brought his knife across Dion's chest, slashing through the cloth as if it were not there. The blade cut into her breast, across her sternum, and down over her ribs. She screamed. She could not help it.

Rafe leapt up. "Stop!" He took two steps forward, cursing under his breath. "Stop, I am here."

"No . . ." Dion moaned. "Rafe . . ."

With his knife poised for another slash, the raider watched the other scout with a slow smile. "Come," he said softly. "Join us."

Rafe stepped forward reluctantly and was surrounded. His bow was removed, his sword unbuckled, his knife taken. Then he was shoved to the ground, his face slammed into the hard-packed earth and his grunt of pain ignored. Hands patted him down, searching for other weapons. The boot knives were discovered. His arms were wrenched behind him, bound tightly so that he grunted again, clenching his teeth against the sharp pain. His hands went numb.

"Stop," Dion whispered.

"Shut up." The first raider backhanded her again. He regarded the scout for a moment. "Kill him." He turned on his heel and dragged her toward the shed.

"No!" Dion cried out. "Rafe—"

There was a gargled cry behind her, and then a ragged drumming of feet against the ground. Dion wrenched herself out of the raider's grip, twisting and standing, shocked, her breathing choked, as she stared at Rafe's writhing body. Blood spurted from his neck. A whining burble escaped him. His body jerked.

Kicking, his legs gouged the dirt until they weakened, stilled, jerked again, and went limp. Dion could not move. Rafe—her scouting partner—was dead. Dead because of her. As surely as the moons rode the sky, she had killed him.

When the raiders grabbed her arms again and dragged her toward the shed, she did not resist. As the door slammed shut and the bar dropped across with a wooden thud, she was frozen on her knees as she had fallen, her mind a blank except for the one thought that screamed and screamed at her consciousness: she had killed him herself.

To the south, across the Phye, Aranur had his hands locked in Hishn's fur. He struggled with the gray beast, forcing the wolf to look into his eyes. "Hishn," he snarled, "where is she?"

The gray wolf snapped at him, locking her gleaming fangs on his forearm, but he did not let go. *Dark.* She whined suddenly. *Dark as a midnight den. Death rots in her nose . . .*

"Is she conscious?" he demanded, grinding his teeth. "Can you reach her?"

She does not listen . . .

"Make her," he snapped forcefully. "Force her to hear."

Hishn growled, shaking her head free of his grip. She paced irritably, pivoting on her hind legs when she was only a meter away.

Aranur looked up at the hand that fell on his shoulder. "Dion is captured," he said harshly to Gamon. "Rafe is dead."

Gamon's face turned grim. "Mount up," he shouted at the group. "Let's go! Now! We make Digger's Gully in three hours."

To the north still, lurking along the trail, Usu waited impatiently. Behind him, the Siker was like a stone herself, she was so still. Soon . . . The wagons rumbled. The dnu snorted. Coming around the bend right about—

"Now!" Usu's arrow flew. There were two raiders in front, two wagons behind them, and three more raiders bringing up the rear. Usu's arrow caught one of the lead raiders. Two others struck the second man, who toppled from his saddle, his scream cut off abruptly as the dnu behind him panicked, racing forward, and trampling him beneath their hooves. The wagondriver snapped the traces, shouting at the dnu to run forward. An arrow clipped his side, another piercing his arm, and he screamed, hunching over on the seat. One of Usu's women jumped the wagon. With an agility born of adrenaline, she swung up, grabbed the traces still clutched in the driver's hand, and kicked the man down. Other bolts struck the other raiders, driving them from their saddles and seats.

Two minutes later, it was all over. The dnu were caught and soothed, the wagons entered, and sacks of food, clothes, and weapons were sorted out. Usu nodded smugly. One more raid like this, and his group would have enough supplies to last till midsummer. By now, the raiders must be feeling the pinch. Usu had taken three full caravans this last month alone. Peyel, his contact in one of the towns, told him the raiders had promised that whoever brought Usu's group in could have them for a month before they would be killed. Long torture. He shuddered. What the raiders would give to find out that he, Usu, manager of the northern forest, did double duty as their executioner . . .

He glanced around. He felt no sympathy for the raiders. What they had done to his county was unspeakable. Even Peyel, who had an easy job as a tavernkeeper, had suffered at their hands. Twice in the last year she had been gone for ninans while she was . . . punished for her remarks. Usu let his lips thin grimly. He would avenge her as he had his own sister.

Several of his people were holding the raiders, pressing their faces to the earth regardless of their wounds, but Usu ignored it. Their pain did not matter. It would be over soon enough. He quelled the uneasiness that always gripped his guts when he watched the Siker.

Walking unhurriedly, the Siker, that silent woman, went to each writhing raider. Not speaking, not looking, simply bending and slitting their throats with quiet calmness, as if she were cutting flowers for a bouquet. She squatted then, waiting patiently for their heels to stop drumming the earth and the blood to slow to a seep. When they were dead, she pulled the siker barb from her pocket and marked them. Three puncture wounds. Left cheek only.

Like her own.

Usu shivered and turned away.

Dion choked in the darkness. The cracks of light that filtered through the wall of the shed showed the bodies like ghosts. A glimpse of a grinning face . . . the gleam of an open eye . . .

Gods keep her from screaming.

Gray voices faded in and out of her mind. The wolves' despair beat against her like dull clubs. To her right, the sliver of light that fell across the hanging body shifted and touched her knee. Her mind was blank.

Wolfwalker, the voices cried. *Hear us. Run with us . . .*

Gods. Gods. Moons that drew the sky so light . . . A chill filtered up from the floor, and Dion shuddered uncontrollably. Death stank in her nose—a smell so vile, so concentrated, in this shed.

A shed. The wolves. Dion blinked. Her cheeks were crinkly. She struggled against the straps that bound her arms together. The blood was already tingling in her shoulders. Soon she would not be able to feel her arms at all. She wondered if it mattered. The wolves . . .

Wolfwalker, Hishn called.

No, she thought dully, that voice was not her wolf. That was a man, far in the distance, a man.

Dione!

She raised her head. She could see the shed more clearly now. The few slivers of light that broke through the thick walls showed her what she smelled. Gods, but the bodies . . .

It is to intimidate you, the voice called. Far away, far beyond her thoughts, the voice insisted on her attention.

"Wolfwalker," she whispered.

Yes. Do you hear them?

"The wolves . . ."

Break free, Dione. You can still take the wolves with you.

There was determination in that voice, and Dion blinked. The dark, the dead . . . She struggled to choke down the bile that rose in her throat. Then she was leaning forward, retching, losing her balance and scrambling to stretch her leg out so that she did not fall into her own vomit.

"Oh, moons," she whispered. "Hishn . . ."

The gray wolf swept into her mind. *I hunger. Bloodlust in my teeth. Wolfwalker—*

"Hishn." Dion got her feet beneath her with difficulty. Her lips were beginning to puff out. "Hishn, I am here." She said the words slowly, as if convincing herself, and when she heard them, she knew it was true. Rafe's death . . . the other wolf-walker . . . The shock of the wolves was running rampant in her, and she must shut it out. She struggled to close the link between them, leaving only the thin gray thread to Hishn in her mind.

She eased between two of the hanging bodies. One swayed, touching her, and she cried out. Her stomach rose. "Oh—" She flung herself against the side of the shed, retching again, coughing and spitting to clear her throat of bile and blood.

She spat one last time, wiping her mouth against her shoulder as best she could, the lashing around her arms keeping them strained back. She had to find something to cut the leather. She crept around the shed, shuddering when she brushed against a body. There was nothing there but the dead. She pushed on the wood of the walls. The door was on that side; she would have to break free on the other. Some of the wood was rotted, but the shed was sturdy for all that. She tried to think. What would Aranur do? Kick the walls down—she almost smiled, breaking off with a whimper as the expression yanked pain into her smashed face. All right, then, what would Gamon do? Test each board, she told herself, then kick the walls down. This time, she did not smile.

Wolfwalker, the gray voice came urgently. *Do you hear me? I am here.* It was Hishn and not Hishn. It was the voice of the wolf in the woods.

"Gray One, you honor me."

I dig.

The scuffling sounds, the scratching in the earth, the sudden smell of wet dirt on top of the dead bodies, and Dion retched again. There was nothing to vomit, and she gagged instead. She leaned against the wall near the digging, then opened her eyes wide. Light . . . the walls were sturdier than she could kick through—at least in less than an hour, but the floor . . .

"Gray One," she whispered excitedly, "it will work!"

Wait.

Time. How long? Would the raiders see? Footsteps approached the shed, and the Gray One fell silent, crouching into his hole so that his body was not above the earth. Dion huddled back against the wall. The bolt was lifted, the door opened, and she blinked, her eyes watering. The raider glanced at the floor, saw her vomit, and grinned. "Like your quarters? Here's more company." He dragged Rafe's body in and, with the help of two other raiders, hoisted it and secured it by its neck to a ring in one of the ceiling beams. "Don't let them talk back, now, you hear?" He chuckled.

The other two leered at her. "Don't go away," one of them admonished. "We'll be wanting to . . . talk," he emphasized evilly, "to you later."

Dion turned her face away, refusing to look at them. They did not wait for an answer, but left unhurriedly, dropping the bolt back across the door. The Gray One behind the shed resumed digging before their footsteps faded.

"Be careful," Dion whispered. "Do not let them see you, or you will be caged again, too."

He did not answer, though Hishn howled in Dion's head, her impatience and frustration growing with each moment. *Scratch, claw the dirt. Rake it back and dig again* . . . His claws scraped the wood, and Dion caught her breath, but he did not stop. Gray light filtered up from the cracks now, though she could but barely see his shape blocking and unblocking the day. She wriggled against her bonds. She had been too dazed to tense up when they lashed her arms together, so there was little slack to use. Wait—the loop above her left wrist . . . She twisted, tightening the cord on her left arm so that she had to bite her lips to keep from crying out. But the right was now slack. She twisted again. Her skin tore. Hishn howled in her head. "Ahhh," Dion cried out softly. She folded her hand and scraped it through the loop awkwardly, leaving flesh and blood behind. Her arm was not yet free, but she could loosen the loop around her left wrist now, and once that hand was out, it took only a moment to wriggle out of the ropes around her arms. She almost cried at the relief when her shoulders came forward. Then the returning circulation began to burn, and she gritted her teeth, rolling her shoulders deliberately to restore the feeling to them. The same with her wrists. Roll, twist, ignore the blood that dribbled from the one.

The Gray One scratched wood again, and this time Dion put her weight on it, bouncing lightly and feeling it give just a little. She glanced over her shoulder. "How deep is it now?"

Soon . . . The wolf was preoccupied, digging furiously at the hole, his body stretched out, then pulled back as the dirt bunched up under his belly and he had to back out and scatter the pile before starting again. Dion shivered. Her tunic gave her little warmth. She stood against the wall, listening, until the sliver of light that now lit one of the bodies' hands gave her an idea. The rope was long enough . . . She gathered the line from the floor, moving to the door and tying one end to the handle. The other end she stretched across to a body: once around the ankle, and a trader's hitch to pull it tight. She stared at the dim shapes with a grim smile. When they tried to open the door, they would have their own surprise. They would hardly expect her to want to keep it closed.

The wolf was still digging. She paced irritably. "Now?"

Soon.

She ground her teeth. Her wrists throbbed, and her knuckles and hands were raw as if doused in acid. The line the raiders used was not smooth.

"Now?" She asked again.

Now.

She tested the boards again, felt their weakness, and drew back. Gathering her focus, she kicked. Her foot bounced off the wood. She said nothing, but breathed in, focused, and relaxed. This time, when she kicked, a sharp crack answered. She froze.

Go. Do not stop.

She kicked again. The crack repeated. On the third try, the board snapped. Jagged splinters slashed up her leg as her foot went through, and she jammed her forearm into her mouth to stop her own scream.

Wolfwalker, the Gray Ones howled. *Pain—burning legs—*

"I am fine," she snarled. "Fine."

She placed her weight on the broken board, and the wood gouging into her legging released. When she pulled her leg free, she was shaking. Grimly, she moved a foot back and kicked again. One minute. Two, and there were three broken boards along the base of the shed. Finally, she broke them off the wall, making a gap as wide as her forearm was long. She stared at the hole, at the gray daylight streaming up from it around a black nose, which eased forward. Dion reached down, touching the Gray One's muzzle.

Hurry, the wolf urged.

She set the broken planks up on the shed floor. Then, head-first, into the hole. Wood splinters raked her back, then her buttocks, but she folded her slender length along the narrow ditch until her head poked outside the shed. Her eyes watered at the light. She could not wipe them. Her thighs seemed stuck. She wriggled, wrenched, and twisted until first one, then the other, loosened and came out another handspan. When her calves scraped across the splinters, she knew she was free.

Hurry, the Gray One repeated. He stood flat against the back-side of the shed, watching her with his gleaming eyes. The gray voices in the background became urgent, and Hishn howled.

Wolfwalker, hurry. The hunter is on the door. The den is no longer safe.

Dion scrambled up, pressing herself against the shed like the wolf. The raiders were in the front. Coming to the shed? She did not know. The dnu—where were they kept? She would have to scatter them before she ran. The larger barn? She eased to-ward the corner of the shed. From where she was, she could reach the barn without the raiders knowing . . .

The Gray One caught her legging in his teeth. *My brothers and sister—*

"I must scatter the dnu first," she whispered. "When the raiders see me then, they must follow on foot. They will bring the wolves with them."

He released her reluctantly. Sneaking like shadows, they ran, crouching, to the barn. Dion crept inside. There were few dnu here, but then, she remembered, there were not so many raiders here, either. Those she and Rafe had found dead on the trail had probably come from this camp. She gathered the four dnu she found. The smells of blood and vomit that clung to her body did not quiet them, and she crooned, soothing them as best she could. Finally, she got them all to the back door at the same time. She led them out quietly, continuing to croon until she set them free on the treeline. They did not show any inclination to go further, so she slapped one of them on the rump. The creature merely turned and glared at her. It was not until the Gray One nipped its heels that the dnu bolted. The wolf bit at the others, but they squealed, and Dion cursed. "Now, Gray One," she muttered, "we begin our run."

"Check the barn!" one of the raiders yelled. They were running now. Dion bolted into the woods, trampling ferns and breaking branches on her way. If they could not follow that trail, then they did not deserve even the name of raider.

"This way—the wolfwalker is gone! Forget the shed—she went out the back!"

"Get the wolves," the leader snarled, "and bring one of the wolfwalkers to help with their cooperation."

Dion glanced back and ran into a branch at neck height. She swore under her breath. Two of the raiders were following her into the woods already. She gathered speed. The Gray One beside her ducked suddenly right, and Dion followed. A path opened up.

Wolfwalker, Hishn howled. *Run!*

Wolfwalker, the Gray Ones sang, freed from their cage. *We come!*

They howled, and Dion's ears rang. Behind her, the raiders caught sight of her and shouted. "This way!" and "She's over here!"

The Gray One in front of her dodged left, and Dion followed. She flung herself down on her hands and knees. Scrambling through the brush tunnel, she hauled herself up on the other side, crouching on the new trail. She paused, noticing how soft the dirt was here. She gouged it deeply with her toes, as if she had leapt to her feet. Glancing back, she caught her breath, then turned and ran.

One kilometer—the trails were flat. The wolves were on her scent now, and when they glimpsed her in front of them they howled. The raiders ran silently, yanking on the neckrope of their captive wolfwalker when he seemed to lag. Two kilometers—the trail began to rise. Dion's breath came in gasps, and she slowed to a walk, her fists pressing against her side to stop the stitch from growing. Three kilometers. Four. The Gray One led her to the main trail, and she ran, knowing that the raiders were close enough to see her, yet far enough to ignore their bows.

Run, Wolfwalker, Hishn howled in her head. *We hear your hunt. We wait . . .*

Aranur, Gamon—they were there, on the other side of the river. Relief washed through her. They must have risked both men and dnu to make the crossing so soon. Aranur . . .

The fifth kilometer came and went, and Dion's ankle turned, throwing her to the ground. She scrambled up, but the raiders had seen. With a roar, they surged forward.

Running. Jumping the trail debris. The wind was rising, and Dion put on more speed. A kilometer yet to go? Maybe more? She could hear the river now, and she knew the raiders could see her clearly. Fast. Faster. Their shouts were not quite drowned in the Phye. The trail crumbled beneath her feet, and she jumped as the side eroded down the long cliff. On—on to the ford.

Howl with us, Wolfwalker, the wolves sang behind her. *Run with the wind.*

Come, she urged them. *Keep with me.* The Gray One who ran with her was in the forest, not on the trail, and the raiders had not yet realized he was there.

There—up ahead. The bend in the river—was the logjam still there? She could not tell. The bank was too high. Please, gods, she prayed, her thoughts jarring with her steps. Her ankle turned, then turned again, and she fell sideways, her knee hitting the ground heavily. Not now, she screamed at it silently. She hauled herself up, ignoring the shooting pain that radiated up her leg. Like Sobovi, like the others, she could run with that. The Gray Ones would hold her up.

Please, moons, just one piece of luck. She rounded the bend. The river rushed by. The logs were there. Hishn snarled in her mind, pacing, raging silently beside the dark shape of Aranur. Close. They were waiting. All she had to do was cross . . .

Here! she screamed back at the wolves. *It is here. You must go with me!*

She did not look back. They were there—she could hear them. The raiders' feet pounded like hers in the earth. They shouted—they had seen the logs stretching across the Phye.

Come, she called to the wolves. *Cross to Ariye.*

She scrambled down the bank, losing her grip on the roots and sliding down into the mud. She landed on her side, the cloying cold of it freezing her tunic to her skin and making her slip again when she staggered up. She clambered up on the logs.

"Shoot her!"

"No—we want her alive. Catch her. She's not going much further."

She hauled herself up, crawling, then standing on the log. She made her crossing in a crouching run. The Gray One with her did not follow. He would wait. He could almost taste the freedom in his mate's mouth.

Wolfwalker, he sent. *Run with the wind.*

"And you, Gray One." She paused and turned back. "Honor will always be yours."

She got ten meters and had to jump to the next log. It shifted beneath her and she froze. Gods—if the dam did not hold—But the force of the river had shoved another snag into the pile; it was merely packing the dam together more firmly. She could see the gully's entrance. Only thirty meters to go, and she would be in Ariye, and then Aranur would take these raiders from her back . . .

She was so close, the raiders did not hesitate. They shouted at their wolfwalker, forcing the wolves onto the logs after her, running recklessly across the dam. The wolves hung back and the wolfwalker was whipped so that he slipped and would have fallen into the Phye but for the collar around his neck. Choking, coughing, retching, he was hauled up by it, his facing turning a swollen red until his feet found purchase again. The raiders cursed.

Water rushed. The wind rose again, chilling Dion through her tunic, and she slipped.

Wolfwalker—Hishn's voice was panicked.

Hishn, I'm all right. She balanced carefully, ignoring the wolves who eased forward only meters away now. When she jumped, she heard their joy like a blast of wind in her head. She landed on the rock with one foot in the water. In seconds, she was up and onto the second boulder. From there, the bank was an easy leap. She jumped. Her ankles sank into the mud, and she struggled to pull them free, throwing herself forward. She had to gain the bluff before the wolves followed her across. Behind her, the first wolf gained the boulders. The raiders shouted in triumph.

The bluff was before her, and she jumped, catching the roots and hauling herself up. Then she was running again, her sweat cold on her sides, and her feet heavy with mud. *Hishn—how far?*

Into the gully. Just beyond the bluegrass. The urgency in the wolf's voice was not lost on Dion, and she sucked at it, letting it fill her with speed. She could almost sense Aranur beside the wolf, pacing as Hishn did, snarling, cursing under his breath.

She was weaving, her breath coming in great gasps, her hands pressed to her sides. She glanced behind and stumbled. Gods—they were only forty meters behind her. She sprinted, her fists clenched with the effort. The gully—only half a kilometer. Just a little farther. Her ankle turned again, and she fell twice. The raiders surged forward. She staggered to her feet and fled.

From the side of the gully, Aranur watched the race with desperate patience. She was running at the end of her endurance now. How far had she come? Four kilometers? Five—and practically sprinting the entire way? Come on, he urged silently. Just to the bluegrass. Just to the edge. Her face was swollen, discolored on one side. Her tunic gapped in the front where it had been sliced across. Aranur's rage grew, but he held it tightly. Dion to safety first. Then revenge. She stumbled, and his jaw tightened. Get up, he shouted in his mind. Hishn snarled, and his silent shout seemed to echo away. Dion's ankle turned again, and she fell heavily this time, tumbling to the side.

Beside Aranur, one of the swordsmen lunged forward. "Let's go," he cried out. "She's down—"

Aranur grabbed his arm. "No," he snarled. "Wait."

"Are you crazy," the man snapped. "They are almost on her. If she falls again—"

"No." Aranur thrust him back. "I give the orders. We wait."

The fighter looked at him as if he were a raider. "What kind of man are you?" he demanded.

Aranur caught his breath. He turned slowly on the other fighter, his eyes like gray ice. The fighter stepped back, his hand half up. Aranur stared at him for a long moment, then turned back. Half a kilometer. Now a quarter kilometer away. Dion ran.

The other man stood stunned. He cursed under his breath. Gamon pointed back to his position, and the man swore again. "What is it with him?" he muttered, glaring at Aranur's back. "Does he want her dead, to force her to run when she can barely stand? Does her life mean so little to him?"

Gamon, watching Dion's staggering run, tested his bowstring calmly and pulled an arrow from his quiver. "She is his Promised," he returned quietly.

The man stared at him in disbelief. As Gamon turned his back on the man, the younger fighter began to curse steadily under his breath.

Aranur watched the race silently. Dion stumbled again, caught her balance, and came on. The wolves stretched out behind her. They made no noise; rather it was the raiders who shouted triumphantly as they gained. Dion's face was twisted with strain. Her fists clenched. Aranur forced himself to remain motionless. Only the muscles jumping in his jaw and the gritted teeth told Gamon that his nephew felt as he did, and he touched Aranur on the arm for a second before moving into place. Beside them, Hishn whined, then snarled. The wolves were running on Dion's heels. The raiders shouted for them to hold her, but the Gray Ones flowed around her instead. She stumbled, put her hand out, and found it grasping a thin gray scruff. There was bluegrass under her feet. Bluegrass . . . She whirled, facing the raiders. "Yaaa," she taunted them.

"Bitch of a lepa!" one of them shouted. "You are—"

The arrow took him in the throat before he could finish. Dion and the other wolfwalker threw themselves to the ground. The wolves scattered. The piercing flight of the arrows was as sudden as it was silent. Someone was screaming. Someone else gurgled obscenely in the grass. Dion huddled down. If the raiders got even one shot off . . .

Aranur raced across the grass. He reached Dion, then ran on to the other wolfwalker, slashing through the tether so that he could get away from the writhing bodies of the raiders. They were dying. The tortured wolfwalker crawled away from them, clutching the wolf who had turned back. Gamon and the others caught up to Aranur, and the tall man, still pumped by the adrenaline, whirled to see one of the men kneeling by Dion, covering her with his own jerkin. Aranur burned. When he strode to her, the other man backed off in a hurry, leaving the jerkin and moving with alacrity to help the others drag the raiders farther into the gully.

Aranur hauled Dion to her feet. "Gods," he whispered raggedly, crushing her to him. "Don't ever do that again."

She locked her hands around his neck and buried her face in his shoulder. They clutched each other for a long moment. Not until Hishn butted Dion's thigh did they break apart.

Wolfwalker, Hishn sent, stretching into Dion's mind with joy at the thought of her name.

"Hishn," she whispered.

Wolfwalker, the other wolves echoed. *The hunt is ours!*

There were four voices that called, and Dion looked back to the river. On the logs, the Gray One who had helped her was crossing, and the wolf that ran to greet him ran with the joy of a mate. She smiled. "Look," she said to Aranur, "they are free again."

The wolves turned as one and howled, their cry echoing through the gully. Hishn threw back her head, and her long howl sobbed back to the sky. Dion shuddered. She was blinded by the sound until it faded. And then the wolves turned and raced from the meadow, leaving only their echo in her mind.

Aranur held Dion away from him, looking at her with a grim expression on his face. She glanced down. His hand caught her under her chin, and he forced her to meet his eyes. "By all nine moons," he whispered then, "you are beautiful." He nodded at her surprise. "You are safe." He took her hand, walking slowly with her back to the gully. He was not even surprised when the boy, Tomi, crept out from the treeline and fell into step behind them.

They reached the ambush camp as the raiders' wolfwalker was being led to it. He sank gratefully down on a log, drinking deeply from one of the bota bags. Then his eyes went to Dion and Aranur, and he stood slowly.

"Dione," he said quietly.

She held out her arms, and they gripped each other tightly. "Wilse." She shook her head, unable to speak, and the other wolfwalker nodded with a crooked smile. There were no more wolfwalkers in Bilocctar. The only one left behind was dead. But the wolves ran free, may the moons curse the raiders to the seventh hell.

Chapter 17

Hiding in the river mud,
Ariyens, gather!
Sneaking through the fireweed,
Ariyens, gather!
Climbing down the Lepa Cliffs,
Ariyens, gather!
Dawn is coming,
Day is near;
Your arrows hunger; your swords are thirsty;
Your hearts are loud in your chest.
Ariyens, gather!

Usu watched the scene from the Slot. The runner, the wolves, the raiders. The raiders gained, and the runner went down, falling, scrambling up, and no longer even keeping ahead of the wolves. Usu lost sight of them as they entered the gully. She was dead, then. The raiders would make sure of that. He was about to draw back and make his way along the Slot Trail when he paused. There was something about that run . . .

He frowned. The raiders had not reappeared, and neither had the runner. A slow smile, grim as death, worked its way onto his face, and Usu regarded the gully opening with a new expression. That runner had had a goal in mind when she bolted from the river. She had not hesitated one step when heading for the draw. Why? If she were trying to outrun the raiders, she would have been better off to head along the riverbank south, into the deeper ravines where the wolves would have trouble following and she could evade the raiders at leisure. No, he decided with grim satisfaction, she had wanted them to follow. There could be only one thing waiting in the draw.

An ambush.

So the Ariyens had come north. He slowly nodded to himself. They either had sent this runner or knew she was coming. The raiders had not reappeared because they were dead. He narrowed his eyes suddenly. The Gray Ones were sprinting out of the gully now, separating and racing away, joined by another who crossed that logjam behind them. The wolves . . .

Could it be? Had the runner freed them? He clenched his fists to his sides. If it was true—if the raiders no longer had their hunters . . . and if the Ariyens were here, north, in enough force . . .

He wormed back from the lip, got to his feet, and hurried to the trail. He exchanged a few words with the man who waited for him there, and when he climbed down from the Slot, it was not along the western trail that he loped, as did the other man, but the east, to find those who came from Ariye.

The evening had darkened the cliffs from the west when Usu approached the Ariyens' camp. He was surprised that he was not challenged. For a long moment, he stopped and watched their camp, uneasy that he should get so close. If this was the best they could do, perhaps it would not be good enough, he worried.

"Good view?"

The calm voice made Usu freeze. He fingered his knife.

"Not a good idea," the voice said dryly. "Besides, we thought you wanted to be friends."

Usu turned his head slowly, moving as unthreateningly as he could. "Ariyen?"

A dark figure separated itself from the shadow of a tree. As it came forward, Usu saw that it was an older man, gray of hair and lean of limb. "Come on down. We've been waiting for you."

"The wolves . . ."

The older man nodded. "Not much goes by that they miss."

A few minutes later, they entered the camp, the curious glances following them into the dim circle that surrounded a sheltered fire pit. With little light cast back up on faces or trees, Usu had to look long and hard to make out their faces. These were fighters, he recognized, who knew their trade. Archers, swordsmen. Lean bodies, taut muscles. For a moment he allowed himself to dream of what he could do if they ran under his command.

The older man halted before a younger copy of himself, and Usu nodded his greeting curtly. Aranur looked at him as if he saw through his soul, and the resistance fighter had to hide his shiver. The tall man smiled. "I have heard of your work," he said quietly. "Welcome."

Usu drew himself up. "I am Usu." He paused. "On the border," he apologized, "I have no other name."

The older man who had brought him in nodded. "This is Aranur." He indicated the tall, gray-eyed figure. "Tehena—a strategist; Dion—"

The resistance fighter recognized her. "The runner."

She nodded.

He frowned, puzzled. "Healer?"

Dion nodded again, raising her hand self-consciously to the silver circlet on her brow.

Gamon offered him some of the stew that still simmered in several of the pots over the fire, but though Usu's mouth watered, he declined. Not when his own people were starving would he take food from this fire. Until the day his county was free, he had sworn to eat no more than he must, saving all he could for the others.

Aranur glanced at his hands, noting their tremble. The hollow cheeks spoke of a hunger that would be grateful for a bite, but it was not Aranur's place to question the man.

"Forgive my abruptness," Usu said instead, "but you are how many here?"

Tehena made a noise of protest, but Aranur shook his head imperceptibly at her as he answered. "Close to eighty."

Usu was silent for a moment. "The raiders' camp in Dog Pocket," he said then.

Aranur smiled slowly, but said nothing.

Usu met Aranur's eyes. This tall man knew what he was thinking, he told himself warily. Could he trust him? It could cost all their lives if he was wrong.

"The raiders are three hundred strong," Tehena said from beside the tall man. Her voice was flat, as if she were discussing a wart or boil, not the destruction of her land, and Usu eyed her narrowly.

"They are unsettled," he returned. "They have lost three supply caravans in half that many ninans."

It was Gamon who said, "Your work, I believe?"

Usu nodded. "We wish to—"

"Join forces," Tehena finished. "You are what, about thirty strong?"

Usu started, stepping back.

"We have not been talking to the raiders," she said disinterestedly. "I figured it from the sizes of the trains you attacked."

He nodded reluctantly. If she was good, she could have figured that. "Around thirty," he admitted, "but there are some who do not fight."

Tehena pursed her lips. "Which puts us outmanned three to one." Her hard expression made Usu nervous, and the smell of the stew distracted him so that he started when she spoke again.

"Three attacks simultaneously?" She turned to Aranur. "I will need this man—Usu—Dion, Sobovi, and, if you are up to it," she added, turning to the wolfwalker rescued from Bilocctar, "Wilse. I will also want you," she said to Aranur, "Gamon, and the maps."

Aranur nodded curtly. Ten minutes later, her questions to the scouts short and to the point, she outlined her plan. Usu nodded again as he answered her, a grudging admiration in his voice, then stood back, letting her finish the details with Aranur and Gamon. These Ariyens were as quick to act as his own group, for which he was glad. With the attack of their last supply train that morning, the raiders were still jumpy, but they would not be expecting another raid on their own camp so soon. They were too many, their camp too strong. And Usu had never attacked twice in the same ninan. For the Ariyens to suddenly swoop down upon them . . .

In front of the resistance fighter, Aranur glanced once more at the lists. A small enough force, he thought, but size was not necessarily strength. He eyed the group thoughtfully as they gathered, nodding their greetings to each other silently. There were over twenty archers in his group, and twice that many swordsmen. There were three wolfwalkers: Dion, Sobovi, and the one they had rescued; and five other scouts. Tehena nodded to him, indicating that she was done with the last few names, and Aranur looked around the group soberly.

"We have never done this before," he stated, acknowledging their concerns. "Most of you came north to set up a camp as we have done in the south. But the raiders have already moved onto Ariyen soil. Usu's group attacked their supply wagons this morning, and they will not be expecting another attack soon. This—" he paused "—is a chance from the moons. It is either move on the raiders now, or wait for them to dig in. If we wait . . ." He shrugged.

"We will never get them out again," Gamon finished. The older man lifted a long message ring. He held up the pole, then handed it around the circle, the map designed on its surface showing each of them the Black Ravines, the Slot, the Phye. He nodded at the wooden ring. "They have been in the north long enough to learn this terrain as we do. They are native here, and as used to the winters as we are. We cannot use the seasons against them, nor can they use them against us. If we let them settle without a fight, we give up this corner of Ariye. They gain a foothold, and from there . . ."

Aranur met the eyes of each man and woman before speaking again. "You know what we must do. Are we ready?"

One of the archers tilted her head at him. "Do we have a choice?" she asked wryly.

He smiled slightly. "Yes," he responded. "Do you want the ground squad or the trail team?"

She grinned. "I'll take the ground squad," she answered slowly. "If we're going to fight, not camp, you won't catch me up on the Slot without a moonwarrior at my side."

The others chuckled. "Where will the wolfwalkers be?" one asked.

Aranur glanced at Dion, then nodded at the other two. "Wilse has agreed to cross with Usu to the other side of the encampment; Sobovi will remain with me, and Dion will be on the cliff," he answered. "Don't count on them to use the wolves to coordinate your attacks," he warned, seeing the hope on their faces. "The Gray Ones are being sent away."

There were surprised looks, but Dion explained. "They cannot be near the fighting. The raiders used them to hunt humans. They must not be used to kill."

"But Hishn and you . . ." The words of one of the men trailed off in embarrassment, and Dion looked at him soberly.

"In defense, yes—when my life was at stake. So, too, for the other wolfwalkers. But this—" She gestured at the ridge over which they would sneak come dawn. "This is not defense. This is deliberate fighting—attack against humans based on rational decisions, not unprecipitated action. This is not self-defense. This is . . . war."

The last word came hard to her, and Aranur squeezed her shoulder. War. The ancient word seemed somehow evil. The ancients had studied war as an art form, as action, as politics, as simple business. But the wars they had known were things belonging to the distant stars. Never had such a thing come to Ariye—or any of the other counties. To create such a thing here . . . He quelled his shiver. He would carry a great burden with him to the moons when he died, may they have mercy on his soul.

Dion's words hung in the air, and Aranur glanced from one face to the next. "War." He repeated her word. Men and women alike looked down before they met his eyes again. "We bring war to Ariye," he said softly. "Let us remember that. This is no simple venge, where a dozen of us ride out after four or five raiders to bring them to justice. This is something bigger which we unleash. If we are unsuccessful—" He paused, letting the words sink in ominously. "—we teach a powerful lesson to the raiders." He nodded at their consternation. "We teach them organization of action, not just the possession of land. We are attacking in force here, on a scale never before seen on this world. If we do not succeed," he repeated, "they will adopt our tactics and absorb them, improve them, until they use them next against us. We will be weaker, the strategy more effective against us than when we used it on them."

One of the men stirred. "How do you know they will even notice what we do?"

Aranur glanced at him. "Because of all the people in Bilocctar there is one who will understand. That one person controls not only the Lloroi, but the raiders."

The other man frowned. ''The raiders I understand, but someone who controls the Lloroi, as well?''

Aranur nodded. ''Longear.''

Even expecting the name, Gamon felt a chill crawl down his spine. Longear. The woman had held Bilocctar in her grip for years. She was the force behind the old Lloroi's expansion into the other counties. She was the genius behind the raiders. What he and Aranur did here was to show her a new weapon she could turn and use against not only Ariye, but the rest of the counties she coveted. Gamon's eyes narrowed. He had fought her before and come out lacking. This time . . .

Aranur followed his thoughts as if they were his own. His gray eyes were cold. ''We must succeed,'' he stated flatly. ''We will succeed. We are fewer, but we are better trained than the raiders. We have the resistance fighters to bolster our numbers. We have surprise. We have determination. More ancient battles were won by those two elements than any other.'' He glanced up at the flattened mountain that loomed over the ridge. ''Rodt, when the first shadows fall across the cliff trail, take your four archers down as far as you can. There are some rough columns there with flattened tops almost like beds. Be careful. It is a narrow trail, and the lepa hunt there in the day.'' He grinned at their faces. ''But don't worry. After a comfy night on the cliff, you should be ready for anything.'' He removed his warcap and ran his hand through his hair; dropping the teasing, he added, ''It will be a long night, but your position is critical. We attack at dawn, when the cliffs are half in light, half in shadow. Down low, your positions will be dark enough to hide you, but the ground will be light enough for us to fight.''

Gamon indicated the small group of archers. ''It's the best vantage point we can give you.''

''We'll count our bolts,'' one of the archers reassured.

Aranur gestured toward the man who stood silently behind him, hiding almost in the shadow. ''Tehena, take your group of archers and follow Usu. He will take you to the mud flats, where half of you will stay until the raiders are driven toward you; the other half will attack the camp. Everyone else''—he smiled faintly—''is with me.'' There was general groaning around the circle.

''Don't get too excited yet,'' he admonished them with a gleam in his gray eyes. ''Those of you who will be going with me will crawl down the south side of Digger's Gully this evening. From dusk to as far into the night as it takes, we will ease our way through the brush until we are within a hundred meters of the raider's camp. We'll stay there till dawn. When we see the signal from the trail archers, we attack from the east.''

''But,'' one of the men broke in, ''the east side of their camp is surrounded by fireweed. No one—''

''No one in their right mind would camp in a meadow of fireweed,'' Aranur finished for him. He grinned slowly. The men and women stared at him.

''If it's any consolation,'' Gamon said sourly, ''I'll be there, too.''

Dion chuckled. Even with her fear of heights, she did not care to trade her cliff assignment for Aranur's task. Apparently, the other archers agreed. Their night on the basalt columns was beginning to look better and better.

Gamon shrugged. ''Those of us in the east will be attacking out of the darkness, for the sun will not have cleared the trees when the signal is given. Those on the cliffs will again have an advantage, since the ravines will keep the sun from your position until two hours past dawn. Those with Usu will not be protected by the sun, but by the mud. You won't have to move into position until just before dawn. Instead, you will camp downstream, then wade up and crawl into the mud in the early morning. You are our shock tactic,'' he said with a faint smile. ''From the raiders' point of view, you will be invisible. The dark shadows from the banks will hide your shapes in the mud, and they will not be able to see where your arrows come from. If you can close the ford to them, the swordsmen can sweep down on them from the east, driving them upstream where the bank grows suddenly steep, and they can be pushed off onto the rocks below. There won't be many who survive that without broken bones of some sort.''

Aranur glanced at them. ''There is one more thing,'' he said quietly. ''Even with our numbers, our strategy, and the help of the resistance group, we are not sure we have the strength to destroy the raiders. Our primary goal therefore is to push them back into Bilocctar. Do not overrun into the thick of them—that will weaken our position and cause us to shoot at ourselves unknowingly. We want to keep them bunched, drive them like oxen to the river. Best if we can destroy them like that. Otherwise, we will simply kill as many as we can as we drive them back to the border."

Gamon looked at each fighter soberly. "Our success depends on the fact that each of us understands our purpose."

"It will be confused fighting," Aranur added. "There will be little light. Stay together. Fight in groups. Gang up on the raiders—don't try to face them one by one. If you are separated from your group, stop, drop to the ground, worm your way back, or stay where you are until you locate your line again. This is critical," he said more sharply as one of the women nodded, bored. "If you are separated and the raiders find you, you are dead." The uneasy silence that followed that remark was proof that he had caught their attention again.

"Most of you have never ridden on a venge," Dion said, her quiet voice a stark contrast to Aranur's commands. "Many of you have never fought outside of a controlled ring." She pointed at herself. "The first time isn't bad—you don't realize at first that it is real. After that—" She shrugged. "You might panic. You might freeze. You might become enraged and run among them like a wild person. The thing to understand," she said as firmly as Aranur had done a moment before, "is that you can't know what you will do until it happens to you. Take Aranur's advice. Stay together. Stay alive."

The woman who had paid little attention before was nodding soberly. Aranur gripped Dion's arm, thanking her silently as he noted the other woman's changed expression. "We have the moons with us tonight," he said softly. "They will be with us tomorrow. Believe in yourselves, and we will win."

Chapter 18

Night,
Which brings the loneliness
and the dark,
Brings also dawn.

It was dusk. Dion edged along the cliff with her heart in her mouth. Basalt shards shifted under her feet, and she eyed the black columns as sweat beaded on her temples and the hum of the Slot vibrated in her bones. Behind her, the archers followed. The trail was visible—just. If only they could have done this in daylight. But then the raiders would have seen them as they descended. As it was, the dusk was their protection and their danger. One misstep . . .

Wolfwalker, Gray Hishn called. The wolf was on a ridge, hunting with the pack, and her images raced through Dion's mind.

Dion paused, one hand on the column beside her, her eyes unfocused. A heart pounded. Was it her? Or the wolf? *You honor me, Hishn,* she managed.

The hunt—run with us! Howl with the pack, Wolfwalker!

Joy filled their voices, and Dion clutched the stones, jamming her fist in one of the cracks between the broken-out columns.

"Dion?"

It was one of the archers, his expression concerned even in the gloom. Behind him, Tomi watched her closely, saying nothing. Dion was not happy that the boy was with her, but she had to agree that he was safer up here, on the cliffs, than he would be with either Aranur or Gamon.

"It's nothing," she said. "Just the wolves."

Down along the curving trail. Down through the dust. They passed the droppings of a lepa, and Dion could not help looking up, searching the deepening gloom for a glimpse of the lepa caves, of the raptors that could tear her from this cliff as if she were a leaf.

How many breaths could be crammed into a second? Her ankle throbbed with every step—the wrap gave it strength, but not relief—and her cheekbones ached. The slash across her chest had scabbed, and now it pulled with every stretch and step. The trail dropped jaggedly, dodging out when columns leaned away from the face. Some were loose, and warnings passed along the line. Don't lean here; touch not that stone. Pale moonlight lit the wall. Crevices split back into the face. Crevices that hid night rodents and snakes. Narrow caves that were black as a moonless night, and glinting with eyes disturbed by her hands . . . and Dion clutched the rocky edges and eased her way on down.

Were these minutes or hours? The moons barely budged in the sky. Her breath came harshly, but not from strain. Darkness did not hide the drop to her left; it plunged away like glass. Down, she staggered. Her knees ached. The jarring of each step became a throb of its own. The trail flattened suddenly, and Dion hurried carefully, her feet gliding out, feeling the path before her weight followed. Rising, the fourth moon eclipsed the fifth as it cleared the trees. Another jog; another bend; another drop, and she slipped in the dust, catching herself on the edge of another column. But the bottom of the trail was in sight at last: The broken rocks where the cliff crumbled into earth was only ten meters away. Twenty minutes, she guessed. It had been twenty minutes down from the top to where she was stopped.

Behind her, the archers passed the boy forward, and Dion pointed to a flattened pocket where he could crouch and sleep.

She settled in beside him, curling and shifting until she found the place where her hips were wedged between two curved spots and her head rested comfortably on a broken plane. Around her, the other archers nestled into the rocks. The wind that howled along the cliff did not touch them except to drop its dust on them like a blanket. One of the archers choked, suppressing his sneeze, and Tomi started. Dion reached out reassuringly. The need for silence was great—their sounds would carry to the raiders like rocks falling into their camp.

Moons crawled. Tomi snuggled into Dion's lap. Her left buttock went numb. Then her shoulder. She shifted, her eyes searching out the stars so that she knew the time. One hour. Two. She dozed, and the rattle of a rock awoke her. She tensed, but it was only the wary steps of a rockrodent, creeping through the motionless humans, confident that though they hunted, it was not he who was their prey. She dozed again, shifting drowsily as her head tilted into a sharp corner of the column. Minutes . . . Hours . . . She came awake slowly, still seeing only dark, but knowing it was near the dawn. She woke the boy with a touch. Pointing, she showed him where to pee, and he did so, the faint sound blending with the wind that gusted along the trail. The other archers were stirring, too, and they took careful turns in the few sheltered places there to do their morning duty.

In the east, the sky was already light. The purple-blue glow flared into pink in the overcast sky, then stretched out seared fingers of red and orange. Dion and the others looked down at the raiders' camp. The lights below were dim, the fires banked in the pits, and the dark hulks of the wagons and cabins sheltering the raider's sleeping bags from her eyes. Dion and the archers could see their surroundings clearly now. They eased farther down the path, choosing spots where the basalt columns stuck up and out from the cliff face. Twice they stepped over narrow chasms, and Dion feared that Tomi would cry out; but the boy, looking into her eyes as he crossed, made no sound. They crouched only twenty meters above the raiders.

Dawn lit the top of the mountain like a dark fire. Shadows splintered across the broken columns with the light, and below, the raiders began to stir. Beside Dion, Rodt, the best archer, watched for the signal, his hand up, open-palmed, indicating that it was not yet visible. The sun crawled out of its eastern den, and suddenly the columns above them were bright gray-black, shining in the morning light, while Dion crouched in dark shadow. Black stones in the dusk; dark stones in the day. The basalt columns stretched out of the broken earth at the base of the cliff. Up, a hundred meters. Two hundred, then three. Broken-out caves darkened the face and hid the lepa who slept and dreamed of bloody meat. The light gray dawn would not bring them out; they waited for the sun. Below their dens, the trails crisscrossed the face. Only one trail went from base to top. One trail, no switchbacks. One straight rise broken only by those blackened columns that jutted into the path and made the trail jog out, then in.

The raiders rose. Sleeping bags were rolled and tossed in the empty wagons. Fires flared up in the pits. The cabins emptied as raiders came out to tend to their morning duties. Rodt's hand was still open-palmed. Tomi glanced from Dion to Rodt and back. The wolfwalker seemed relaxed, but her eyes, alert, cataloged the movement below, noting each position, each piece of cover the raiders had.

Rodt hissed. His palm closed into a fist. A sudden roar erupted from the fireweed line, and the raiders, as one, leapt to their feet. Archers fired. Screams answered. Aranur's men fired first, then scrambled to their feet and surged forward. The raider's camp was in an uproar. Two of Dion's archers fired flaming arrows, and the cabin roofs and wagons caught fire. Smoke curled up. They fired again, and flames sprouted suddenly, taking hold of the wood and racing along it as if the wood were a steep hill and the fire were water. How many had they taken out? Smoke formed a column blasting apart in the wind and blackening their view. "Down!" Dion shouted as a volley of arrows flew up toward them. The archers dropped back, one not soon enough. Shafts of wood struck the rocks around them, and one of the barbs cut across a woman's cheek. She screamed, and her partner cut the bolt from her face, dragging it through where it had punctured the other side of her jaw. She moaned, spitting blood, but her partner lashed a pad to her face. Resolutely, she wiped her blood-slick hands on her trousers, then reached again for her bow.

Dion fired at one of the figures that ventured out from behind a cabin and followed with another bolt as the first one struck flesh. When a second figure raced across the porch, the wind gusted. Her third bolt went astray, skittering harmlessly across one of the water barrels beside the porch.

Fire stretched down the sides of the cabins now, and the raiders ran from within. Aranur's men had gained the camp. The raiders, confused by the noise and the dark, gave way. With a roar, Aranur leapt forward. Dion held her breath as the smoke blew back against the cliff, stinging her eyes and blinding her to the action. From all over the camp, raiders raced to face the threat from the east. Behind them, from the west, two dozen figures leapt up from the dark, shooting into the raiders' backs, then dropping back to the ground. Half the resistance fighters crawled forward like dogs, hidden in the green-black growth, while the other held back, waiting for their turn. The raiders turned, crying out that there was attack from the river side. Their confused force was split, some running to the west, some east, no one commanding their frantic energy. The resistance group reached the edge of the camp in less than a minute. A knot of raiders obeyed a furiously shouting figure and shot blindly into the shadows. Behind them, the fire silhouetted their forms for the resistance fighter's arrows and cast dancing shadows forward to confuse the raiders' eyes. A dozen men from the camp gave up and fled. More ran from the unseen death. Two seconds, three, and then the resistance group leapt up and surged forward. Silently, they raced into the camp, slashing as they went. One of the fighters went down under two raiders. Another tumbled, an arrow sticking out of his thigh. It snapped off with his hideous scream, and he dragged himself to the scant shelter of a broken barrel, thumbing another arrow to his bow as he crawled. Huge gaps of space opened up and shifted as the raiders ran for the attackers, then fled to the river. The Ariyens poured in.

Smoke shifted, and Dion saw Aranur. He was leading a group between the wagons, circling and cutting off a smaller band of raiders against the burning walls. He cut, he lunged, and she held her breath. Gamon was beside him—she could not mistake his whirling blade. She clenched her fingers on her arrow, but there were no clear shots for her to take. Two, then three raiders fell before Gamon and a swordswoman. The ground was split between bodies and running men. Aranur tumbled. Blades flashed. Then he leapt away, motioning silently as he left another body behind. The others chased after.

"Look!" Tomi pointed.

"What?" Dion followed his finger, but could see only raiders in the camp.

"Peyel!"

"Peyel?" Dion searched the grounds for the figure to which he pointed. The woman from the tavern? The woman who had told Moira to take her children to the Sky Bridge?

"The raiders—" His voice was urgent. "They have her."

"Where?" Dion scanned the action quickly. Between the gusts, she could shoot into those who held the woman, freeing her to run back to the resistance group if she was not wounded.

"There—no!" Tomi shouted gleefully. "She is free of them."

Dion stared. Dark hair, small figure—that was no resistance fighter. That was—

"Longear," she whispered. "Longear!" she shouted, blinded by her rage.

The woman below did not hear her, but Dion was already moving. "Stay here," she snapped at the boy. She scrambled down the path, passing the other three archers. They looked up, startled, but she did not pause to explain. Intent only on reaching the melee below, she jumped the gaps in the columns and landed like a goat, ignoring the pain that shot through her weakened ankle. Longear. It was like a chant in her blood. The children taken and killed . . . the wolves whipped and beaten. She slipped and slid along a dusty spot, keeping her body on the trail only by jamming her fist into a crack and swinging violently around to fetch up hard against a column. Her eyes blacked out for an instant with the force. She pushed herself upright and leapt on. Longear. If any of the raiders reached the trial block, she swore it would be that one. There was no way in all the nine hells that Dion would give Longear a chance to cross the river with the others. She flung herself down the trail. In her mind, the gray echo swelled. Hishn cried out for her to run. Gray strength flooded her senses, making her dodge the strike of a startled night snake before she knew it was there. Her nose choked in the smoke and smells of blood. Her feet danced on the edges of the blackened columns, leaping from one to the next before her balance caught up with her and swayed her forward.

She vaulted the last boulder, refusing to lose the seconds it would take to circle. Landing hard, she glared forward, her eyes locked on Longear's slight form. She pulled her sword. Stab to the left. Block. Duck under a raider's arm and run forward again. Longear still did not see her. Halfway to the resistance group, Dion was halfway to her. Longear did not look back. The woman dodged the raiders, and Dion followed. No one cut at Longear—the resistance fighters and raiders both knew her for one of their own. Someone tumbled out of the dark and caught Dion a blind blow on the ribs. She tumbled, rolled, and came up with dust in her eyes. She shook her head and scrambled for her sword, ignoring the struggling forms and continuing her chase with deadly, single-minded intent. Longear paused, glancing back, but a raider blocked her view, and she did not see Dion jam her sword into the heavy man's gut, only to wrench it free and leap around to catch up to her in seconds.

Bloodlust, bared fangs . . . Hishn's thoughts were caught up in Dion's emotions. *Tear the flesh and drive down the prey . . .*

Dion lunged and grabbed Longear by the hair. "Longear!" she screamed, dragging the woman down into the dirt.

Longear reacted instantly. Kicking, striking, she fought like a watercat. Dion ignored her blows. She slammed her elbow into Longear's sternum, then her gut. The woman doubled over. Gasping, she kicked at Dion's knees, and the wolfwalker drew back, spinning an ax kick into the other woman's neck. Longear dropped like a stone.

Dion grabbed her by the hair and rolled her over. It took an instant to bind the woman's hands, one more to heave her up and over Dion's shoulder. Light as Longear was, Dion staggered with the weight. Sobovi was suddenly beside her, and Dion glanced up.

"Go," he shouted, his eyes unfocused. "I will guard you."

A raider lunged, but Sobovi felt him coming and crouched suddenly, slicing across the raider's calves. The man screamed, and Sobovi whirled, slicing across the man's hamstrings as he hobbled, then crashed to the ground in agony, clutching his legs. Dion ran on.

The hunt, the wolves sent. *The hunger grows . . .*

Dion staggered to the first of the boulders. Sobovi was at her side. He passed her, hauled himself up the first broken column, then reached back down for Longear. Around them, an evil shaft splintered stone and Dion stiffened. Sobovi flung himself back. "Drop her!" he shouted.

"No!" Dion refused. She shoved Longear up. He cursed, then grabbed the woman by her arms and dragged her up. Dion scrambled behind. Longear was beginning to come around, and she struggled against Sobovi's grip. "Hurry," he snapped.

Dion looked back. Someone—a woman—was running toward them from the resistance group, but another arrow smashed into stone, and there was no time to wait for the woman to arrive.

"Go," Sobovi said. "I'll help her."

Dion did not argue. She grabbed Longear's arm and dragged her over the boulders. The smaller woman cursed as her shins banged against the stones. Dion dug her fingers into a pressure hold on Longear's elbow, and the woman writhed. "Get your legs under you or lose them," Dion snarled.

From behind, the other figure reached the boulders. Sobovi hauled the woman up urgently. Dion was already up on the next set of columns. Longear staggered in Dion's wake, her balance jerked with Dion's stride. Dion was not gentle, and the other woman's knee was wrenched in a crack as she slipped. "Damn you, Dione," Longear swore. "I'll burn every finger from your hands for this."

"You'll burn in hell," Dion snapped back. "Now go!"

Up, they scrambled. Dion's chest heaved with the steepness of the climb. It had taken seconds to run down; it was a dozen times that long to go back up. In the back of her mind, the gray echo grew, and she closed it off abruptly.

The cliff dropped away where the hot springs down below ate into the wall. Longear hugged the face, slowing deliberately. Dion jerked her forward. Longear looked back. Raiders were running for the cliff trail now, and she laughed softly, watching them come. Dion's jaw tightened. She slammed Longear against the cliff face and ground one of her hands into the stone. Longear screamed, and Dion hauled her up. "Move!"

From below, a roar rose up, and a mass of raiders surged onto the columns. From above, Dion's archers shot carefully, then fell back, their bolts piercing leather and flesh alike, but the curve of the cliff blocked them from the trailhead, and over a dozen raiders reached the first broken column within seconds. Dion no longer dared to look back; Longear eyed the edge of the trail with calculation. "Don't even think about it," Dion snapped.

"Why not?" Longear growled. "You can't keep them from your back forever. They will advance, and you will fall back, and in the end, they will catch you, you will die, and I will win as I always have."

Dion ground her fingers into Longear's elbow, hauling her forward again, but this time, the other woman grinned, the strain of the expression showing only in the sweat that beaded on her forehead. "Have you forgotten that I always win, Dione?" she taunted. "It was what, a year ago we last met?"

A year ago, Longear's whips had burned their way into Dion's back. Dion tightened her jaw. A year ago, Longear had set a boy to die in the fighting rings. A year ago . . . She stared at Longear, her jaw trembling from the force with which she ground her teeth. Longear laughed. Dion took a step forward, dragging her unwillingly on, then paused, turned swiftly, and jammed her elbow back into Longear's gut again. The woman gasped, and Dion pulled her forward unresisting.

They reached the archers' position, and Dion hauled Longear past them to safety. Tomi jumped up, staring at the two. Dion ignored him, slamming Longear into a hole in the columns, her chest heaving, her eyes dark with fury.

"Peyel?" the boy asked hesitantly.

"Stupid child," the woman muttered, her dark eyes glittering at him like a snake.

The boy stared at her.

"She is no friend of yours," Dion said harshly. "That is Longear, leader of the raiders."

Someone moved behind her, and Dion glanced back. "Longear," the soft, hoarse voice whispered.

Dion turned and froze. "Namina?" she whispered, stunned.

Longear, staring at the newcomer, struggled to her feet. "You—" she snarled.

Namina stared at her, drinking in her figure. The three healed scars in her cheek pulsed red.

"Siker," Longear hissed.

Dion looked from one to the other. The puncture marks. Siker. Namina. The raiders' bodies with their throats slashed . . . Longear's nemesis. Namina?

Tomi edged away from the three women. Longear glanced at him, then back to the other, silent woman. "Namina, mate to the late Lloroi," she mocked. "You surprise me. I will have to be more thorough next time." She looked at the wolfwalker. "Want to know what I'll do to her this time, Dione? Or to the child? Just because of you?"

Dion's hand snaked out involuntarily and slapped her.

Longear laughed, softly, evilly. "See how easy it is to hit someone whose hands are bound? Fills you with a sense of power, doesn't it?"

Dion felt sick. From below, Rodt shot at the raiders on the trail, falling back toward her. "Dion, get going—up the trail," he yelled. "We cannot hold them off."

"No," Longear said gleefully. "You cannot keep them back, can you?"

"Shut up," Dion snarled.

"Dione, you haven't the guts to shut me up now or ever."

Dion clenched her fists, then grabbed Longear by the arm and dragged her along the path. Tomi scrambled after her, and Namina followed the boy like a ghost, silent and determined.

Someone screamed from below, and Dion half turned, only to whirl back as she felt Longear tense. Longear subsided, leering at her sudden fear, and Dion cursed under her breath. Aranur, she begged in her mind, look up . . .

Wolfwalker! The howl was long in her mind, and Dion's lips curled back. *We hunger* . . .

Longear looked at Dion and grinned at her unfocused eyes. Just a meter forward, there was a narrow spot in the path . . .

Dion stumbled. Longear shoved. Namina threw herself forward—

"Damn you," Dion swore. She crawled up on the trail, out of Longear's reach. Longear raised her eyebrow. Namina's left hand was clamped on the woman's arm, her right hand on the hilt of her knife. Dion got to her feet. "Can you keep hold of her?" she asked Namina. The blue-eyed woman did not nod, but her eyes burned her acknowledgment. "Then go." Dion pointed up the path. "I'll follow with the boy."

Someone else screamed, and then Rodt was running up the trail, Sobovi and two archers hard on his heels. "Go!" he yelled urgently, waving them past as he halted and turned back for the last archer. The last woman in the line whirled and set an arrow to her bow, barely pulling back before the shaft flew away. The dull thud of its strike was hidden by a cry, and she whirled and raced after the others. She covered only a few meters when she went rigid. She staggered forward, her mouth open in a soundless scream. Rodt leaped forward. She fell lengthwise in the trail. Rodt grabbed her shoulders, turning her, staring into her eyes until she began to kick. "Moons make your passage safe and sure," he choked. He did not wait for the death rattle to finish before he took her half-full quiver, cursing his clumsiness, and finally put an arrow to his bow. He drew back and waited a bare second before the first raider rushed around the bend. The running man took the bolt deep in his chest. The raider on his heels fell back with a curse. Rodt sent another shaft after him, then turned and fled up the trail.

From below, Aranur watched the line of fighters race and stop, crouch, and jerk their way up the cliff trail. Rodt had had only three archers with him besides Dion. Two were already down, their bodies shoved off the trail by the raiders. Sobovi—he had seen the wolfwalker run to help Dion—was up with the boy, and there were now two other figures on the trail. Dawn folded their shadows onto the face of the cliff as he watched, and he cursed while he ran toward the trail. There were almost two dozen raiders following them up the wall. The three or four who had already died hardly dented the number that were chasing Dion. He risked a look around the edge of a cabin, throwing himself back as a raider swung his sword in a short, vicious arc. The blade bit wood where Aranur's chest had been. Aranur lunged, rushing him. Ducking and slashing, Aranur stabbed his blade through the other man's guts, wrenching the blade up to disembowel him. Gamon, beside him, beat aside another sword, following the blow with an elbow to the second raider's head. They drove the raiders back, forcing them to the river while the camp blazed behind them. The crackling of the fire was punctuated by the crash of timbers inside the collapsing cabins. Smoke stung Gamon's eyes and leached the air from his lungs until he staggered to keep up with Aranur. Just a little farther, and the trailhead up the cliff would be clear. Someone shouted Gamon's name, and Aranur threw a glance over his shoulder. It was Tehena, the skinny woman directing a group of swordsmen toward the trail after them. She halted, waiting for Aranur and Gamon, and they dodged past a clump of fighters to join her.

"They're halfway up." She pointed. "If we don't go now, the raiders will have us in their sights before we get to the first boulder."

Aranur nodded, forcing his way to the front. "I'll lead," he said tersely. The others fell back. He jumped up on the boulder, hauling himself up the next broken column until he reached the smooth part of the trail. Then, sword out, he ran.

Far ahead on the trail, Rodt shoved Sobovi onward. "I'll hold them here," he snapped. "Take the healer and run for the top."

"No," Dion resisted stubbornly. "We'll stay with you."

"Just leave me your arrows, Healer. This pocket is well-protected."

Sobovi gave him a long look, then unslung his quiver and handed it over. Dion stared at him, then shut her mouth. If she stayed with Rodt, Tomi and Namina would be in even greater danger. She unslung her quiver without a word, handing it over. She touched Rodt quickly on his chest, and he returned the gesture gently. "See you at the top," he said with a lopsided grin. Dion turned and was gone. Sobovi followed without a word.

Rodt glanced after them, the sweat beading on his brow. He looked inside his jerkin. The red stain was beginning to discolor the leather behind the small hole. "See you," he whispered, "on the path to the moons, Healer."

Above, Namina propelled Longear on. Longear's eyes narrowed as she looked back at Dion and Sobovi, noting that the archer was no longer with them. "He's hit, isn't he?" she said with satisfaction.

Dion gave her a grim look, but did not answer.

"You might as well give up now, Dione," the dark-haired woman suggested. "You haven't the brains to outthink me, nor the guts to do me in. My raiders are on their way up—don't think your one pitiful archer is going to stop them."

Dion cursed under her breath, and Longear laughed. "They

won't let me go, Dione,'' she taunted. ''I am their bread and butter, their power, their wealth. Without me, they are nothing, and they know it. They will follow you to the ends of this world to get me back.''

Tomi stared at her, and Dion touched his shoulders gently. ''She was never Peyel as you saw her. She was always Longear,'' she said softly.

''She is Peyel,'' he said stubbornly. ''She told the others when to escape.''

Longear's eyes glittered. ''I told them when to run,'' she admitted with evil glee, ''and told my raiders where to find them when they did.'' She grinned, the expression stretching the evil across her face. ''They trusted me so easily,'' she said, shaking her head at her own disbelief of their naïveté. ''To them, I am Peyel, a woman who grew up on the border with them—a cousin to some of those fools.'' She laughed. ''Did you never wonder how I knew the terrain so well, Dione? I ran those trails when you were wasting away becoming a healer.'' She made the word an insult, and Dion clenched her fists. ''Go ahead. Hit me.'' Longear laughed again.

Dion glared, her breath burning in her lungs. *Gray rage. Blood in my fangs. Wind in my teeth, and the hunger growing in my belly. Rage at the raiders who laid their fire across my back . . .* She struggled to control the images that rose in her head, managing only to motion Namina on. Namina did not let up on Longear's arm, but gripped her more tightly as she dragged her along.

They staggered past another broken-out column, stepping around it, then over a split in the cliff. The last two archers paused. They crouched, waiting behind the column. Sobovi and Dion hauled themselves on. *Wolfwalkers!* the Gray Ones called across the ridge. Dion's eyes unfocused. The trail grew wide, then narrow, as she forced the images from her mind. She pressed her hands to her sides, gasping for breath. Ahead of them, Tomi trailed doggedly after Namina.

How far had they gone? Halfway? More? Dion heard a cry, and she flung herself toward the lip, watching the arrow-pierced body of one of the archers fall to his death. A moment later, the other archer followed, his dark hair streaming back, his arms limp as his body tumbled. He had been dead before he fell. The raiders kicked him off. Dion stared. Sobovi cursed, calmly, steadily. He drew his sword. Then he began to run—down the trail.

"No!" Dion shouted at him.

Sobovi did not listen. The tide of gray was in him, rising with his rage. Death—there was only death in this hunt. He met the raiders head-on. They clashed. One raider slipped and fell from the cliff. Sobovi stumbled. The ringing storm seethed in Dion's head, and she saw through Gray Yoshi's eyes. The sword that slashed Sobovi's ribs tore into her own, and she staggered. "On!" she screamed at Namina. "Go!" She clutched her arm, feeling the shocking break where Sobovi's bone had been smashed by a sword. She ran. She stumbled. Behind her, Sobovi fell. She threw her head back and howled. Sobovi died.

Namina staggered to a stop, her chest heaving. Longear's hair was plastered to her forehead by sweat. Tomi crouched on the trail. "Give up, Dione," Longear croaked. "That other wolf-worm is dead. You have lost again."

"Of all the—raiders on this—cliff," Dion snarled between breaths, "you are the one—I swear will not—walk away unscathed."

Longear began to laugh. "Stupid woman. Don't you see? The men behind you are mine. The camp below was mine, and will be mine again. The county west—that is mine. And the one to the east, your Ariye, will be mine, as well. The trick you pulled at dawn—I know it now—it was one of the ancient ways of war. I had not thought to use them yet, but now—" She paused grimly. "The next time your precious Ariyens try to fight by numbers, they will go down the same way—in droves." She pointed with her chin. "You will never take me to the trial block. You cannot even judge me here, when you know who I am and what I do to your precious Ramaj Ariye." She laughed coldly. "You can kill a man in battle, but you can't kill in cold blood, Dione. And you," she taunted Namina, "never even had the guts to speak your name in a quiet room. Nothing you can do here will make a difference. I will be back in my base this evening, and you will all be dead."

"No," Dion protested.

Longear snarled. "The raiders on this trail will not let you reach the top of this stupid mountain, Dione. Even if you did reach the top, what then? Do you think to hold off a dozen swords with your healer's band? You are stupid enough to try to fight them, but so what? You will go down, like the other fools on this trail, and I will be rid of you and the one child who knows I am both Peyel and,'' she taunted, ''Longear. I will have everything I had before. I will have lost nothing but a few raiders.'' She shrugged delicately. ''They are easily replaced.''

Dion stared at her.

''Oh,'' Longear added as if an afterthought, ''and the boy, Dione? Just so you know. I think I will keep him for myself.'' A slow grin, like the death smile of a skull, stretched across her face. Tomi shrank back.

Dion could not move in her horror. ''This cannot be allowed to continue,'' she whispered, agonized.

Namina looked at Dion and blinked. She tightened her grip on Longear's arm.

Longear looked at her and laughed. ''You are worse than nothing, Namina. Dione at least can fight me. You cannot even speak.''

Namina's blue eyes stared through Longear's soul. ''I had not had a need,'' she said. Her soft, hoarse voice was barely a whisper. She stepped forward. Her hand tightened on Longear's arm. When she stepped from the cliff, it was again in silence.

Dion lunged forward. ''No!'' she screamed. ''Namina!''

The two bodies plunged strangely, one still and spread on the air like a bird, the other twisting, kicking, screaming, as it fell. The only link between them was the hand of Namina on Longear's arm. The air curdled with Longear's scream. Then there was silence.

Dion stared after them. The first raider on the trail after them eased around the corner and, seeing the wolfwalker at the drop, surged forward. Tomi shouted. Dion scrambled to her feet, swinging up with her sword and a handful of dust at the same time. The raider yelled in rage. Someone had her arm, urging, pulling her away, and she followed, running blindly after the boy. *Wolfwalker,* the tide of gray raged. *The hunt—the hunt is on the heights. Run with us! Run high!*

Dion and Tomi scrambled around another balanced column, rocking it as they grabbed for its support. ''Go!'' Dion shoved the boy away. She flung herself at the cliff, jamming herself between the face and the stone. The boy stopped, turning back, standing dumbly as she strained. Her lips grimaced; her neck muscles stood out. "Gods!" she screamed. The column rocked forward, swung back—Dion gasped, her legs jammed back against her—then slowly, agonizingly slowly, tipped out.

The column rumbled. Rocks crashed to the trail. The massive piece of stone fell across the trail and began to roll. A man screamed, followed by the grisly fading shriek of another man. Dion and Tomi ran. They did not look back.

Gray storms sweeping the ridge. Wolfwalker! We come!

Gray Ones . . . She could not close her eyes to the surging tide of strength. It blinded her, and she stumbled, the boy clutching her arm as she fell to her hands and knees. She crawled. The raiders' curses were loud as they clambered over the stone and followed grimly up the trail.

"Here," Tomi screamed at Dion, dragging her sideways. A gap in the stone met her groping hands. "Up." He pushed futilely at her back.

Dion clenched her fists, clearing her eyes. The slit of a cave beckoned just above her head. The raiders would come around that last bend any second. Once the raiders saw her, the dark arrows would drive her and the boy from the trail in a minute. Even if the arrows missed, she and Tomi could not survive the fall. She looked at the slit again, the senses of the wolves drowning her nose in the trail, the crushed leaves, the musky scents of the males, the lepa . . .

The lepa. She went rigid. The cave was a lepa den. Dion clutched Tomi's arm. If they disturbed the beast . . . She glanced at the sky. It was an hour past dawn. One hour. There were no shadows in the sky. Was it sleeping? Or had it roused to hunt? Gods, the raiders would be here any second. She licked her lips, trembling. She put her fist into the crack and drew herself up. Moons of mercy, moons of light, she prayed. Her foot found purchase between the columns. Guide me in the darkest night . . . Her hands found the lip of the cave. Keep me safe from evil spirit . . . She pulled herself up.

There was nothing there.

She hauled herself in, twisting and reaching down for the boy. "Quick," she breathed. He was light as a stick, her strength multiplied by the power of the wolves. His knees banged on the stone and he whimpered, but he made no other sound as she dragged him up, pulling him into her arms and crouching beside him in the cave. The smells choked them both.

No more than half a minute passed. The rasping breaths of the raiders, their muttered curses, filled the air. Scrabbling sounds followed them where their hands searched for support along the trail. They passed. A second later, an arrow shot across the entrance to the cave. Dion flinched. The gray rage in her head made it hard to see, and she edged forward, looking down along the trail. Gods, it was—

"Aranur," she cried out.

The man leapt forward, reaching up to grasp her hands. "By the moons, you are safe!"

"The raiders—"

"Twenty meters ahead, no more." He motioned for her to climb down. As she slid over the lip, he stepped back, bracing himself in case she slipped, then steadying her as she landed on the trail. The boy followed, sliding into his arms. Behind Aranur, Gamon glanced up, his hands on his thighs as he caught his breath with difficulty. As Aranur grabbed the boy, Dion stepped back toward Gamon, and the older man wrinkled his nose. The reek of the cave clung to her body. He shivered. Lepa. He looked up again. Did she not know the death she had risked? He glanced at her face, white and sweating in the gray light of dawn. No. She knew.

"Come on," Aranur snapped. "We can still catch them."

Dion stopped him. "No," she said urgently.

"They will gain the top and run for Bilocctar."

"They will go nowhere." She looked up at the rim of the cliff, her eyes unfocused. "The wolves are waiting," she whispered.

Aranur stared at her.

Rage, wolfwalker. Hungry death. Man smell, hot smell, sweat-stink in the wind . . .

She nodded to herself. Rage. The images shifted, blending and separating so that she saw from a hundred eyes. The dark, lupine shapes crouched on top of the flattened mountain, waiting, listening, lifting noses to the wind. The hum burned in their bones. The first raider reached the top and staggered onto the flat. Wind swept the sweat from his face. He gasped, forcing himself away from the edge. The mountaintop was narrow here. Thirty meters—no more than that. Flat and smooth, the material of the ancient Slot reached across that expanse. The raider's sword and knife were stuck together, the studs in his leggings gluing the blades to his thigh.

The Gray Ones waited.

The second raider dragged himself up. A third. A fourth. The eighth one laughed, and Dion heard the echo as if the woman's mouth were in her ear. Nine and ten. Twelve. Fourteen. They crawled away from the edge, regaining their feet, watching the rim warily. Wind whipped dust into their eyes. They held up their hands to guard their faces while their chests heaved and their mouths hung open to suck air into their starving lungs.

The Gray Ones moved.

Unseeing, the raiders staggered toward the path that ran along the top. They stopped.

A tide of gray shadows slunk along the Slot. Hackles rose. Teeth bared. The raiders grabbed at their swords. They could not raise them from the scabbards. The Gray Ones advanced. Waving their arms, the men shouted at the wolves to send them back. The creatures did not hear. Or, hearing, did not care. Their rage ran deep, ran red. They circled in. The raiders backed toward the Slot. One woman came too close to the edge and clutched another man for support. The wolves did not pause. Shouting, the raiders ran at the Gray Ones, fighting the wind to break through that tide of gray. Fangs slashed. A Gray One yelped. Someone screamed. One of the raiders was gone, falling over the edge of the Slot and into the humming channel below.

Howl, Wolfwalker, the gray beasts raged. *The hunt is on the heights!*

Two raiders went down under the crush of gray; two more fell from the rim. Another faced the fangs at her throat and jumped, clutching the Gray One and taking it with her. The wolves howled, furious. The tide turned to a frenzy.

Then there was silence.

The wind howled across the flat. The Gray Ones slunk away. The mountaintop was bare except for the bodies. Below, in the slot, the sprawled forms were tiny on the smooth tiles of the ancients, a gift from the memory of the wolves. The only movement was the shadow of the lepa hovering over the Slot, circling, circling in the sky.

Epilogue

Aranur and Dion faced each other on the ridge behind their new home. Gamon was there, by Dion's side. Aranur's other uncle, the Lloroi, stood beside his nephew. A boy, two youths, the hard-faced woman Tehena, the mate of the Lloroi, and three men waited in the summer wind. A wolfpack stood in the trees on the edge of the meadow that topped the ridge, and their yellow eyes gleamed.

"Let this stone reflect my love," Aranur said softly. His tunic was pulled away from his chest, as was Dion's. His long fingers touched the blue gem held lightly to her sternum by the waiting studset. "Let this promise be as enduring. By the wind and"—he smiled faintly—"the wolves; by the nine moons; by the stars; know that my love, my respect, my home, are yours."

Dion's soft voice repeated the words, her hand touching his chest as lightly as his had done hers. Their hands dropped and clenched. They gripped each other tightly, staring into each other's eyes. Gamon and Tehena stepped forward. They nodded to each other, then, at the same instant, pressed the studguns against Aranur and Dion's bared sternums. The shocks of the studs stunned the two with an instant, fading pain, and the wolves in the treeline threw back their heads and howled.

Gamon grinned in satisfaction. "Let those who hear and those who howl be witness to this mating."

Tehena nodded curtly. The Lloroi and his mate exchanged a long, smiling look. Aranur pulled Dion's shirt back over her shoulders, and she did the same for him. Gray eyes met violet ones. They stood for a long moment, feeling the newness of the blue gems set above the purple ones. The studs ached deeply, reaching into their bodies with the coral growth that would bind the gems permanently to their bones. Hidden now, the two stones, one purple, one blue, shone over their hearts and rasped beneath their tunics. A year they had waited for this.

Gamon, Tehena, the Lloroi—those who had gathered turned to walk away. Aranur and Dion did not notice. They were full of each other, standing in the wind, standing above their home, holding each other together.

Tomi stared at them, his eyes dark in the mask of his face. When he turned away, he stumbled. Gamon stretched out a hand to steady him, but he jerked away.

"Tomi," Gamon said.

The boy halted.

"Where are you going?"

"They are mated," he said in a low voice. "They are a family now."

"Yes," said Gamon simply.

The boy turned away, his eyes blurred, his feet finding the path with difficulty.

"Tomi," Gamon said softly.

He halted, but did not look back.

"Why are you going?"

"They won't want me to stay anymore," he whispered. "And Moira said I have to find a family."

"You already have." Gamon pointed at Dion and Aranur. "Give them a ninan, boy. Their home will be ready by then for you too."

The boy did not respond. But when Gamon held out his hand

small fingers felt their way into his grip. He did not speak, only closed his hand about the fingers lightly, and Tomi, his face still wary, walked with the old man, instead of behind him, back to his home.